Praise for

Monica Burns

"Burns doesn't disappoint!"
— *rtbookreviews*

Monica Burns writes with sensitivity and panache.
— Sabrina Jeffries, nyt bestselling author

"powerfully done…the scenes between Tobias and Jane mesmerized me. I loved it."
— Joey W. Hill

"No one sets fire to the page like Monica Burns."
— eCataromance

"Definitely recommended reading."
— The Romance Studio

"Ms. Burns is masterful at escalating the sexual tension and suspense with her characters."
— Coffeetime Romance

Forever Yours

The Forevermore Series, Book 2

by

Monica Burns

Copyright © 2022 by Kathi B. Scearce
ISBN 978-1-948505-12-3
Cover Design: Maroli Design Services

Kathi B. Scearce dba Monica Burns—Maroli SP Imprints
P.O. Box 75072
North Chesterfield, VA 23236

Publishing History
Digital 1.0 edition / 2022
Print 1.0 edition / 2022

Acknowledgements

With thanks to Kris Bloom, Megan Bloom, Maria Ferrer, Lesley Field, Donna Nalbandian Woerner Homschek, Debbie Punko Hoopes, Mary Anne Landers, Laura Polito McEleney, Sue Moorhouse, Margaret Springett, Charlene Whitehouse, Maggie Whitworth, Norah Wilson and Karen Wyman for brainstorming series titles in my Historical Romance Addicts Too reader group. You ladies are awesome!

Family Tree

For those who have not read Forever Mine or if it's been some time since you've read the book, you might find yourself slightly confused in the prologue as to whom Anna is interacting with. If you'd like to see the rough outline of where the characters come from, you can download a pdf or view the image on my website at this URL — https://monicaburns.net/treefms2.

Table of Contents

Acknowledgements   v

Famly Tree   v

Prologue   1

Chapter 1   8

Chapter 2   29

Chapter 3   42

Chapter 4   66

Chapter 5   83

Chapter 6   94

Chapter 7   101

Chapter 8   109

Chapter 9   126

Chapter 10   133

Chapter 11   141

Chapter 12   150

Chapter 13   166

Chapter 14 184

Chapter 15 201

Chapter 16 212

Chapter 17 223

Chapter 18 236

Chapter 19 246

Chapter 20 264

Chapter 21 279

Chapter 22 290

Chapter 23 299

Chapter 24 315

Chapter 25 333

Chapter 26 348

Chapter 27 373

Chapter 28 388

Chapter 29 410

Chapter 30 428

Chapter 31 439

Chapter 32 453

Epilogue 473

Author's Note 497

Prologue

Brentwood Park, 1966

"**G**randmama Anna. Grandmama Anna." The childish cries of excitement echoed in the hall outside of Anna's bedroom.

"Girls, *stop*." The sharp command from Anna's granddaughter failed to stop the pounding of feet that grew closer.

Harsh coughing wracked Anna's body, but she managed to push herself upright in her bed. Just as she'd settled into the pillows, Annabelle and Frances bolted into the room. The weariness and pain assaulting her body vanished at the sight of her two great-granddaughters. Arms outstretched, she welcomed the girls as they launched themselves up onto the bed beside her. With a child on either side, she wrapped her arms around them and held them close.

"*Girls*, get off that bed this minute," Sarah Jane Marbury scolded. "Grandmama Anna isn't feeling well."

"Leave them be, Sarah Jane," Anna rasped. "After tonight, I won't see them or you for a very long time, and you know how much I love having them near me."

"You know I don't want to go home tomorrow, Granny."

"I know, sweetheart, but I will miss them, and I want to spend as much time with them as I can these last few hours.

Perhaps we might all have supper here in my rooms?"

"Surely that would be too much excitement for you. You should be resting." Her granddaughter's gentle chiding echoed with a hint of worry.

"For fuc—balderdash," Anna snapped as she stopped herself from using the one word in her vocabulary that Céleste had never been able to completely banish. Sebastian would have chastised her sternly for uttering it in front of the children, although there had been times when he found it amusing and even wickedly arousing. It made her heart tighten as she pushed the pain away to keep it from showing. In the next difficult breath, she could hear Sebastian's voice in her head. *Not long now, my love. we'll be together soon.*

Anna didn't know if it was her imagination or just wishful thinking, but she chose to believe it was her dark angel speaking to her. Deep in the back of her head, she heard Sebastian's laugh as if teasing her for doubting, when she'd always been adamant about such things when he'd been alive.

Sarah Jane eyed her with disapproval, but her granddaughter's eyes sparkled with laughter. Her granddaughter had been privy to her colorful language on more than one occasion when Anna had thought she was out of earshot. Pressing a tender kiss to her grandmother's forehead, Sarah Jane busied herself adjusting the pillows to make her more comfortable.

As her granddaughter fussed with her pillows, Anna marveled at how much she looked like Victoria, but she possessed Sebastian's arched looks and disapproving expressions. When she'd finished fluffing the pillows, Anna caught her granddaughter's hand in her own.

"I need you to do something for me, sweetheart," Anna said softly over the top of her namesake's head and pointed toward her nightstand. "There's an envelope with a letter of instructions for you in the drawer. You'll need to ask Simmons to come to the house as it needs to be done before the evening is over."

Puzzlement furrowing her brow, Sarah Jane retrieved the items. Concentration made the younger woman arch her eyebrows, much in the same way Sebastian had when he was contemplating something. As Sarah Jane's gaze skimmed over the letter Anna had written to the young woman a few days ago, her granddaughter's confusion gave way to another emotion entirely. Anna knew she should have handled the matter herself weeks ago, perhaps even longer than that, but she'd procrastinated.

If she'd not been so stubborn about seeing the doctor, she could have had her solicitor amend her will herself. Instead, she'd unfairly placed the burden on her granddaughter's shoulders. A task that needed to be done by the end of the day if she and Sebastian were to find each other in the future. The letters and clock needed to remain in the family until the right time, which meant Sarah Jane and the girls would need to know the truth of what was to come. Deep down inside, a small voice murmured the real reason she'd obstinately put off doing what her granddaughter would have to do for her.

But with each passing day, the truth had become a villain she'd been forced to acknowledge. She was no longer as certain about her beliefs as she'd once been. It was why she'd not attended to the matter herself. Worse, she was afraid. What if she'd been wrong her entire life and there wasn't anything beyond the veil? What if she'd been wrong to believe she and Sebastian would have another life together in the future?

An image of her lover, supporter, best friend, and husband formed in her head, and for a brief moment, pain clawed at her insides. It eased to a bearable throb after a moment, and Anna dragged in as deep a breath as she was capable. No, she wouldn't allow her mind to dismiss what her soul knew to be true.

She wasn't wrong. There had been too many signs over the years to believe anything but her soul and heart. She was convinced her next big adventure lay directly before her, and Sebastian would be a part of that adventure. The thought filled her with an unexpected excitement for what lay ahead, and it lightened her spirits.

"I don't understand, Granny."

Sarah Jane looked up from the letter. The moment their gazes met, her granddaughter's eyes widened. Anna raised her hand in a silent command for the younger woman to remain silent.

"No questions, Sarah Jane. You know I'm seldom wrong, and I'm ready." Anna smiled as she tried to alleviate her granddaughter's fear. "It's my last wish."

How like her grandfather she was. Sebastian had loved all their children equally, and his grandchildren had been a joy for him until his last breath. But Sarah Jane had been different. While she'd acquired the beauty of her paternal grandmother, Victoria, her granddaughter had been the most like Sebastian in personality and temperament. There had always been a strong bond between the two of them. Tears made her granddaughter's eyes shimmer in the late morning light.

"Oh, Granny." Sarah Jane's words were barely audible as she grabbed Anna's hand. "You mustn't—"

"You know better, sweetheart. Even your grandfather learned not to question me." Anna released an unladylike snort of laughter.

Her granddaughter choked out a laugh, but there were tears in her eyes as her fingers squeezed Anna's hand. A moment later, just like Sebastian would do when he was deeply upset, Sarah Jane hid her pain and sorrow. From where she was snuggled up against Anna, her namesake blew out a breath of exasperation.

"Grandmama Anna, are you and Mama done talking? I

have something to tell you." The child's voice echoed with impatience. Anna stroked the little girl's brow in a tender gesture.

"I'm sorry, crumpet. You have my complete attention now." As Anna's gaze focused on her great-granddaughter, young Anna nodded with satisfaction. The sunny smile that curved the child's features lightened Anna's heart.

"We found turtles down by the pond."

"*You did?*" Anna exclaimed as an overwhelming love for her great-granddaughters filled her heart. Opposite her younger sister, Frances nodded with enthusiasm.

"Grandfather says they're probably the grandbabies of the turtles his Uncle Edmund used to find in the pond."

"I'm sure they are. What else did you do?"

"We had a picnic with apple cake, just like the picnics Grandfather said great-grandfather Nicholas and his Uncle Edmund liked," young Anna said with a grin. "It was very good. We saved some for you, too."

"Then I'll have it for dessert tonight when you have supper with me."

"We're going to eat with you here in your rooms?" Frances gasped with pleasure.

Whenever Anna ate in her rooms, all etiquette rules were abandoned. It was an indoor picnic with candles, a ghost story, and a cheery fire where they roasted marshmallows. It was a tradition Anna had done when Jane had been a little girl. The custom had started even further back when it was only Sebastian and herself, but those picnics had invariably ended in a pleasure that could still make her heart race.

"It's not been decided yet." The moment Sarah Jane expressed a reluctance to comply with her plans, Anna settled her stern gaze on her granddaughter.

"It *has* been decided, Sarah Jane Thornhill Marbury."

The use of their mother's full name made both girls' giggle. Sarah Jane glared down at her daughters for a moment before resignation crossed her features. Her acquiescence to her grandmother's decree made the two girls shout with glee.

"Since Grandmama Anna says we are to have supper with her, we need to leave her to rest."

"But she isn't going home to New York with us. She's staying here at Brentwood Park with Grandmama and Grandfather, and we won't see her for a very long time," young Anna said with a mutinous twist of her lips. Not bothering to bargain with her mother, Frances caught Anna's hand in hers and carried it to her cheek.

"She's right, Grandmama Anna, and I don't want to go home without you telling us the story," Frances said in a pleading voice. Even at eleven, it was obvious the child was going to be a great beauty. Frances had the same silky dark hair as Sebastian and long, sooty eyelashes highlighted the girl's warm brown eyes.

"Now you know better than to ask that Frances Lillian Marbury," her mother said sternly. "Granny hasn't been feeling well."

"Are you saying *you* don't want to hear the tale again?" Anna's lips parted in a small laugh, followed by a cough, as she looked at her granddaughter. "As I recall, you begged me to tell you the story on a regular basis when you were little."

"You weren't ill then." The fear in Sarah Jane's reply was emphasized by the dismay in her sapphire eyes. Anna reached out and caught her granddaughter's hand.

"And we both know it won't hurt to tell the story one last time."

"You *mustn't* say that Granny." Tears welled in Sarah Jane's eyes again as she shook her head in protest. Gently squeezing the younger woman's hand, Anna smiled.

"How many times do I need to remind you that parting is only for a brief time? Energy doesn't die. It simply changes form," Anna said in a matter-of-fact fashion Sebastian would have approved of.

Anna closed her eyes as the pain rushed up to the surface again before she could bury it. The image of her dark angel filled her head, and tears pricked at her eyelids as she struggled with the hole that had opened in her heart the night Sebastian had died.

"That's quite enough. We're going to leave Granny—"

"No," Anna whispered as she opened her eyes and met Sarah Jane's gaze, knowing it was the last time she'd be able to share the story. "I want to tell it one last time. I want to hear it again."

"Oh please, mama, please let her tell the story."

"Yes, mama, *please*."

The childish pleas made their mother hesitate as Sarah Jane looked at Anna. Fear flashed in the younger woman's eyes, and Anna squeezed her granddaughter's hand in a sign that all would be well. With a slow nod, Sarah Jane gave her permission.

"I need to go call Simmons, but I'll be back in a few minutes. Go ahead and start without me, or the girls will pester you non-stop."

Sarah Jane kissed Anna's cheek, then hurried from the room in a sign she didn't want to be gone any longer than she had to. A familiar excitement pulsed through Anna as she smiled at her granddaughter, then turned her attention to the girls cuddled against her. With a mischievous grin, Anna winked at each girl as her heart lightened. In the back of her head, she heard Sebastian's familiar deep laugh at her love of telling their story.

"Let me see, where should I begin?" she said quietly.

Chapter 1

"You *do realize* the entire evening is going to be nothing but men leering at you, don't you?"

The disapproval in Nicholas's voice said he was running at full throttle with the protective big brother attitude tonight. Nora had known her costume was going to raise her brother's eyebrows, but she hadn't expected his reaction to be this bad.

The door of the limo they'd rented for the evening quietly popped open, and Nora scowled at her brother before she accepted the driver's hand to help her exit the vehicle.

Not about to give Nicholas extra fuel to continue his rant, Nora refrained from flirting with the driver as he assisted her out of the car. She said a quiet thank you, then walked to the corner of the street to wait on Nicholas and Victoria. Her brother had always acted as the stereotypical, over-protective big brother, but Victoria's pregnancy had seemed to increase Nicholas's alpha tendencies when it came to his wife and sister. Her sister-in-law took it in stride as apparently Nicholas had acted the same way when they were man and wife in 1897.

Unfortunately, on the few occasions when her sister-in-law rebelled against his autocratic manner, Nora became the target of Nicholas's mother hen behavior. It didn't happen often, but tonight her Egyptian costume had set him off.

It wasn't like she couldn't handle herself. Six years of Wing Chun classes with Tanaka-sensei had taught her when to run and when to fight. Not only that, Nicholas had never seen her go up against two classmates at one time. Her skills didn't qualify her as championship material, but she was more than capable of fighting off an attacker. Nora also knew her height and weight would make someone think she would be harder to overpower than someone smaller.

Despite being five foot ten, Nora would never be able to call herself slender or willowy. She was curvy everywhere. All the beer she drank on poker night probably didn't help with the calorie intake, and she had a *major* weakness for turtle cheesecake and chocolate. No, chocolate wasn't a weakness. It was an addiction.

The word moderation didn't exist when it came to chocolate, and it was hard to control a chocolate addiction when one hated going to the gym. So, she compensated with three Wing Chung workouts a week under the stern eye of Tanaka-sensei. It wasn't necessarily a strenuous workout, but it did keep her muscles in shape. When she was traveling, she was usually able to find a school that was open to guests.

The loud thunk of a car door slamming shut made her look over her shoulder to see Nicholas and Victoria walking toward her as the limo pulled away from the curb. She looked back at the long line of cars waiting to unload other gala attendees. It had been the right decision to suggest their driver let them out at Stanhope Gate and Park Lane across from the Dorchester.

The weather had been lovely all day, and the temperature was warmer than usual for late May, which was one of the reasons she'd made the suggestion. It would make for a pleasant walk from the street corner to the ballroom's outside-entrance on the side of the hotel. A wolf whistle echoed out of a passing car as her brother and sister-in-law joined her, and Nicholas scowled at the car's occupants before casting another look of disapproval in Nora's direction.

Annoyed by her brother's I-told-you-so look, she rolled her eyes at him while they waited for an opportunity to cross the street. Nora heard her sister-in-law make a soft sound, and she turned her head toward Victoria, expecting to see her smiling. Nicholas had apparently heard it as well and jerked his head toward his wife.

Victoria arched her eyebrows at them with a complacency that said she wasn't surprised by their quarreling. Nicholas muttered something under his breath as he turned his attention back to the street, then ushered them forward to the pavement that split Stanhope Gate as it merged into Park Lane. Despite her aggravation with her brother's judgemental opinion about her costume, she couldn't help feeling proud of how handsome he looked.

It was as if the Earl of Guildford had stepped out of the picture in the book she'd given him almost a year ago, as he'd sat watching over Victoria in the hospital. Her sister-in-law had surprised Nicholas more than a week ago with the formal evening dress that was a replica of the evening clothes he'd worn in their past life together. For herself, Victoria had given the dressmaker a description of a ball gown she'd worn when the two of them had been married in 1897. The day the costumes were delivered to the house the couple had bought recently, Nora had insisted Victoria model the gown for her husband.

She'd made her brother stand at the foot of the stairs, then announced her sister-in-law with a loud ta-da. Her brother's reaction had been that of a man knocked off his feet as he'd watched Victoria descending the stairs. Clearly oblivious to everything except each other, Nora hadn't bothered to say goodbye to the couple. Instead, she'd quickly shown herself out the front door.

The memory of how she'd stood outside their house that day trying not to cry made her heart twist in her chest. She wanted what her brother and Victoria had, but in recent weeks, she'd come to accept the odds probably weren't in her favor. Not everyone got a second chance at happiness.

Behind her, a low whistle of appreciation made her glance over her shoulder to see a small group of men waiting to cross the street. Nicholas stiffened beside her, but before he could turn around, Nora saw Victoria place her hand on her husband's arm in a silent plea for him not to react. A rumble of sound echoed out of him as Nicholas guided them across the other lane of the street onto the pavement.

"What did I tell you," her brother snapped as the three of them walked toward the side entrance of the hotel. His autocratic behavior was reminiscent of an alpha male in the past, and Nora smiled up at him sweetly.

"I've got it. Why shouldn't I flaunt it?" At her unabashed manner, Nicholas uttered a low sound of anger.

"*Because*, Nora *Annabelle* Barrows, some asshole might take it as an invitation."

"Then he's going to be in for a surprise, isn't he?"

Nora glared fiercely at her brother not because of his over-protective behavior, but because he'd used her full name. Uncle Charles had been the only one she'd allowed to use her middle name, although her uncle had always called her Anna, unless he was angry, then he had sounded just like Nicholas had a moment ago. Uncle Charles always said she looked more like an Anna than a Nora. Regret swept across Nicholas's face before concern replaced it.

"A few years of martial arts classes doesn't make you a ninja." Nicholas's dismissal of her reply was harsh and fierce. "Hell, I thought the chauffeur's eyes were going to pop out of his head when you walked out of your flat to the limousine. I've not seen a guy move so fast to open a door since

Jamieson ran out—"

A barely audible groan escaped her brother. Nora's anger vanished as she was forced to hold in her laughter at his befuddled look. Lately, her brother had been remembering a great deal about his life in 1897, when he and Victoria had fallen in love. Their time together in the past had been short, but both of them had said on more than one occasion it only made them appreciate each other all the more here in the present.

Nicholas opened the side entrance door into the hotel for her and Victoria, his frustration emphasized by a brotherly noise of irritation. As they entered the small breezeway between the outer door and the hotel's ballroom lobby, Nora couldn't resist teasing her brother.

"Was he this uptight in 1897, Victoria?"

"I think he's mellowed with age." The onetime Countess of Guildford laughed as she moved through the interior door into the ballroom lobby. Her amused reply earned her a scowl from her husband, but Victoria simply laughed again and patted his arm. "Stop being a worrywart, my lord."

"You enjoy doing that, don't you?" Nicholas's disgruntled look made Victoria pause for a brief second to kiss his cheek before turning away with another laugh.

"Yes, I do. It sort of evens the playing field, reminding you that bossing me around here in the present isn't as easy as it was in the past. Although you know it wasn't all that easy then either." Victoria tossed the words over her shoulder as she moved deeper into the hotel lobby. "Besides, your sister really does know how to take care of herself, and her costume isn't *that* outrageous."

"The two of you wait here, and I'll get our bidding paddles."

Nicholas's scowl said he'd heard his wife's defense of Nora but had chosen to ignore it. Instead, he kissed Victoria's cheek before moving to stand in line at the registration table.

Across the lobby, Nora saw an older couple eyeing her with surprise before they turned away from her with a shake of their heads in a silent condemnation of her choice in costume. One side of Nora's mouth tugged her lips into a grimace of self-doubt with a quick glance down at her outfit. Maybe she *had* gone a bit overboard.

When the invitation had arrived for tonight's historical costume gala and charity auction, she'd known immediately she would go as Hatshepsut. One of the most successful pharaohs in ancient Egypt, Hatshepsut had ruled for more than twenty years. Although Nora had always had a fascination with ancient Egypt, her real inspiration had come from a recent acquisition of late-Victorian era jewelry.

She'd found the jewelry at an estate sale while on a trip to New York last year. Whoever the original owner had been, they'd either had a deep interest in Egypt or a deep knowledge of the era. The wide collar had been the focus of the design of her costume. Made of a lightweight gold filagree, five large garnet scarabs adorned the collar and were separated by bright blue glass beads. The collar was too ornate for a normal night out, but for the gala, it was perfect. Now, as she glanced down at her attire, she was beginning to second guess her choice.

Floor length silky, almost transparent, white fabric completely hid her legs until she moved. With each step she took, the inner and outer layers of panels that formed her skirt fluttered, swirled, and parted in a gentle flurry of movement to reveal teasing glimpses of her long legs. Her top was a soft beige with a mesh of netted material layered over it, which was adorned with brightly colored blue and gold beads.

Overall, the costume would have been considered fairly sedate if it wasn't for the neckline that plunged downward almost to her belly button. The first time she'd tried on the top she'd been worried about it slipping out of place and revealing a hell of a lot more than she wanted to show off. But the costume designer had eased her concerns by adding a sheer piece of fabric in the middle of the top. It created the illusion nothing was holding the material in place. To further strengthen the daring design, the weight of the gold collar necklace had been used to hold the covering in place, and small snaps had been added at the back and front part of the shoulders to help stabilize the gold collar. To complete the look, she wore a dainty gold diadem as well as ornate gold arm bands.

There was only one thing she didn't like about her costume. It had no pockets, and she'd been forced to ask Victoria to hold her license and a few pound notes, which her sister-in-law had added to the discreet inside pocket she'd had sewn into her bodice. Nora felt almost naked without her phone, but she hadn't felt like holding it the entire evening. A light touch on her forearm jerked Nora out of her thoughts.

"Don't you dare let *anyone* make you feel ashamed of your costume." Victoria smiled in exasperation as she glanced at Nicholas. "You look stunning. Just like a queen of ancient Egypt. I'd never be able to pull off wearing anything like it. I don't have your figure or your self-confidence. Not to mention, I'm big as a house with junior here."

Admiration and ironic amusement filtered through her sister-in-law's voice, as she touched her stomach. Nora squeezed Victoria's hand in a gesture of affection and gratitude for the support. Six months into her pregnancy, her sister-in-law was radiant.

"You are *not* as big as a house. You look beautiful. My brother doesn't even have to say it for me to know he thinks the same thing. The man adores you." At Nora's compliment, Victoria blushed, then darted a glance at Nicholas, who was speaking with someone behind the registration table. A second later, Victoria turned her head back to Nora.

"Where's Seth?" Her sister-in-law's quiet curiosity was evident in her gaze as she studied Nora. "We thought he'd be bringing you tonight."

"I broke things off with him a couple of weeks ago."

"A couple of—but I thought you were crazy about the guy." Eyebrows shooting upward, Victoria stared at her in surprise.

"He's a self-centered ass, and I didn't like the way he embarrassed me the night I ended things." Nora grimaced in irritation as she remembered the incident in front of the restaurant they'd gone to almost three weeks ago.

"Embarrassed you?"

"It wasn't a big deal." The lie made her insides twist with renewed humiliation. "He just illustrated how terribly wrong he was for me."

"Oh, Nora, I'm so sorry."

Victoria wrapped her arm around Nora's waist in a half-hug of warmth and love. The two of them had become quite close since Victoria had emerged from her coma and married Nicholas. Although she often felt like a third wheel, Victoria constantly reassured Nora she wasn't. At the commiseration, Nora shrugged.

"Don't be. I'm better off without the sorry fuck. Besides, seeing you and Nicholas together only raises the bar when it comes to what I want from a permanent relationship."

Before Victoria could reply, Nicholas returned. As her brother halted at his wife's side, he bent his head to whisper something in her ear. Victoria smiled with happiness as she looked up at him. Suddenly feeling as though she were an interloper, Nora turned her head away from the couple.

She hadn't been lying when she'd told Victoria the happiness her sister-in-law shared with Nicholas had raised her standards when it came to a relationship. The memory of the night she'd ended her relationship with Seth flitted through her head. She'd been considering ending things with him for about a month, but his reaction to her clumsiness three weeks ago had pushed her over the edge. It wasn't as if she'd deliberately meant to spill wine all over his new suit. Seth's reaction had made her feel as if she'd taken a knife to a Titian or Rembrandt painting. His over-the-top reaction of disgust and anger had made her cringe with humiliation as people seated around them had watched his reaction with varying degrees of disgust and pity for her.

It had only taken a minute of embarrassment before her own anger rose to the surface. Without hesitating, she'd told him they were through, and she'd walked out of the restaurant while placing a call for a black cab. Her only regret was that she'd not had another glass of wine to dump onto the bastard's head. Nora breathed a soft sigh.

For some perverse reason, the universe kept sending her toads to date. It wasn't as if she were asking for a knight in shining armor to sweep her off her feet. Hell, he didn't have to be tall, dark, and handsome either, although she wouldn't complain if he was. The kind of guy she wanted was someone who loved her so much that the only woman he saw was her.

She wanted, no needed, someone who would call her beautiful on a bad hair day. A man who would kiss her even with morning breath. She wanted a guy who was willing to go to hell and back for her, even though she was more than capable of fighting her own battles. Her idea of Mr. Right was a man who believed in her when it came to anything she wanted to do.

Perhaps that's what she wanted the most. A man who would cheer her accomplishments and comfort her when she failed to meet an objective, while encouraging her to try again. Nora knew it was a tall order. Few people found the type of love Nicholas and Victoria had. In the back of her head, a small voice whispered that Sebastian had been that kind of man.

Without hesitation, she squashed the thought. Nope, she refused to go down that slippery slope. Even if she was the reincarnation of Anna Reddington, Viscountess Starling, it changed nothing. If her dark angel hadn't found her by now in this lifetime, he never would. Nora winced slightly at the odd nickname she'd come to associate with Viscount Starling.

It had first popped into her head when she was reading Victoria's journals while her sister-in-law had still been in a coma. Every time she'd read the name Sebastian, she'd envisioned a tall, dark-haired angel from hell scowling at her. For weeks after reading Victoria's journals, Nora had found herself thinking Sebastian was just around the next corner. She winced as she remembered the pain and disappointment that had slammed into her every time her dark angel hadn't appeared. All she'd done was set herself up for heartache.

The sudden sound of Victoria gasping jerked Nora out of her thoughts, and she turned toward her sister-in-law. Wincing with discomfort, Victoria dragged in a deep breath as Nicholas's fingers caught her by the chin and forced her to look at him.

"We're going home." The concern on her brother's face was emphasized in his voice, which was tight with concern. Victoria waved his words aside.

"*No.* We're *not.* The baby's just kicking a little bit harder than usual. I'm perfectly fine." The look the two exchanged made it clear Victoria wasn't leaving until she was good and ready. Frustration darkened her brother's handsome features.

"You are a stubborn woman, sweet witch."

"Yes, I am. And you know you wouldn't have me any other way, my lord. It's not like I've not been through—" Tears suddenly shimmered in Victoria's blue eyes, and Nicholas grimaced with equal pain.

"It's all right, my love. He was happy, and I came to terms with the way events played out." Nicholas tenderly kissed his wife's temple. "We're together now, and that's what counts."

"Yes, and I don't want to waste a single moment here in the present." Victoria nodded as she pulled a thin catalog out of her husband's hand. "Now, what were the pieces you were interested in looking at tonight?"

Over the top of Victoria's bent head, Nora saw her brother's worried look, and she bobbed her head in a gesture of reassurance. His reluctant nod revealed just how worried he was about Victoria, and Nora offered up a small prayer that the couple would have a happy and long life here in the present. Victoria uttered a soft exclamation of excitement.

"*Anna*. Is this the clock you were talking about the other day in the shop?" Victoria winced and jerked her head up to look at Nora. "Lord, I've done it again. I'm so sorry, Nora."

"Stop. How many times do I have to tell you it's okay to call me Anna? I kind of like it."

She smiled at her sister-in-law as Victoria reinforced her apology with a squeeze of Nora's hand. It was the truth. There was something comforting about Victoria using the shortened version of her middle name. Ever since coming out of her coma, Victoria was continuously calling her Anna. It was a natural reaction on her sister-in-law's part, as Victoria frequently said how much Nora looked and acted like the Viscountess Starling.

Nora pushed her thoughts aside and bent her head to look at the auction catalog page Victoria had turned to. Excitement made her heart skip a beat as she stared down at the picture in the catalog. Nora didn't know why, but the first time she'd seen the clock on the auction website, she'd wanted it. She'd known better than to just push the feeling aside and had made up her mind to bid on it if it was still up for sale. Fingers lightly brushing over the image of the tall, grandfather clock, she tapped on the location listed on the page.

"I'm going to go look at it." As she met her brother's curious gaze, Nora realized she didn't want anyone with her when she found the clock. Determined to keep the couple from accompanying her, she smiled at her brother. "Nicholas, show Victoria those two chairs I mentioned yesterday and see if she likes them. I think they'd be perfect for your living room with that round table Victoria loves so much."

Nora didn't wait for a reply and spun around on her heel to move quickly toward the main hall where the auction items were on display. It didn't take her long to find the grandfather clock, and as she approached it, several people were examining it. Fear slashed through her as she considered the possibility she might not have the winning bid when the clock came up for auction. Impatiently, she waited for the people to leave. She wanted to examine the majestic time piece more closely and without commentary from others. The people didn't seem to be interested in moving away quickly, and Nora blew out a breath of exasperation.

"I see you've found my clock."

The soft words made Nora jerk her head toward a woman who had seemed to appear out of nowhere to stand at her side. A twinkling blue-eyed gaze met hers as she took in the elderly woman's appearance. There was something familiar about her, but Nora couldn't pin down where she'd seen the woman before. Suddenly, the woman's words registered in her head, and Nora's heart sank. Had the clock already been sold at the auction held earlier in the day for items of lesser value?

"This is your clock?"

"It is until it's sold this evening. It is lovely, isn't it?"

"Yes, I'm already in love with it.

Relieved the clock hadn't been sold yet, the tension in Nora's muscles eased slightly as the group in front of the clock moved away. She took several quick steps forward and stretched out her hand to run her fingers across the intricate carvings on the polished mahogany cabinet. The wood was warm beneath her fingertips, and in that instant, Nora knew she'd sell everything she owned to buy this clock. The elderly woman joined her in front of the tall, imposing piece of furniture and laughed softly.

"You have the same look my great-grandmother always did whenever she told me and my siblings the story about how she and my great-grandfather met and fell in love." The woman's smile vanished and was replaced by a sadness. "The clock belonged to my great-grandfather, and when Grandmama Anna died, she gave it to my sister. But Frances passed away a few months ago, and I have to sell it."

"Oh," Nora said with a small amount of guilt for wanting the clock so badly. "I'm terribly sorry for your loss. Wouldn't you rather keep it with you instead of selling it?"

"If I did that, then they might not find each other again." The elderly woman's lips twisted as if enjoying a private joke as she looked up at Nora with amusement. "My name is Anna Marbury Langford, by the way."

"Nora Barrows."

"I like the name Annabelle."

The woman's odd reply made Nora jump. How did the woman know her middle name was Annabelle? A whisper drifted through the back of her mind, but Nora ignored it. As she studied Anna Marbury's profile, the old woman gave a sudden, sharp shake of her head, and she uttered a sound as if reaffirming a thought.

"No, tonight's the night. I can feel it. Besides, it won't fit in the small apartment I'm moving to."

"Well, if I win the bid for it tonight, I promise I'll take good care of it."

The woman didn't seem to be listening as she studied the clock with a wistful smile. Suddenly, her smile grew mischievous as she grinned up at Nora.

"It has a secret compartment. My great-grandmother showed it to me once. She said it used to hold important documents. Would you like to see it?"

"Absolutely."

"You'll have to help me." The elderly lady's grin broadened as she stepped forward to open the door of the large clock. "I'm shorter than I used to be, and even as a young girl, I had trouble reaching the lever. But you're quite tall and should be able to reach it easily. It's close to the top on the left."

"Excuse me, touching the items up for sale is prohibited."

Nora jerked her head to look over her shoulder and saw a tall woman glaring at them. She immediately stepped back from the clock, while Anna Marbury muttered something under her breath. The stern-looking woman wore a plated name badge that identified her as an employee of the firm in charge of the evening's auction. The woman pushed past Nora and the old woman to close the clock's door. The soft click of the latch falling into place made Nora wince.

"I apologize. I'm bidding on it this evening and wanted to examine it a little more closely."

"That's no longer possible," the woman said in clipped tones. "It was sold earlier this afternoon."

Stunned by the woman's abrupt announcement, Nora stared at her slack-jawed, while Anna Langford's features became ashen. The moment the old woman swayed on her feet, Nora took hold of her hand to help steady her, while the woman's other hand clutched at Nora's arm.

"Sold?" Anna Langford's voice quavered as she stared at the auction house employee in horror. "It was supposed to be sold at this evening's auction, not the one this afternoon."

"The owner pulled it from the list at the last minute, as they received a firm offer for it."

"But I *didn't* pull it." Anna Langford's expression was

one of panic. Her hand suddenly clutched Nora's arm tightly as she looked up at her. "It has to be a mistake. I *know* it was supposed to be sold to you this evening."

"There you are, Granny. I was beginning to worry about you." A young woman joined them and bent to kiss the elderly woman's cheek.

"They've sold the clock, Annabelle," the woman said with a note of desperation in her voice. In the back of her mind, Nora realized the woman had confused her with her granddaughter when they'd introduced themselves. It was a fleeting thought that became lost in the chaotic emotions flooding her body. Her granddaughter sighed.

"I know, Granny. I explained that to you at lunch. We received a much larger amount than what the auctioneer said he could get for it."

"But it was supposed to be sold to this young woman, Annabelle." Clearly distraught, the elderly woman's eyes teared up as she clung to Nora's arm. The old woman used her free hand to grab hold of her granddaughter's arm. "You have to get it back, Annabelle. It needs to go with this young lady. Grandmama Anna said so. She's the one who's supposed to buy the clock."

"That's not possible, Granny." Concern crossed the young woman's face at how distraught her grandmother had become. "It's already been paid for, and the money transferred into your bank account."

"Then give it back. The clock was meant for this young woman," the elderly lady insisted fiercely as her panic escalated. Her granddaughter shook her head.

"It's not possible. I knew I shouldn't have agreed to bring you this evening, it's obviously been too much of a strain for you. Let me take you back to the hotel room."

The young woman wrapped her arm around the elderly woman's shoulders and gently forced Anna Langford to release Nora's arm. Still in disbelief the clock had been sold,

Nora stared at the two women with her heart in her stomach. The young woman glanced up at Nora and sighed softly.

"I apologize. She gets this way sometimes. Losing my Aunt Frances has been very difficult for her."

"I understand," Nora choked out as she suddenly felt like crying.

"We must do something, Annabelle," the old woman said with a small sob in her voice. "I promised Frances. She must know about the letter from Grandmama Anna."

With an apologetic shake of her head in Nora's direction, the young woman murmured something in her grandmother's ear and gently guided the old woman away. The auction house employee directed another arctic look in Nora's direction in a silent reminder not to touch the clock before she disappeared into the crowd.

Unable to move, an icy chill slid over Nora's skin until she was shivering. What had just happened? Why did she feel as if she'd just had her heart ripped out of her chest? It was just a damn clock. Nora stared at the large piece of cabinetry with its intricate carvings that edged each side of the grandfather clock.

The design was a combination of English wildflowers that met at the top in a bouquet of carnations inside a heart. While the carnations inside the heart struck her as odd, she knew they represented something important. It was like an elusive memory just on the edge of her conscious mind, she couldn't pull forward.

"Over here, Jesse. Isn't it splendid?"

The exultant note in a woman's voice made Nora glance over her shoulder to see two women close to her age moving toward her. They smiled at her politely as she stepped out of their way. Without any hesitation, one of the women pulled open the glass door of the grandfather clock. Golden blonde hair swinging gently against her cheeks, she peered inside, while the woman called Jesse shook her head as she admired the clock.

"It's fabulous, Bethany. Bash must be thrilled."

"He doesn't know about it yet," the blonde-haired girl said. "Mom and Dad saw it this morning, and they bought it for him. It's his birthday present."

"That's one *hell* of a birthday present," the girl called Jesse exclaimed.

"I know, but we all know it's exactly like the one in the drawings he's been doing since he was a kid. Mom said it's worth every penny they spent." The young woman tucked a lock of hair behind her ear as she closed the clock's glass door, then stroked the intricate carving on the clock's edges with her hand.

"Would he be willing to sell it?" The moment she asked the question, a swirl of hope eased the ache in Nora's chest. Both women turned their heads in her direction in curious surprise.

"Sell it? You mean the clock?" the blonde asked in amazement. She shook her head. "I doubt it. In fact, I'm pretty sure it would be an emphatic *fuck no*, from my brother."

"Right."

Nora jerked her head in a nod of understanding as she accepted the inevitable. For the second time in minutes, her entire body ached as if she'd just been thrown to the mat by Tanaka-sensei. The woman called Jesse took a step forward and touched Nora's arm as she swayed slightly.

"Hey, are you okay? Hell, you look like you're ready to pass out or something. Bethany, did you see any chairs around? She looks like she's gonna collapse any second."

"I'm fine," she whispered.

Nora swallowed the bile rising in her throat as she gently tugged her arm free from the petite woman's grasp. Despite the soft protests from both women, she turned and walked away. Behind her, the young woman called Bethany murmured something to her friend with what sounded like a note of awe in her voice. In response, her friend Jesse gasped loudly.

"*Oh fuck.* You're right. Go find Bash while I do something to keep her here."

The quiet exclamation barely reached Nora's ears as her stomach began to churn violently. Certain she was going to throw up, she hurried away from the clock in search of the nearest bathroom. She rushed out of the ballroom to find the ladies room, and a few seconds later, she was heaving her insides out like someone who'd mixed numerous shots of hard liquor with two or three bottles of wine.

Trembling, she pressed her hands onto the sidewalls of the stall to keep from sinking to the floor. God, what the fuck was wrong with her? She had to have caught a bug, and her disappointment at losing the clock had exacerbated it. Deep inside, a voice shouted she was wrong, but she ignored it. A quiet knock on the stall door made Nora jerk her head up.

"Hey, umm…are you okay, hon?" The disembodied voice echoed softly in the air. "Is there something I can get for you? Someone I can call, maybe?"

Nora recognized the voice of the woman called Jesse, and she suppressed a sigh of annoyance before grabbing some toilet paper to wipe her mouth. God, the last thing she wanted was to have someone mothering her. She just needed to get the fuck out of the hotel and go home. Whatever she was coming down with, was obviously *not* going to be pleasant.

Inside her head, she heard a voice jeer at her for blaming her reaction on a bug. Nora ignored the sarcastic rebuke echoing through her mind. The bitter residue of bile in her mouth called for water, even though she really didn't want to have to deal with the woman who'd followed her into the bathroom. She shivered as she flushed the toilet, then slowly turned to open the stall door. Jesse's worried look as she emerged from the stall made Nora grimace.

"Thanks, but I'll be fine. It's just a bug I must have picked up." The words caused a loud snort of disagreement to echo in her head.

"Are you sure?"

"Yes."

Nora nodded and moved to the basin where she ran cold water to rinse out her mouth, then splashed some on her cheeks. She straightened and looked into the wall mirror to see the other girl frowning at her.

"Look, Jesse is it?" She arched her eyebrow to emphasize the question, and the girl bobbed her head. "I appreciate your concern, but I'll be fine."

"Yes, but…it's just that…well, I promised Bethany that I'd keep you here while she went to get…went for help."

"As you can see, I don't need help. I just need to go home."

"Where's home?" Jessie blurted out. Nora turned around to stare at the girl in surprise. The girl blushed. "I'm sorry, I just thought maybe you might need help getting home."

"I'm a big girl. I can manage on my own," she muttered with annoyance as she remembered giving Victoria her license and the few pounds she'd brought with her. "I'm actually here with someone. I'll get them to take me home."

The thought of finding Nicholas made her wince. The last thing she wanted to deal with at the moment was trying to explain to her brother about the clock. Especially when she couldn't even explain it to herself. If Uncle Charles was here—she pushed the thought aside. He wasn't, and she would have to deal with this alone. Whatever *this* was.

"If you're sure," Jesse said in a hesitant voice. The girl glanced at the exit door, before she suddenly smiled with inspiration. "I have an idea. Why don't you sit down in the lounge area here, and I'll go find your friends?"

There was something about the girl's insistence that

made Nora narrow her gaze at the younger woman. Color rose in Jesse's cheeks, and Nora shook her head.

"Thanks, but you don't have to worry about me. I'm feeling much better." It was a lie. She felt ready to throw up again. An image of the clock filled her head, and Nora's heart twisted in her chest.

Without waiting for the girl to reply or protest, Nora walked out of the ladies room. She walked toward the ballroom, then stopped at the entrance. What she really wanted was fresh air, if one could call it fresh air in London. Tomorrow, she'd pack a few things and go to the country for a couple of days. That was *if* she could manage it without throwing up.

Satisfied with her plan of action, she walked quickly toward the side exit of the hotel. She paused briefly at the registration desk and arranged for someone to find Nicholas and Victoria and tell them she'd be waiting for them outside. The moment she descended the steps to stand on the pavement, she dragged in a deep breath of air. In the short time since they'd arrived at the Dorchester, night had settled over the city.

The air was still warm from the day's sun, but goosebumps layered her skin. Rubbing her hands up and down her arms, Nora shivered. What the hell was wrong with her? It was a clock. Just a damn clock. Why was she acting like a passenger on the Titanic, frantic to find something that would float because all the life boats were gone?

Fingers gently massaging her temple to ease the headache she'd suddenly developed, she began to pace the pavement. In the distance, she heard an incoherent shout. It was more of a bark of sound than anything else, but it made her turn around to study her surroundings. The sound whispered through the air again, and she jerked her head toward Hyde Park across from the hotel's side entrance. Despite the darkness, she could just make out the silhouette of someone standing on the edge of the park grounds. It was impossible to tell if the person was watching her or someone else.

"Oh, for fuck's sake, Nora *Annabelle* Barrows. Pull yourself together. There's no one watching you."

The moment her words faded away, another shout filtered its way through the air. Once again, she stared at the silhouette across the street just a few feet from the park's perimeter. This time, she could have sworn someone was calling her name, but two cars whizzed past her, drowning out the cry. The shout came again, and this time it was clearer, and she was certain whoever was in the park had shouted the name Anna.

Without thinking, she stepped forward and heard a horn blare loudly. She jerked her head toward the sound and was blinded by headlights. It happened so fast, she didn't have time to register anything except the impact.

Chapter 2

March 1895

The stone floor was cold against her body as Anna groaned with pain. She blinked as she pressed the heel of her palm against her head. God, every muscle in her body ached as if she'd fallen out of the Falcon's crow's nest. The only thing that might hurt worse was the way her head was throbbing.

Soft sobs echoed in the air, and she blinked again. Where the hell was she? The last clear memory she had was being dragged from the Blue Mermaid by Hamish and Smitty after a profitable evening. She'd been quite pleased with the amount of money she'd won. It had been more than enough to buy several new books before the Falcon left port in a few days.

Anna slowly pushed herself into a sitting position and patted her sides. The jacket she'd been wearing with the money hidden inside the concealed pocket was gone. She dragged in a sharp breath as she suddenly realized her new leather boots and wool pants had been replaced by a lightweight chemise. Her mouth twisted with confusion as she studied the white garment for a moment.

It reminded her of clothing she'd seen on murals inside the pyramids at Giza, when Uncle Charles had taken her to the ancient monuments as a child. An Englishwoman would consider the garment indecent and fit only for a whore. But Anna knew it would have been a practical garment for a woman of royal blood or a priestess in ancient Egypt. It would have made the heat of the Egyptian sun more bearable. The only problem was, she wasn't in ancient Egypt, and the chemise was definitely inappropriate for England's damp weather.

Worse, it was the only thing she wore. She was going to be a target for every sailor on the docks looking for a woman, willing or not. Although the thought was an unpleasant one, it didn't terrify her. Uncle Charles had taught her well, and she was confident she could defend herself if necessary. Unfortunately, her fighting skills hadn't done her any good on the way back to the Falcon with Hamish and Smitty.

Short flashes of the events that had happened after leaving the tavern flitted through her head. The memories caused her to grimace with regret. None of this would have happened if she'd not followed her friends, and occasional bodyguards, to the Blue Mermaid. Uncle Charles was going to rain the fires of hell down on the heads of the two sailors the moment he learned of her disappearance. Not that there was anything Uncle Charles could say to the seamen that would make them feel worse than they were probably already feeling. She was certain Hamish and Smitty would be ridden with guilt. But there wasn't anything the two seamen could have done to prevent her kidnapping.

Anna released a rueful sigh. The two sailors were completely blameless for her current predicament. She'd known Hamish and Smitty never would have agreed to take her with them. But for almost two years now, she'd been sneaking off the Falcon, dressed as a young sailor, to follow her friends to whatever tavern they visited.

No one had ever been the wiser as Anna had always been exceedingly careful to ensure she wasn't seen leaving or returning to the Falcon. She'd also been discreet about not winning too much to avoid drawing attention to herself. But she'd become too cocky, especially believing she could easily defend herself, and her luck had run out.

Uncle Charles wasn't going to just have Hamish's and Smitty's head. Her uncle would most likely renew his efforts to make her leave the Falcon and stay in England to enter society. In fact, Anna was certain he would insist she do so after this escapade, possibly even ordering her to do so.

"*Damnation*," she said softly. "You've made a cockup of things this time, Anna."

Her plan had been to earn a few pounds gambling at cards, then wait for her friends to leave and follow them out of the tavern. The two men hadn't even realized she was in the Blue Mermaid until a small crowd had gathered around the table where she was winning handily at cards.

It wasn't until she'd seen Hamish glaring at her from a few feet away that she realized she needed to leave the game voluntarily, or her friend would end it for her. After she'd claimed her winnings, Smitty and Hamish had followed her out of the tavern. Hamish, who'd known her since she'd first stepped onto the Falcon at the age of eleven, had been furious.

Her friend had been cursing up a blue streak beneath his breath as he'd tugged her toward where the Falcon was docked. In the process, she'd stumbled, and her cap had fallen off, sending her hair tumbling down over her shoulders. That had made Smitty choke out a low curse of dismay, but Hamish hadn't responded.

Instead, the tall, strapping sailor had slapped at his neck as if bitten by a bug. Smitty and she had both done the same while the three of them continued forward. Seconds later, Hamish had stumbled then turned to stare at her in horror before he had dropped like an anchor at her feet.

On the other side of her, Smitty saw Hamish sinking to the cobblestones, and he'd quickly tugged her forward to escape danger. But like Hamish, the stocky sailor had stopped dead in his tracks to fall silently onto the cobblestones. A split-second later, she'd followed her friends and tumbled downward into a dark void. It was the last thing she remembered until she'd woken up on this cold stone floor in nothing but a decadent chemise. An undergarment someone else had put on her.

"*Bloody hell*," she gasped in horror.

The thought of a stranger undressing her and replacing her clothes with the lightweight slip of material was mortifying. Anger spiraled through her at the violation. If she found the man who'd dressed her in this garment, she'd serve up the bastard's ballocks to the sharks. Suddenly, Anna jerked with dread as she tentatively touched her inner thighs. In the next breath, a wave of relief rolled over her. Her skin bore no traces of a man's seed, and she wasn't sore. Thank God for Céleste's detailed instruction in the ultimate intimacy between a man and a woman.

Over the past five years, her uncle's mistress had taught her a great deal about what happened when a man and woman were in bed. If Uncle Charles ever discovered how much Céleste had shared with Anna about the pleasures of the flesh, there would be fireworks between the couple. Still, she was grateful for Céleste's teachings. It was how she was certain no one had violated her while she was unconscious.

Goosebumps formed as a shiver skimmed across her skin. *Christ Almighty*, she was cold. Hands rubbing her arms in an attempt to warm herself, she peered into the darkness that bordered the patch of moonlight blazing a narrow trail across the stone floor from a small window above. A sudden flash of light in front of her made her jerk in surprise.

Blinded by the intensity of the beam, she shielded her eyes with the back of her hand, trying to see what was beyond it. A second later, something hard slammed into her chest, and the impact sent her crashing back down onto the stone floor. Pain sliced through her, and she grunted. Poseidon's balls, that hurt. As if from a distance, she heard someone call her name before the light winked out.

Oh God, now wasn't the time for one of her clairvoyant episodes. Anna didn't move for a moment as the force of the impact that had thrown her violently back into the cold stone made her body ache. After a long moment, some of the pain and tension ebbed from Anna's muscles, and she slowly sat up again, steeling herself for the light to reappear. When it didn't, she breathed a sigh of relief.

Anna slowly became adjusted to the darkness again and began to study the dark corners of her prison cell. At least, that's what she thought it was. There were shadows huddled together in different spots, while in other places she saw only one shadow cowering in the dark. In the distance, she thought she heard chanting.

"Hamish? Smitty?" she called out quietly, hoping her friends had been brought with her. Instinct said she was the only one who'd been taken. Her heart twisted in her chest.

"They aren't here." The quiet words drifted out of the darkness behind her, and Anna jerked her head to look over her shoulder.

"Who's there?"

"Sarah. I'm Sarah Trafford."

Anna scrambled to her feet, then turned to peer into the darkness to see who was speaking. The quiet whisper of sound on the stone floor accompanied the appearance of a golden-haired woman stepping out of the deep shadows. As the woman called Sarah ventured closer, Anna drew in a sharp hiss of air the moment the dim light revealed the other woman's countenance.

Sarah's lips were swollen, and a small trickle of dried blood clung to the corner of her mouth. Even in the darkness, Anna could see the woman's jaw was beginning to show a dark bruise. Anger sped through her. Whoever had hit Sarah deserved to be hung by the neck from a ship's yardarm until dead. She'd seen far too much violence inflicted on those unable to defend themselves. A painful memory whispered in her head, but she buried it in an instant.

"Did you see where they took my friends?"

"No, I didn't even see who took me prisoner."

"And the others?" Anna gestured toward the shadows huddled against the walls of the cell they were in.

"They were here before me." Sarah's voice echoed with a myriad of emotions, but the girl's fear dominated her reactions.

With a nod, Anna quickly worked her hair into a braid to keep it out of her way, tying off the end in a knot. When she finished, she walked toward the outline of a door. She knew it was a futile gesture, but she tested the handle, anyway. It gave way only a fraction in a silent confirmation it was locked. Next, Anna turned her attention to the hinges that held the door in place.

Flakes of rust covered her fingertips as she tested the pins to see if they were loose enough to remove. It was a miracle someone had managed to open and close the door. Anna released a harsh breath. She was in trouble. It wasn't the first time, but this was definitely the worst situation she'd ever been in.

The soft chanting she'd heard earlier had resumed, and she pressed her ear to the door, trying to make out what the voices were saying. Most of it was unintelligible, but at certain points the chanting peaked in volume as the voices cried out the name Hatshepsut.

"Can you tell what they're saying?" Sarah's soft whisper next to her ear made Anna start violently as her hand swung up and stopped within a hairsbreadth of the other girl's neck.

"*Fuck.*" Anna jerked back from the other woman, her voice a soft, harsh whisper of surprise and fear. "Don't *ever* do that to me again. I could have hurt you."

Although the room was barely lit by the stream of moonlight, Anna saw the other girl staring at her in wide-eyed shock. Anna winced slightly. It was unlikely the woman had ever heard the foul curse, let alone from a woman. Céleste would be disappointed if she ever learned Anna had used the word in front of someone other than the ship's crew.

The Frenchwoman had been trying for years to strike the word from Anna's daily vocabulary. While her friend had succeeded for the most part, there were still times when it was the best curse at Anna's disposal. This was one of those times.

It helped release some of her trepidation. And she *was* afraid. Anna hated to admit it. Fear was a weakness, but something deep inside said she might not be so lucky to escape whatever was on the other side of the door. Anna rolled her shoulders in a silent apology.

"All I heard was the name of a pharaoh from ancient Egypt. Hatshepsut."

"Oh God," the girl's voice was a low moan of terror as she sank down to the floor with her back against the door. Something in the young woman's expression made Anna's stomach lurch violently.

"*What?* Tell me what it means." Anna knelt in front of Sarah. The young woman appeared to be in shock, and her cheeks were wet with tears. When the other girl didn't say anything, Anna grasped her by the shoulders and gave her a hard shake. "*Sarah*, tell me what it means."

"It means we're going to be sacrificed in their unholy ritual." Sarah's words were so soft, Anna wasn't quite sure she heard her correctly.

"Ritual? What kind of ritual?"

"They're praying to Hatshepsut for eternal life," Sarah whispered as she looked at Anna in horror. "They need blood…the blood of a virgin for the ritual."

"Don't be absurd," Anna snapped as she heard the

resignation in the other woman's voice. "What the hell makes you think that?"

"I'm a journalist. I've been investigating the recent disappearances of young girls from the docks and certain parts of the East End." The woman flinched as if remembering something unpleasant. "For the past two weeks, I've been following Viscount Farthington because I'd learned he had connections to an Egyptian cult of Hatshepsut worshipers."

"But Hatshepsut was a pharaoh, not a goddess," Anna said with a shake of her head.

"They believe Hatshepsut is a conduit to the Egyptian god of chaos."

"*Apophis.*" Anna breathed the word with alarm.

Uncle Charles had mentioned more than a year ago that a cult worshiping the ancient Egyptian god of chaos had been discovered in Cairo. It was why she'd not been allowed off the ship the last time they'd docked in the capital city of Egypt. Normally she could persuade her uncle to let her leave the ship with Hamish and one or two other sailors for bodyguards. But her uncle had been adamant in his refusal, stating it wasn't safe, and that they weren't staying in port long enough for her to visit any of the ancient tombs.

At twenty-six, she was no longer obligated to answer to her uncle, but Anna had never gone against his explicit orders since she was a child. It would hurt him deeply if she were to flagrantly disobey him. She'd learned that lesson when she was eleven, shortly after Uncle Charles had assumed guardianship of her and she'd gone to live on the Falcon.

Anger and defiance had insulated her from the pain she'd endured before her uncle had brought her to live with him on his merchant ship. It had been that same defiance that led her to climb up to the Falcon's crow's nest after Uncle Charles had told her not to.

When Hamish had brought her down to the main deck

to where her uncle was standing, his look of disappointment had been crushing. The devastation had become even greater when he'd simply turned and walked back into his cabin without saying a word to her. It was the last time she'd deliberately disobeyed him.

An image of her uncle filled her head. Tall, dark, and handsome, he'd been the romantic image of a pirate the day he'd strolled into The Red Gables inn and rescued her from a life as a scullery maid. He'd been her champion ever since, and she knew he'd blame himself if something were to happen to her. *Christ*, Hamish and Smitty would never forgive themselves, either.

Footsteps echoed outside the door of the cell, and Anna darted away from the door with Sarah following her lead. Apprehension made Anna tremble as the door's rusty hinges screeched loudly and the door slowly swung open. Four men, dressed in monks' robes, entered the cell, and screams filled the air as the shadows came alive with girls and women scrambling to get as far away from the door as possible.

Anna didn't move from where she stood in the moonlight. Her stance defiant, yet relaxed, she focused her mind on the critical lessons her uncle had given her. In her head, she heard him telling her to remember that the place of battle was just as important as the time. If she wanted to escape, she needed to wait before she attacked.

"This one," one of the monks uttered harshly as he pointed to Sarah, before swinging his attention to Anna. "And that one."

Sarah cried out in terror and began to struggle as two monks pulled her toward the door. Anna didn't resist as the other two cowled figures pulled her out of the cell and down a narrow hallway. They emerged from the corridor into a large area that had been transformed into a replica of an ancient Egyptian temple similar to the one she'd seen in Luxor several years ago.

The sight of the altar, with two masked figures in gold ceremonial robes behind it, sent Anna's heart crashing into her chest. It was little more than a stone slab, but the dark stains on the top of the altar's surface made her mouth go dry with fear. Sarah had been right about the sacrifices. Aware that she was on the verge of giving in to her fear, Anna forced herself to focus on using whatever was at her disposal to escape.

Her gaze surveyed the scene as quickly as possible, noting where braziers were, how high the torches were attached to the columns, and anything she could use as a weapon. Off to her right, she saw stairs leading up to a second floor. There were two doors at the rear of the temple, and she prayed they led outside and to freedom.

As the monks led her forward, they came close to one of the braziers lighting the temple area. In a flash of movement, Anna quickly bent her arm upward at the elbow in a blaze of motion to slam her fist into the nose of the man on her right. As he uttered a low cry of pain, the monk released her arm to press his hand to his face. Without hesitating, Anna kicked her leg backward and hooked her foot behind the man's calve. With a hard tug, she sent the man crashing to the floor as she pulled his leg out from under him. The monk on her left jerked to a halt, and with a well-practiced move, she whirled away from him on the tips of her toes in a pirouette. In one fluid movement, she lifted her leg as she came full circle and planted a hard kick into the man's back.

The strike propelled him forward into the open flames of a brazier. The monk screamed in pain, and she allowed herself a brief second of satisfaction before she saw the other monk starting to stand. Without hesitating, she landed a kick straight into the man's neck.

He gurgled and clawed at his throat as he lost the ability to fill his lungs with air. In front of her, the two monks who'd been dragging Sarah toward the altar turned to see what was happening behind them. Anna raced forward, and in the back of her head, she heard her uncle telling her where and how to cause the enemy the greatest damage. She released a flurry of strikes that sent the two men staggering away from Sarah.

"The doors behind me. *run*," she snapped as she saw the other girl standing rigid where the monks had left her. The sight of more cowled figures heading toward them made Anna lunge for one of the torches on the wall, which she handed to the girl. "*Go. Now.*"

As if coming out of a trance, Sarah grabbed the torch and raced toward the doors. In the back of her mind, Anna prayed she hadn't directed the girl into a dead end. She didn't have time to do more than utter a word of prayer before she forced herself to focus on the new threat. She counted four monks running toward her as other members of the cult appeared confused and uncertain as to what was happening.

Anna glanced behind her and saw two more cowled figures trying to close in on her from the right. There was a time to fight, and there was a time to run. Only a fool would stay to fight right now. Without a second thought, Anna whirled around and raced after Sarah. She'd almost reached the door the other girl had disappeared through when a rough hand grabbed Anna's braid and dragged her to a halt.

Pain assaulted her scalp, and a blast of fury burned its way through her. As she began to fall backward, she instinctively flipped her body and landed on all fours like a cat. In the next breath, she lunged forward and shoved her head hard into the stomach of the man trying to stop her.

The loud grunt above her became a shriek of pain as she drove her fist into the man's crotch. The man instantly released his grip on her hair and staggered away to fall to the floor, sobbing like a baby.

Anna sprang upright and was immediately forced to duck as another monk charged at her with a torch. The flame of it singed her cheek, and she tried to fight back the anger pounding its way through her as it began to take hold of her senses. Uncle Charles had always said anger was her worst weakness, but at the moment, she wanted to send every one of these bastards to hell.

As the torch swung back toward her again, Anna darted to one side and planted her foot into the monk's leg with a savage kick. The loud snap that filled the air said her foot had connected with a kneecap. With an agonized cry, the man fell to the ground. Anna didn't have time to think as, out of the corner of her eye, she saw another hooded figure coming at her from the left.

Her fury taking control of her, Anna spun around on the ball of her foot to face her next attacker. The anger surging through her added power to her blow as Anna drove her fist into the man's solar plexus before she struck a hard blow with the side of her hand into her attacker's throat.

The icy rage flowing through her became cold satisfaction as she saw the man fall. She only paused for a fraction of a second before she looked up to see two more monks heading toward her. Gun shots suddenly filled the air, and the monks heading toward her pulled up short. Anna jerked her head toward the gunfire as well, then back to the cult members. One monk turned and fled, while the other one lunged toward her.

Anna quickly balanced herself on her toes and just as he was in arm's reach, she threw her leg up then outward in a vicious kick to the side of the man's head. Anna spun around to face another monk charging her, and everything suddenly moved in slow motion as if she had been thrust into a dream. The moment Anna saw the blade descending toward her chest, she twisted her body away from her attacker to avoid the sharp weapon. Adrenalin flowed through her as she struck out, and the side of her hand landed a vicious blow to the man's neck. The knife clattered against stone as the monk stumbled backward, then plopped down to the floor in a sitting position. With a sharp kick, she slammed the heel of her foot against the man's head.

More shots rang out, and Anna turned to see several policemen chasing monks who were now fleeing the temple like a flurry of cockroaches being exposed to light. In front of her, a young man was staring at her in amazement and dismay. For a moment, she stood frozen, preparing herself to do battle again.

As she met the stranger's gaze, Anna saw his mouth move, but his voice was little more than a whisper in her ears. Something warm spread across her chest, and she looked down to see a large spot of blood spreading across the top of her chemise. Oh God, Uncle Charles was going to be so disappointed with her. It was the last thought in her head as she slid to the floor.

Chapter 3

Sebastian Reddington, Viscount Starling, took a drink of brandy and stared into the flames of the fireplace. His evening at the opera and a late supper at Rules with friends had proven to be quite enjoyable, despite Lady Margaret's absence. She'd sent word earlier in the day that she was feeling under the weather and would be unable to join him for the evening.

For more than a month now, he'd enjoyed Lady Margaret's company on frequent occasions, and he found her an intelligent, pleasant companion. In fact, he'd even begun to contemplate the possibility of proposing marriage to her. It was time he settled down and produced an heir. The thought made him wonder what bedding Margaret would be like. Not that it mattered, a mistress could easily satisfy his need for bed sport if a wife failed to find pleasure in the bedroom.

A twinge of guilt nipped at him for being a hypocrite, but he quickly dismissed it with the reminder that women weren't to be trusted. Not even Margaret. The memory that accompanied the thought tightened the muscles in his body. It vanished at the abrupt sound of the front door crashing open, followed by his brother's cries for help in the foyer. Puzzlement twisted Sebastian's mouth at the urgency and panic in Alexander's shout.

His younger brother wasn't normally excitable, but there was a distinct note of fear in Alexander's voice. Setting his brandy snifter on the fireplace mantel, Sebastian quickly strode across the floor of his study and out into the main entryway of Starling House. The sight of Alexander covered in blood, while holding a woman who appeared lifeless in his arms, made Sebastian's mouth grow dry with fear.

"You're hurt," he exclaimed as he rushed to his brother's side.

"No, but she is. I think she's dying, Bash." The horror in his brother's voice deepened Sebastian's concern. What the devil had his younger brother involved himself in and with whom? "We can't let her die, Bash. It will be my fault."

"Come. Give her to me. I'll take her upstairs while you fetch the doctor."

Alexander carefully laid the woman in Sebastian's arms, then stood staring down at her for a moment before he looked up at him.

"You should have seen her, Bash. She was magnificent."

The look of awe and admiration in his brother's voice made Sebastian frown. Whatever Alexander had embroiled himself in, it couldn't be good. Out of the corner of his eye, he saw his butler enter the foyer. Concern flashed across Hodgekiss's features as he took in Alexander's appearance. His brother was well-loved by the staff, and his butler's worried look wasn't surprising given Alexander's blood-stained appearance.

"You can tell me about it later. In the meantime, the woman needs a doctor. *Now go.*" Sebastian turned and started up the steps. "Hodgekiss, have Mrs. Osbourne send up towels, hot water, and bandages to the green room, and send someone to find my mother, wherever she is this evening."

When he reached the second floor, he strode quickly down the hall to the guest bed chamber. A soft moan of pain drifted out of the woman in his arms, and Sebastian jerked his gaze downward. Her eyelids fluttered open for a moment, and she stared up at him with bewilderment, then fear before she sank back into unconsciousness.

It was impossible to ignore the fact that she was lovely, which explained his brother's interest in the woman. Even *he* felt the strong stirrings of desire just from a cursory inspection of her curves. The indecent chemise she wore left little to his imagination, and he couldn't help picturing her in his bed.

The thin, almost transparent material did little to hide her lush thighs and full breasts. She had a body like the portrait of *La Grande Odalisque* painted by Ingres. Sebastian released a quiet snort of disgust at his musings. The woman appeared to be badly injured, and he was a reprobate for allowing her tempting curves to stir lust in him. From her current state of *en déshabillé*, he could only assume his brother had paid a visit to one of the higher-end brothels tonight.

That or his brother had taken a mistress. The thought made his jaw clench with irritation. It didn't bother him that his brother might have taken a mistress. But Alexander needed to understand there were some women a man needed to avoid at all costs, no matter how lovely and enticing she was.

The last thing his brother needed was a mistress that came with a less than savory past. He couldn't see the extent of the woman's wound, but it was obvious she'd been attacked. Perhaps by a jealous lover? And what had Alexander meant when he'd said the woman had been magnificent?

Whatever had happened, he would have to monitor the situation closely. His younger brother was generous to a fault, and most women managed to hide their traitorous natures with great skill. They especially excelled at deceiving men such as Alexander by playing on their kind hearts.

Sebastian gently laid the woman on the bed, then pulled

a small portion of material away from her shoulder, trying to determine the extent of her wound. Despite his efforts to ignore her physical attributes, it was impossible to miss the soft swells of her breasts, or how the chemise had fallen between her thighs to reveal even more of her long legs. They were legs made to wrap around a man's waist as he buried himself inside her.

If there was one thing he couldn't fault Alexander for, it was his ability to choose a woman made for pleasure. Behind him, a gasp of dismay filled the air, and Sebastian turned his head to see his housekeeper, Mrs. Osbourne, enter the room and hurry toward the bed.

"Mr. Hodgekiss sent me, my lord." The woman moved to the opposite side of the bed and released another quiet sound of horror.

"I've sent my brother for the doctor, but it appears she may have lost a great deal of blood. I can't tell how badly she's injured, but we need to ensure the bleeding has stopped."

"I shall see to her, my lord." The housekeeper nodded in his direction before looking over her shoulder at the household maid standing in the doorway. "Lucy, make sure some warm water is brought up with the hot as well. We'll also need vinegar to clean her wound before the doctor arrives. My lord, if you would, please, leave me and Lucy to take care of the young lady. We need to remove this…this garment she's wearing, then put her under the covers."

Sebastian noted the disapproval in Mrs. Osbourne's voice. It emphasized just how indecent the injured woman's garment was. A hand suddenly clutched at his arm in a display of strength that surprised him, and he jerked his head toward the woman on the bed. For the amount of blood staining her bodice, her grip on his arm was amazingly strong. He looked down into dark chestnut eyes, glazed with pain. She stared up at him for a moment in confusion before horror darkened her gaze. Her grip on his arm tightened.

"Sarah." The soft, cultured notes of her voice vibrated with fear.

"Is that your name? Can you tell me where your family is? I shall send for them." Sebastian studied her intently, hoping she'd give him something he could use to find whoever was responsible for her.

"Sarah. Where is…Sarah?"

Who the devil was Sarah? Again, Sebastian's alarm grew as he considered the depths of the quagmire Alexander had clearly stumbled into. It made him believe that whatever had happened, the entire affair was far from circumspect, which meant a scandal. The last thing he wanted was for the Reddington name to be dragged through the gossip columns. Before he could question her, her fingers dug painfully into his arm, and he winced.

"Where…where is she…I need to know…"

The woman's voice trailed off as her eyelids fluttered closed. Sebastian frowned as he studied her pale features for a moment. Despite looking as if Alexander had pulled her out of a brothel, the woman's genteel voice forced Sebastian to question his original impression of the woman.

"Sebastian?"

The sound of his mother's voice made him stiffen as a familiar antipathy tightened his muscles. Slowly turning around, he coldly eyed the woman who'd given birth to him. With a worried look, she glanced at the woman in the bed, but waited for him to answer her unspoken question as to what had happened. It was obvious from her evening gown she'd just arrived home. For a fraction of a second, Sebastian was glad she was here. He immediately dismissed the emotion. Their discord had been set in place for years, and it was something he had no intention of changing.

"Alexander brought her here a few moments ago. He's gone for the doctor."

"Did he say who she was?"

"I didn't question him. I felt it more imperative to summon a physician to tend to her wound." His reply made his mother nod, and Lady Harding pulled off her evening gloves as she prepared to take charge of the situation.

"Leave her to Mrs. Osbourne and me."

She moved deeper into the room, and while she didn't look at him, it was obvious she was waiting for him to leave. With a sharp bob of his head, Sebastian left the guest room and made his way back down the stairs and into his study.

In the space of just a few short moments, the quiet ending to a pleasant evening had dissolved into chaos. The memory of his younger brother standing in the hall covered in blood with the unconscious woman in his arms made Sebastian frown. As he stared down into the fire, he picked up the brandy snifter he'd left on the mantel and finished the remainder of his drink. He could imagine any number of scenarios to explain the injured woman upstairs, but he discarded them one after the other.

With a grunt of irritation, he knew he'd have to wait for an explanation of the evening's events until his brother returned. He didn't have long to wait before voices echoed in the foyer. Moving quickly toward the study door, Sebastian reached the entryway, just as his brother had taken his first step up the staircase.

"Alexander, come into the study. Our mother is with…the patient, and Dr. Johnson will see to her care." Sebastian nodded at the man who'd stopped behind Alexander. "Doctor, take a left at the top of the stairs. Your patient is in the second room on the right."

His brother hesitated, then with a reluctant nod, Alexander stepped aside to watch the doctor climb the stairs for a brief moment. Sebastian cleared his throat to capture his brother's attention, then turned to enter his study, with Alexander following him. Guilt and worry made Alexander appear older than his twenty-two years as Sebastian watched his brother move to the liquor cabinet.

Alexander pulled out a bottle of Sebastian's best cognac and splashed a large quantity of the liquor into a glass. The younger man tossed down a stiff amount of the alcohol then repeated the action. Sebastian frowned at his brother's silence. Tired of waiting for answers, he cleared his throat in a manner that indicated he wanted an explanation.

"It's not what you think, Bash," the younger member of the Reddington family said as he turned around.

"It's rather difficult not to think the worst, considering the way the woman's dressed. Is she your mistress?"

"*No*, she's *not* my mistress," Alexander snarled. "*Stop assuming* every woman you meet is unworthy of kindness, respect, or even love, Sebastian."

The sharp words were all the more harsh as his brother used his given name instead of the name his youngest siblings had used since they were old enough to talk. The anger and disgust in Alexander's voice made Sebastian stiffen as he defended himself against his brother's accusation.

"I can assure you that I hold Lady Margaret in the highest regard. I am also considerate and kind in my dealings with her. While I've not yet offered for her hand, I believe we are well matched."

"Well matched? What about love?" His brother's voice was filled with contempt, perhaps even a hint of pity. Sebastian didn't like the way it made him feel.

"Love is not required to produce an heir."

"The only kind of man capable of making such a statement is one without a heart or the ability to forgive his mother for marrying another man so soon after his father's death," Alexander said with caustic vehemence. "But I consider you a lost cause. Anna is *not* my mistress, and I did not find her in a brothel."

"Then perhaps you can explain the manner of her

clothing, or rather, the lack of it?"

"If you would stop interrupting me, I'll tell you." The sarcasm in his brother's voice made Sebastian eye the younger man with irritation.

"Then explain."

"Anna risked her life to save the woman I intend to marry."

"*Marry*," Sebastian exclaimed with astonishment, suddenly remembering the woman upstairs, and how she'd demanded to know if Sarah was safe.

"Yes, marry. I've already offered for Sarah's hand."

"You've proposed?" Sebastian snapped as he considered the possible ramifications of his brother's actions.

"Yes. And before you assume the worst of her, as you have Anna, Sarah is the daughter of Baron Trafford. So, she is more than suitable to become my wife. She will support me in whatever path I choose where my future is concerned. She will do me credit in every way a *loving* wife should."

While news of his brother's intentions was startling, Sebastian experienced a rush of relief the Reddington name would not be involved in a scandal. An image of his mother floated through his head, and he viciously buried it. Alexander shoved a hand through his hair as he glanced at Sebastian in a rebuke of cold anger, silently making it obvious he knew what Sebastian had been thinking.

"*Now*, are you going to keep your mouth shut, and *let me speak?*"

The angry disgust in his brother's voice and expression made Sebastian jerk his head in a gesture of compliance. For a momentary instant, he suddenly felt as if their roles were reversed, with Alexander playing the part of the older brother, chastising the younger.

As he waited for his brother to continue, Sebastian's thoughts focused on the woman upstairs. Her hand had gripped his arm so fiercely as she'd demanded an answer to her question before she'd succumbed to her injury and fallen unconscious again.

It was becoming apparent with each passing second that he had misjudged the woman, and he frowned with regret. He was not so unfeeling as to think ill of someone who was fighting for their life. But in his defense, the woman's state of déshabillé had not lent itself to the formation of a favorable opinion.

In the back of his mind, he heard a snort of contempt. Thinking the worst of the woman hadn't simply been based on her inappropriate dress. He slammed the door on the memory that accompanied the thought. When Sebastian remained silent, his brother's reaction was one of cold satisfaction. His head bowed as he studied the floor, Alexander shook his head as if trying to put his thoughts in order. After a brief moment, he raised his head.

"I know you're familiar with my interest in Egyptology, but I've not shared the depth or extent of my fascination with the topic. Mainly because I know you will find the pastime less than conducive to defining a promising future for me."

Alexander frowned at Sebastian. It was the same angry scowl his younger brother had worn when Sebastian had recently offered to secure a commission for him in the Army. Something Alexander had immediately rejected.

"For the past year, I've been studying ancient Egypt with others who share my fascination with the culture."

Startled by his brother's revelation, Sebastian arched his eyebrows as Alexander turned back to the liquor cabinet again. The younger man poured himself another drink and, looking over his shoulder, silently offered to pour Sebastian one as well. When he refused his brother's offer with a shake of his head, Alexander splashed more of Sebastian's best cognac into a snifter, then tossed it down in one gulp.

While Sebastian wasn't miserly with his cognac, Alexander's sudden propensity to drink with abandon was disturbing. Particularly when his brother didn't bother to savor the flavor of one of the finest brandy's Sebastian had ever found. He quickly clenched his jaw to refrain from commenting. Alexander turned back to him, holding his fourth glass of liquor.

"I met Sarah a few months ago at a lecture on the *Book Of The Dead* hosted by Wallis Budge at the British Museum. It was as if we'd known each other all our lives. We even manage to finish each other's sentences more often than naught."

Alexander stared down into his glass of brandy, and Sebastian noted the brief smile of happiness and hope curving his brother's mouth. His brother's disposition had always been cheerful and pleasant, but his smile displayed an emotion he'd never seen in Alexander before. It told Sebastian his brother would not be swayed in his intentions to marry the young woman he'd set his cap for. Sebastian could only hope his brother didn't fall prey to the heartache their father had. A second later, Alexander's features hardened with grim rage. He took another swallow of liquor before continuing.

"Like me, Sarah has an avid interest in Egyptology. Our interests are so closely aligned we've even discussed traveling to Egypt for our wedding trip, although I'm not about to agree to such a trip now."

Unyielding determination thinned his brother's lips. It was a sign that he would not change his mind on that score. Perhaps his brother was not completely at the mercy of the woman he had emphatically said he intended to marry. Another strong swig of drink found its way down his brother's throat, but Sebastian's disapproval became concern as he saw how badly his brother's hand shook.

"Come sit down, Alexander." His concern reflected in his quiet command, Sebastian gestured toward one of the chairs in front of the fireplace, but his brother refused with a wave of his hand.

"Once I'd ensured Sarah and Anna were safely in my carriage, I told Sarah I would escort her home, and that Terrence would bring Anna here. Sarah objected vehemently to that plan. She demanded I bring her with me to Starling House so she could tend to Anna herself, but I refused. My future bride can be incredibly stubborn on occasion, but Sarah's mental state is incredibly precarious given the ordeal she's been through."

Raw fury slashed across his brother's face as his fist hit the top of the liquor cabinet in a violent strike that caused the cabinet to visibly shudder.

"They hit her, Bash," Alexander's voice was hoarse and dark with rage. "She fought them when they tried to remove her clothing, and the bastards hit her."

"Good God," Sebastian muttered at the implications of what had happened to Alexander's bride-to-be.

"They dressed her and Anna like concubines in a Pharoah's harem," his brother choked out. "I can only thank God Sarah fell unconscious before they stripped her. It spared her being cognizant during the debasing act. It's bad enough she will never forget the humiliation of it, but if they—"

The sudden explosive crack filling the air made Sebastian start with surprise as Alexander slammed his still half-full snifter down onto the cabinet's wood surface. The fragile goblet shattered beneath the force of his brother's violent act, and his brother muttered something unintelligible as he looked around for something to clean up the glass and the substantial amount of liquor spilling across the cabinet's surface.

"Leave it," Sebastian said quietly, and his brother nodded.

Guilt settled on Alexander's tormented features, and it made Sebastian's gut twist viciously. It was easy to follow his brother's train of thought, and he could tell Alexander would blame himself if his fiancée had been violated.

From his brother's current state, he was convinced Alexander thought he was to blame for Miss Trafford's ordeal. Sebastian rejected the possibility. His brother was one of the best men he knew. The only blame to be assigned was to the bastards who'd taken the women prisoner. Alexander drew in a deep breath. With suppressed violence, his brother began to prowl the floor.

"As I was saying, Sarah fiercely protested my initial plan to take her home while Terrence brought Anna here. I argued with her for several moments, but it was only when I agreed to be the one to bring Anna here while Terrence escorted her home that Sarah relented. She said I was the only one who could explain the entire situation to you. As usual, my wonderful bride-to-be was right. Terrence doesn't know you like I do. You would have brow beaten the man, perhaps even ordered him to take Anna to the hospital."

"Do you—"

"Don't deny it, Sebastian." His younger brother wheeled to a halt to confront him with a savage expression of contempt. "We both know you can be a cold-hearted bastard sometimes. You've proven it repeatedly where our mother is concerned. But as your brother, I had the power to ensure Anna received protection here, with or without your permission. Terrence didn't."

The insult flung in his direction made Sebastian go rigid. It was a disparagement that stunned him. If Alexander knew the truth about their mother, he wouldn't judge Sebastian so harshly. But to know his brother believed him so callous and lacking in character that he would have refused the woman care in his house cut deep.

He would never have been so indifferent to insist she be sent to the hospital instead of caring for her here. Sebastian had seen how badly the woman had been injured. But for

Alexander to believe him capable of such an act and brutally accuse him of uncaring behavior in such a derogatory fashion chilled him.

It was something his brother had never done before. The idea that Alexander saw him as a man unworthy of respect was almost a physical blow. He'd always tried to be the kind of man his siblings could be proud of, particularly Alexander and Francis. Sebastian loved all his siblings deeply, and their happiness was paramount to his own. It was why he'd shielded them from the truth about their mother. He'd never wanted them to experience the betrayal and pain he had.

The way his brother scowled at him with such disdain deepened the wound his brother's words had inflicted. It was as if Alexander had eviscerated him with one swift stroke. The younger man turned away from him with a disgusted shake of his head. The gesture further emphasized Alexander's poor opinion of him, and Sebastian flinched. His brother returned to prowling back and forth across the study's carpet.

"For the past year, Sarah has been writing articles for the Times under her mother's maiden name of Evans."

"Do you mean S.B. *Evans?*"

Amazed, Sebastian stared at his brother in disbelief. There were very few who didn't find Evans's articles intriguing and informative. Even he enjoyed reading them. Alexander bobbed his head.

"Yes. While most of her writings focus on recent archeological finds in Egypt, she has researched general topics as well, including unusual items of interest." Alexander inhaled a deep breath. "Sarah and I were to attend a lecture at the museum last night, but when I arrived to collect her, the household was in an uproar. Sarah had been missing since early yesterday morning. Lady Trafford was in her room under a doctor's care, while Lord Trafford was understandably highly agitated with fear and worry. When the man informed me of events, I was equally shaken, perhaps even more than the baron, because I knew what Trafford didn't."

His brother stopped speaking again as his pacing brought him to a halt in front of the window, looking out at Charles Street. Although Sebastian knew the only thing his brother could see was a reflection of himself, Alexander's rigid stance suggested his brother was seeing something completely different. Sebastian could only surmise Alexander was reliving the moment he'd learned his intended had been taken. With a shake of his head, his brother continued, but kept his back to Sebastian.

"More than a month ago, Sarah uncovered information that suggested a cult worshiping, Apophis, the Egyptian god of chaos, had migrated from Cairo to London. They believe that if they raise this god from the underworld, they'll become immortal."

Alexander's statement made Sebastian grimace at the foolishness of such beliefs. His brother turned to face him and waved his hand in agreement.

"Yes, yes, I know how ridiculous that belief is. But Sarah learned this cult was supposedly using the blood of virgins as part of their worship rituals. It made sense because we both knew Scotland Yard was working on the disappearance of young women known to be chaste. However, the police were focused on the possibility that Jack had returned."

"*Christ Jesus,*" Sebastian muttered beneath his breath.

Jack the Ripper as the papers had called him, hadn't been active for several years now. If the man had returned, the city wouldn't be safe until the police caught the sadistic monster. Alexander's expression was grim as he met Sebastian's gaze.

"They've managed to keep their investigations out of the papers, mainly because the few bodies that have been found were in the Thames completely intact except for slashes to the wrist and throat."

Alexander paled at his statement, and suddenly the puzzle pieces began to fall into place for Sebastian. Crossing the floor to the liquor cabinet again, his brother found a clean, more solid glass to fill. He quickly poured another large portion of brandy and tossed it down his throat before facing Sebastian again.

"When I learned Sarah was missing, I immediately contacted an inspector I know at Scotland Yard. Inspector Pratt had also heard the rumors about the cult, and he'd been following up on various pieces of information he'd uncovered despite being ordered to drop the direction of his investigations. We've been working together since last night trying to find Sarah. A few hours ago, we were able to isolate three possible locations where the rituals were taking place. Pratt gathered a few officers who were loyal to him, and we set off to search the buildings. The first location was empty, but the second building we'd pinpointed was the right one."

"And the woman upstairs? You mentioned protecting her."

"Several of the cult members escaped, and the inspector and I are concerned they'll come after Sarah and Anna to protect their identities." Before his brother could finish speaking, Sebastian strode toward the study door.

"*Hodgekiss.*" In seconds, Sebastian's loud summons resulted in the butler emerging from the back hall. "Send Portman to twelve Hooper Street and inform Thomas Scully, I expect him here within the hour with six of his men to guard the house."

"*No,* tell the man he's to send three of those men to the Trafford residence at seven Harcourt Street," Alexander said sharply over Sebastian's shoulder. Sebastian nodded in the butler's direction.

"Do it. And tell Portman he's not to return without

Scully and his men. There's no telling how quickly he'll find the man." As Hodgekiss hurried away, Sebastian turned around to see his brother studying him with a small measure of respect.

"Thank you," his brother said quietly. "I was unnecessarily harsh with you a few moments ago."

"I am not the man you think me, Alexander. At least, I'm not quite as bad as you suggested." At his quiet reply, his brother nodded.

"I know that. I've simply not been thinking straight since yesterday when I learned Sarah was missing. I'm deeply worried about her, and Anna as well. They've both been through an ordeal that would test even the bravest man's courage." Alexander paused for a moment as the look of admiration Sebastian had witnessed on his brother's features earlier, returned.

"But to do what Anna did...it almost defies the imagination."

"I've no doubt your Sarah is just as courageous."

"No, you don't understand. Sarah *is* strong and courageous, and I *am* proud of her. She didn't collapse in hysterics like most women would. But even she is in awe of what Anna did." Amazement and awed disbelief crossed Alexander's face as he met Sebastian's gaze. "*My God, Bash,* you should have seen her. I've only seen a handful of men in the Limehouse Causeway fight like Anna did. I saw her drop three men to their knees sobbing in agony in less than a minute."

At his brother's description, Sebastian frowned. Only immigrants from the most eastern regions of the Asian continent lived in the causeway. It was one of only two places in London, possibly England, where one could learn the fighting skills Alexander was describing. The woman upstairs wasn't an immigrant. She was an Englishwoman. Not only that, but her voice was also that of a gentlewoman.

While it was impossible to tell if she was of noble birth or simply a well-educated commoner, the possibility of her being a resident of the East End, let alone the Limehouse Causeway, seemed highly unlikely. What woman of breeding could fight in the way Alexander described, let alone be taught such a skill? His doubt must have been obvious as his brother objected to Sebastian's dubious reaction.

"It's the truth, Bash. She moved as if she were a bolt of lightning. None of the men I saw attacking her laid a hand on her until the last one. The bastard had a knife and charged at her from behind. I couldn't reload my gun fast enough to get off a clean shot, and I was too far away to stop the bastard from stabbing her the moment she turned around."

Remorse darkened Alexander's features. It was obvious his younger brother held himself responsible for the woman's injury simply because he hadn't been fast enough. Sebastian was certain Alexander had done everything in his power to keep the woman safe from harm. Now, as he studied the younger man, he suddenly realized the carefree, somewhat reckless, young rogue had become a man overnight. The regret on Alexander's face remained, but his admiration and astonishment were equally visible as he met Sebastian's gaze.

"I was still loading my weapon when the son of a bitch crashed to the floor, clawing at his throat. She took the bastard down as if she had swatted a fly. If not for the blood, I would have thought her untouched by the blade. Even then, she was still prepared to fight. She spun around, anticipating another attacker. It wasn't until I reached her that she looked down at her shoulder. She looked surprised. It was as if she'd only just realized she was hurt. A moment later, she collapsed."

Alexander shoved his hand through his hair in a state of bewilderment as if questioning the scene he'd just described. His brother's disbelief vanished as he lifted his head to study Sebastian for a moment. Sebastian's continued skepticism must have been evident as Alexander straightened his shoulders in a manner that said he was offended that Sebastian doubted him.

"I'm *not* exaggerating, Bash," he bit out with fierce resentment. If they had been living in the distant past, Sebastian was certain Alexander would have challenged him to a duel for calling his word into question. "I can tell you don't believe me, but I've never seen anything like it. She's the one who ordered Sarah to run, while she stayed behind to fight. Sarah and I owe her a debt that cannot be repaid."

Alexander's shoulders suddenly sagged as he rubbed the back of his neck. Wearily, his brother crossed the floor to the chair Sebastian had pointed to earlier and sank down into the seat. His brother's head fell backward to rest on the chair's padded cushion in unmistakable exhaustion. Everything about Alexander emphasized the strain he'd been under over the past twenty-four hours. Sebastian winced as he realized he'd added to his brother's stress by doubting Alexander's word.

Sebastian remained silent as he tried to envision the scene his brother had described. The idea of the woman upstairs possessing a skill such as Alexander described wasn't simply unusual, it was unheard of. Where could she have learned an art form few people outside a small collective of men in the East End knew? Sebastian grimaced. The woman was a mystery, and while mysteries intrigued him, they could also be dangerous. That a woman was involved made it even more so.

"If only we'd gone to the warehouse before the first one we searched. We would have arrived in time to prevent Anna's injury." Alexander's words were filled with defeat, and Sebastian immediately disagreed with him.

"*No one* could have done more than you or the police in what I'm certain had to be a chaotic scene. You are not responsible for the actions of a group of fanatics."

Sebastian's fierce objection to Alexander's misguided belief that he was in some way responsible for tonight's events made his brother stare at him in surprise. The younger man disagreed with a shake of his head, then looked away once more. Concerned for his brother's state of mind, Sebastian quickly changed the direction of their conversation.

"Do you know anything else about the woman other than her first name?"

"No. Nothing." Alexander said as he pinched the bridge of his nose before looking up at Sebastian. "We'll have to wait until she's coherent to learn more."

"Actually, we have a small clue as to how to find her family."

At the sound of his mother's voice, Sebastian glanced over his shoulder to see Lady Harding standing in the study's doorway. She didn't cross the threshold, and he knew why. His study was the one room in the house that both of them had agreed she would never enter. In a flash of movement, Alexander was on his feet, and closing the distance between himself and their mother.

"How is she?"

"The doctor is still with her. You're unhurt?" Lady Harding gently touched Alexander's cheek with concern as she stared down at his blood-stained shirt.

"I'm fine."

"You said you believe you know how to find her family." Sebastian's voice was devoid of emotion as he spoke. His mother glanced at him before she turned her attention back to Alexander, ignoring Sebastian's unspoken question.

"And Sarah? Is she safe?"

Lady Harding's question made Sebastian start with surprise. His brother had told their mother about Alexander's future wife. Had Alexander not told him about his marital intentions because he feared Sebastian would object? The answer filled Sebastian with remorse. Perhaps Alexander had been right to call him a cold-hearted bastard.

"Terrence took her home, but I am worried about her, Mama. She is terrified. What she's been through…"

"Then go to her," his mother said softly.

"I cannot. I gave her my word that I would stay until the doctor apprised me of Anna's condition. She will want to know how badly Anna is hurt."

"The doctor will be down shortly, and we will know more then. Given our guest's injury, I believe you are right about Sarah. I cannot begin to imagine the trauma she and the young woman upstairs have suffered." A tender smile curved his mother's mouth as she briefly inspected Alexander's blood-stained shirt. "I also think you should change. You do not want to alarm Sarah in thinking you were hurt as well."

Alexander grimaced, and with a sharp nod, he darted around their mother and bounded up the stairs. Lady Harding arched an eyebrow at Sebastian, then turned and walked across the foyer into the salon. Sebastian followed his mother across the main hall, and as he entered the main parlor, his mother was sitting down on the settee.

"You will need to send someone to the docks, Sebastian." His mother's quiet statement made him jerk in surprise.

"The docks?"

"While Mrs. Osbourne and I were waiting for the doctor to arrive. We were forced to move the young woman two or three times. The pain brought her into a somewhat conscious state, albeit only for a few seconds." His mother winced with regret. "Although her voice was little more than a whisper, Mrs. Osbourne and I were able to discern the words falcon, uncle, and ship."

"Do you think her uncle is a passenger on a ship called the Falcon?"

"I think it more likely her uncle is a merchant who owns

a ship called the Falcon. Despite that horrifying garment she was wearing, her voice indicates she's well-educated. And while her loveliness hasn't suffered from it, she's clearly spent too much time in the sun."

Sebastian frowned at this new piece of information. The woman upstairs was becoming more intriguing with each passing minute. His mother's suspicions that their guest came from a home of some standing matched his own. As for her appearance, he deliberately shoved his mother's words out of his thoughts. It only reminded him of the desire that had assaulted him when he'd carried her up to the green room.

"And you heard nothing other than those three words?" At his question, his mother frowned slightly.

"Now that I think on it, she did mention a Hamish and another name that might have been Smith. It could be her uncle's name or perhaps a husband. But if we can find a ship called the Falcon, I'm confident we will find her family. But I suggest the sooner we search for them, the better." Lady Harding's expression grew more troubled as she stared off into space. "Her wound is deep, and I'm uncertain what the doctor will say. I purposely did not mention it a few moments ago. I fear Alexander might believe himself responsible for the young woman's injury."

"Your suspicions are correct. He said as much when he gave an account of what had happened this evening."

Clearly surprised at Sebastian's reply, Lady Harding studied him for a brief moment, then nodded and looked away. The awkward silence filling the room made Sebastian feel the urge to explain the plan of action he'd taken.

"I sent Portman earlier to find Thomas Scully with the message he's to come here immediately. I'll have him place guards in front of the house and the Trafford's. When he arrives, I'll have him assign one of his men the task of searching for Anna's family as well."

The moment he mentioned the woman by her first

name, his mother arched an eyebrow at him, but remained silent. Confused by his informal reference to the woman he'd carried upstairs, Sebastian frowned. The idea of Anna dying affected him in a way he didn't understand. He quickly dismissed the feeling and attributed his reaction to a compassionate concern for the woman.

He had no desire to see Anna die. With everything Alexander had told him, the woman had saved lives tonight. She deserved to live, unlike those who'd murdered innocent women. He also didn't want Alexander to inflict any more guilt on himself. His brother had already assumed too much responsibility for tonight's events.

Silence fell between them once more, and Sebastian moved to stand beneath the portrait of his father that hung over the room's fireplace. It was always like this between him and his mother. Cold, awkward, and even painful. He didn't like the way it made him feel, but his mother's betrayal wasn't something he could ever forgive. Sebastian had idolized his father, and he'd witnessed Levi Reddington's unhappiness as the result of his wife's infidelity. His jaw tightened at the memory of Alexander announcing he'd proposed to Sarah Trafford.

"You knew about Alexander's decision to marry." Sebastian continued to stare up at the painting of his father.

"Yes," she replied softly. The moment he spun about on his heel to face her, his mother shook her head slightly with umbrage. "You seem surprised Alexander would confide in me."

"No…yes. In a matter such as marriage, I am surprised he didn't speak with me first." Sebastian cocked his head slightly as he contemplated his brother's reason for speaking to their mother about his plans to marry before bringing it to Sebastian's attention.

"So you could persuade him to change his mind?" Lady Harding sighed with what might have been a note of sorrow in her voice. "He will be happy."

"Like you and father were?" The icy question sliced through the tension to the raw wound underneath as he turned to look up at his father's portrait once more.

"There are some things that cannot be explained," she said. "If I could have spared you…"

Lady Harding's voice died away as Sebastian whirled around to eye her with contempt. She immediately flinched, then paled beneath his glare.

"You mean you would have kept on lying."

"I would, and *always will*, do anything to spare *any* of my children pain, Sebastian. Despite what you think of me, I am not ashamed of anything I've done, nor do I have any regrets."

Sebastian was on the verge of lashing out at her again, when the doctor entered the salon. Lady Harding immediately rose to her feet to question him.

"How is she?"

"Asleep at the moment, my lady. I've given her some laudanum to help alleviate any discomfort she might have tonight. We only need to be concerned if she develops a fever. If that happens, send for me at once."

Footsteps pounded against the stairs and across the hall as Alexander charged into the salon. His expression dark with worry, his younger brother looked at the doctor.

"How is Anna? Will she live?" At Alexander's question, the doctor nodded.

"Yes, I believe so. The laceration was deep, but despite the loss of blood, her pulse is strong, and she's clearly in good health."

"Thank God," his brother exclaimed with relief.

"Alexander, go to Sarah."

At their mother's quiet order, his brother moved quickly to kiss Lady Harding's cheek. He paused for a moment to nod at Sebastian then raced from the room. A moment later, the front door closed with a loud thud as Alexander left the house. Dr. Johnson cleared his throat.

"I've done all I can for the moment, my lord. I've given your housekeeper instructions as to the young woman's care, and I'll return in the morning to see how she's faring."

"Thank you, Dr. Johnson." Sebastian nodded his thanks.

The doctor bowed first to his mother and then him before leaving the main parlor. Lady Harding walked toward the salon doorway a second later. Before she stepped into the foyer, she paused and looked over her shoulder.

"I did love your father, Sebastian. If he were here, he would tell you the same thing." The words made Sebastian stiffen, and he narrowed his gaze at her.

"Forgive me, my lady. But given my knowledge of certain facts, I find it impossible to believe you." The frost-bitten words made her blanch, but she didn't look away.

"If you love your brother, and I am certain you do, don't try to persuade Alexander to change his mind about marrying Sarah. He has always looked up to you. I do not wish to see either of you hurt."

Despite the discord between them, Sebastian heard the heartfelt plea in her voice. It did not surprise him that she would express concern for his brother, but for her to include him as well, startled him. Almost as if she could read his mind, a sad smile twisted her lips, and she shook her head.

"A mother never stops loving her children, Sebastian, no matter how much her children might despise her. Good night."

Lady Harding left him standing in the salon staring after her, still startled by her words.

Chapter 4

Anna blinked as she stirred beneath the covers of her bed. Staring up at the ceiling, she tried to remember where she was. Everything in her head was like a dream, with intangible pieces of information. Sitting upright in the bed, she drew in a sharp hiss of air as her shoulder silently howled a protest at her movement.

What the devil had she done to—the Cult of Hatshepsut. Like angry waves crashing across the Falcon's deck during a storm, memories from the night before rolled through her head. Hamish and Smitty falling to the cobblestone street. The two priests behind the altar in their black and gold robes. The monks dragging her and Sarah into their temple.

As the image of the young woman danced through Anna's head, it was followed by the face of the man who'd attacked her and the glint of steel in the dim light as the knife descended toward her. Anna's stomach lurched at the memory before more images flooded her head. The police and the young man who'd been with them. The man's stunned look of disbelief had made her look down at her chest, and she'd suddenly realized she'd been stabbed.

More images flashed in her mind, a tall woman whose voice had held a soothing note as she and another woman hovered over her. The memory of the doctor and the pain when he'd sewn up her wound. The recollection caused Anna's stomach to churn once more before all the faces in her head became wisps of smoke, until only one countenance filled her mind.

Of all the images, the tall, dark-haired stranger was the most vivid. There had been something about him that was so familiar. She didn't remember how she came to be in his arms, but she remembered his heat. It had been as if a dark angel from hell had soared up out of the fiery depths of the earth to warm her as he carried her up a flight of stairs.

Even the quiet, authoritative sound of his voice had stayed with her as she remembered him asking if her name was Sarah. The memory made Anna draw in a sharp breath. She'd been asking the stranger what had happened to Sarah. He'd not answered her. Had the younger woman escaped? Was she uninjured?

With a tug of her good arm, Anna quickly threw the bedcovers aside and slid out of bed. The room spun around her as she tried to stand, and she took three quick steps forward to grab hold of the post at the foot of the bed. Eyes closed, Anna pressed her forehead into the warm wood of the bedpost for a moment until her stomach settled down.

Her equilibrium restored, Anna disregarded the pain in her shoulder as she walked unsteadily to the door and pulled it open. Clinging to the doorjamb, she stepped out into the corridor, looking up and down the hallway, hoping to find someone who could tell her what had happened to the young woman she'd met last night. At least she thought it was last night. God knows how long she'd been unconscious.

One hand braced against the wall, Anna saw a stairway a short distance from her room and began to work her way toward it. She was only a few feet from the steps when a tall figure emerged from the stairwell and turned away from her to walk in the opposite direction. The man had only gone two steps when he came to an abrupt halt in the middle of the hallway. In a sharp move, he whirled around to stare at her in disbelief. Her dark angel from last night.

"*Damnation, woman*," he exclaimed with what sounded more like irritation than concern as he strode quickly to her side. "What the devil are you doing out of bed?"

"Sarah. I need to know what happened to Sarah." The energy that had enabled her to leave her room suddenly vanished, and Anna pressed her back into the wall to keep from sliding to the floor. "Is she all right?"

"Miss Trafford is unharmed and safe in her own home. You, however, dear lady, are not," he growled with obvious aggravation.

The world shifted suddenly, and Anna gasped in surprise as he swung her up into his arms, then headed back toward the bedroom she'd left. Snug against his chest, she curled her arm around his neck to hold her head at a more comfortable angle. An unexpected, tantalizing awareness swept through her as her senses exploded with unfamiliar sensations.

His arms, strong and sturdy as a ship's mast, held her snug against a solid chest that molded her body into his. The intimacy of her dark angel's embrace sent Anna's heart skidding out of control as the heat of him melted through her nightgown. It was a fiery sensation that sank through her pores into her veins, where it made her blood burn hotter than a summer sun.

Unsettled by her reaction to him, Anna tried to dismiss her acute awareness of him as nothing more than an overactive imagination. In the back of her mind, Anna heard a snort of mocking amusement. She peeked up at him. With hair the color of a starless night when the Falcon was at sea, everything about him shouted the word dangerous.

Céleste had taught her a great deal about physical attraction, but nothing her friend had taught her had prepared her for a moment such as this. The strength of the emotions flowing through her was exhilarating, and Anna couldn't help wondering what it would be like to kiss this man. With an unshakable certainty, she knew his mouth was capable of teasing and arousing a woman until the only thought in her head was the pleasure his caresses promised.

Now Anna understood what Céleste had meant when her friend had warned her there were some men who could bring a woman to the brink of something wicked and sinful with barely a word. Her friend's voice echoed loudly in her head. *You must avoid this kind of man at all costs, ma petite cherie, unless you want your heart broken.*

As if suddenly aware Anna was studying him, her dark angel glanced downward, and eyes as black as coal studied her intently. They glittered with an emotion that made her throat close until it was difficult to breathe. For a fraction of a second, she thought he might actually oblige her with a kiss. The thought shot a delicious anticipation through her, and her tongue darted out to wet her lips. The moment she did so, his beautiful mouth tightened into a hard, firm line, and he looked away from her.

Anna frowned in puzzlement at his stern manner. No, not stern. He was angry. The vague memory of the tension radiating off him as he'd carried her upstairs last night made her realize he'd been equally incensed then, too.

"You're angry with me."

"I beg your pardon?" He came to an abrupt halt in the doorway of her bedroom to look down at her in amazement.

"I can only assume it's because I'm an imposition, for which I apologize," she said in a pragmatic tone as she frowned. "If you will send word to the Falcon at the West Indies Dock, berth twenty-three, my uncle will come for me."

She didn't look away from him. Instead, she tipped her head to one side to watch him with curiosity as she waited for his answer. A soft rumble of sound whispered out of him as he looked away from her again and strode to the bed.

He leaned down to set her onto the mattress, and his face came within mere inches of hers. The moment their gazes locked, something wicked flared in the dark eyes, studying her with such intensity it threatened to steal her breath away. Immediately, her heart raced out of control again, and a frisson streaked across her skin.

She'd seen a man's eyes blazing with fury before, but what she saw in her dark angel's hot gaze was a different kind of fire. It hinted at something utterly sinful, and it held the promise of an inferno that would consume every inch of her with pleasure.

Mesmerized, she didn't move. She had the oddest sensation she'd experienced this moment before, and it had ended in something wild and unrestrained. The thought made her body tighten everywhere. In the next breath, her nipples hardened to stiff peaks that ached for his touch. It was a wicked sensation she knew she shouldn't feel, but with each passing second, the ache grew stronger. Almost as if he could read her thoughts, his gaze shifted downward. She knew she should fold her arms across her chest as any respectable young woman would, but she didn't.

Their eyes met once again, and a muscle twitched in his cheek as if he'd clenched his jaw with great strength. The sound of her heartbeat thundered in her ears while she struggled to breathe normally. Every inch of her was aching for something she desperately wanted to experience.

The realization made Anna lick her dry lips once more. For a mere instant, she was certain he'd leaned closer until his mouth was almost touching hers, before he abruptly jerked upright as if she'd slapped him. With his sharp retreat, the hot, sultry warmth of him vanished, replaced by a strong sense of frustration and disappointment. For the first time in her life, she understood what Céleste meant as to how a man could ravish a woman with just his gaze.

Her dark angel had done just that, and Anna was

struggling with the way her body was reacting to him. The man had ignited something dangerous inside her, but it was a danger she wanted to embrace. An emotion she couldn't decipher flashed across his face before he muttered something beneath his breath.

"You are not an imposition." The words were rough and harsh as he directed a dark look in her direction. "Do not leave this bed again until the doctor gives you permission to do so."

"But I don't…" Her voice trailed off into thin air as he strode from the room without stopping to hear what she had to say.

Frustrated, she glared at the door he'd closed behind him. Damn the man, she didn't even know his name. For someone who said she'd not offended him, the man acted as if she'd done just that. Irritated by his cold, abrupt manner, she huffed a sound of indignation. The man was rude.

Worse, she'd behaved like a wanton, not even attempting to hide the way her nipples had stiffened until they ached. But then she'd never done much of anything society would consider chaste and prudent. She was a grown woman, and at twenty-six, she was considered a spinster by most people.

Her mind flitted back to the way he'd stared at her. Céleste had once described how a man could use his mouth to tease a woman's nipples before working his way down to more intimate places. A rush of heat surged through Anna's body as an erotic image formed in her head. It was a tantalizing picture of her dark angel teasing her body with his mouth.

The sensitive spot between her legs tightened with anticipation at the imagery taking root in her head. While she'd occasionally contemplated taking a lover, it had never been a thought she'd considered seriously until this moment. The men she'd met were either too long in the tooth or simply not interesting enough to stimulate her mind, let alone her body. But she instinctively knew her dark angel would be able to skillfully introduce her to the art of pleasure.

Not that she needed an actual introduction. She was well-educated in what happened between a man and a woman. All she lacked was practical experience. The image of a dark head nestled between her thighs made Anna's body tense with arousal. What would it be like to be pleasured by her dark angel in such an intimate fashion? Her eyelids fluttered closed as her body responded to the images flooding her mind.

Suddenly, she released a sharp gasp of dismay, and her eyes flew open as she swept the pictures in her head into oblivion. Poseidon's balls, what in the name of God had come over her? Lusting after a man she didn't even know. And to top it off, he was an obnoxious jackass. Still, she begrudgingly had to admit he'd at least had the decency to carry her back to her bed when she'd been on the verge of fainting in the hall.

But it didn't excuse his behavior. He'd not even said he would send word to Uncle Charles as to her whereabouts. She was certain her uncle, Céleste, and the others would be deeply worried about her. Any delay in notifying them she was all right would cause them unnecessary anxiety. She also wanted to know if Hamish and Smitty were all right. Instinct said they were, but she wanted to be certain.

Anna squirmed slightly, using her back and uninjured arm to adjust the pillows behind her. When she was satisfied with their position, she leaned back into the soft bedding. Her shoulder was hurting after the strain of leaving her bed, but she was grateful it wasn't as excruciating as it had been last night. When the doctor had sewn up her wound, she'd felt as if she were a ripped sail Smitty was repairing. She'd been given a strong dose of laudanum, but it had done little to ease the pain of the needle and thread piercing her skin until after the doctor was finished.

At the sound of the bedroom door opening, Anna saw a tall woman enter the room. The faint memory of the same woman holding her hand as the doctor had sewn up her wound whispered its way through her head. From the first stitch to the last, the woman had held her hand and stroked her forehead while murmuring soft encouragement.

It was the same motherly attention she would have received if Céleste had been with her. There was the slightest hint of silver in the woman's dark hair, which was upswept into a fashionable coiffe. A kind smile tilted her mouth as she walked toward the bed.

"Well now, I see you're awake. You had us quite worried last night." Laughter suddenly danced in her dark eyes. "And you *must* be feeling much better, as my son informed me of your valiant effort to find out what happened to Miss Trafford."

"If your son is the man who car—escorted me back to bed a few moments ago, I doubt he used the word valiant," Anna said as her mouth quirked with ironic skepticism. "I'm more inclined to think he used the words foolish or addle-brained where my behavior is concerned."

"I believe the words he used were impetuous and fool-hardy, which are not quite the same thing," the woman said with a laugh. "However, I've no doubt finding you in the hallway in your nightgown was a shock to Sebastian. He holds himself and others to a high standard of propriety."

"Meaning he's a prude," she muttered beneath her breath as she remembered the man's behavior.

The moment the older woman drew in a quick breath of surprise, Anna realized her comment hadn't been soft enough. The woman's astonishment made Anna wince, and her cheeks grew hot with embarrassment. It had been an unforgivably rude comment, especially as the woman and her son had taken her in and cared for her.

As she prepared herself to apologize, the woman suddenly laughed out loud with genuine amusement. Startled, Anna stared at her in bewilderment. With a reassuring gesture of her hand, the woman sat down on the side of the bed and smiled.

"You are very astute, my dear. Sebastian can be arrogant, inflexible, insufferable, and sometimes even unforgiving." An odd emotion darkened the woman's gaze for a brief second, then disappeared as she smiled. "But despite those flaws, my son is a good man."

"I'm terribly sorry." Anna cringed as she met the woman's amused look. "I've been told many times that I'm far too blunt."

"I find blunt honesty refreshing," the woman said with a twinkle in her eye. It was obvious the woman knew how much her son's behavior had annoyed Anna, despite her best effort to hide it.

"But he didn't even acknowledge my request to send word to my uncle."

"I've no doubt it must have been terribly aggravating to feel you weren't being heard. However, it simply confirmed what we suspected last night, when you implored us not to let the Falcon sail without you. Sebastian sent someone to the docks early this morning to find your family."

"Thank you," Anna said with a sigh of relief.

"Now then, I think introductions are long overdue. I am Lady Harding, and you are in my son's home, Starling House. My second oldest son, Alexander, brought you here last night and told us your name was Anna."

"Yes, Anna. Anna Sawyer. I don't remember anyone called Alexander, but then I remember little of anything after the last attack." She frowned slightly at the thought. In truth, she suddenly realized the only thing she remembered vividly, other than the doctor's unpleasant needle and thread, was her dark angel. Lady Harding's arrogant son.

"Alexander was with the police when you and Sarah were found last night," Lady Harding said quietly. "Although, Alexander's description of the event is quite extraordinary. He and Sarah say you're the reason she's still alive, and quite possibly the other kidnapped women as well."

Lady Harding's words sent a chill streaking through Anna. Until now, she'd not allowed herself to consider how fortunate she was. The horrifying images from last night that had surfaced when she'd awoken returned to viciously assault her senses. The unwelcome memories of cowled monks, insidious chanting, and the menacing figures dressed in gold and black robes at the altar flooded her head.

Every detail of her ordeal swept over her with a savagery that tightened her chest, making it difficult to breathe. A shudder rippled through her followed by a disorientation and lethargy she knew well. Unable to move, Anna found herself sinking into a familiar state of a waking dream. Every sound in the room became muffled, as if she'd slipped beneath the ocean's waves.

In the next breath, a rush of wind blew across her skin. The strength of it was strong enough to billow out the Falcon's largest sail. The brute force of it sent her catapulting forward at an alarming speed. Unintelligible voices whispered above her, their words echoing in her ears as if from a great distance. Little more than a soft whirr of sound, the indecipherable words were impossible to understand, but fear and shock vibrated through them.

Strange images swept before her as she lifted her head slightly. In front of her was something that looked like a train carriage, but she knew it wasn't. Hovering over her was a young woman with pink hair and a small gold ring on her nose that reminded anna of the one Smitty wore in his ear. The young woman looked terrified, and anna tried to stretch out her hand toward her in an attempt to reassure her that all would be well.

Out of the corner of her eye, she saw a man and a woman, dressed in clothing similar to Lady Harding and her son, pushing their way through the ghostly shapes hovering over her. Everything about the couple was so familiar. It was as if she'd always known the two, yet she was certain she'd never met either of them. The man viciously shoved someone aside to reach her, and the terror on his face made her flinch as he knelt beside her.

Anna felt the strength of the stranger's grip as he squeezed her hand tightly in his. The stirring of familiarity continued to grow until it was a tangible sensation cascading through her. Surprise made her shiver slightly as she felt her hand flex and tighten around the man's. Although she could see his lips moving, his voice was little more than a fluttering of sound just out of reach.

As the auburn-haired beauty that was with him awkwardly knelt by the man's side, the connection between her and the couple only grew in strength. Anna knew they were married, and the woman's fear matched that of her husband's. A soft whisper drifted across her senses as the most beautiful, sapphire eyes Anna had ever seen stared down at her with a look of helpless horror. The moment she realized the sound was a name, it danced away into the ether.

The woman was *enceinte*, and something about the fact struck anna as oddly familiar. In the next breath, confusion flooded her as she realized the child the woman carried was the couple's first, and yet she knew they'd had a child together at another point in time. With her free hand, anna reached out to touch the woman's stomach.

An image of a man who looked remarkably like the stranger holding her hand flitted through her head. A second later, vicious shock pulsated through her body. The stranger's hand became a painful grip around hers, and she heard him shout the name Nora. The man's shout was muted by another male voice calling her by name. Never had she ever heard her name spoken with such strength, passion, and intensity. There was a note of command in the voice that demanded she respond, and Anna tried to turn toward the unseen man when another shock jolted her body.

Suddenly, she found herself hurtling backward with breath-taking speed. In the next instant, it was as if she was falling from a great height, and she jerked hard as she hit the mattress. She uttered a soft cry as the world came back into focus, and she met Lady Harding's alarmed gaze.

"Good heavens, child," the woman exclaimed softly as she clasped Anna's hand in hers. "Are you all right?"

"Yes…forgive me," Anna whispered and closed her eyes as the fatigue that usually accompanied one of her spells settled over her. After a long moment, she looked at Lady Harding again, who was eyeing her warily. "The doctors say I have a very mild form of epilepsy. Whenever I have a spell like this one, it's usually brought on by stress. I think last night qualifies as stressful."

"Oh, my dear girl." Lady Harding's suspicious air quickly dissolved into obvious dismay, and Anna quickly reassured the woman.

"Please don't worry. It's not painful. Most of the time, it's only for a few seconds, and few people ever realize what's happening. It's as if I'm in a dream until the spell ends."

Anna deliberately omitted the fact that her spells always involved seeing occasional glimpses of the future or pieces of information about people. Although what she'd just experienced a moment ago was unlike anything she'd seen before. Wherever she'd been, it had been unlike any place she was acquainted with, and yet it had felt familiar too. She needed time to think it through if she was going to make sense of it.

Uncle Augustus was the only person Anna had ever told about her visions. She'd been seeing things since she was little, but only her uncle knew her secret. As a child, she'd been afraid of the things she would see, but Uncle Augustus had told her to accept her ability as a gift and not to fear it. But her uncle had also told her it was best if she didn't tell others as most people would react in fear. She'd followed her uncle's advice in keeping her ability a secret. She'd not even confessed to Céleste, and most certainly *not* Uncle Charles. He'd been upset for weeks after the doctor told them she had a mild form of epilepsy. God knows what he would do if she were to tell him she could see things others could not.

Anna suppressed a groan of alarm. Ballocks, if Uncle Charles were to discover she'd had a spell on top of last night's events, things would go from bad to worse. It was going to be difficult enough to persuade him to let her set sail with the Falcon when the vessel left dock in a few weeks.

While they both knew he had no real say in what she did, she loved her uncle dearly and had no wish to worry him. Anna also knew she might still be in danger if any of the cult members had escaped. The bastards might think she could identify them. She'd be a fool to walk the docks without Hamish or Smitty at her side, even during the day.

Bugger it, she should never have followed her friends to the Blue Mermaid tavern last night. Anna released a disheartened sigh as she realized she had no one but herself to blame for this entire mess. But then, in all likelihood, Sarah and the other women would be dead. That was worth the price of losing even a small bit of her freedom. Aware that Lady Harding was still studying her with dismay, Anna leaned forward slightly.

"Please don't mention this to my uncle. It upsets him when I have a spell."

"But my dear, surely he should know what's happened." Lady Harding shook her head in objection.

"*No*, you must promise me you won't say anything. I've no doubt Uncle Charles will be worried enough as it is when he learns I was injured last night. I have no wish to upset him all the more."

"I'm not certain—"

"I *must* insist, my lady," Anna said emphatically at the woman's hesitant expression, then smiled with as much charm as she possessed. "Besides, as I always remind Uncle Charles, I am in exceptional company. Julius Caesar had epilepsy as well. It was called the falling sickness then, but it didn't stop the man from rising to power."

"Julius Caesar, indeed." Lady Harding raised her eyebrow as a small smile twisted her lips. "Very well, I'll not mention this to anyone."

"Thank you," Anna said quietly. Relieved the woman wouldn't say anything to her uncle, Anna relaxed back into the pillows. "Uncle Charles must be worried half out of his mind, and I only hope Hamish and Smitty escaped unharmed. At least they'll be able to tell my uncle what happened."

"Hamish and Smitty?"

"My friends… and occasionally my bodyguards. Uncle Charles likes me to have one of them with me whenever I disembark the Falcon." Anna released a quiet sigh as she accepted the fact that from this point forward, she would have an escort for some time to come whenever she stepped off the Falcon. Guilt nipped at her as she recalled how this entire adventure had begun. Puzzlement clouded Lady Harding's features.

"I don't understand." Lady Harding's brow furrowed with confusion.

"While I'm of age and can do as I wish, I do my best never to worry Uncle Charles. It makes him feel better when I agree to Hamish or Smitty accompanying me wherever I go." Anna paused as her lips twisted with self-disgust and chagrin. "Although, despite my protests when they're trailing along behind, there have been moments when I've been glad they were looking over me. I confess to having a reputation for stumbling into trouble."

"How often do you travel with your uncle?"

"All the time. The Falcon is my home."

"You live *on* the *ship*," the woman exclaimed with obvious dismay. "Have you no one you could stay with here in England?"

"I have a cousin that Uncle Charles wanted me to stay with a few years ago, but I convinced him to let me stay on the Falcon. There's no other place I'd rather be. I love the sea. It's beautiful, no matter the time or weather."

"And yet your voice sounds as if you attended a French finishing school."

"That would be Céleste's doing." Anna smiled as the Frenchwoman's features filled her head. "She's tutored me in French, Italian, and German, philosophy, and opera. Uncle Charles has instructed me in mathematics, astronomy, and history. Hamish and Smitty have taught me how to navigate and hoist a sail, among other things. Although Céleste has tried quite hard to instruct me on the subject of etiquette, that is one skill I've failed at consistently."

"And this Céleste, who is she?" At Lady Harding's question, Anna stiffened.

She'd shared far too much information already, and the last thing she wanted to do was have anyone think unkindly of her closest friend and confidant. The relationship Uncle Charles and Céleste had was socially frowned upon, and while it was unorthodox, the couple cared for each other deeply.

If he'd had his way, Uncle Charles would have married Céleste years ago. But no matter how hard her uncle tried to convince the Frenchwoman to marry him, Céleste refused. She said she would never give up her independence. Anna emerged from her thoughts to see Lady Harding studying her with curiosity.

"Céleste is a family friend." Anna's short, cryptic reply sent Lady Harding's eyebrows shooting upward as if to say she knew Anna wasn't telling her everything.

"I see," Lady Harding murmured.

The older woman studied Anna for a brief moment, obviously debating what question to ask next. A knock on the door prevented the older woman from asking any further questions. Lady Harding rose to her feet as a maid stepped into the room.

"Dr. Johnson is here, my lady."

"Show him in, Lucy."

Lady Harding nodded at the girl, who quickly stepped out into the hall, and a second later, the doctor entered the room. Anna's mouth twisted in dismay at the sight of the man. The last time she'd seen him hadn't been a pleasant experience. The doctor smiled cheerfully at her as he crossed the room to set his medical bag on the bedside table before he sat on the side of the bed.

"Well now, young lady, you are looking much better than I expected this morning," Dr. Johnson said jovially as he popped open a pocket watch, then caught her wrist between his fingers to check her pulse. "How are you feeling?"

"My shoulder hurts like hell," she said without thinking.

The reply sent the doctor's eyebrows arching upward as he stared at her in surprise and disapproval. Behind him, Lady Harding released a soft gasp of dismay. Anna winced, then consoled herself with the thought she'd not used a stronger oath. That would have been far worse. When the doctor finished taking her pulse, he nodded toward her shoulder.

"If I may, I need to examine my handiwork to ensure an infection hasn't set in."

At the man's request, Anna twisted her mouth in a grimace before she reluctantly pushed her nightgown off the injured shoulder. His manner brisk and matter-of-fact, the physician quickly probed at the wound. The moment she drew in a hiss of pain, he apologized, then gently pulled the nightgown closed.

"Well, young lady. You are very fortunate the knife didn't strike two inches lower. I'm not sure you'd still be with us if it had." Dr. Johnson's face was somber for a moment before he smiled. "But I'm pleased with the way your injury looks, and I think you should be able to get out of bed for an hour or two tomorrow."

"Tomorrow," she exclaimed softly.

"Yes, tomorrow, and you'll need to remain convalescing for the next week. No exertion of any kind. I'll be back in the morning to see you again. In the meantime, I expect you to rest. Sleep is an excellent healer."

"But I cannot—"

"You will do exactly as the doctor says, Anna. Not another word."

Lady Harding's expression said she would brook no argument from her, and Anna nodded. Deep inside, she admitted she was grateful for the order. Leaving her bed when she'd first awakened and then receiving her strange vision, had left her exhausted. Satisfaction lightened Lady Harding's still lovely features as she leaned over the bed and patted Anna's hand.

"Now do as Dr. Johnson said. Sleep."

With a soft word to the physician, the older woman escorted the man out of the room. As Lady Harding pulled the door shut behind them, Anna released a sigh. She didn't feel sleepy, but she was extremely tired, and she hadn't been lying when she'd complained about her shoulder hurting. Careful of her shoulder, Anna adjusted her pillows, then began to clear her thoughts as Uncle Charles had taught her. In moments, she was drifting off to sleep, and the last thing that flitted through her mind was an image of a dangerous, dark angel called Sebastian.

Chapter 5

Sebastian massaged his forehead with his fingers. His headache had been with him for most of the morning, as he'd only had a few hours' sleep. After his mother had left him in the salon last night, he had met with Scully several hours later. The two of them had agreed that the man would provide security for both Starling Place and the Trafford home until Scotland Yard confirmed they'd found all the cult members responsible for Sarah's and Anna's ordeal.

Alexander had sent word first thing this morning that his fiancée was recovering, but his brother had heard nothing from Inspector Pratt. Less than a half hour ago, a message had arrived from Scully that he'd received Sebastian's message as to the precise location of the Falcon, and a message had been left with the ship's captain.

It irritated him that Scully had taken so long in getting a message to Anna's family when Sebastian had sent directions to the man right before luncheon. As for Anna, the doctor had left Starling House hours ago with the prognosis she would make a complete recovery.

Now, as Sebastian tried to review a report on the livestock at Birchwood, his country estate, his concentration was constantly interrupted by Anna's lovely features. It was unlike him to find his thoughts so consumed by a woman, but he'd been unable to stop thinking about her. Then again, it was hard to ignore how intriguing Anna was.

Alexander's description of how the woman had fought off several men seemed almost too extraordinary to believe. But his brother was not a liar, nor was he prone to exaggeration. That left Sebastian with only one explanation. Alexander's story had to be the truth, no matter how outlandish it sounded. Unable to help himself, Sebastian tried to envision his guest doing what his brother described.

It was a difficult thing to imagine. Yet he already knew how unusually strong she was. For a woman who'd suffered an injury that had stained her chemise and Alexander's shirt dark with so much blood, her strength last night had surprised him. The memory of Anna's grip on his arm as she'd demanded to know whether Alexander's betrothed was safe created a vivid image of her in his head.

She'd stared up at him with dark brown eyes that were the color of roasted chestnuts that had been polished until they sparkled like sunlight. Despite the pallor of her skin, Anna's complexion wasn't the pale, cream-colored look most Englishwomen had.

Just as his mother had pointed out last night, there was a soft golden glow to her skin. It was as if the sun had kissed her gently while a dark pink rose had brushed across her mouth, leaving her lips stained with color. Then there were her full-figured curves that had filled his dreams last night. When he'd awoken this morning, he'd been hard as iron and found it necessary to take himself in hand to ease his cock's hungry need for some form of satisfaction.

Last night, he'd compared Anna to *Le Grande Odalisque*. He'd been wrong. She didn't possess the worldly look Ingres's model did. Anna looked more like Titian's painting, *Flora*. He had always enjoyed Titian's work, and he had no doubt the grand master would have eagerly used Anna as a model. With her full, voluptuous curves and lush thighs, she possessed all the attributes of one of the grand master's models. And God almighty, her breasts. When freed completely from any material, her beautiful, rounded breasts would spill out and overflow into a man's hands.

When he'd found Anna in the upstairs corridor this morning, he'd been amazed to find her standing, let alone having almost reached the stairway. Worse, his immediate reaction to her had been one of intense lust. Forced to carry her back to the guest room, one alarm bell after another had pealed loudly in his head at the way his body had reacted to hers.

But it was her forthright manner that had thrown him completely off balance. Although Anna had mistaken his inner turmoil as anger, he'd been stunned at how easily she'd read him. No other woman had ever done that with him before, and he didn't like it. Women weren't to be trusted, and a woman who was intuitive enough to come so close to pinpointing the source of his struggle was dangerous.

Sebastian released a low, angry sound of self-disgust. He was a blackguard to even lust after the woman. Not only was she a guest in his home, but she'd also been through a traumatic experience. His fascination with her was that of a lascivious degenerate, and most definitely not the behavior of a gentleman. Another harsh noise passed his lips. He needed to focus and push all thoughts of the woman out of his head.

Deliberately, he forced himself to focus on the report he'd been trying to comprehend for more than three hours. If his progress continued at such a slow pace, he would be forced to forego dinner at the club with Nicholas. Over the next two hours, he managed to review almost three quarters of the report before he heard Hodgekiss answer the front door. A moment later, the soft echo of an authoritative voice drifted into his study.

"I am here for my niece, Anna Sawyer."

Sebastian was on his feet in a split-second and striding

toward the foyer. As he emerged from his private sanctuary, he saw an odd collection of visitors standing in the hall. The one who appeared to be the leader of the group was tall and distinguished looking. He wore the uniform of a ship's captain and had tucked his hat under his arm. The man was flanked by a woman dressed in the height of fashion, and behind the couple stood a large burly sailor, and another sailor of slighter build.

"Good afternoon, I'm Viscount Starling. Your niece has been a guest of mine since last night." At his quiet greeting, all heads in the small group turned in his direction. The master sailor stepped forward and extended his hand.

"Captain Charles Wentworth," the tall man said as he shook Sebastian's hand, then gestured toward the others. "May I present Céleste DuBois, a family friend, and my men. I understand you're responsible for rescuing my niece from her kidnappers."

"Actually, it was my younger brother, Alexander, who performed that service. He brought her here so we might tend to her injuries."

"She's been injured? The messenger said nothing about her being hurt," the captain exclaimed as his face grew ashen and the woman gasped in dismay. "All I was told was that someone had secured her freedom from her kidnappers."

Captain Wentworth glanced at the largest of the two sailors behind him. Like his captain, the seaman had become pale beneath his tanned, weathered features. The burly man muttered something unintelligible beneath his breath and looked at the other sailor. The guilt and deep regret on both men's faces made Sebastian think the two men might have been charged with Anna's safety and failed at their task.

"Your niece has received the best of care, and the doctor says she will recover within the week."

"A week?" Captain Wentworth frowned in confusion. "How was she injured?"

"While trying to escape her kidnappers, she suffered a deep knife wound—"

"*Mon Dieu! Charles*, I want to see her *now*."

Horror threaded its way through Céleste DuBois's soft, distinctly Parisian accent. The Frenchwoman's hand clutched at Captain Wentworth's sleeve, and the man covered it with his larger one. Sebastian frowned, irritated that Scully's man hadn't provided the sea captain with the full details of Anna's condition. Although from the varied reactions of fear, concern, and anger exhibited by the small group, he didn't think knowing the full details before arriving at Starling House would have made any difference. It was obvious Anna Sawyer was well-loved by those standing in his foyer.

"I can assure you that your niece is going to recover."

"Take me to her at once." Captain Wentworth's voice echoed with the stern authoritativeness of a man used to having his orders obeyed. The command made Sebastian stiffen. While he understood the man's concern and desire to see his niece, Sebastian wasn't accustomed to being dictated to by anyone, especially in his own home. With a stiff nod in the sea captain's direction, Sebastian looked at his butler, who was standing off to the side.

"Hodgekiss, please escort Captain Wentworth and Miss Dubois to Miss Sawyer's room, and have one of the footmen show his men to the servant's dining hall."

The moment Sebastian uttered his name, the butler stepped forward to lead the way upstairs. Wentworth turned and murmured something to the two sailors. The largest of the sailors frowned but jerked his head in compliance. A rustling of silk made Sebastian turn his head to see his mother descending the staircase. The Falcon's captain turned back toward the stairs, and Lady Harding gasped loudly.

"Charles."

His mother's look of stunned amazement became an animated smile that reminded Sebastian of how she used to smile when he was a child, before she betrayed his father. At the sound of his mother's voice, Captain Wentworth stared thunderstruck at Lady Harding descending the staircase. Sebastian's mother increased the pace of her descent at almost a run, and the sea captain hurried forward to meet her at the foot of the stairs.

"*Good God, Lily.* Is it really you?" A broad smile lightened Captain Wentworth's features, and he captured Lady Harding's outstretched hands in his. "Whatever are you doing here?"

"Sebastian is Levi's and my oldest son," Lady Harding said with a nod in his direction as she kissed Captain Wentworth's cheek.

"*Of course! Starling.* I was so worried about Anna, I didn't make the connection, but then Levi was always just Levi to all of us.

"*You're* Anna's uncle?" his mother asked with amazement.

"Yes, she's Serena's daughter. So, this is Levi's boy." Wentworth turned his head to study Sebastian for a moment, then returned his attention to Lady Harding with a somber look. "Since he introduced himself as Viscount Starling, that must mean Levi is gone."

"Yes, Levi died a little more than a year after Augustus."

"I am truly sorry, Lily. He was a good man, and I know how much you loved him."

At the man's statement, Sebastian released a barely audible snort of disgust. Captain Wentworth knew nothing about his mother or her treacherous nature. His mother darted a look in his direction before she nodded in reply to the captain's comment.

"I can say the same about Augustus. His unexpected death was a devastating shock to…to both of us."

His mother and Wentworth exchanged a silent look Sebastian found puzzling. It was as if they were commiserating with each other about something more than just the loss of two people dear to them. Sebastian immediately dismissed the thought. Despite her protests to the contrary, Sebastian knew his mother had never loved his father.

"As it was to Serena and me. Losing Augustus in the way we did was painful." Anna's uncle suddenly winced as he turned and stretched out his hand to the Frenchwoman standing behind him. The woman immediately moved forward to take his hand. "Forgive me, Céleste. Allow me to introduce Lady Starling. Lily, may I present Céleste Dubois, a close family friend."

"It's Lady Harding, now. I married a little more than a year after Levi's passing." Sebastian's mother smiled warmly at Céleste DuBois and stretched out her hand to the other woman. "I'm delighted to meet you. Anna mentioned you when we spoke a short time ago. It's obvious how dear you and Charles are to her."

"How is she? May we see her now?" The note of anxiety in the Frenchwoman's voice made Lady Harding squeeze the other woman's hand in a consoling gesture.

"Of course, forgive me for being so thoughtless. Seeing Charles was such a shock. As for how Anna is, considering everything she's been through, I think she's doing quite well. Come, let me take you to her." Sebastian's mother gently pulled Céleste Dubois toward the stairs. "And you must stay for dinner, Charles. We have a great deal of catching up to do. Hodgekiss, will you please tell Cook we have two guests for the evening meal, and please show the other gentlemen to the servants' dining room for a meal as well."

"Thank you, Lily, but we cannot—"

"Nonsense, I insist. I want to hear about everything you've been doing all these years. Sebastian won't mind, will you?" Lady Harding looked at him, and he was startled by her resolute expression that dared him to contradict her.

Sebastian bowed slightly toward the captain.

"As my mother said, you must stay for dinner."

"Then we accept." The Falcon's captain smiled warmly in Sebastian's direction before turning his attention back to Lady Harding.

"Excellent." His mother's animated smile returned as she pulled Céleste DuBois toward the stairs. "Come, I know Anna's as anxious to see you as I know you must be to see her."

Captain Wentworth nodded at his men for a second time, then turned and followed his mother up the stairs. Hodgekiss escorted Captain Wentworth's men toward the rear of the house, leaving Sebastian standing alone in the foyer feeling somewhat bewildered by what had just happened. How did his mother know Anna's uncle? The way the master sailor had spoken of Sebastian's father indicated the man had been a friend of both his parents. Since Sebastian couldn't remember ever having met the sea captain, he could only assume the man had known his parents before Sebastian was born.

Still mulling over this new development, Sebastian wheeled about on his heel and strode back into his study. The grandfather clock struck the quarter hour as he entered the one place in the house that was his sanctuary. Soft and lilting, the chimes sent a gentle melody through the air. It was an almost melancholy sound, and Sebastian turned his head toward the tall clock. It had been his father's prized possession. As a boy, he'd often entered the study to find the man he'd admired and loved standing in front of it with a sorrowful expression.

Delicate English wildflowers were carved into a thin layer of dark mahogany wood that formed a frail, lace-like border on the top, bottom and sides of the furniture's front. Cornflowers, forget-me-nots, and scarlet pimpernels were entwined in a garland that met at the top of the timepiece in a bouquet of carnations inside a heart.

A replica of the wood carving of the heart and carnation bouquet had been painted on the face of the clock, where the carnations were painted a soft green. It was an unusual color that had always puzzled him, but he'd never questioned his parents as to whether it held any meaning. It was the lace-like carvings that were his favorite part of the clock. The flowers were so lifelike that, as a child, he'd always expected them to release a soft fragrance.

Sebastian's mother had given the clock to his father for their tenth wedding anniversary. An irony given her behavior that followed only a year later. Just before his twelfth birthday, he'd seen his mother in the arms of her lover. Harding had always been a frequent guest at Starling Place. The man had been a friend of his father's, which made his mother's and Harding's betrayal all the more heinous.

As a child, his sister Lydia had always come to him whenever she had a nightmare, and it had been no different the night he'd learned the truth about his mother. Lydia had pleaded with him to retrieve her favorite doll from the parlor so she could sleep. He might never have been the wiser if he'd not given in to his sister's pleas. On his way back to the nursery with Lydia's doll, he'd seen his mother and Harding, standing in the doorway of his mother's rooms, locked in each other's arms in a passionate kiss.

Harding had been the first to see him standing in the hall, staring at them. The moment her lover had abruptly pushed her away, Sebastian's mother had murmured a protest before the man had silently nodded toward Sebastian standing in the middle of the hall.

Until that moment, he'd adored his mother, but after that night he'd felt nothing but contempt for her. Sebastian had confronted her privately the following morning. He'd denounced her with a blistering scorn, but she'd offered no defense of her betrayal. Instead, she'd stood before him with a look of deep pain on her face.

From that day forward, he'd spoken only to his mother when it was necessary or when he needed to avoid arousing his father's suspicions as to the rift between him and his mother. Nor had he broached the subject of his mother's betrayal with his father. The idea of hurting the man he loved and respected by revealing Lady Starling's infidelity had been unthinkable for Sebastian. It would have destroyed his father.

Fortunately, he'd returned to Eton a few weeks later, which had enabled him to maintain distance between him and his mother. Little more than a year after his father's death, Lady Starling had married her lover in a private ceremony and became Viscountess Harding.

When Harding had died almost ten years ago and a distant relative had taken control of Harding's properties, Sebastian had done his duty and offered his mother a home. The two of them had lived under the same roof in an uneasy truce ever since, but Sebastian made it a point to avoid his mother as much as possible.

With a sound of disgust, Sebastian returned to his desk. Thank God his father had never discovered his wife's infidelity. He was also grateful his siblings remained in the dark as to their mother's betrayal of her marital vows. Sebastian hadn't kept his mother's secret for her sake. He'd done it to protect his siblings from the pain of knowing their mother was an adulteress. A pain and disappointment he still felt, even to this day.

Sebastian muttered an oath that he'd even acknowledged being disillusioned with his mother's betrayal of his father. Irritated with himself, Sebastian sank down into his desk chair. He flicked a small stack of papers aside with his fingers, then reached for paper and pen. He'd write to Lady Margaret with an invitation to escort her to the Dyston affair if she had recovered by tomorrow night. He would enjoy an evening free of distractions and all thoughts of his mother.

In the back of his mind, a mocking voice reminded him there was one more woman he needed to stop thinking about. The problem was, he didn't think Anna would be as easy to drive from his thoughts as his mother.

Chapter 6

"Anna."

The voice sounded as if it was far away, but when she heard her name again, it was closer. Was it her dark angel calling to her? Again, she heard her name. No, it wasn't him. Sebastian's voice had vibrated across her skin like a smooth, fiery brandy. God, his eyes had been so dark and piercing. It was as if he could see into the very depths of her soul.

"Anna."

This time, she recognized her uncle's voice. Her eyes fluttered open, and she saw her uncle and Céleste on either side of her. Immediately, her eyes blurred with unshed tears at the deep worry and fear on their faces.

"Anna, my darling girl." The gruff note in her uncle's voice sent a tear sliding down her cheek as his hand tightened around hers.

"Oh, no, *ma petite*, do not cry. There is no need to cry, *cherie*," Céleste exclaimed softly as she wiped the wet drop off Anna's cheek. As the Frenchwoman leaned forward to brush her lips against Anna's brow, she fought back the tears. She turned her head slightly to look at the man who'd been her guardian for so long.

"Hamish? Smitty?" she whispered as a wave of fear for her friends swept over her. "Are they all right?"

"They're hale and hearty. Although they've been snarling at everyone as they've been deeply worried about you, as we all have."

"You mustn't blame them, Uncle Charles. They didn't know I'd followed them."

"Of that I have no doubt." The quiet resignation in her uncle's reply filled her with guilt and tears blurred her vision.

"Oh, Uncle Charles, I'm so sorry. I know you must be so disappointed in me for being so foolhardy. I should never have followed Hamish and Smitty."

"Disa—you are *not* a disappointment, Anna. You are kind, extremely intelligent, adventurous, and sometimes too impetuous and confident for your own good, but you are most definitely *not* a disappointment." A small grimace of amusement tugged at his lips before he sobered. "I am simply relieved you are all right. You *are* all right, aren't you?"

The fear she saw in his eyes told her the real question he was asking. Without thinking, she pushed herself upright. The sudden movement tugged on the sutures in her shoulder, and the movement shot pain across her chest and down her arm.

"*Poseidon's balls*, that hurts worse than an ass caning."

"I think that answers your question *mon amour*." Céleste smiled in Charles Wentworth's direction before she arched an eyebrow at Anna and shook her head. "But you, *ma petite*, we absolutely *must* work on your vocabulary."

Anna winced at the gentle chiding. The memory of shocking Sarah with her cursing added to her chagrin. She knew most people thought foul language indicated one was of common, lowborn status. But when she cursed, it eased any anger, fear, or pain she was experiencing. It was an honest and straight-forward response to a situation.

Despite Céleste's personal disdain for certain social mores, the Frenchwoman had made it her mission to teach Anna how to follow the conventions of society. Her most challenging task had always been that of eliminating Anna's love of salty words from her vocabulary.

The idea that she'd made her mentor feel as if she'd failed in her teachings made Anna squeeze the older woman's hand in a silent apology. The Frenchwoman smiled at her with amusement, indicating Anna had been forgiven. Now that her shoulder pain had eased to a small throb, she turned her head toward her uncle.

"In answer to your question, I'm fine. No one touched me."

It was a half-lie, because someone had stripped her clothes and put her in that ridiculous chemise while she was unconscious. But she refused to upset her uncle and Céleste even more than they already had been.

"They needed young women who were…" Anna paused as she fumbled for the best way to describe what the cult members wanted. "…untouched in order to sacrifice them."

"*Sacrifice?*" Captain Wentworth's face paled, and Céleste drew in a breath of horror. Their obvious deep consternation caused Anna to frown.

"Didn't anyone tell you what happened?" she asked in a quiet, hesitant voice.

"I didn't give Starling time to tell us much of anything, and seeing Lily was such a shock, I failed to ask her for details."

"Lily?" Confused, Anna tipped her head to one side as she stared at her uncle in bewilderment.

"Lady Harding. She's a childhood friend. Your Uncle Augustus and your mother were friends with her, too." At the mention of his siblings, a shadow of sorrow darkened his features. Anna quickly caught his hand in hers.

"I miss them, too." Her uncle nodded, then cleared his throat. "As I was saying, all we know is what Hamish and Smitty told us about your abduction. The messenger didn't tell us anything other than you were safe here in Starling House."

Anna grimaced at the worry and concern she saw on their faces. She wasn't sure what to tell them that wouldn't alarm them even more, but she knew better than to hide the truth from her uncle.

"It was the Hatshepsut cult we heard about in Cairo. I was in a holding cell. When they came for me and a woman called Sarah, I waited until we were out of our cell before I tried to escape." Anna twisted her mouth in self-disgust as she remembered her anger had almost gotten her killed.

"*Christ Almighty*," her uncle breathed as he and Céleste stared at Anna in stunned horror.

"I tried to keep your lessons in my head, but I lost control of my anger. I let my guard down, and I didn't see the man or his knife until it was too late. The police had arrived by then, but it was so chaotic. I remember little of anything after that."

"When I find these whoresons, I'll see them hang, if I cannot kill them myself."

The quiet, deadly resolve in Charles Wentworth's voice, combined with his oath, emphasized his unforgiving, harsh fury. It was a rare occasion when she'd heard her uncle curse, and she jumped slightly at the rage clouding his features. She couldn't remember ever seeing him so angry. His serenity and calm in even the worst of storms was something she had always tried to emulate. But at the moment, Uncle Charles was anything but serene. The moment Captain Wentworth narrowed his eyes at her, Anna stiffened.

"I made a mistake not sending you to stay with Georgina six years ago," he said in a voice tight with frustration.

The memory of their argument shortly after she turned twenty pushed its way to the forefront of Anna's mind. A few days after her birthday, her uncle had expressed his wish that she go live with their cousin for a season. It wasn't until she'd cried out her mother's name in the heat of their argument that her uncle's resolve had weakened.

Bitterness had filled her voice as she reminded him as to his sister's terrible fate. She'd emphasized her mother had been forced to marry a brutal, vile man. A man who had beaten Anna's mother regularly until the day she'd stabbed him to death in self-defense. Several hours later, her mother had thrown herself off a bridge into a nearby river. But not before she'd left Anna at the Red Gables Inn where Captain Wentworth had found her almost a year later.

Although it was unlikely Georgina's husband would have the authority to force her into an unwanted marriage, Anna had raised it as a possibility. But it was when she mentioned her mother that she knew her uncle wouldn't send her away. Anna knew it had been unfair, even cruel in some respects, to mention her mother, but she'd been desperate to stay on the Falcon. It was the only home where she'd truly been happy. It was a place where she had the freedom to be herself.

Ever since that terrible argument, her uncle had only mentioned Georgina when he received a letter from the woman. Her cousin had even sent one or two letters to Anna asking her to come for a visit. She'd torn up the missives. If her uncle had realized she was as loyal and obedient as the sailors who manned the Falcon, her fate might have been different.

Over the past several years, Anna had arrived at the belief that her uncle had always known she would have obeyed him in the matter. But he'd chosen not to wield that power over her. He'd allowed her to have a say in her life. Since she'd come of age, he'd mentioned the topic less and less. Anna was grateful for that. Now, hearing him express regret at not having sent her to stay with their cousin made Anna's chest tighten with dread.

If there was anything she understood about her uncle, it

was how protective he was over those he loved. He would go to hell and back to keep her and Céleste safe. He was also a fair and honest man, who was a strong advocate for his men. It's why the sailors who manned the Falcon were like family. Every member of the crew had been in her uncle's service for years. The last sailor her uncle had taken on had been almost ten years ago. The ship's crew wouldn't hesitate to follow their captain's every order without question or protest.

Anna was no different. Just like every man on the Falcon, Anna always followed her uncle's orders without argument. Her fingers curled around the bedsheet in a tight grip as she met his gaze steadily.

"You know I would be bored to tears. I would miss life on the Falcon, you, Céleste, and everyone else. There is no other place where I could be happy."

Her words were met with silence, and the moment she saw the inflexible thinning of his lips, Anna's heart sank. The silence stretched out between them until it was difficult to breathe. She knew what he was about to say, but she held out the hope she was wrong.

"We both know I don't have the authority to control your actions, Anna, but I'm asking you to indulge me by remaining in London." His voice was intractable as he met her gaze steadily. "It's time you experienced something other than life on the Falcon."

"But I'm happy on the ship. I love being at sea."

"I understand that, but for once, I am going to insist you agree to my request." Arms folded across his chest, her uncle eyed her sternly. "It's time you meet others your own age, perhaps even a young man."

"If you're suggesting it's time I was married—don't. I have no intention of marrying." Anna shook her head as she tried to convince her uncle not to make his request an outright order. "It's highly unlikely I would find a man with your qualities, and it's pointless to bother looking. Staying with Georgina would be a waste of time."

"While you flatter me, my dear, I am not the paragon you seem to think I am." He smiled as he turned his head toward his paramour. "A fact Céleste can attest to, can you not, my love?"

"I will not deny there have been moments when I find you quite stubborn, but I could never be happy with anyone other than you."

The Frenchwoman stretched out her hand to her uncle, who immediately captured it and raised it to his lips. The look the two exchanged was one of deep love, and Anna was certain she would never find a love as rich and rewarding as what Uncle Charles and Céleste had. Her uncle focused his gaze on Anna once more.

"I'll send word to Georgina today. I'm sure she'll be more than delighted with the prospect of introducing you to her and Herbert's circle of friends. A few parties and a ball or two will make you see there's more to life than the Falcon."

Anna swallowed a reply and nodded reluctantly that she would do as her uncle wished. Relief swept across Charles Wentworth's features, and he leaned forward to kiss her forehead.

"Thank you, Anna," he said with a smile. "I promise it won't be as bad as you think. In fact, I believe you might find it quite enjoyable."

Any other time, Anna might have fought harder to make her uncle reconsider his decision. But his relief at her agreement to stay with Georgina was far too great for her to offer up a single protest. The one thing she was certain of was the fact that Uncle Charles was wrong. She wouldn't have an enjoyable time. Worse, she could already feel the walls closing in on her as if she'd been put into a cage.

Chapter 7

Sebastian sat at the head of the table, eating his meal in silence. For the most part, he'd been able to block out the conversation between his mother and Captain Wentworth as they reminisced about their childhood. Occasionally, the sea captain would address Sebastian with either a question about his father or a polite observation as to the story he and Sebastian's mother were sharing with Céleste DuBois.

Although Sebastian had been polite in his replies, he'd not taken part in the conversations the other man had tried to pull him into. Eventually, the man had ceased his efforts to include him, and Sebastian found himself breathing a sigh of relief. Dessert had just been served when he heard his mother exclaim an objection to something Captain Wentworth had said. Sebastian laid his spoon back into place, as he gave his full attention to the conversation. What the devil were they discussing?

"You never did like someone saying no to you." Captain Wentworth eyed Lady Harding in amusement.

"I won't deny being determined to having my own way, but you forget I know your cousin. Although I've only spent a few moments with your niece, it was long enough for me to tell you it's a mistake to put her in Georgina's care."

"You're being unfair to Georgina," the sea captain

disagreed with a slight shake of his head.

"No, I'm being realistic. Your cousin is a kind, sweet woman, but Georgina's social circle is filled with people much older than Anna. It doesn't help that your cousin's interests are limited to needlepoint, playing the piano, running a household, and being an obedient wife." Lady Harding arched her eyebrow imperiously as she met Captain Wentworth's gaze with a steely determination. It was an unflinching resolve Sebastian had never witnessed in his mother until today. "You might as well suffocate the poor girl now, because if you don't, Georgina will do it for you. Is that what you want? Do you really want Georgina to crush Anna's spirit?"

"Of course not," Wentworth exclaimed.

"Then leave her with me."

At his mother's adamant words, Sebastian stiffened. What exactly was his mother proposing to do when she insisted Wentworth leave Anna with her? The sea captain frowned as if contemplating his mother's words, but didn't reply. Sebastian's mother leaned forward to steadily meet her childhood friend's gaze.

"I did not *have* to make the offer, Charles. I proposed you leave Anna here with me, because I *want* to do it. It's been five years since Caroline's debut. I would love the chance to do it again. Not that Anna will be considered a debutante given she's well past the normal coming out age, but I'll see to it she meets all the right people, and you know I always did enjoy shopping."

Sebastian's mouth went dry at Lady Harding's words. *good God*, had his mother just asked Captain Wentworth to leave his niece here at Starling House? Alarm bells went off in his head at the thought of Anna remaining here. Even in his mother's care, Anna's continued presence in Starling House had the makings of a disaster. Sebastian tried to swallow as Captain Wentworth turned his head to look at him, but his mouth was too dry.

"This is *your* home, my lord. Do you have any objection to your mother's proposal?"

The matter-of-fact note in the man's voice reminded Sebastian of Anna's straightforward manner. Now her uncle was asking if Sebastian had any objections to the man's niece staying under his roof with his mother as a chaperone. Sebastian experienced the instantaneous sensation of having walked into a trap.

Bloody hell. Yes, he had objections. The memory of how close he'd come to kissing Anna when he'd placed her back in bed this morning forced him to suppress a groan. God help him, when her nipples had stiffened and peaked, an unparalleled lust had surged through him at a blistering speed.

Worse, he knew she'd been aroused too. Maybe not to the extent he had, but Anna's arousal had been evident when she'd not hidden herself from his eyes like any other inexperienced woman would. He'd known at that precise moment she wouldn't object to his kiss or his touch. His cock stiffened slightly at the memory.

It brought him full circle back to the problem at hand. It was one thing to be tempted for a few days, but having Anna in the house for an indefinite amount of time was one of the most dangerous things he'd ever faced. God help him if he lost control and indulged his base needs by bedding her.

Sebastian's gaze swung to his mother, and the unflinching look she directed at him made his muscles grow taut. Lady Harding didn't say a word. She simply narrowed her gaze. But he recognized it for the silent challenge it was. For the first time since Lady Harding had returned to Starling House almost ten years ago, he remembered his mother's indomitable will. She'd hidden it beneath the surface as she'd agreed to all the expectations he'd laid out upon her return.

Not once had she questioned his dictates. The only dictate she'd refused to accept had been the allowance he had tried to bestow upon her. He remembered her quiet dignity as she'd rejected his decision to support her financially. Sebastian suddenly realized how badly he'd deceived himself into thinking he actually controlled his mother.

Like all the women he'd ever met, his mother had merely chosen not to make their relationship any more contentious than it had been since his childhood. An invisible net wrapped itself around him until his body protested the restraint. The glint in Lady Harding's dark gaze convinced him there was no alternative he could suggest that his mother would even consider agreeing to.

"I can see you are troubled by the thought of Anna—"

"Forgive me, Captain Wentworth, I have no objections at all to your niece's continued stay with us." Sebastian lied as he forced a smile to his lips and met the man's concerned gaze. "I was simply considering any consequences there might be to your niece's reputation when people learn she's a guest here. While my mother's sponsorship will make Miss Sawyer's stay here above reproach, the question of her relationship to our family might be used by some who take pleasure in creating scandals where none exist."

"Then we shall say that Anna is the niece of a distant cousin." Lady Harding smiled with triumph at Sebastian before turning back to Captain Wentworth. "It's not that far from the truth. Levi and I always looked on you, Augustus, and Serena as part of our family."

Anna's uncle hesitated and shook his head in disagreement. For the first time since the discussion of Anna's fate had begun, Céleste DuBois spoke up.

"Lady Harding is correct, *mon cher.* You know, as well as I do, that Anna is far too intelligent to be condemned to a life that is filled with little but needlepoint, no matter how sweet and kind Georgina is." Céleste's hand rested on the captain's arm as she sent him a soft, pleading look. It suggested the woman was more than just a family friend the master sailor had introduced her as. "I saw the look on her face when you were so insistent that she go stay with Georgina. Just like the men you command, she has always followed your wishes if she thought it was an order."

"But I didn't order her to go. The last time I broached the matter, she fought vehemently to stay on board the Falcon, and I didn't order her to go then either. She barely put up a fight this time," the sea captain said with a look of confusion. "She's of age. She knows I cannot force her to go."

"I know that Charles, but *she* saw it as an order. She's not disobeyed an order from you since the day she climbed up to the crow's nest when she was eleven. Worst of all, I believe Anna will come to resent you for forcing her to go stay with Georgina. I have no desire to ever see that happen. Even asking her to remain here at Starling House might be a mistake."

Captain Wentworth stared at the Frenchwoman for a long moment before he nodded, then turned his head toward Sebastian's mother.

"If you're sure about this, Lily, then I will accept your generous offer. Naturally, I will pay all of Anna's expenses while she's under your care."

The moment Wentworth agreed to Lady Harding's proposal, Sebastian barely managed to contain the groan pushing its way up his throat. Christ Almighty, he was in the fire now. Unwilling to show any hint of his growing alarm, Sebastian looked down at his dessert. Charlotte Russe was a particular favorite of his, but somewhere along the way, his appetite had vanished. Eager to escape the ongoing conversation as to plans for Anna's stay at Starling House, Sebastian cleared his throat.

"If you will excuse me, I have estate business that requires my attention."

Rising from his chair, Sebastian bowed slightly, then

strode out of the dining room as if the hounds of hell were baying at the table. In seconds, he was behind the closed door of his study. His only sanctuary other than his bed chamber.

"*Damnation*, Starling. Why didn't you simply say no?"

The room crackled with the strength of his anger and frustration as he stared blindly at his desk. The answer was simple. He'd been caught off guard by Lady Harding's insistence that Anna remain here under her charge.

Only when she'd silently dared Sebastian to object to her proposition had Sebastian reluctantly agreed to Anna remaining at Starling House. A loud snort of self-disgust blew past Sebastian's lips as mocking laughter resounded in his head for refusing to admit he'd agreed for a different reason altogether.

With a shake of his head, Sebastian silenced his inner voice's taunting laughter. All he needed to do was arrange his schedule so he would see as little of Anna as possible. Another snort of laughter echoed through his mind, and it infuriated him. Sebastian shoved his fingers through his hair until his hand cradled the back of his neck.

"I am no longer a school boy incapable of controlling his base needs," he snarled to the empty room as he struggled with how to deal with his predicament.

The club. He would spend more time at his club. He could even spend a couple of weeks at Birchwood. He'd invite Nicholas and several other friends to join him for several long weekends filled with cards, drinking, and the occasional hunt for the pheasant he enjoyed so much.

Then there were the two house parties he'd been invited to. Sebastian had put them on the pile of invitations to decline, but now he was forced to reconsider that decision. Perhaps a short and simple liaison with a young widow might be just the thing to purge the lust Anna aroused in him.

At the very least, it might ease some of his body's painful demands. One's hand was a poor substitute for the pleasure of a woman's body flexing tightly around his cock. The thought quickly evolved into an image of Anna writhing beneath him as he drove his body into hers. The speed with which his body responded to the erotic vision made him release a groan of torment as he fought to push the vision out of his head.

With a jerk, he began to pace back and forth. What had he been thinking about before his mind had entered the hellish heaven that involved erotic imaginings about Anna? A liaison. Yes, a short-term liaison at a house party. Perhaps a short weekend in the country was precisely what he needed. A momentary diversion from his current state of affairs would be quite welcome at the moment. Sebastian immediately rejected the idea.

Liaisons could become complicated. Invariably, a woman's thoughts turned from a short-term relationship to a much longer one. Sometimes the woman in question would even try to make the liaison take on a much more permanent form. No, the last thing he needed at the moment was one more complication. Christ Jesus, he was a fool. He'd known almost from the first moment he'd laid eyes on Anna that she was dangerous.

Her effect on him had been challenging enough. But he'd comforted himself with the belief it was a temporary state that would resolve itself when she was gone. Not in his wildest imaginings had he even contemplated Anna might remain here indefinitely. Sebastian grunted as he continued to pace the floor.

Still, if he occupied his days and evenings with business matters, Lady Margaret, and friends, he would be able to avoid temptation. It was doubtful those activities would completely purge his lustful, erotic thoughts where Anna was concerned, but it was a start. A low groan broke past his lips. God help him avoid temptation and the cataclysmic consequences he was certain would follow if he surrendered to his body's demands.

Chapter 8

"No, Lord Asquith. I cannot agree to that." Sebastian rejected the request of the older man seated behind the desk. "I refuse to put Miss Sawyer's life in danger."

"As I understand it, the young lady is quite capable of taking care of herself," the Home Secretary replied, his eyes narrowing as his mouth thinned with irritation.

"Based on the account my brother shared with me, that is my understanding as well." Sebastian eyed the man with icy disdain. "Nonetheless, as a member of my household, I'll not allow Miss Sawyer to be used as bait to draw out the Hatshepsut cult members who've managed to elude Scotland Yard. And while my brother isn't here, I know he, too, will refuse to put his fiancée at risk."

"Dammit, Starling, Miss Sawyer and Miss Trafford are our best chance at catching these bastards."

"Lord Guildford and I will find another way to draw out the Hatshepsut cult members who are still at large." Sebastian turned his head toward his best friend, the Earl of Guildford, who was seated next to him. The two of them had met their first year at Eton and formed a steadfast friendship. Now he watched Nicholas nod in agreement.

"We're both aware of how sensitive this matter is, my lord," Nicholas said in an even-tempered voice, but Sebastian heard his friend's irritation. "However, I feel certain it's possible to find these cutthroats without endangering Miss Sawyer or Miss Trafford. If you would allow Lord Starling and me to do some investigating of our own, we can provide you and the Commissioner with regular updates as to our progress."

"I'll not deny we could use the help, my lord," Sir Bradford said in a tight voice. "I've assigned a number of men to work with Inspector Pratt, but it's almost impossible for my men to question a peer without any kind of evidence."

Lord Asquith leaned back in his chair, eyebrows furrowed in frustration. He studied Sebastian in silence for a long moment, before he made a sound of anger and threw himself forward again. His hand slapped the top of his desk before he pointed a finger at Sebastian.

"I will expect a weekly report as to any findings in the investigation. You're to work hand in glove with the Commissioner and this Inspector Pratt of his." With an arrogant wave of his hand, the Home Secretary dismissed them. "That will be all, gentlemen."

Sebastian's jaw clenched at the man's demeanor but said nothing as he rose to his feet and offered Asquith a slight bow. Nicholas did the same, and they strode out of the Home Secretary's office with Commissioner Bradford on their heels. As they reached the outer offices of the Home Secretary, the commissioner cleared his throat.

"My lords," he said with a slight note of hesitation in his voice. Sebastian and Nicholas came to a halt and turned to face the man. The commissioner's embarrassment was evident as he cleared his throat again. "I wish to apologize."

"Apologize? For what?" Sebastian frowned in bewilderment.

"I'm afraid I'm responsible for Lord Asquith knowing about Miss Sawyer's…her rather unusual skill in self-defense. Several officers witnessed her ability, and it was impossible to omit that detail in my report." Sir Edward heaved a sigh. "If I had known his lordship would suggest Miss Sawyer be used as bait, I would have provided the Secretary with an…abbreviated report."

"I don't blame you, Sir Edward," Sebastian said with a shake of his head before he looked over the commissioner's shoulder at the outer door of the Home Secretary's offices. "Lord Asquith is the one who proposed the plan. From your reaction, I know you were as offended as we were by his suggestion."

"Thank you, my lord. I'm also grateful for your offer to assist in the investigation. It's a delicate matter to question a peer of the realm," the commissioner said with a grimace. "I'm certain your subtle inquiries, as well as Lord Guildford's, will be of immense value. Naturally, all our files are available for review at your convenience."

"Perhaps now would be a good time. Nicholas?" Sebastian turned to look at his friend, and the earl nodded.

"Now is fine with me. I've no plans until later this afternoon when I'm meeting with the Prime Minister."

"Excellent. It's my hope you'll be able to make headway with the investigation where my men have not." Sir Edward nodded his head with satisfaction and not a small measure of relief. The commissioner pulled his watch from his vest pocket and glanced at it, then lifted his head. "I shall meet you in my office in, say…half an hour?"

When the man received nods from both Sebastian and Nicholas, the commissioner smiled and continued on his way out of the building. Sebastian didn't bother to watch the man depart as his gaze focused on the outer door of the Home Secretary's office.

"I can't believe the bastard had the audacity to suggest Anna and Sarah be offered up as bait."

Sebastian's jaw clenched as he remembered his disbelief and anger when the Secretary had made his proposal. With a final glare at the door to Asquith's office, he turned away and caught Nicholas eyeing him with surprise. He arched an eyebrow at his friend.

"I confess to being stunned by the man's suggestion as well, but I think I'm more astonished that you refer to Miss Sawyer by her first name," Nicholas said as he began walking toward the building's exit. "It's unlike you to step outside your normal rules of propriety."

"Anna is a relative, and it's difficult not to address her by her first name when she's living under my roof and my entire family refers to her as such."

Sebastian knew it was a misleading statement given his thoughts about the woman. But he wasn't about to admit to lusting after Anna, not even to his best friend. He tightened his jaw with irritation. He needed to find a way to keep the woman from disturbing his thoughts, especially at night. Sebastian glanced at Nicholas and saw his friend's eyebrows arched in obvious skepticism. Aware of how well his friend knew him, Sebastian returned his attention to the doors in front of them that led out into the street.

"I think perhaps it's her courage and fortitude, which makes me think of her as Anna. Like Sarah, who will soon be a member of my family," he clarified his familiar mention of his future sister-in-law without glancing in Nicholas's direction. "Anna is lucky to be alive. It's impossible to forget that if Anna's knife wound had been just a little bit lower, she would be dead right now."

"Well, to ensure *Anna* and Miss Trafford remain safe, we've our work cut out for us."

Nicholas's reference to work was far more accurate than either realized. More than four hours later, the two of them were still sifting through a large stack of documents detailing all the events leading up to the night Anna and Sarah had escaped being sacrificed by the Hatshepsut cult. Sebastian had taken his jacket off more than two hours ago, and now stood up to stretch his back, then stretched his arms as well.

"I'm beginning to think this is hopeless," he muttered with a sense of defeat. Nicholas immediately offered words of encouragement.

"We still have a few files to go through."

"But none of them mention any peers of the realm."

"Miss Trafford's notes have been added into this file," Nicholas said as he tapped the file in front of him. "Alexander's fiancée has been quite thorough in her investigation of the Hatshepsut cult."

"Does she mention anything, or anyone in particular?" Sebastian turned toward his friend, who still had his head bent over a thick file.

"She mentions Viscount Farthington and a couple others, but Farthington is mentioned repeatedly in Miss Trafford's notes." Nicholas looked up from the papers he was reviewing to meet Sebastian's gaze. "The young lady notes the man appears to have a number of connections that are worth investigating further."

"Didn't Farthington host one of those mummy-unwrapping parties a couple of months ago?" Sebastian frowned as he tried to recall where he'd heard about the event. His frown deepened as he remembered where. "Margaret. She mentioned she'd attended the affair with her niece."

"Interesting," Nicholas said. "Although I can see where she might believe that nonsense about immortality."

"What are you implying, Nicholas?"

"Nothing, but you must admit the woman is quite preoccupied with her appearance." Sebastian's friend bent his head again to continue reviewing the open file in front of him. "I would think the idea of immortality would appeal to her."

"I know you don't care for Lady Margaret. However, as I'm seriously considering extending an offer to her, I hope you will think kindly of her. I believe we will do well enough together."

"Then you're a fool," Nicholas snapped. "Have you learned nothing from my own situation? The sight of my wife fucking the footman hours after our wedding is nothing I would wish on any man."

"But I'm not in love with Margaret."

"I was in *lust*, not love, and that lust died a quick death when I found the footman humping the bitch from behind."

Nicholas's deep bitterness made Sebastian wince. He disliked seeing his friend so unhappy. Vickie had played Nicholas for a fool. His wife's blatant affair with the Earl of Fane less than three weeks after she married his friend had been one of deep humiliation for Nicholas. Not even Sebastian had seen through her displays of genuine adoration of his friend.

But Vickie had wanted to marry up the social ladder, and she'd achieved that goal. Nicholas's only consolation was the return of his family's ancestral home, that had been lost in a wager more than three hundred years ago. Sebastian moved to the window where he could see the Westminster Bridge crossing the Thames.

The difference between him and Nicholas was that at least he and Margaret had several interests in common. She was also pragmatic like him, and he knew her desire to be married was most likely a need for financial security. According to gossip, her first husband had left her with limited funds. Behind him, Nicholas muttered an oath.

"I spoke out of turn, Sebastian. I simply have no wish to see you humiliated by Lady Margaret as I have been by my wife."

"I promise you, I am well-prepared for Margaret to take a lover, *after* she's produced my heir," Sebastian said in a detached voice as he turned back toward his friend. "I have no illusions when it comes to a woman's ability to be faithful to her marriage vows. Marriage is nothing more than a means to an end. It ensures the continuation of one's lineage."

"A cynical point of view, but one I understand." Nicholas shrugged. "However, it still leaves the question of whether Lady Margaret is involved in the Hatshepsut cult."

"While I have doubts as to her involvement, I know she's mentioned an interest in the subject on one or two occasions. I'll question her under the guise of investing in an archeological expedition based on the Set's current level of enthusiasm."

"Then I'll follow up on Farthington. The man enjoys the sound of his own voice. I have no doubt I'll be able to convince him to expand on his interest in Egypt's ancient era." Nicholas closed the file he'd been reviewing. "I need to go, or I'll be late for my meeting with Rosebery. He's an affable fellow but doesn't like it when someone is late."

As Nicholas hurried out of the small office Sir Edward had provided for their use, Sebastian retrieved his coat at a more leisurely pace. Pushing his arms into the sleeves of the garment, he considered Nicholas's remarks about Margaret. It was obvious his friend disapproved of her. Was it possible Nicholas had seen something in the woman that Sebastian had missed?

He'd not been lying when he'd said he had no expectations of Margaret remaining faithful if she became his wife. His only expectation was for her to provide him with an heir. Lady Margaret was amiable enough, and she abhorred scandal, so they were in accord on that point. He was certain life with her would be reasonable, if not boring.

But then, boring meant peace and quiet. Something he'd not experienced since Anna had arrived at Starling House a week ago. His nights had been filled with erotic fantasies, while he'd spent his days desperately filling his hours with as many things as he could, simply to avoid thinking of her. Sebastian released a grunt of irritation as he left Scotland Yard and made his way home.

A short time later, he was walking through the front door of Starling House. Sebastian had barely removed his hat and gloves when he heard a loud thud echo out of the salon. His stride long and fast, Sebastian strode into the main parlor, expecting to find someone lying on the floor. Instead, he saw Anna seated in the window seat, trying to reach a book that had fallen to the floor below.

"Dammit to hell." At the vicious oath, Sebastian stared at Anna in stunned disbelief. It took him several seconds before he found his voice.

"I beg your pardon?" he bit out between clenched teeth.

Anna jerked violently and almost tumbled out of the window seat as her eyes met his. Dismay caused her lips to fall open slightly as she stared at him in surprise, while he struggled to comprehend that he'd just heard the woman utter a curse. Not a strong one, but it wasn't the strength of the curse that troubled him so deeply. It was the fact that the woman had said it. Said it in his house. Anna winced beneath his harsh glare of condemnation.

"I'm sorry. My shoulder is still tender. It hurts if I move too quickly."

Sebastian accepted her explanation and apology for her unladylike language with an abrupt jerk of his head. Fully expecting her to stand up, he moved forward, intent on picking up the book on the floor. When Anna didn't climb out of the window seat as he approached her, a knot formed in his throat. With the hem of her gown riding up her legs, almost to her knees, her posture resembled that of a seductress intent on arousing him.

It was working.

Firm, shapely calves, he remembered all too well from the night she'd first arrived, were exposed in all their glory. There was an aura of innocence about the way she was sitting. Her relaxed posture was so natural that he was certain she had no comprehension as to how inappropriate it was for her to expose herself in such a manner. Worst of all, she was clearly unaware of how tempting she looked or the effect she was having on him.

Transfixed by her, a primitive emotion surged through his veins as he fought to control the images flooding his mind. Sebastian's body tightened at the thought of his hand caressing her ankle before he allowed it to move upward. His hand flexed as he imagined his fingers stroking their way up to the lusty thigh hidden beneath her skirt, then even further to explore the heat of her sex.

When she didn't move to cover her legs, his gaze shifted to her face. Puzzlement furrowed her brow as she studied him, before a sudden flush of color rose in her cheeks. As if suddenly realizing how improperly she was sitting, she awkwardly scrambled out of the window seat.

The instant her gown covered her legs, his mind shouted a protest. He ruthlessly crushed the silent objection. What was it about this woman that he found so enticing? So much so that it was difficult to think straight whenever he was near her. Anna wobbled on her feet, and Sebastian instinctively caught her in his arms to keep her upright. The heat that barreled through him the moment his arms wrapped around her made Sebastian's heart slam into his chest with the blunt force of a sledgehammer. Frozen in place, he held her in his arms as he stared down at her.

Anna's wide-eyed surprise vanished as her plump, pink lips parted slightly, and her eyes took on a soft, sultry expression. Without thinking, he slowly lowered his head toward her tempting mouth. A split-second later, he jerked violently and released her, then put several feet between them. What the devil had he been thinking? He'd almost kissed the woman.

"Forgive me. I only meant to keep you from falling. It's not like me to take advantage of such a situation," he said, keenly aware of the charged emotion layered beneath his apology. A mischievous smile curved her delicious mouth.

"I wouldn't have minded at all if you had kissed me." Her brown eyes darkened. "I was hoping you would."

Shocked by her confession, Sebastian didn't move as she bent over to pick up the book he'd meant to retrieve for her before he became distracted. A second later, he heard her draw in a sharp breath.

"Fuc—bugger it."

In a noisier environment, her almost inaudible curse would have gone unheard. But here in the quiet salon, he heard her clearly. Sebastian didn't know whether to be offended and appalled by the oath or amused by her obvious effort to utter a less offensive one. He knew he should have condemned her language immediately, but he stopped himself as he saw the look of pain on her face as she straightened upright in a quick, sharp movement. Sebastian immediately stepped forward and picked the book up off the carpet.

"Perhaps you shouldn't move so quickly when reaching for something, particularly a heavy book."

The moment her eyes widened in surprise, he bit back a smile. About to hand her the leather-bound text, Sebastian glanced down at it and frowned at the title etched in gold on the cover. Eyebrows raised in surprise, he stretched out his hand to return the book to her. As she accepted the heavy volume, Sebastian clasped his hands behind his back.

"Is that normal reading material for you?" At his question, she blinked in surprise before she smiled and nodded.

"Ancient Egypt has fascinated me since my uncle took me to the Pyramids at Giza as a girl."

"You've been to Giza?" At the surprise in his voice, she smiled as if she were recalling several pleasant memories.

"Several times, as well as Luxor, Cairo, Marrakesh, India, and numerous other places. Uncle Charles says visiting a place will help you remember much more about its history than if all you do is read about it in a book." She tipped her head to one side as she looked at him with curiosity. "Have you traveled?"

"I have." His mouth twisted in a smile as he remembered the enjoyment his trips had brought him. "Like you, I've been to a number of places as well. I've spent time in Morocco, Paris, Rome, Venice, Athens—"

"*Athens*." Her enthused excitement lit up her lovely features. "I've always wanted to visit Greece. The Falcon has never sailed close enough to it for us to stop. What is it like?"

"Beautiful. Almost as beautiful as—"

Sebastian stiffened at the realization he was about to confess how beautiful he found her to be. Puzzlement made her tip her head in a silent request that he continue. The knot he'd swallowed a few moments ago returned to wedge itself solidly in his throat. He'd told himself he needed to keep distance between the two of them, and he was failing miserably at the task. He shook his head as if his thoughts had been interrupted, which wasn't far from the truth.

"I shall let you return to your reading."

"I was actually doing research." Anna looked down at the book in her hand as if contemplating its contents.

"Research?" Speculation made him narrow his gaze at her. Even on short acquaintance, he had surmised Anna Sawyer was far more intelligent than most of the women he knew. Instinct told him the word research wasn't a careless choice of words with her.

"Yes, I know several members of the Hatshepsut cult escaped the police, and I wanted to learn more about the cult."

"There's no need to be frightened, I can assure you that every precaution has been taken to protect you and Miss Trafford."

"Yes, Uncle Charles said you'd arranged for protection,

and I thank you for doing so. It's just that I wanted to see if I could find any references to the cult." The response heightened his concern.

"To what end?"

Sebastian grew still and narrowed his gaze at her. The moment Anna hesitated, he couldn't help thinking she was trying to hide her real intent. Alarmed by her hesitation to explain herself, Sebastian took a quick step forward to tower over her. It was a deliberate attempt to intimidate her into answering his question, but deep down, he knew it was a futile effort.

He was correct. Clearly annoyed by his efforts to force her to answer his question, her mouth tightened with irritation and more than a hint of defiance. When she remained silent, a harsh breath escaped him.

"I *asked* you a question, Anna."

Exasperation furrowed her brow. It was a reaction one might expect of a woman unused to explaining herself. The determination he'd already witnessed in her could easily indicate a stubborn streak as well. Sebastian narrowed his gaze at her again, and a sound of aggravation escaped Anna. With disgust, she rolled her eyes at him.

"I was simply *curious*. I'm quite knowledgeable about Egyptian history, and I've never heard of any cult associated with Hatshepsut." Anger clouded her lovely face, and indignation straightened her spine. "Egypt prospered under her reign. Hatshepsut proved a woman can be just as strong a leader as a man, even better than some. But I think someone wants to attribute her success to a god, not her leadership skills."

Anna's answer was quite reasonable, and while it didn't completely alleviate his concerns about her motives, it eased the tension in his muscles. Her outrage that Hatshepsut might have been maligned by the cult demonstrated her admiration for the ancient pharaoh. Her defense of the long-dead ruler also suggested she might support the suffrage movement.

It was a social issue he was sympathetic to, but he also knew change took time. Still, the idea that Anna's interest was nothing more than academic in nature didn't rule out the possibility of deeper motivations. But he needed to take her at her word, despite his misgivings.

"Why do I think the word *simply* takes on a whole new meaning when you say it?"

Despite his decision to take her at her word, he heard the note of irony in his voice. Immediately, she scowled at him. Sebastian responded with a look that challenged her to deny he was wrong. Despite his best efforts not to be amused by her annoyance, his lips twitched as he fought not to laugh.

"Captain Wentworth warned me that you have an adventuresome nature and a tendency to research or investigate things that attract your attention."

The puff of air she blew past her lips stirred the tendrils of brown hair that had escaped her upswept hair. Anna twisted her mouth in resignation as she averted her gaze from his. With an exaggerated sigh of defeat, she shrugged, then met his gaze and smiled.

"Guilty as charged. Uncle Charles has often said I'm far too curious for my own good." Laughter sparkled in her eyes as she laughed at herself. "And he's correct that I have a somewhat intrepid spirit. One that has landed me in trouble on more than one occasion. I know it frustrates and worries Uncle Charles sometimes, although he hides it well."

"He is quite worried about you, but I assured him that you would be safe here." At his quiet statement, Anna nodded with understanding. With a small shake of her head, she suddenly stared off into space, a haunted look on her face.

"I love him very much. Uncle Charles is the father I never had."

"Never had?"

"My father was a monster. When he died, I was glad. I knew he would never be able to hurt my mother again. But she died a short time after he was gone."

Bitterness filled her harsh and unforgiving words, and he stared at her in shock. The sudden realization that her father had been abusive made his body tighten with outrage and revulsion. A man who beat a woman deserved to be shot like a rabid dog.

"How old were you," he asked gently. Anna turned her head to meet his gaze as if startled to realize she'd shared something about herself she hadn't meant to. She turned away from him again.

"I was ten. Uncle Charles has been my hero since the day he came to the Red Gables Inn a year later and took me to live with him on the Falcon."

"The Red Gables Inn?" There was something about the anger, pain, and sorrow in her eyes that made him want to pull her into his arms in an effort to soothe her. He quickly crushed the emotion.

"I was a scullery maid at the inn for almost a year after my parents died before Uncle Charles found me."

"A scullery maid," Sebastian exclaimed softly. It was the last thing he had expected her to say.

"My mother arranged it before she—" Anna didn't finish her sentence. It was clear she didn't want to discuss the past, but something prompted him to try and probe a little deeper.

"Forgive me for dredging up unpleasant memories, I merely find it difficult to imagine you as a scullery maid."

"It's in the past, and I buried it long ago. My life started anew when Uncle Charles found me."

She shook her head in a way that signaled she wasn't about to reveal any more about her past. Sebastian didn't have time to ask her anything else as the sound of voices in the foyer floated through the air and into the salon. A second later, Alexander entered the room with a young woman on his arm. Beside him, Anna gasped with delighted surprise.

"*Sarah.*" Excitement and delight filled Anna's expression, and she quickly laid her book on the window seat, then hurried across the room to hug the other girl. "I'm so happy to see you. Are you well?"

"Yes, thanks to you." Sarah returned Anna's smile and squeezed her hands while kissing one of Anna's cheeks and then the other. "You saved my life. Alexander and I can never repay you for that gift."

"So, you're Alexander." Anna's gratitude was reflected in her smile as she extended her hand to his younger brother. "Lady Harding told me you were the one who brought me to Starling House the night Sarah and I...the night we met. Thank you."

Alexander carried Anna's hand to his lips and brushed his mouth across her knuckles. For not the first time in the past week, Sebastian realized once more how much his brother had matured. While he knew it could not have been an instant transformation, he marveled at how he'd missed the change in Alexander.

"Thanks are unnecessary. As Sarah said, we can never repay you for what you did. I hope you are well and fully recovered?"

"I am quite well, thank you." Anna turned her head and nodded in Sebastian's direction. "Although Lord Starling did not catch me at my best a few moments ago when I tried to pick up the book I dropped."

"It was a heavy book," Sebastian said in a dry voice as he remembered her clear effort to soften her language.

Sebastian swallowed a laugh as Anna cast a threatening glance his way. He turned his head toward his younger brother and noted how Alexander drew himself up even taller as he directed an arched look at Sebastian.

"Bash, I don't believe you've had the honor of meeting

my betrothed, Miss Sarah Trafford."

Alexander turned to look at his betrothed for a moment before he looked back at Sebastian with an air of defiance. The memory of Lady Harding telling him not to interfere with Alexander's marital plans made him clear his throat. He closed the distance between him and the young couple, then bowed toward his future sister-in-law and politely kissed the hand she offered him.

"It is a true pleasure, Miss Trafford. From all the accounts I've heard, my brother has chosen well. I am honored to welcome such a lovely, brave woman into the Reddington family."

His brother and his fiancée appeared thunderstruck by his words. Sarah was the first one to react to his quiet greeting. A flush filled the young woman's cheeks as she offered Sebastian a small smile.

"Thank you, my lord. I shall do my very best to make Alexander happy."

"Just having you at my side makes me happy, my love."

The depth of emotion in Alexander's voice startled Sebastian. It was clear his brother's feelings for Sarah Trafford ran deep. Even if his mother had said nothing about the relationship between him and Alexander, he would have known at this instant not to question his brother's choice of bride. A teasing smile on his lips, Alexander turned back to Anna.

"And has my big brother been treating you well?"

Despite the playful question, Sebastian heard the underlying current of tension in his brother's voice. As Alexander shifted his gaze from Anna back to him, Sebastian saw a belligerent glint in his brother's eyes.

"Lord Starling and Lady Harding have been very kind."

"I have no doubt as to our mother's kindness, but Bash can be quite contrary at times, especially where our mother is concerned."

At the quiet note of anger in Alexander's statement, Sebastian stiffened and narrowed his eyes at his younger brother before he turned toward Anna and Sarah.

"If you will excuse me, I have business to attend to."

He'd only gone two steps when a shock of current spread across his chest. Sebastian jerked to a halt and looked down to see Anna's hand resting on his arm. His gaze quickly shifted to her brown eyes, which reflected a warm softness.

"I would like to hear more about Greece at another time, Sebastian. That is if you would be kind enough to indulge me."

Her request eased some of his tension, and a small smile touched his lips as he stared down at her. Without thinking, he caught her hand in his and brushed his mouth across her fingertips.

"I'd be happy to do so," Sebastian murmured.

A small tremor reverberated out of her as they looked at each other in silence. Suddenly aware he was still holding her hand, Sebastian released his grip on her fingers with a quick jerk. He glanced toward his brother and saw Alexander watching him in amazement. With a sound of aggravation, Sebastian strode quickly out of the salon.

Chapter 9

As his brother disappeared from view, Alexander released a low sound of astonishment.

"By the Gods, however did you manage to make my brother so amenable?"

"That was amenable?" Anna lifted her shoulders a fraction as she looked at Alexander with skeptical amusement.

"If you knew my brother even half as well as I do, that was practically a warm smile where Bash is concerned when it comes to anyone outside of the family, except for Mama, of course." Amazement furrowed Alexander's brow. "I've never seen him look so conciliatory toward a woman before, not even Lady Margaret."

"Lady Margaret?"

"The woman he's considering as his future wife."

At Alexander's revelation, Anna flinched as disappointment sliced through her. Her dark angel was contemplating marriage. Anna didn't understand why the news twisted her insides in such a painful manner. She barely knew the man, and he was far too cantankerous and pompous for her to be upset by the thought of him marrying another woman.

No doubt the woman was every bit as boring as Sebastian was. A voice in the back of her head chastised her for being so unforgiving. There was something about her dark angel that made her believe he wasn't quite as dull as he tried to make everyone believe. The ludicrous thought made her smother the sigh threatening to reveal her conflicting feelings.

"Come," Alexander said cheerfully as he silently urged her and Sarah to have a seat. "I want to hear how you came to have such amazing skills as I saw that night in the warehouse. Where the devil did you learn to fight like that?"

"My uncle was my teacher. He learned his skills from a monk he met shortly after signing onto his first merchant ship. Uncle Charles exercises every day on the after-deck, and I've always enjoyed watching him. Every movement he makes is strong, powerful, and graceful. It wasn't until I was fourteen that I realized his exercises could be used for self-defense.

"The Falcon had docked in Cairo, and we spent the day in the souks. While returning to the ship, two sailors tried to convince Céleste to leave Uncle Charles and go with them. When she refused, the sailors tried to drag her away. Both men were on the ground in seconds.

"I'd never seen anyone move so fast before in my life. From that day forward, I begged Uncle Charles to teach me. He refused repeatedly until the day he saw a new crew member trying to kiss me. The sailor was gone before we set sail, and the first day at sea, Uncle Charles gave me my first lesson. I think he thought I would eventually lose interest, but I never did."

"Amazing." Alexander's reaction was filled with respect and admiration as he turned to Sarah. "I don't know if you saw or even remember Anna fighting, my love, but she was a sight to behold."

"I was not as good as you think," Anna murmured with a grimace as she remembered how she'd lost her focus.

"I'm not sure what you consider good versus

exceptional, but to do what you did is extraordinary in my book." Alexander's emphatic tone indicated she wasn't to argue with him. Sarah leaned forward to touch Anna's hand.

"If I wasn't so certain of Alexander's love for me, I would be jealous of his obvious admiration."

Sarah's attention turned to her fiancée, and the two stared at each other for a long moment in an unspoken language Anna recognized. The young couple reminded her of her uncle and Céleste when they exchanged glances. For a brief moment, Anna found herself experiencing a small touch of envy.

It lasted only a moment as she reminded herself that men such as her uncle, and now Alexander, were rare creatures in the world of men. It was highly unlikely she would ever find a man forward-thinking enough to love her without trying to mold her into what society believed a woman's role should be. Color flooded Sarah's cheeks as she looked at Anna.

"Forgive me, Anna. I'm easily distracted these days," she said as her cheeks became an even darker pink. "But I agree with Alexander. Although I only saw you fight for a brief moment, it's obvious you're the reason both of us are here today. Alexander would have arrived too late."

"Thank you," Anna murmured as their admiration and praise caused her own cheeks to burn with embarrassment. She shook her head in protest. "But I'm not the only one who saved lives that night. If not for you, those other women would have died because no one was looking for them as Alexander was for you."

"And yet, there are still a few members of the cult the police have yet to find." Sarah's trepidation vibrated in her voice, and Alexander immediately wrapped his arm around her to pull her into his side, then kissed the other woman's temple.

"I've told you that you're quite safe, my love. Scully's

men will be guarding you, as well as Anna, wherever you are, from now until every one of those blackguards is caught."

"About that," Anna said with renewed excitement. "I found something that might be of help in finding the ones who escaped the police that night."

Leaping to her feet, Anna hurried to the window seat to collect the two books she'd left lying on the cushions. She quickly returned to her seat and opened the volume she'd been reading when Sebastian had first entered the salon.

"Listen to this," she exclaimed softly as her finger began to trace its way across the page. "There was, however, an obscure group that believed Hatshepsut was a worshiper of Apophis. It was whispered that the god of chaos promised her immortality if she sacrificed numerous innocents in his name. The sacrifices were always presided over by Hatshepsut herself and one of her priests."

Anna looked up from the volume at the couple seated across from her. Excitement had lightened Sarah's features as she leaned forward.

"There were two priests at the altar that night," the young woman exclaimed.

"One of them was A *woman*." Both Anna and Sarah spoke simultaneously, as their gazes locked with triumph.

"We need to look for a woman who—"

"*Absolutely not*." Alexander's harsh objection was sharp and fierce as he interrupted and glared at Sarah. "If you think I'm about to let you put your life at risk again, Sarah Elizabeth Trafford, then think again. That goes for you as well, Anna."

"I am a journalist, Alexander. It's what I do," Sarah said in a firm voice as she eyed her fiancée steadily.

"And you almost died because of it," he snarled.

"And I still might if we don't find out who's behind this cult and its horrific actions." Sarah sighed as her fingers brushed across Alexander's cheek. "You know as well as I do that Scully's men cannot be everywhere. I'm still vulnerable, and the only way I know how to be safe is to fight back and find these…these—"

"Bastards." Anna supplied the word she knew Sarah was looking for but couldn't say.

"Yes," Sarah said with a blush as she nodded her agreement, while Alexander stared at Anna in shock. With a sheepish grimace, Anna shrugged her shoulders slightly.

"I speak four languages, one of which is completely unacceptable in polite company. I've tried to abstain, but I have significant moments of failure, much to your brother's dismay."

"I can imagine." Alexander's eyebrows shot up with just a hint of judgement, which was quickly overshadowed by amusement. As if suddenly realizing he'd been distracted from the original conversation, Alexander returned his gaze to his fiancée. "As I was saying about you and Anna searching for these dangerous criminals, I forbid you from pursuing this new piece of information, Sarah. It's too—"

"You *forbid* me?" Sarah snapped as she glared at her betrothed.

"Perhaps that was the wrong choice of words."

Alexander winced at Sarah's reaction, and he immediately tried to placate her by catching her hand in his to kiss it gently. The gesture did nothing to appease Sarah's outrage. If anything, her displeasure deepened, and Alexander sighed.

"All right, *definitely* the wrong choice of words. I'm simply asking you not to place yourself in harm's way, my darling. You have no idea the fear I experienced while Inspector Pratt and I were searching for you."

"I understand that Alexander, but I can't bear to live the way I'm living now. Always looking over my shoulder, never sure where danger might exist." Sarah's features softened as she touched Alexander's cheek with her fingers and eyed him steadily. "Is that what you want for me? Do you want to reduce me to a mouse afraid of her own shadow?"

"Of course not." Alexander's voice was filled with tenderness as he leaned forward and kissed Sarah's cheek.

"Then allow me to do what I'm good at. I promise I will consult you on everything, and I'm sure we can count on Anna to do the same."

"Absolutely," Anna said with a nod. "I have no wish to throw myself into a dangerous situation, but I refuse to live in fear either."

"I don't like this at all." Alexander's grim expression slowly changed to one of resignation in the face of Sarah's inflexible determination. "But I know you will investigate no matter what I say, and it's better to know what's happening than being left in the dark."

"Thank you, my darling."

Sarah leaned forward and kissed Alexander on the mouth before she drew back and blushed prettily as if suddenly realizing she'd done something unconventional. Alexander chuckled at her pink cheeks.

"I knew from the moment we first met that life would be one adventure after another with you, my love." Alexander turned his head toward Anna. "As for you, it's obvious you're a woman of many talents. What else can you do that might be put to good use in our quest?"

"Well, I'm well-versed in ancient Egyptian and Roman history, and I'm exceptionally good at winning at Brag." At Anna's confident statement, Alexander arched his eyebrows in skepticism.

"Exceptionally good?"

"Good enough to take your money off the table," she said with a laugh. "I have three trunks of books upstairs that were bought with my winnings."

"May God have mercy on my soul." Alexander groaned as he pressed his hand over his heart. "My bride-to-be is an intrepid journalist, and we are friends with a woman who possesses skills that exceed mine in language, history, and self-defense. If her gambling skills surpass mine, then I truly am a lost soul."

"I have no wish for you to lose your soul, only a few pounds. I can always use a new history book." Anna laughed at Alexander's askance expression, and Sarah entwined her arm in her fiancé's and kissed his cheek.

"I shall console you if you lose, my darling."

"That is a comforting thought." Alexander laughed as he arched his eyebrows at Anna. "Heaven help the man who falls in love with you, Anna Sawyer. He'll never know another moment's peace or serenity ever again."

"Since I've no intention of marrying, the men of this world can sleep easy at night, knowing they'll be spared such a terrible fate." As she saw the looks of surprised dismay on her friends' faces, she waved away their unspoken words of protest. "Besides, we have more important things to discuss at the moment, specifically how to go about finding our high priestess of Hatshepsut."

Chapter 10

Anna ran along the upstairs corridor, knowing that if Lady Harding or Céleste were to see her sprinting toward the main stairs, she'd be chided for her unladylike pace. The constant reiteration of this rule or that, had left her ready to cover her ears the next time someone reminded her to behave as a lady.

She was certain she could expect more behavioral constraints in the coming weeks and months before she was able to sail on the Falcon again. But at the moment, she couldn't care less that she wasn't moving with decorum. Hamish and Smitty had finally been free to visit and were waiting for her in the salon.

The entire time she'd been convalescing, Lady Harding had been emphatic in her refusal to let Anna receive the two sailors while confined to her bed chamber. Since then, the two sailors had been busy making the Falcon ready for her next voyage, and they'd been unable to visit. Knowing she wouldn't be on the ship when it sailed made her heart ache, and the bars of her cage closed in on her once more.

Halfway down the stairs, her feet slipped on the carpet, and if not for her fingers wrapping around the bannister, she would have landed at the foot of the staircase. She muttered a soft curse and came to a halt as Sebastian stepped out of his study to stare up at her. It was impossible to tell if his expression was one of concern or disapproval.

"Are you all right? It sounded as if you'd fallen." The concern in his voice warmed her heart.

"I just slipped. I think the heel of my shoe managed to get caught in the hem of this dress."

Annoyed by her clumsiness, she glanced down at the floral gown she was wearing and waved her hand in disgust at the dress. A quiet sound echoed out of him, and she immediately raised her head and narrowed her gaze at him.

"Are you laughing at me?"

"Not at all." His reply was just a little too smooth for Anna's liking, and she was certain she saw a glint of laughter in his dark gaze. "I'm simply relieved not to find you sprawled in a heap at the foot of the stairs."

This time she was certain he was struggling not to laugh, and she barely managed to keep from insulting him with a word she knew was unseemly. Irritated by her inability to counter his mockery in her usual manner, she made her way downward with her chin tilted at a haughty angle.

"I think it more likely you're disappointed you weren't able to chastise me as to some impropriety with that pompous, disapproving deportment of yours," she sniffed as she reached the bottom of the stairs.

Pleasure zipped through her as she saw him stiffen. So, the man didn't like being called pompous. Delighted her barb had struck a nerve, she smiled sweetly at him. Perhaps insulting someone didn't require an obscenity if one kept their wits about them.

The low rumble of anger she heard echoing out of him made her smile become a grin as he spun away from her. Gleefully, she made a face at his back as he disappeared into his study. Remembering her friends, she quickly crossed the foyer to the salon.

The moment she crossed the room's threshold, the jaws of the two sailors sagged in stunned amazement. Her friends stared at her in silence for a long moment before Hamish chuckled with amusement and Smitty burst out laughing.

"Ye look like a trussed up little pigeon." Hamish's chuckle became a laugh, while his gaze skimmed over her and skepticism lifted his eyebrows. "All dressed up and ready to be served on a platter at the captain's table."

"Ye clean up real pretty, lass." Smitty grinned as she glared at the two of them.

"That's right. Go ahead. Enjoy yourselves at my expense," she sniffed with annoyance and gritted her teeth as she glared at her friends. A second later, she smiled and hurried forward to give each of the sailors a tight hug. "Just remember, I can still drop both of you on your arses, you overblown double-baggers."

"I don't doubt that at all." Hamish nodded sagely, then grinned. "We saw you drop the cap'n *one* time."

Anna scowled at the tall, burly man who was her uncle's first mate. His grin widened, then with a shake of his head, the sailor's features took on a fatherly concern.

"Now then, first order of business. Has your wound healed?"

"Yes, I'm completely recovered." Anna grimaced as she remembered Dr. Johnson sewing her wound closed. "Although I now know what a sail must feel like when Smitty is stitching it up."

"That bad was it," Hamish murmured as he glanced at Smitty with a sly grin.

"I know how to sew, ye old dog." Smitty grunted with disgust. "My canvas stitching is the best the Falcon's ever seen."

Anna folded her arms across her chest and shook her head with a smile as she cocked her head to one side to look at the side of Hamish's head, just below the ear.

"Hamish, is my memory failing? Wasn't there someone on the Falcon who had to stitch up a cut on your face a couple of years ago?"

"Cut? You mean this one here?" Hamish's expression was solemn as he touched the large scar bordering the edge of his jawbone. Anna bit back a smile as she saw the mischief in his eyes and offered a nod of confirmation.

"Yes, that's the one. I'm trying to remember who stitched it up for you. Hmmm. Who was it? The name is just on the tip of my tongue." Anna tapped her forefinger against her chin as she stared up at the ceiling as if she were trying to remember.

"Now, don't the two of ye start up with that again." A dark frown settled on Smitty's brow as he uttered a noise of irritation. "It would have been a beautiful job if this chowderhead hadn't been three sheets to the wind. It took four men to hold him still."

Anna and Hamish looked at each other innocently before they laughed loudly, and Smitty's scowl blackened even more. The man mumbled something beneath his breath, and Hamish snorted as he playfully shoved against his friend's shoulder.

"You're right, Smitty. Ye did the best ye could with a raging bull. We were just poking fun at you, you miserable old salt." Fists pressing into his waist, Hamish tilted his chin and struck a pose. "I had one dove say it made me look exciting and dangerous."

"Exciting and dangerous to who? The seagulls?" Smitty grinned smugly at his friend, and Hamish blew off the other sailor's comment with a wave of his hand.

"I'll remember that next time we play cards." The moment Hamish spoke, a thick silence fell over the three. Anna flinched as the two men stared down at the floor. Anna swallowed the knot that had formed in her throat.

"I haven't told you both how sorry I am that my actions put the two of you in harm's way. I never would have followed you to the Blue Mermaid if I'd known what might happen."

"Ah, lass, we might have been angry with ye for following us, but we're proud of ye for defending yourself so well against those bast…men." The way the big man stumbled and corrected his language made Anna's heart sink. Already Hamish was looking at her differently. He was treating her like a proper lady, and not the Anna he knew as a friend. An equal. Still, Hamish's praise made her heart twist in her chest. God, how she was going to miss these men. They'd looked out for her from the first moment she'd boarded the Falcon.

"Hamish is right. We were a mite worried about ye when we came to our senses, but we knew ye could handle yourself." Smitty shook his head slightly as she arched her eyebrows at him. "All right, we were both worried sick. We scoured the docks for you from early morning into the night."

"Oh, Smitty. Hamish," she exclaimed softly as tears welled up in her eyes. "I don't know what I'm going to do without you. I'm homesick already, and the Falcon won't set sail for several weeks yet, or at least not until Céleste and Lady Harding are done clothes shopping for me."

"Homesick? For the Falcon, lass?" Smitty's eyebrows became almost a straight line as he studied her in puzzlement.

"Yes, you salty beast," she exclaimed. "Homesick."

"Why ever would ye be homesick, lass?" Hamish looked around the parlor in confusion. "As I see it, ye have a lot more room here than you did on the Falcon."

"But it's *not* the Falcon, you big oaf."The ferocity of her statement made Hamish look at her in surprise.

"Well, of course it's not, Anna." Her friend's bewilderment was emphasized by Smitty as he mumbled something similar. Hamish eyed her with puzzlement. "Are ye denying you don't like it here?"

"Didn't I just say I was homesick?"

With a look of dismay, Hamish stepped forward as if ready to pull her into a bear hug when he froze. Hamish gave the best comfort hugs, and they were almost impossible to escape, but the hug she expected never materialized. Instead, his hand patted her awkwardly on the shoulder. Stunned by his reticence to hug her, Anna stiffened as Hamish cleared his throat.

"All right, all right, you probably shouldn't be hugging us so much, now that you're a proper young woman." Even his voice sounded odd as he eyed her uncomfortably. It was almost as if he—

"*Hells bells*. You think I won't ever return to the Falcon," she said tightly. As she glared at them, both sailors averted their gazes. Anna immediately drew in a breath of dismay and anger. "*Damnation*, do you *honestly* think I want to be here? That I'll stay?"

"We didn't say that lass." Smitty's gruffly muttered response only increased Anna's anger.

"*Ballocks*. You didn't have to, I can see it in your faces."

The invisible cage confining her to a world she didn't want any part of, grew smaller once again. Disgusted that her friends thought her fickle enough to give up her life on the Falcon so easily, she blew out a harsh breath of anger.

"You're *both* arseholes for even *thinking* I want to be here. I'd give anything to be on the Falcon when she sets sail in a few weeks."

"Anna."

Somewhere in the back of her head, she heard Hamish say her name, but it didn't stop the growing homesickness, fear, pain, loneliness, and frustration raging completely out of control inside her. An intense fury held her tight in its grip as she planted her hands on her hips and eyed her friends with the scorn they deserved. With the horse's bit between her teeth, she fiercely berated the two men for thinking her so disloyal to her family on the Falcon.

"Do I *look* like a fucking bampot? I've even thought about becoming a goddamn stowaway just to escape this prison Uncle Charles has condemned me to."

"*Anna.*"

Hamish's voice wasn't loud, but the sharpness of his tone was one she rarely heard from him. Anna paused in her furious rant to defiantly meet his gaze as she allowed him to speak. Her friend's silent reprimand didn't quiet her anger, but when he cast his gaze toward the salon door, ice sluiced through her veins at the thought Lady Harding might be standing behind her.

Slowly, she turned around and saw Sebastian's towering figure in the doorway. His mouth was a thin line of angry disapproval, and she saw the silent condemnation in his eyes. The way his gaze was pinned on her gave her the sensation of being an insect he'd impaled on an invisible entomologist's board.

"I could hear you from my office, Anna. Are you in need of assistance?"

The man made his question sound like a polite query as to her well-being, despite the obvious reference to having heard her cursing in his office. The harsh disapproval flaring in his dark eyes heightened her anger and fear. Everything about him represented the cage that had slowly been shrinking in on her, inch by inch, from the moment she'd unwillingly agreed to Uncle Charles's request that she remain in London.

It wouldn't be long before everything she loved and held dear would be ripped from her completely, leaving her with nothing. The terrifying thought was like adding oil to Anna's fury as she took in the censure in Sebastian's expression. A need to strike out at the man who represented her prison made Anna's eyebrows shoot upward in a supercilious manner.

"If I *needed* any assistance, my lord, *you'd* be the *last* person I'd call for help." Anna spun away from him to glare at her friends, who were studying her with uneasy expressions and obvious remorse. "As for you two. I don't think I've ever been so disappointed in anyone in my entire life. For you to even *think* I'm happy to leave the Falcon says a great deal as to what you really think of me. Especially when you can see for yourself the life I'm being condemned to."

With a sharp movement of her hand, she gestured toward Sebastian, whose tall figure was growing blurry as she fought back tears.

"Anna. Please lass, we—" Hamish flinched as she cut him off with a sharp gesture of her hand.

"Go back to the Falcon. Both of you. I can't bear the sight of you anymore."

Anna barely managed to keep the tears from streaming down her cheeks as she raced toward the door. A strong hand latched onto her arm.

"Anna—" The vicious swipe of her fingernails across the back of his hand made him draw in a pain-filled hiss of air. "*Damnation.*"

"You're a goddamn hypocrite, Lord Starling," she said fiercely as she blinked back tears of anger and helplessness. "Let me go before I drop you to the floor like a sack of feed."

The instant she was free, she shoved her way past Sebastian and fled up the stairs to her room.

Chapter 11

Sebastian took three steps toward the stairs when a strong hand settled on his shoulder and forced him to a halt. Startled, he turned his head to see the tallest of the two sailors holding him in place.

"No, lad, let her go. She's hurting, and she's terrified. She's about to lose her home, her family, and her freedom. Everything she's known for more than fifteen years is being ripped away from her like a scab off a wound."

As if suddenly aware that his hand was still on Sebastian's shoulder, the burly sailor released his grip and quickly stepped back from him. The man twisted his knitted cap in his hand as he met Sebastian's gaze, then looked away.

"We'll be on our way. If the lass wants to see us again, she'll send for us," the tall sailor said in a gruff voice as he looked toward the empty stairwell. "Let's go, Smitty. Hopefully, she'll send for us again before the Falcon sails."

The two sailors mumbled a quiet goodbye and nodded their heads in Sebastian's direction before heading toward the front door. Sebastian reciprocated with a bob of his head as he watched them leave.

When the door closed behind Anna's visitors, Sebastian glanced down at the back of his hand, where small traces of blood marked where her fingernails had raked across his skin. Christ Jesus, she was right. He *was* a hypocrite for holding her to a standard he'd failed to live up to himself. Sebastian glanced at the empty stairwell as he remembered the stark terror on Anna's face as she'd fought to free herself from his grip.

It was obvious the sailor called Hamish knew her well. The sailor's insight had been emphasized by the fatherly look the man had worn as he'd stared up at the top of the stairs. The other sailor's expression had mimicked Hamish's, but it was the deep concern on Hamish's rugged, weathered features that bothered Sebastian.

Troubled by Anna's distress and panic, Sebastian raked his fingers through his hair. Even despite their short acquaintance, he'd come to see her as a woman of great strength and courage. To see her reduced to tears was worrisome. He wasn't uncaring about her distress. In fact, he cared more about her unhappiness than he wanted to.

"Sebastian."

At the stern note in his mother's voice, Sebastian lifted his head to watch Lady Harding descend the stairs at a fast pace.

"My lady," he said quietly as he bowed in her direction the moment she reached the bottom of the staircase.

"What have you done?" The sharp question made him start slightly as he stared at his mother in surprise.

"Done?"

"Anna has locked herself in her room, and I can tell she's sobbing into a pillow to deaden the sound." Lady Harding narrowed her gaze at him.

"I am *not* responsible for Anna's distress," he said through clenched teeth.

"*Then who is?* You're the *only* person in this house who wields his tongue like a sharp blade to inflict the most damage possible." His mother eyed him with something that bordered on contempt as her gaze skimmed over him as if finding him wanting. "I have tolerated your condemnation of me because I refuse to explain myself or my actions to you, but you will *not* treat Anna as you do me. Do I make myself clear?"

Stunned by his mother's anger, Sebastian stared at her, completely at a loss for words. Not once could he recall ever having seen her so angry, and Sebastian wasn't sure how to react. When he didn't say anything, Lady Harding jerked her head as if satisfied that his silence was his agreement to do as she demanded.

Before he could offer up a single word protesting her unjust accusation, his mother whirled around and stalked back up the stairs. With a snarl of anger, Sebastian stormed into his sanctuary and slammed the study door behind him.

Ever since Anna's arrival, his mother had become increasingly difficult to avoid. As he recalled Lady Harding's fierce defense of their guest, Sebastian huffed a breath of exasperation. It didn't please him to admit it, but his mother wasn't the only one who felt the urge to protect Anna.

Sebastian bowed his head to stare at the pattern of the rug beneath his feet. When he'd heard Anna's raised voice floating into his study a short time ago, he'd been torn between indignation and amusement at her earthy language. Despite the inappropriate words that flew from her beautiful mouth, the one thing it emphasized was her blunt honesty. She held nothing back.

In his mind, he saw a pair of beautiful chestnut-colored eyes shimmering with unshed tears. Seeing her in pain had aroused a need in him to gather her up in his arms and allow her to sob against his shoulder for as long as she wanted. It had been a reminder that for all her strength and confidence, Anna wasn't invulnerable. A knock on his study door drew him out of his thoughts, and Sebastian turned to see Alexander standing in the doorway.

"Bash, I need to speak with you."

His brother's voice echoed with quiet concern, and

Sebastian gestured for Alexander to come in and shut the door behind him. Since the night his brother had appeared in the foyer with Anna in his arms, Sebastian had come to see his younger brother in a different light. Almost overnight, their relationship had gone from a parent - child relationship to that of equals.

Alexander no longer needed his counsel as an older brother. Instead, his brother simply needed someone to listen as he worked out his own solution. Sebastian had also learned quickly that his brother liked to collect his thoughts before speaking.

"Come sit down."

Sebastian sank down into a chair by the fire and pointed to the one opposite him. Alexander's thoughtful look as he joined Sebastian was more that of distraction than anything else, and Sebastian studied his brother with amusement.

"Something tells me you're not really here to talk."

"What?" Alexander's gaze focused on Sebastian with bewilderment for a brief moment before he grinned sheepishly. "No, I wanted to discuss Anna with you, but I'm not quite sure how to begin."

The moment Anna's name passed his brother's lips, Sebastian's entire body tightened with something akin to alarm. Had his brother suddenly decided to shift his affections from Sarah Trafford to Anna? The possibility set Sebastian on edge as a wave of possessiveness slammed through him. Tension held him rigid as his fingers curled around the wood at the end of his chair's padded arm rest.

"Are you having second thoughts about Miss Trafford?"

"What?" Alexander stared at him in amazement before laughing. "God no. For better or worse, there will never be anyone for me but Sarah."

"Clearly a man in love."

The moment the words rolled off his tongue, Sebastian experienced a twinge of envy at his brother's happiness.

Sebastian quickly crushed the emotion. He was quite content with his life, or rather the life he had planned out for himself. An image of Lady Margaret filled his head, but in the space of a single breath, Anna's face replaced Margaret's. Once more, his muscles knotted with tension as he met Alexander's surprised gaze.

"You say that as if you envy me." His brother narrowed his eyes to study Sebastian intently.

"No," Sebastian lied smoothly, with a shake of his head. "I'm simply delighted to know you're happy. It's all I've ever wanted for you, Francis, Caroline, Emily, and Lydia. Your happiness has always been of the utmost importance to me."

"And I hope you know we feel the same about you." Something in Alexander's voice made Sebastian frown. Concerned that his brother might broach the topic of his intentions toward Lady Margaret, Sebastian moved quickly to redirect the conversation to Alexander's original subject.

"I'm pleased to hear it, but as I recall, you came in here to discuss Anna, not my happiness."

"Right," Alexander said in a distracted voice as he eyed Sebastian carefully for another moment then bobbed his head. His brother leaned forward in his chair as his brow became furrowed in a frown of concentration. "About Anna. Terrence has mentioned her several times to me, and I wondered what you thought about him as a potential suitor for Anna."

"*What?*" Stunned by the idea of Alexander's friend courting Anna, he stared at his brother in disbelief. As his amazement eased, it was replaced by the same possessive emotion he'd experienced only a moment earlier. "Terrence is completely unsuitable."

"Why would you say that?" Alexander asked with a look of surprise. "He's in line for an earldom that's quite lucrative, and he's a likeable chap."

"Likeable and a title are not what Anna needs."

"What makes you so sure about that?"

"Because he could never make her happy." The moment Sebastian spoke, he realized his mistake as Alexander stared at him in stunned amazement. Desperate to convince himself and his brother that his response was completely that of an observer, Sebastian made a dismissive gesture with his hand.

"I say that as someone who just witnessed her emotional state at seeing her friends from the Falcon." Sebastian grimaced at the question visible on Alexander's face. "One of the sailors said the Falcon has been her life for a very long time. The man didn't say it, but I think the only reason she's here and not onboard her uncle's ship is because she agreed to stay in London at Captain Wentworth's express wish. A wish I think might have been more of a command she didn't want to disobey."

The memory of tears collecting on long, dark eyelashes made Sebastian release a soft sound of irritation. Wentworth had been wrong to keep her in London. After what he'd witnessed a short time ago, he was certain she was longing desperately for the Falcon.

"I see," Alexander said quietly as he stared into the fire. "Then it would appear you're correct that Terrence is completely wrong for her. The man gets seasick at the sight of a rowboat."

"I suggest you forget trying to find a suitor for Anna and tend to your future marital status," Sebastian said with a sense of relief at having navigated the question of Anna's need for a suitor without any stunning revelations on his part.

"Well, that's relatively easy for me, but Sarah is another story. Ever since Anna made it clear that she has no intention of marrying—"

"Anna said she *didn't* want to marry?"

Sebastian stared at his brother in amazement. What woman didn't want a husband and family? He understood Anna was different, but to state she'd never marry was unusual, even for her.

"That was my reaction too," Alexander said with a shake of his head. "But she was emphatic about the matter. Naturally, my intended, like most women in love, doesn't believe her."

"Then your Miss Trafford is in for a rude awakening. If there's one thing I've learned about Anna in the short time she's been here, it's that not only does she speak her mind, but she generally means what she says."

"That's my opinion as well, but Sarah is convinced it's up to us to find Anna a husband."

"Good God," Sebastian muttered. "Spare me from the machinations of a woman's efforts to ensure everyone is happy simply because she is."

"I can agree with you somewhat." Alexander chuckled at Sebastian's reaction. "But honestly, I think Anna could make the right man quite happy. He'd never be bored, that's for certain."

"And the unfortunate soul would live in constant fear of her saying something completely inappropriate in mixed company. Correction, *any* company for that matter."

"She does have a way with words." Alexander grinned. "Much to my somewhat pompous brother's scandalized sense of propriety."

"Since when did I earn the title of being pompous," Sebastian snapped as he remembered Anna insulting him with the word.

There was *nothing* pompous or proper about the way he felt whenever Anna was near. If Alexander had even the slightest inkling as to Sebastian's erotic thoughts about the woman, his brother would be horrified and disgusted.

"There's no need to be upset, Bash. You've always been that way," Alexander said with a chuckle before sadness darkened his face. "But when Father died, you became almost fanatical about it. The only thing that kept the rest of us from pummeling you into the ground whenever you reprimanded us for some minor indiscretion was Mother."

"Mother?" Sebastian snarled softly. "What in God's name did she have to do with my expectations as to your behavior? When Father died, it was my responsibility to ensure all of you did nothing to shame his memory."

"That's what Mother said." Alexander shrugged in agreement. "She defended you stalwartly every time one of us complained about your rules and expectations as to the proper way you expected us to behave."

"What do you *mean*, she defended me?" Sebastian demanded as his brain tried to wrap his thoughts around the idea of his mother defending his actions to his siblings.

"Exactly what I said. She defended you," Alexander bit out as a spark of anger suddenly flashed in his gaze. "Mother said you were doing your best to honor Father's memory by setting a good example for us. She defended you even when you treated her with disrespect. Even when I was ready to come to blows with you about your vicious treatment of her, Mother defended you."

Alexander's bitterness was evident as he rose to his feet and scowled down at him. The look of disappointment in his brother's expression reminded Sebastian of the night Alexander had called him a cold-hearted bastard.

"What happened to make you despise her so badly, Sebastian? She's a kind and thoughtful woman. And God help her, she still loves you even despite your obvious disgust for her."

"This is *not* a subject I will discuss with you, Alexander. And this is the *last* time you will *ever* speak of it to me again. Is that clear?"

The palms of his hands hit the leather arm rests of his chair in a loud crack of sound. Rising to his feet, Sebastian towered over his brother as fury snapped every muscle in his body taut and unyielding. Alexander took a quick step back from him, his hands raised in the air in a display of surrender.

"Very well, I'll not broach the matter with you ever again." His brother's gaze narrowed with a resolute stubbornness, a trait Sebastian knew they both owed to their mother. "However, it's *my turn* to make a demand of my own. If you *ever* show our mother any disrespect in front of me again, I will make you *pay* for it in the most *unpleasant* manner possible. Is that clear?"

Sebastian jerked slightly at the vicious note of acrimony in his brother's voice as Alexander threw his own words back in his face. Somewhere in the back of his mind, Sebastian experienced the beginnings of shame, but he ignored the emotion as he acknowledged his brother's edict with a rough bob of his head. With a nod of satisfaction that he'd made his point, Alexander turned and walked out of the study.

As Sebastian watched the study door close behind his brother, he was forced to acknowledge how badly his entire body ached. Every inch of him hurt as if he'd been in a local tavern brawl. Sebastian had always known Alexander disapproved of his abrupt manner with their mother, but never had his brother delivered an ultimatum to him as he had just a moment ago.

The warning in Alexander's voice had been distinct and filled with purpose. His brother's word of caution had been more than just a shot across the bow. There had been something about Alexander's attitude that suggested his brother knew precisely what fine he would levy if Sebastian failed to meet Alexander's edict. Sebastian tried not to think about what that penalty might be, but it was impossible not to let his mind consider different possibilities. Whatever it was, Sebastian knew Alexander was more than ready to bring all manner of hell raining down on his big brother's head. It wasn't a pleasant thought.

Chapter 12

A quiet knock on the study door made Sebastian look up from his newspaper to see Anna standing in the doorway. It was the first time he'd seen her since yesterday when she'd left him and her two friends watching her run up the stairs. Sebastian rose to his feet and gestured for her to enter.

"Are you certain?" She arched her eyebrow as her pink lips curved in a small smile.

"Certain of what?"

"Allowing a woman to walk on what is clearly hallowed ground. You don't have plans to sacrifice me to some ancient god, do you?" she said with a laugh. "Because if you do, I should warn you that I'll put up a good fight."

"This is not hallowed ground," he said as his jaw tightened with irritation. The woman was mocking him.

"Then why isn't your mother allowed in here?" Anna crossed the threshold and began looking around the room. The curiosity in her question was reflected on her face as she walked toward a bookshelf to peruse the titles.

"My mother and I have an agreement as to what space we occupy within Starling House." Puzzled, he watched Anna pull a book off the shelf and open it to slowly turn the pages.

"I like your mother very much." She replaced the book, then moved toward the grandfather clock to stare at it in fascination. "This is beautiful."

"It belonged to my father. He received it as a wedding anniversary present from my mother."

"She must have loved your father very much." Her misguided observation made Sebastian snort with disgust. At the sound, Anna looked over her shoulder at him in surprise. He shrugged.

"My parents were ill-suited for one another."

"They were?"

Anna eyed him in bewilderment before she turned back to the clock. She stretched out her hand to stroke the wood, and he heard her draw in a sharp breath before he saw her straighten and stand motionless in front of the clock. There was something odd about her posture and how still she was, which prompted Sebastian to go to her side.

The bewilderment on her face as she stared at the clock puzzled him, but it was her ashen features that worried him. Gently, Sebastian touched her shoulder. With a violent jerk, she jumped away from him. The moment their eyes met, his concern deepened. There was nothing in her gaze that said she even saw him standing in front of her.

"Anna. What is it? What's wrong?"

The moment his quiet voice filled the small space between them, her transfixed expression slowly disappeared. She blinked and pressed her fingers into her forehead. It was as if she'd been sleepwalking, only to awaken in unfamiliar surroundings. Confusion darkened her eyes as she stared at him for a moment, then shook her head slightly.

"Nothing, forgive me. I sometimes have moments where I get so lost in thought I forget where I am."

"You didn't look as if you were just lost in thought," he replied as he studied her carefully. "You looked as if you were about to faint."

"Clearly you're prone to exaggeration." A small smile tilted her mouth before she rolled her eyes with obvious chagrin. "And I forgot why I came here in the first place. I wanted to know if you could help me visit the British Museum without your mother's or Céleste's knowledge."

"*Without* their knowledge?" He cocked his head to one side in surprise.

"Yes, if the two of them find out I want to visit the museum, I'll be forced to dress as if I were being presented to the queen." Her grimace of distaste made Sebastian chuckle. His reaction earned him a fierce glare, and he laughed again.

"I seriously doubt you would be required to wear a presentation gown to the museum."

"Maybe not," she said with a wry twist of her lips. "But it will become a major expedition, when all I want to do is visit the Egyptian wing without having to stop every few feet and be introduced to someone."

"The Egyptian wing?" Sebastian narrowed his gaze at her, and she nodded with enthusiasm.

"Yes, I've heard wonderful things about the museum, and I would particularly like to see the Rosetta Stone. This is the first time I've ever been in London long enough to go." She took a quick step forward and pressed her palm into his chest. "Could you ask Hodgekiss to secure a hack for me? He won't do anything without your say so, and I'd be incredibly grateful."

The moment Anna's hand pressed into his chest, a shock of electricity vibrated through him. It felt as if he were a lightning rod, and she was the lightning. His involuntary reaction to her touch was to draw in a deep breath. Instantly, he realized his mistake.

He couldn't remember ever having breathed in such an intoxicating smell in his life. The exotic scent of jasmine filled his nose with just a trace of vanilla. It was a light, enticing fragrance that was as unique as Anna was. The hint of a smile touched her lips as if she were Circe determined to make him do her bidding.

"Please, Sebastian."

"No. It's too dangerous for you to go alone."

Sebastian stepped back from her with a shake of his head, then quickly put several feet between them. It was the only way to avoid tasting her kissable lips, which wouldn't just be a pleasurable thing to do. It would be an exceedingly *dangerous* thing to do. His gaze slid to her mouth, which was parted slightly in stunned disbelief before it suddenly took on a defiant twist of anger.

"*Dangerous*? It's the *middle* of the day. I won't be gone for more than an hour or two. And I wasn't asking your permission. It's not as if I'm thinking of going down to the docks on my own."

"*That* you will most *definitely* not do," he bit out between clenched teeth at the thought of something terrible happening to her like the last time.

"Then send one of the footmen with me, if you're so damn worried I can't protect myself," she said angrily. "Or send one of the men you have watching the house. I've seen them from the windows. Surely one of—"

"If you would let me *finish*." Sebastian fixed his exasperated gaze on her, and while her mouth was set in a mutinous line, she remained silent. "Now then, as I was about to say, if your heart is set on going, *I'll* take you to the museum."

"You will?"

Her disbelief became amazement, and the moment her lips parted again, Sebastian suppressed a groan. Was he really thinking about dropping himself into the fire where this woman was concerned? Apparently, he'd already done so. With a sharp jerk of his head, he confirmed his offer.

"Yes. Collect your hat and gloves. I'll have Hodgekiss find a hack for us."

"Oh thank you, Sebastian." Happiness made her face

glow as she threw herself forward into his arms and kissed his cheek.

The softness of her mouth against his skin was only the briefest of caresses, but it was enough to make him feel as if one of his sparring partners had slammed him to the floor with a harsh blow. She pulled away from him, completely oblivious to his reaction.

Excitement lighting up her face, Anna smiled at him, then bolted from the study. As she disappeared through the doorway, Sebastian walked unsteadily to his desk. Christ Jesus. He was insane to escort her to the museum. The logical side of his brain snorted in disgust. It was a simple trip to the museum in the middle of the day.

Despite his reservations, he'd made the right decision to be her escort. If he'd said no, he was certain she would have found a way to go with no one knowing, and that was far too dangerous given his discussion this morning with Inspector Pratt.

Shortly after breakfast, Sebastian had met Nicholas at Scotland Yard to meet with the inspector. The man had been thorough in his update on the search for the Hatshepsut cult members, but his frustration at his inability to find those responsible for Anna's and Sarah's kidnapping was evident.

Although he'd been polite about the matter, Pratt had been blunt about his belief it would be difficult to find or prosecute the guilty parties. Sebastian understood the man's dilemma and had stated he and Nicholas would continue to do everything they could to help the inspector find the culprits.

Sebastian muttered an oath beneath his breath before walking out into the foyer and calling for Hodgekiss. The butler was in the hall in seconds, almost as if he'd been hovering nearby in the expectation of being needed. Sebastian asked the man to secure a hackney, then moved to collect his gloves off the cabinet in the entryway. Hodgekiss returned to the entryway to announce a hack was waiting for him, and Sebastian turned toward the stairs as he heard Anna running down the steps.

As she reached the foyer, her eyes sparkled with excitement as she pressed her straw hat down on her head, then used a long hat pin to secure it. Sebastian offered her his arm, steeling himself for the moment she touched him. With a brilliant smile, she slid her hand into the crook of his elbow. Even though he'd prepared himself for her touch, it did nothing to lessen the strength of its effect on him.

In minutes, they were seated side-by-side in the hackney that rolled forward. Sebastian turned his head to see Anna enthralled with everything she saw. Amused, he settled back in his seat and allowed himself to simply enjoy watching her excited reaction to everything. As he studied her, Sebastian noted something odd about her hat. He leaned forward in curiosity as his gaze focused on three quill stubs, minus their feathers, pressed inside the ribbon band encircling the bowl of her hat.

The moment he pulled the quills free, Anna jerked her head toward him. Holding up the broken feather tips, he arched an eyebrow in her direction and waited for her response. Color flushed Anna's cheeks, and her shoulders sagged slightly as she released a sigh of annoyance.

"They looked ridiculous, and one of them kept tickling my nose. It was annoying as hell." Her eyes widen slightly as he eyed her sternly, and she winced. "I'm sorry. I *am* trying."

"I suspect your tongue is less controllable when you're upset or excited," he murmured.

Sebastian met her gaze steadily as the memory of her fleeing up the stairs yesterday filled his head. Almost as if she knew what he was thinking, she stiffened and looked back out on the scenery. When she didn't comment on his observation, Sebastian stared down at the broken quills in his hand.

Unable to help himself, he chuckled as he envisioned Anna trying to puff a wayward feather away from her face. Out of the corner of his eye, he saw her look in his direction, and he lifted his head to smile at her.

"I was simply wondering how many times you had to blow the feather away from your face before you sent it to its death." He grinned as she eyed him in surprise, then laughed at his teasing.

"Just once." At her mischievous smile, he shook his head in amusement, and she shrugged. "I tried telling Céleste and your mother how annoying they were, but the two of them were already swooning over another hat by then."

"Do you mean to tell me you broke the feathers off in the *shop*?"

"It had already been added to the bill, and since it was mine to do with as I wished, I removed the offensive things." Anna rolled her shoulders in an insouciant shrug before her mouth twisted ruefully. "Although, if I had known doing so would send the hatmaker into a frenzied hysteria, I probably would have waited until we were out of the shop."

Sebastian laughed out loud at her reply, and Anna laughed with him. As their laughter died away, Anna studied him for a moment, then sighed.

"I lied to you earlier."

"Lied?" Sebastian frowned in curiosity.

"Yes, I didn't really come to your study to ask to go to the museum."

"I see, then what *did* bring you to the devil's lair?" Her eyes widened as she stared at him for a long moment before she quickly looked away as if embarrassed.

"I came to apologize." Regret filled her soft voice. "I'd already planned on getting a hackney myself, but I lost my courage when I reached your office, so I asked you to have Hodgekiss fetch me a carriage instead."

"Apologize for what?" Sebastian eyed her in

puzzlement, and Anna shook her head in regret.

"I know I drew blood when I scratched you yesterday, and I'm sorry for having injured you."

"There's no need for an apology. You were upset."

Sebastian's quiet reply made her wince again, before she nodded and looked out on the passing landscape once more. She remained silent for several moments, before she darted a glance in his direction, then looked away again.

"You're really quite nice when you're not acting so stuffy and stiff-necked."

"I beg your pardon?" Sebastian grew rigid at her remark, and she darted another glance at him, then sighed.

"See, I can't even compliment you without offending you."

"*That* was a compliment?" He arched his eyebrows in disbelief.

"Of course it was. Do you think I would say you're nice when you're glaring at me and imagining what punishment you'd like to administer first?"

Instantly, every muscle in Sebastian's body hardened. Punishment? The woman had no idea how many ways he'd envisioned teasing and tormenting her. Her hand touched the back of his, and it was as if someone had burned him with a fire poker.

"See, you're *already* imagining some terrible punishment to inflict on me, aren't you?" Her voice was a soft breeze in his ear, and he growled with frustration at her teasing.

"I can assure you *any* punishment I administered would be *far* from painful, Anna. *And,* I am *quite* certain you would be pleading for mercy faster than you could imagine."

The suppressed violence in his reply caused Anna to stare at him in surprise. In the next instant, her brown eyes darkened with awareness. Immediately, his heart slammed into his chest. Christ Jesus, did she actually understand what he'd meant? If she didn't, then that clever brain of hers would put it together for her soon enough.

"Then I shall do my best not to make you act on said punishments." The quiet words made Sebastian suddenly ache for the chance to show her just how pleasurably he could punish her. As he met her gaze, a smile bolder than Circe's curved her lips. "Although, I *am* curious as to how a punishment could be so pleasurable that one would need to cry for mercy."

The warm, brown eyes that met his had taken on a sultry look that dragged the air out of his lungs. Good God, she did understand what he'd meant. The hack rolled to a halt in front of the British Museum, and Sebastian threw himself out of the small, two-seat carriage before the vehicle had even come to a complete halt. Without looking at her, Sebastian helped Anna out of the vehicle, then silently ushered her toward the steps leading up to the museum's main entrance.

Tension throbbed between them, and he immediately regretted allowing himself to glance down at her. She was studying him intently with a small, enticing smile tilting her lips. Sebastian couldn't remember ever having seen a mouth so kissable in his entire life. He swallowed hard as he realized if they'd been alone somewhere, he'd be kissing her now.

Sebastian suppressed a deep groan as he realized he was swimming in deep, dark waters. As they entered the building, Sebastian saw the sign directing patrons to the Egyptian exhibit. With an abrupt gesture, he pointed toward the wing's entryway and guided Anna toward the opening.

As they entered the hall dedicated to the ancient era, Sebastian heard Anna draw in a breath of excitement. His gaze immediately swung to her face, and he was struck by her expression of delight as she looked around her surroundings. Unlike most women he knew in the Set, Anna didn't even attempt to hide her fascination or happiness at being in the museum.

Sebastian recalled the last time he'd been here. Several

months ago, he'd accompanied Lady Margaret to the opening of a new section of the Egyptian wing with artifacts found in Luxor by one of the museum's expeditions. If he'd not known how eagerly Margaret had been looking forward to the exhibit, he would have thought her bored the entire time they were in the museum. Anna's rapt attention was the complete opposite. A small gasp escaped her, and Anna grabbed Sebastian's arm.

"There it is."

The excitement in her voice was an almost tangible sensation as she tugged on his coat sleeve in an attempt to drag him toward the Rosetta Stone. As they approached the large stele, Anna released her grip on his coat, and quickly stepped into an opening made available when another visitor moved away. Sebastian remained a few feet away, watching her strike up a conversation with a young woman who had taken a spot next to Anna.

"Charlotte, come. We'll be late for tea." The sound of Margaret's voice made Sebastian turn around. As his gaze met hers, a smile of pleasure curved her lips. "*Sebastian.* What a delightful surprise."

"Margaret," he said quietly as he bowed and brushed his mouth across the back of the hand she offered him. "A pleasure to see you, as always."

"What brings you to the museum today? I didn't think you cared for Egyptian artifacts."

"I brought a distant cousin of mine to the exhibit. My mother is making plans to introduce her to society soon."

"You have such a good heart, Sebastian. I hope the young lady appreciates your sacrifice." Lady Margaret turned her head away for a moment. "Charlotte, please."

The young woman Sebastian had seen speaking with Anna quickly appeared at Lady Margaret's side and curtseyed when Margaret introduced the young woman as her niece. Out of the corner of his eye, Sebastian saw Anna join them as well, and he smiled down at her.

"Did you manage to memorize the markings yet?"

"No, but give me a few more hours." The sound of Anna's laugh shot a bolt of pleasure through him.

"Is *this* your mother's protégé, Sebastian?" Eyebrows arched in surprise, Margaret's gaze swept over Anna with a look that bordered on pity. "When you said your mother was introducing her to society, I expected someone *much* younger."

Muscles tightening at her disparaging manner, Sebastian narrowed his eyes at Margaret. Just as he was about to defend Anna, an irreverent laugh passed her lips.

"If my Uncle Charles had had his way several years ago, perhaps I would have met your expectations. Unfortunately, I now fall into the category of women my age or *older* who seem desperate to capture a husband."

Anna's cheerful, almost self-deprecating reply, held just enough of a steely edge to indicate she'd understood Margaret's veiled insult. The moment Margaret's eyes narrowed in antipathy, Anna's eyebrows shot up in a silent challenge for the other woman to complain at having been called out for her rude behavior.

Despite Anna's ability to defend herself, he experienced a strong need to protect her. Irritated by Margaret's discourteous manner, he suddenly wished he could offer the woman a curt nod of farewell and walk away, dragging Anna with him. Instead, he made the necessary introductions.

"Lady Margaret, may I introduce Anna Sawyer? Anna, this is an acquaintance of mine, Lady Margaret."

"Acquaintance?"

Lady Margaret stared at him in surprise and with more than a hint of irritation. Annoyed by Margaret's treatment of Anna, Sebastian didn't bother to correct his characterization of their relationship. As he made the introduction, Anna extended her hand to Margaret.

The moment the two women shook hands, Anna uttered a soft, unintelligible sound and quickly jerked her hand free of Margaret's. Startled by Anna's reaction, Margaret's face suddenly reflected anger at what she clearly believed was a slight. Sebastian frowned with disapproval, but it evaporated the moment he saw Anna's pale features reflecting an emotion that resembled horror. She quickly averted her gaze, but not before he saw something he couldn't define darken her eyes. An apologetic smile on her lips, Anna turned back to Margaret.

"I apologize, my lady. My gloves created a small amount of static electricity. I hope you did not suffer the same." Anna bowed her head to massage the hand she'd offered to the other woman.

"It appears I was more fortunate than you, Miss Sawyer. I experienced *no* such discomfort." Not waiting for Anna to reply, Lady Margaret smiled up at Sebastian. "I hope to see you soon, my dear. Will you be attending the Rothschild's ball next week?"

"I've not made my plans yet," Sebastian replied quietly. Something about Margaret's question made the tie around his neck seem to tighten. It was more than apparent to him that Margaret was asking if they would be attending the ball together. Any other time, he would have automatically said yes, but something made him remain silent. For a fraction of an instant, he thought he saw anger in Lady Margaret's blue eyes, but it was gone as she smiled at him.

"Of course, now if you'll excuse us, we really must be going, or we'll be late for tea at Lady Markham's." Lady Margaret smiled at him as she touched her niece's arm. "Come along, Charlotte."

As the two women walked away, Sebastian turned his head toward Anna. She was staring after Lady Margaret and her niece with an odd expression on her face. Sebastian frowned slightly.

"Is something wrong?"

"What?" Anna jerked her head toward him.

"You seemed fascinated with Lady Margaret and her niece."

"How long have you known her?"

"Margaret?" he asked in puzzlement as he saw her bob her head. "We've been acquaintances for over a year now, I think."

Anna nodded, then turned away and moved to one of the exhibits lining the wall. Perplexed by her quiet demeanor, Sebastian stared at her in confusion. The glow and excitement that had been on her face from the moment he'd offered to bring her to the museum had dimmed. Sebastian snorted softly and dismissed the fanciful thought.

For the next hour, they roamed the hall, with Sebastian always standing a few feet away. At first, he'd tried to engage her in conversation about one artifact or another, but after a few polite replies, she would move on to the next exhibit. To say he was baffled was an understatement. The woman had been so excited to come to the museum, and now she appeared detached from everything around her.

Exasperated, he grunted softly and turned his attention to a presentation of canopic jars found in an ancient tomb. Finished reading the display information, he turned toward the exhibit Anna had been standing at. When he didn't see her, Sebastian quickly glanced around the room. Anna was nowhere to be seen, and a sudden sting of fear lashed into him. Where the devil was she?

Worried, he began to methodically search the exhibits off the main wing. It wasn't until he reached the farthest part of the Egyptian wing that he heard her laughter. Relief surged through him at the sound, and he followed it into a small library. She was standing with a man of medium height who said something that made her laugh. The pair were studying a book in front of them, and as Sebastian drew closer, he recognized Wallis Budge, Keeper of the museum's Egyptian and Assyrian antiquities.

"So you think it's possible?" Anna asked.

"Anything is possible, Miss Sawyer," Budge replied. "But I would need more time to research the possibility."

"I couldn't ask that much of you, Mr. Budge. Perhaps I could come back and read some of the texts here in the library?"

"Of course, I would naturally be curious as to anything you find."

Sebastian cleared his throat as he drew near, and Anna immediately straightened upright to study him as he approached the table. Although she smiled at him, it held none of the warmth it had held much earlier. Thoroughly confused by her retreat behind a polite façade, Sebastian came to a halt at the library table.

"You disappeared. I was worried when I couldn't find you."

"There was no need to worry. I met Mr. Budge here, who's been very helpful with some of my questions about the exhibits."

"And it's been a delightful conversation, Miss Sawyer," the older man said as he pulled off his spectacles to clean them. As he hooked the wire rims over his ear lobes, he smiled at them both. "Unfortunately, I have a meeting with one of the museum's chairs and must take my leave. I'll leave word at the front desk as to my giving you permission to use the library any time you wish, Miss Sawyer."

"Thank you, Mr. Budge, that's very kind of you."

"I'm happy to help. Now, if you'll excuse me, I really must run."

With a small bow, Budge gathered up some papers that were lying off to one side and hurried from the room. Silence filled his wake, and Anna met Sebastian's gaze, then looked away.

"I'm ready to leave if you are."

"You intend to come back again?"

"I'd like to." She avoided his gaze, and it annoyed him. They'd been having a pleasant outing, but everything had changed for some reason. "It will depend on how many fashion excursions your mother and Céleste have planned for me in the next two weeks."

"If you do return, you're not to come without an escort. Is that clear?" At his soft command, Anna stiffened.

"The last time I checked, you were not my guardian, Lord Starling. I don't require your permission to come and go as I please."

"I didn't say you needed my permission to come here. I said you were not to come without an escort."

With a jerk of her head, Anna silently agreed to his wishes, then quickly skirted the table and headed toward the library's exit. As she passed him, Sebastian caught her by the arm and pulled her to a halt. The fire streaking across his hand made him quickly release her.

"Something's troubling you. Tell me what it is."

"Nothing's troubling me." With a shrug, she started to move away again. Sebastian brought her to a halt once more and glared at her.

"*Don't* lie to me," he snapped. "I don't know what's happened, but something has upset you."

"Even if I told you what was wrong, you wouldn't believe me, so I'd prefer we simply drop the matter right now."

"What the devil is that supposed to mean?" As they scowled at each other, Anna rolled her eyes at him.

"It means I'm ready to go back to Starling House."

Without waiting for him, Anna stalked to the exit and disappeared into the main section of the Egyptian exhibit. Damn it, the woman was prickly as a hedgehog, and it had all started when he'd introduced her to Lady Margaret. Sebastian frowned as he hurried after Anna. As he reviewed the conversation between the two women, he tried to determine what might have been said that would account for Anna's sudden change in mood.

Sebastian entered the main hall of the Egyptian exhibit and saw her walking quickly toward the exit. His long legs easily closed the distance between them. Anna was just about to walk through the main doorway when Sebastian reached her. His hand caught her elbow to ensure she didn't exit the museum without an escort. When they were outside, he ushered her down the wide steps and quickly hailed a hackney. A moment later, a cab rolled to a halt in front of them, and Sebastian assisted her into the vehicle. As the small carriage rocked into motion, he turned his head toward her.

"Anna, you do know you can trust me, don't you?"

The quiet question hovered in the air between them for a long moment without her reply. Sebastian was about to question her again when Anna turned toward him.

"I trust you."

The soft words held the faint sound of something he couldn't identify. Before he could push her once more to explain what was wrong, Anna leaned back in her seat and closed her eyes, an obvious sign she had no wish for conversation. Frustrated, Sebastian leaned back as well, and the rest of the short trip home was done in silence.

Chapter 13

Anna leaned back and allowed her head to rest on the back of the settee. Eyes closed, she tried once more to understand the meaning of the two visions she'd had the day Sebastian had taken her to the museum. The first had been in his study while she'd been admiring his grandfather clock.

It was a beautiful timepiece, and she'd been unable to resist stroking the rich mahogany of the furniture. The instant she'd touched the clock, she'd seen her Uncle Augustus laughing as if he was conversing with someone behind him that she couldn't see. He'd looked so happy.

Happier than she'd ever seen him in all the time she'd ever spent with him. It had made her heart lighter to see just how contented he'd looked. In her vision, Uncle Augustus's laughter had suddenly deepened, and as his face had faded from view, a letter had fallen out of his hands to slowly spiral down until it landed at the base of the clock. A moment later, the letter had slowly faded away like the rest of her vision.

Anna had no idea what it meant, and worse, she had no one to help her make heads or tails of what she'd seen. But the image of her uncle had been more puzzling than anything else. Her reaction to touching Lady Margaret's hand had been much more alarming. Almost from the first word the woman had spoken, Anna had disliked her. Arrogant and condescending, Lady Margaret had irritated her so much that if they'd been at sea, she would have found a way to push the woman overboard.

But it was when their hands had touched that Anna had struggled not to cry out at the bleak darkness that surrounded the woman. There had been no clear images, only a black veil of something unpleasant. There had been the sensation of drowning in a whirlpool that sucked her down into a dark pit where only fear and pain existed.

It had frightened her so badly she'd been unable to avoid jerking away from the woman. Perhaps worst of all was the desperation she'd sensed in Lady Margaret. The emotion seemed to feed the woman's determination to be Sebastian's wife, and Anna was convinced the woman would do whatever it took to achieve her goal.

Frustration sailed through her at her inability to make any sense of it all. If only she had someone she could talk to about what she'd seen. She'd considered telling Sarah and Alexander, but over the years, she'd learned to keep her talent hidden. She knew how uncomfortable people could be when it came to an ability such as hers.

The sound of voices out in the main foyer broke through Anna's thoughts, and she immediately straightened in her seat. The last thing she needed was for someone to see her reclined on the settee as if she were still on the Falcon. It would be considered unladylike. Her insides tightened as her cage closed in once more.

"Anna, I've come bearing news and bringing friends."

At the sound of Alexander's cheerful voice, Anna turned her head to see Alexander and another man walking into the salon. Instinctively, her muscles grew taut with tension as she quickly rose to her feet. With a smile, she stretched out her hand to Sebastian's brother.

"Hello, Alexander. What a nice surprise. Isn't Sarah with you?"

"That's the news. We've been at the British Museum doing research, and she sent me to fetch you."

"Did she say what she's found?" Anna exclaimed with excitement. Perhaps it wouldn't be necessary to tell her friends about her special gift after all.

"No, she refused to tell me anything. She said I had to wait until I arrived with you in tow," Alexander said with a grin. "But before you go to fetch your things, I'd like to introduce my friend Terrence Sheffield, Viscount Eastcote. Terrence, I know you're already aware of who Miss Sawyer is."

The tall young man standing just behind Alexander quickly stepped forward and captured Anna's hand in his to brush his lips across her knuckles. He was what Céleste would call a devastatingly handsome man with his sable-colored hair and handsome face. In the back of her mind, a small voice compared him to her dark angel and found the viscount lacking. Eastcote straightened but didn't let go of her hand, as he eyed her with an admiration that made her cheeks grow hot.

"I am delighted to finally meet you, Miss Sawyer. I am an enthusiastic admirer of yours. I was with Alexander the night you were injured. I think what you did was extraordinarily brave."

"Thank you," Anna said as her face became hotter beneath the young man's ardent gaze, and she gently extracted her hand free of his. "It's kind of you to say so."

"It is a fact." Eastcote's emphatic statement made Anna wince at the viscount's look of admiration. "I know you've not yet attended any social functions, but I was hoping I might persuade you to let me call on you tomorrow."

"It's kind of you, but my schedule is not my own. I am at the beck and call of Lady Harding and my friend Céleste Dubois."

Anna smiled politely at the young man as she suddenly

realized Alexander's friend appeared interested in being more than a simple acquaintance. Immediately, a resounding no echoed loudly in her head. A suitor was the last thing she wanted. It would only make life that much more complicated.

"Then I shall plead my case to Lady Harding." The viscount's confidence made Anna's heart sink. The man was definitely intent on making her life more complicated. Alexander clapped a hand on his friend's shoulder in a gesture of consolation.

"Somehow, I don't think my mother is going to be open to you calling at Starling House until Anna's been properly introduced to the Marlborough Set, Terrence."

"Perhaps not, but I shall entreat her, nonetheless."

Viscount Eastcote's determined look made Anna suppress a groan of dismay. Heaven help her. Was this what she had to look forward to once she'd been introduced to society? Suitors calling on her left and right? God, she wished she'd never followed Hamish and Smitty to the tavern that night. In the back of her head, a voice reminded her that if she hadn't, she never would have met her dark angel. At least meeting him was worth the headache of a few male admirers.

"Well, you'll have to plead your case another time, old man, because Sarah is waiting on us, and I do not like to keep my intended waiting. Now fetch your things, Anna, so the three of us can be on our way."

With a bob of her head, Anna hurried from the salon and up the stairs to collect her hat and gloves. In less than two minutes, she was running down the steps to the foyer. As she reached the marble floor, Sebastian's study door opened, and she drew in a breath of surprise as he stepped into the main hall. The moment he smiled at her, Anna's heartbeat accelerated, and her chest tightened as the air left her lungs. Damnation, what was wrong with her?

"Good afternoon, Anna. Are you off on another shopping excursion?"

"No," she said breathlessly as she struggled to hide how the sight of him affected her. "Alexander and Lord Eastcote are taking me to the British Museum."

"Eastcote?" Sebastian's terse, one-word question made Anna look at him in surprise. She didn't have a chance to respond as Alexander and the viscount emerged from the salon.

"Afternoon, Bash." Alexander cheerfully greeted his brother before turning to Anna. "Ready?"

"Yes." Anna nodded, then blew a harsh puff of air past her lips. "The devil take it. I forgot to let Lady Harding know where I'm going."

"I'll see to it that she's informed as to your whereabouts." Sebastian's silent look of disapproval as he rebuked her for cursing, was made all the more harsh because of how quietly he'd chastised her. Anna winced beneath his gaze before he turned to Alexander. "And *you* are *not* to leave her alone while you're at the museum. Is that clear?"

"Give me *some* credit, Bash." Alexander's eyebrows shot up as he stared at his brother in surprise. "I'll see to Anna's safety just as carefully as I do Sarah's."

"See that you do," Sebastian said in a tight voice before he nodded to the viscount. "Eastcote."

The viscount barely had time to bow in Sebastian's direction before her dark angel turned around and went back into his study. The door closed behind him with a hard thud, leaving the three of them staring after him in amazement.

"What was *that* all about?" Alexander turned to Anna. Bewildered, she shook her head. Sebastian's brother frowned slightly before an odd expression crossed his face and he muttered. "No, that couldn't be it."

"Couldn't be what?" Viscount Eastcote eyed his friend with confusion. Alexander met their puzzled gazes with a startled look that said he'd not realized he'd answered his question out loud.

"Nothing." A reflective gleam in his eye, Alexander glanced at Sebastian's closed study door for a second before he dismissed whatever he was thinking with a shake of his head. "Come on, I left one of Scully's men with Sarah, but her mother says she still has terrible nightmares, and I don't like leaving her alone except when the woman gives me no choice, as she did a little while ago."

With his hand on her elbow, Alexander ushered Anna outside and into a waiting carriage. Sliding across the seat to the window, she glanced out and saw a boy standing across the street. He was scrawny and small, and there was a blank expression on his face. Their eyes met from across the street, and in a flash of movement, he was gone.

Any other time, Anna would have dismissed the incident as simply a child caught staring. But with everything that had happened since the night she'd been stabbed and her vision about Lady Margaret, she'd become even more vigilant as to possible threats around her.

"Is everything all right, Anna?"

"What?" She turned her head toward Alexander, who was studying her with concern.

"You look worried."

"Do I?" She forced a laugh. "Worried isn't the word I'd use. Frustrated is more appropriate."

"If Bash is being difficult—"

"*No*, it's not Sebastian," she interjected. "I'm just becoming increasingly weary of my daily visits to the dressmakers."

"What woman doesn't enjoy shopping?" Lord Eastcote's assumption that every woman loved to do nothing all day except shop struck a nerve, and she eyed the man with annoyance.

"*This* woman," she bit out through clenched teeth. "I ask you, why in heaven's name do I need four different dresses to wear from morning to night every single day?"

"To drain the pockets of men who pay their wives' seamstress bills." Alexander chuckled with amusement.

"Such an explanation would not surprise me, but I think it's something much more insidious."

"Insidious?" The viscount eyed her with open skepticism.

"Yes, it's to restrict our freedom. Far too many men treat women as second-class citizens. What better way to keep women in their place than by distracting them with a shiny object, just like one does with a cat."

"I see."

The uneasy note in Eastcote's voice only strengthened Anna's growing belief that the man had never given much thought to a woman's place in society. The realization made Anna bite back a smile of triumph. Without even realizing it, Alexander's friend had given her the very weapon with which she could use to fend off the viscount and any other man who might come calling.

"I'm not sure you do, my lord." Anna shook her head with disapproval at Eastcote's reply. "Women are viewed as property by the majority of men, and I have no intention of becoming someone's property."

"I knew there was more than one reason Sarah likes you so well, Anna." Grinning, Alexander shook his head. "If I didn't already know Sarah was of the same mind before the two of you met, I'd hold you responsible for my bride-to-be's reformist thoughts."

"Are you saying you disapprove of her opinion?" Anna narrowed her gaze at Alexander.

"Not at all, and I've no doubts that Sarah would lambast me if I were to speak out against the suffragette cause." Alexander's expression indicated the topic was one battle he knew to give a wide berth. He grinned. "Sarah's mind is one of the things I love the most about her. She can hold her own in a debate with great skill."

"*That*, I cannot do." Anna shook her head and laughed. "I have a tendency to lose my temper far too easily. Despite my uncle's instruction, mastering control of it remains elusive. Although I excel at hiding the fact that I'm holding the winning hand in a game of Brag."

"You play Brag?" Viscount Eastcote's question was filled with amazement as he studied her with a scandalized stare.

"I see that I've shocked you." Anna winced at the viscount's obvious dismay, and she made a mental note to be cautious with who she shared that particular talent. "It's a game I learned while spending time on the Falcon."

"I see."

Eastcote's second instance of I *see* within a minute of each usage convinced her the viscount clearly had an aversion to women who spoke their mind. Thank God she wasn't attracted to the man, because the last thing she could ever do was be subservient. Beside her, Alexander chuckled.

"We still need to arrange a time for you to demonstrate your skills."

"I am free on Thursday evening, although it's unlikely your brother will approve of our gambling, especially if I'm playing." Anna frowned, then smiled as she eyed Alexander with mischief.

"Quite true." Alexander nodded with a grimace of resignation.

The moment the idea flitted through her head, Anna knew Sebastian would stridently disapprove. She also knew Lady Harding and Céleste would be appalled if they caught her in the act. But the longer she thought about the idea, the more she wanted to attempt it.

Although she had no doubt that if someone other than her inner circle discovered her brazen escapade, the scandal would definitely have repercussions. Still, the thought of escaping the confines of society's rigid rules for women, lifted her spirits. Even if it was only for a few hours, being free of any expectations from society would be worth the risk. Somehow, she needed to break free of the cage she'd been in since Uncle Charles had persuaded her to remain in London.

"I'm willing to wager all my winnings at our game of Brag if you meet me at your club Thursday night at nine o'clock."

"At my club?"

Alexander stared at her in confusion, while the viscount did the same. Suddenly, Alexander's gaze narrowed, and for a moment it was as if Sebastian was seated next to her with a look that dared her to argue with him. She didn't give him time to reply as she tried to goad him into accepting the bet.

"Well, do we have a wager?"

"*Absolutely not.*" Alexander's fierce rejection of her idea made Anna wince at his adamant tone. "Not only would I lose my membership in the club if we were caught, but far worse would be the fact that Bash would have my head, and I prefer to avoid that even more than losing my club membership."

"I don't understand," Eastcote said with bewilderment.

"She's proposing to disguise herself as a man and entering our club to play Brag."

"*Good God.*" Eastcote's features grew ashen as he eyed her with harsh disapproval. "To quote Alexander, absolutely not."

"Then let me add a caveat to our wager. If you recognize me outside your club or if the reception desk realizes I'm not what I appear, then I will concede the wager to you." Anna smiled slowly. "*But*, if you do not recognize me immediately, and no one questions my presence, you will direct me to the nearest table where I promise I will trounce you at a game of cards."

"*Christ Jesus*, you're mad." Alexander rejected her suggestion with a vicious wave of his hand.

"No, I would never have proposed the wager if I wasn't confident of my ability to pass muster." Anna smiled at both men.

"*The answer is still no*." Alexander glared at her. "We will make arrangements to play a game of Brag on a night that Sebastian is out for the evening."

"As you wish." Anna sighed with disappointment as she saw her chance for a few hours escape from her cage disappear. "Although I think my proposal would be infinitely more enjoyable."

"It would be nerve wracking." Alexander's disapproval was harsh, and Eastcote nodded.

"I concur with Alexander."

"We'll not mention this again. Is that clear, Anna?"

Again, Anna experienced the sensation of being pinned beneath Sebastian's censorious gaze. Disconcerted by the resemblance between the brothers, Anna nodded her agreement. She smiled at the two men as if trying to placate them, but she was determined to prove them wrong. Sometime in the near future, Alexander and Lord Eastcote would have no choice but to follow through with her plan. It was simply a matter of time.

§ § §

"Anna, listen to this."

The restrained excitement in Sarah's voice was a welcome sound from the monotonous words Anna was reading. She lifted her head from the stack of old letters a Lady Braithwaite had sent to her husband while he'd been assigned to Cairo by the Army.

"What?"

"Jerome Osborne, second Viscount Farthington and William Mitford, fifth Earl of Cookham, agreed to fund an expedition to the Northern Monastery in 1817 and again in 1826."

"The Northern Monastery?" Alexander studied his betrothed in bewilderment.

"The cliffs of Deir el-Bahri. It's where Hatshepsut's temple was found by Thomas Young." Anna answered his question as excitement began to build inside her. "But none of the writings in the temple made any sense until Champollion deciphered the Rosetta Stone."

"But what does it have to do with the cult?" The viscount looked even more confused than his friend. Exhilaration filled the smile Sarah directed at Lord Eastcote.

"The third Viscount Farthington and Cookham are acquaintances. Cookham is at least ten years younger than Farthington, and I've not seen any evidence of the two being connected." Excitement flushed Sarah's cheeks. "But my sources have confirmed Farthington has a specific interest in Egyptology like his father. I've also tracked both men to two different mummy unwrapping parties."

"You mean the ones like Dr. Pettigrew hosts?" Eastcote frowned with curiosity.

"*Yes*. It's done for entertainment's sake, not for science." Sarah's fierce response conveyed her revulsion for the practice.

"Does it say what artifacts they brought back to England?" At Anna's question, Sarah quickly skimmed the page of the open book in front of her. She jerked her head to look at Anna.

"They brought back stone rubbings of the hieroglyphics from both expeditions."

"Champollion translated the stone's hieroglyphs in 1824. No doubt they were able to translate their stone rubbings and had to have found something of specific interest for them to organize a second expedition." Anna tapped her forefinger against her lips, as she contemplated what information the men might have discovered that had compelled them to form a second expedition to the Northern

Monastery.

"Well done, my love, well done." Alexander beamed with pride as he looked at his fiancée from across the table where the four of them were seated. Sarah smiled back with a look of excitement and satisfaction.

"So, what do we do now?" The viscount's question made Anna turn her head toward him as her lips twisted in a wry grimace.

"Nothing. Unless we can find out what the rubbings say, we have no way of knowing what prompted the second expedition. Without more information, there's nothing connecting the current Viscount Farthington to the Hatshepsut cult."

"I agree." Sarah sighed with resignation.

"Unless, of course, someone was to find the rubbings themselves." Anna straightened in her chair as an idea filled her head. "Sarah, didn't you say Lord and Lady Farthington were hosting one of the largest events of the season at the end of next month? I wonder if Lady Harding and I have been invited. It wouldn't be difficult to—"

"What? To attend the affair and find a way to sneak into the man's study and look for papers we aren't sure even exist? *No, you will not.*" Alexander's voice held the same steely inflexibility she'd heard in Sebastian's voice numerous times. "This is where I am definitely putting my foot down."

"Well, I was thinking more along the lines of encouraging Farthington to talk about his interests and perhaps persuading him to show us the rubbings." Anna smiled as she met Alexander's stern gaze, and his suggestion set her brain churning over the idea. "Although searching his study isn't a bad idea either."

"God help me." Alexander uttered an unintelligible sound as the viscount slapped his friend on the back in a gesture of disgust.

"Excellent show, old man. Give her an idea she *hadn't*

thought of." Ignoring Eastcote's sarcasm, Alexander narrowed his eyes at Anna.

"You are *not* to search the man's study, and if you think to ignore me, Anna Sawyer, I won't hesitate to tell Bash what you're up to. He'll make you wish to God you'd never ever thought of doing it."

"But I didn't think of it," Anna said with a grin. "You did. Will you tell Sebastian that too?"

"If it keeps you out of trouble? Yes. Better that he rains hell fire down on my head for giving you the idea, versus him learning after the fact." Her friend's brow wrinkled in a dark frown of irritation. "Be grateful I've not mentioned your participation in our current investigations."

"Alexander is right, Anna. Searching the man's study is far too dangerous." At Sarah's quiet support of her fiancé, Anna rolled her shoulders in a small shrug.

"Very well, but I can at least engage in a conversation about his interests. Does that satisfy everyone?"

"Yes," Sarah nodded in agreement. Alexander simply grunted and nodded with displeasure, while his friend did the same as he studied Anna with a troubled expression.

The sound of a soft chime made the viscount pull his pocket watch from his vest and pop it open. He glanced at the timepiece, then looked around the table as he snapped it shut and returned the watch to his vest pocket.

"It's five o'clock, and I have a dinner engagement."

"Already?" Sarah gasped as she looked at Alexander in dismay. "We'll be terribly late for dinner with my parents if we don't leave right away."

Anna looked in Alexander's direction, and his expression dared her to even suggest that she stay and continue reading. With a resigned sigh, she began to gather up the letters she'd been reading. Alexander quietly offered to place them with the documents he'd been reviewing. She extended her hand outward to hand the letters to him, and the moment their fingers brushed against each other, a jolt shook Anna's body. The spell happened so quickly it took her a moment to realize she was standing in the middle of what she realized was Lady Harding's sitting room.

Alexander's mother was seated in a chair near the window that overlooked the back of Starling House. Mother and son were arguing while Alexander paced the floor in front of the viscountess.

"You should have told me." Alexander stopped pacing the floor and shook the papers in his hand as he frowned darkly at his mother. "You should have told all of us."

"How could I?" Lady Harding grew pale as she stared up at her son. "It was difficult enough when Sebastian—"

"What?" Pain tightened Alexander's features for a moment before his expression became one of raw fury. "Do you mean to tell me that you told Sebastian, but left the rest of us in the dark?"

"No," Lady Harding exclaimed in anguish. "I told him nothing. He only knows…he saw James and me…when Sebastian confronted me, I couldn't tell him the truth. He was so hurt and angry, so I said nothing. Even if I had, I doubt he would have believed me. Levi wanted us to tell him the truth together, but I refused to drive a wedge between the two of them."

"Sebastian deserves to know the truth. He's treated you unfairly all these years and needs to know that. You must tell him, Mama, all of it," Alexander exclaimed vehemently as he held up the papers in his hands.

"No. I'll not do that to him." Lady Harding sprang to her feet to stare up at her son with a fierce look of determination. "After all this time, he would see it as just one more betrayal. Look at your reaction to the truth. Are you going to say you aren't angry?"

"I'm not angry." Alexander denied the question, then uttered a dismissing grunt as his mother eyed him sternly.

"All right, yes, I was…am angry. You should have told me when you and my…when you and James were married. I was old enough then to know the truth."

"Please understand, Alexander. I was terrified of what might happen if I told you everything. Sebastian was already lost to me. I could not bear it if you or…" Lady Harding's voice trailed off as she sank back down into her chair. Alexander quickly moved to where she was seated and wrapped his arm around her in a consoling manner.

"I understand, Mama. In a way, it's a relief to know the truth."

"Then can you not imagine what learning the truth would do to Sebastian? It won't be just one more betrayal in his eyes. It will be the ultimate betrayal of a father to his son."

"He still deserves to know the truth. You owe him that much."

"No. I will never tell him, and you won't either. I will have your word on that Alexander. You will swear to me that you will never tell Sebastian the truth." As Lady Harding pinned her son beneath a harsh, determined gaze, Alexander nodded his head with obvious reluctance.

"I won't tell him."

"Swear it, Alexander. Swear as if your hand was on the good book. Swear that you will not tell him."

"I swear." At her son's quiet reply, Lady Harding's features relaxed. Her fears alleviated, the viscountess closed her eyes and drew in a deep breath. Alexander blew out a harsh breath of frustration. "My oath not to tell Sebastian the truth does not mean I think you're right to hide it from him."

"Even if I agreed to tell him, Sebastian would never believe me. The only way he might believe me is if he were to find letters like these." Sadness and pain flitted across Lady Harding's face.

"Are you telling me there are more?" her son snapped viciously.

"It's possible, but I don't know. I didn't even know these existed until you found them and brought them to me." The viscountess's hand pressed down into a stack of letters in her lap before she nodded toward the papers Alexander held in his hands.

"Christ Jesus."

"It's highly unlikely your father kept any correspondence he exchanged with Augustus. Levi knew their discovery would create a scandal that would make the entire family pariahs. The trunk must have been amongst all of Augustus's possessions your father brought home after the funeral. I have no doubt Levi would have destroyed these if he'd known they were there. It never occurred to me to go through the attic after Levi died. If I had, I would have found these and destroyed them."

"But if there are more letters, we need to find them before someone else does."

"And exactly how to you propose we set about searching for them?" Lady Harding's stern gaze was harsh as she stared at her son. "If you really want to arouse Sebastian's curiosity, then, by all means, turn this house upside down in your search. But if there are more letters, I'm confident they'll not be discovered any time soon."

"Just like no one would find these in that old trunk?" There was a thin layer of sarcasm underlying his words as Alexander held up the papers in his hand and scowled at his mother. Lady Harding glared back.

"That trunk had been there for years and still would be if you hadn't pried open the lock instead of asking me about it. I would have known what it was immediately, and you would never have seen this correspondence." Lady Harding winced as she released a long breath, then looked at Alexander. "I'm sorry, dearest. This is all such a shock."

"And if there are more letters, where would they be?"

"You said there weren't any other trunks in the attic that

were locked, which means there's only one other place Levi might have placed them, and no one will find them, not even Sebastian."

The scene in front of Anna began to fade, and from a distance, she heard people saying her name. Panic threaded its way through the voices as they grew stronger in her ears. Anna swayed on her feet as her friends came into focus.

"*Sit down*, Anna," Sarah said with stern sharpness. Without apology, her friend forcibly pushed her down into her chair.

"What the devil just happened?" Alexander demanded. "One minute you were handing me correspondence, and the next you were staring at me as if you were hypnotized."

The familiar lethargy sweeping through her made Anna close her eyes at the questions. Dear God, of all the times to have a spell. Worse, this was the third one in two days.

"I have these spells occasionally," she murmured. "It's nothing to be concerned about. I'll be quite all right in a moment."

"Nothing to—you need to see a doctor." Sara looked over her shoulder. "Terrence, would you summon a hack, please? Alexander and I will assist Anna to the exit."

"I'm fine," Anna interjected with a shake of her head as she saw the viscount sprint out of the small library they'd been given use of by Mr. Budge's staff.

"Sarah is right, you need to see a doctor." At Alexander's comment, Anna dismissed it with a wave of her hand as her lethargic reaction slowly ebbed away.

"I've already seen doctors for my condition. I'll be quite all right in a minute."

"Condition?" Alexander's eyebrows arched upward.

"I have a mild form of epilepsy," she said with a small shrug. Along with visions, too, she added silently.

"*Epilepsy*. Like Julius Caesar?" Sarah stared at her in amazement. Anna forced a smile to her lips.

"Yes, like the great man himself. I've never had actual convulsions. I'm simply unable to move or speak for short periods of time. Usually, the episodes only last a few seconds, but clearly this one was a bit longer than most."

"*Bloody hell*," Alexander muttered before he fixed his gaze on her. Anna straightened in her chair at his reaction.

"You're not to tell anyone about this, not even Lord Eastcote. I prefer people not know."

"And *what* exactly do you expect us to tell him? He was here when it happened," Sarah snapped impatiently.

"I'll tell him I have a medical condition that I prefer not to discuss."

Anna met Sarah's gaze steadily, and the other woman slowly nodded her head in agreement. She turned her head toward Alexander, and he raised his hands in a gesture of surrender. Satisfied her friends would remain silent, Anna nodded, then stood up and smiled.

"Don't look so down in the mouth. I'm fine, truly I am," she chided them as she began to walk toward the door. The couple looked at each other, and Anna glanced over her shoulder, then stopped to release a harsh breath of frustration. "Stop dawdling. I believe you said you're expected for dinner, and at this rate, you won't arrive until breakfast."

Despite their reluctance, the two of them quickly gathered their things and followed Sarah out of the room.

Chapter 14

Anna drew in a shallow breath of apprehension as she left her bedroom and slowly walked toward the stairs. Damnation. This was even more frightening than the first time she'd disguised herself as a boy and disembarked the Falcon to follow Hamish and Smitty to a tavern.

Then her fear had only been that of being caught. This evening was something altogether different. It didn't help matters that the torture device she was wearing was so tight it was difficult to breathe normally.

Tonight was her first introduction to the Marlborough Set, and she was terrified. At least she could be thankful her identity had been kept private when it came to Scotland Yard's investigation of the Hatshepsut cult. Notoriety of that kind would have made her even more of a spectacle than she expected to be this evening.

But then the police were keeping *everything* about their search for the leaders of the secret society out of the papers. That made it difficult for Sarah to gather information in their own search for the man and woman who had been at the altar that night. Last night Anna had experienced a vision with a woman wearing the robes of the ancient pharaoh Hatshepsut.

She wasn't one to frighten easily when it came to her visions, but last night she'd been afraid. There was something evil and dark about the woman. The gold mask covering her face had been even more lifeless than a marble statue, which only emphasized the soullessness of the woman.

Whoever the woman in her dream was, they were a member of the peerage. If she'd had doubts before, she would be convinced of the fact now. Yet even her vision hadn't frightened her nearly as much as the thought of tonight did.

For the past month, she'd been poked and prodded by dressmakers. She'd suffered the indignity of trying on hats that made her look ridiculous and fought fiercely to have flowers and ruffles removed from the gowns that had been ordered for her. It had become her daily mantra to vehemently protest the female fripperies she was informed she needed.

Anna winced at the memory of her protests. For the first time, she realized there might be a good use for the silk fan she held tight in her grip. She glanced down at the closed fan and offered up a small prayer of gratitude that she had something to hold on to that kept her hands from shaking so badly.

Céleste had chosen the muted gray silk fan because the Frenchwoman had said it complemented the rich, vibrant tones of Anna's royal blue gown. The thought of her friend made Anna come to an abrupt halt in the middle of the corridor, where she swayed as if she were on the deck of the Falcon as it rode the waves.

Yesterday morning, the ship had set sail carrying her family with it. She'd pleaded with her uncle and Céleste to stay one more night, but they'd refused. When Uncle Charles appeared to be wavering at her renewed pleas, Céleste had quietly and firmly ended the discussion with the declaration that Anna needed to stand on her own two feet. Céleste's reassurances that she'd be fine had done little to ease her fears.

"*Bloody hell*," she gasped softly as her stomach lurched with a sickening sensation.

Frozen in place in the upper hallway of Starling House, Anna choked back the bile threatening to rise in her throat. She'd never been seasick a day in her life, but she suspected this was what it must feel like. It didn't help that the corset Lucy had put on her was making it difficult to breathe.

Closing her eyes, Anna struggled not to whirl around and run back to her room with the intention of never coming out of it again. The soft rustling of material caught Anna's attention, and she saw Sebastian's mother moving toward her. As the older woman reached her, Lady Harding linked arms and gently pulled her toward the stairwell.

"You look lovely, Anna. I fully expect you to be surrounded by a dozen young men eager to make your acquaintance within the first hour of our arrival."

"If I don't retch all over my gown first," she muttered in response. Lady Harding laughed softly.

"You'll be fine, and I've managed to secure reinforcements for this evening," the older woman said. "Although I confess to being more than a bit surprised by his volunteering for the duty."

"Volunteering?" Anna's nausea vanished as she looked at the viscountess in confusion.

"Sebastian offered to be our escort this evening."

At Lady Harding's statement, delight warmed its way through every inch of Anna's body. As they reached the top of the stairs, Lady Harding urged her forward. Anna was halfway down the staircase when Sebastian emerged from the salon.

He glanced in her direction before turning toward the footman holding his hat and gloves, then quickly turned back to study her in silence as she made her way down to the foyer. Anna saw his throat bob as he stepped forward to take her hand in his and carry it to his mouth. As Sebastian's lips brushed across the silk glove covering her hand, a small current of electricity shot up her arm.

"You look exquisite this evening, Anna."

As always, Sebastian's voice vibrated across her skin as if he'd caressed her with his hand. It set her heart pounding, and heat burned her cheeks as she murmured a soft word of thanks. His gaze locked with hers, and her mouth went dry at the fire she saw flare in his gaze before it disappeared.

"Thank you for offering to be our escort this evening, Sebastian," Lady Harding said with quiet politeness, but Anna heard the note of confusion in the other woman's voice.

"I am happy to do so, my lady."

There was a stilted note in Sebastian's voice that made Anna suddenly wonder if serving as their escort tonight had been his idea or someone else's. If he was accompanying them as the result of coercion or out of a sense of duty, Anna would rather he just remain at Starling House. She refused to be a duty he felt obligated to perform. Straightening her shoulders, she narrowed her gaze at him.

"You sound like a man who's been given no other choice *but* to escort us this evening," she said with a fierce note of steel in her voice. "If that's the case, I would prefer you remain here."

Sebastian was in the middle of accepting his hat from Hodgekiss, and the moment she spoke, he jerked his head toward her and met her gaze with a look of astonishment. Beside her, Lady Harding uttered a soft sound that might have been a laugh she was struggling to suppress.

"Well?" Anna snapped as she watched Sebastian stiffen beneath her displeased look. "Did someone twist your arm and tell you it would be in your best interest to escort us this evening?"

"*No.*" Sebastian's features hardened into an unreadable mask. "I thought since your uncle wasn't here that you might find me a suitable stand-in should you need rescuing from an unwanted suitor."

"Rescuing?"

Anna stared at him wide-eyed with surprise as laughter rose in her throat. Almost immediately, Sebastian's beautiful mouth tightened into a thin line of indignation, while his posture became stiff and rigid. Poseidon's balls, the man was serious. He also appeared decidedly uncomfortable at having been caught in the act of doing something thoughtful and kind.

It was an incredibly sweet gesture that warmed Anna's heart even more than when Lady Harding had said Sebastian was to be their escort for the evening. As their gazes locked, Anna was certain she saw something remarkably like disappointment in his gaze. Then, with a blink of his eye, he cloaked his discomfort with the demeanor of a blasé nobleman eyeing her with pompous disdain.

Eager to see the man behind the mask once more, Anna stepped forward to lightly touch his arm. Beneath her hand, Sebastian's muscles were hard as knotted ropes of rigging. It made Anna realize he wasn't just disappointed by her reaction. She'd injured his pride as well. Although she didn't see him flinch, she saw him struggling not to jerk away from her touch. Sebastian's eyebrows rose in a cynical look as he glanced down at where her hand was resting on his arm.

"I think that is one of the nicest things anyone has ever done for me, Sebastian. Thank you." The moment she smiled up at him, Sebastian's arm muscles relaxed and became flexible steel beneath her fingers. He studied Anna intently for a long moment before a small smile tilted one corner of her dark angel's beautiful mouth.

"You're welcome." The slight bow he offered her as he murmured his reply was accompanied by a sudden glint in his dark eyes that made her heart skip a beat. He stepped out of her way, then gestured for his mother and Anna to precede him out the front door to the carriage.

The ride to Sheringham Place was a relatively short one, but Anna's stomach began to churn again, and she was only able to take in small breaths, which didn't allow her to help settle her stomach. Huddled in the corner of the carriage, she barely heard Lady Harding speaking to her. When a strong hand touched hers, Anna started violently as she focused her gaze on first Sebastian and then his mother.

"I'm sorry? Did you say something?"

"I was saying you shall be fine if you will just breathe." Lady Harding eyed her with a hint of concern, and for a moment Anna stared at the older woman in confusion. With a shake of her head, Anna released an unladylike snort of sarcastic amusement.

"I'd be thrilled if I *could* breathe, but Lucy laced up this damn torture device so tightly, I'm barely able to walk naturally, let alone breathe."

The dark sound rumbling out of Sebastian made her wince. She looked up at him to silently plead forgiveness for her language. Her dark angel's exasperation was clearly evident, but she could have sworn she saw a spark of amusement in his black eyes. Lady Harding uttered a soft sound of dismay and leaned forward to press her hands on either side of Anna's waist.

"Dear Lord," she exclaimed quietly. "Lucy must have misunderstood my instructions. I told her not to worry about making your waist look small."

"Do we need to return to Starling House?" Sebastian's quiet question vibrated with something that might have resembled concern, and Anna shook her head.

"No. The sooner I get this evening over with, the better." She tried to draw in a deep breath, only to feel lightheaded a moment later.

"Then if you refuse to return to the house, my mother will need to redo the laces of your corset once we reach the

Sheringham's. The alternative is a fainting spell that will guarantee you a prominent position in the gossip columns tomorrow morning."

The decisive statement of action made Anna and Lady Harding jerk their heads toward him in surprise. Exasperation tugged at Sebastian's mouth as he eyed them with detached amusement.

"I am not unacquainted with the lengths women go to when it comes to making their figures as enticing as possible."

"Perhaps not, but it's hardly the sort of observation I'd expect of you."

Lady Harding directed an arched look at her son as she struggled to hide her amazement. If Sebastian's mother had expected him to apologize, he did not. Instead, he folded his arms across his chest and looked at the two of them with a great deal of male aggravation. When he remained silent, Lady Harding turned back to Anna.

"Despite my son's astonishing remark, Sebastian is correct. When we arrive at the Sheringham's, I will need to adjust your laces. It will make the evening far more pleasant."

Lady Harding patted Anna's hand and offered her a soothing smile before she reclined back into the squabs of the carriage seat to stare at her son in puzzlement. Despite her miserable physical state, Anna focused her attention on mother and son. In the past two weeks, she'd rarely seen the pair say two words to each other. When they *did* speak, it was because they had no other choice but to do so.

Tonight was the first time she'd witnessed Sebastian speak to his mother without his usual cold, condescending manner. The more she thought about it, the man was being quite pleasant, and Lady Harding appeared completely confounded by her son's behavior. Anna saw Sebastian glance in his mother's direction before his jaw clenched, and he averted his gaze to stare out the carriage window.

The remainder of the ride was conducted in silence, and

when their vehicle rolled to a stop in front of Sheringham Place, Sebastian quickly stepped out of the vehicle. With a quiet command that they were to stay where they were, he disappeared for a moment. After what seemed like an eternity, he returned and offered his hand to his mother to assist her out of the carriage. He murmured something to her, and Anna saw relief lighten Lady Harding's features as she nodded. Sebastian turned back to the carriage and extended his hand to her.

"Come, I've arranged for a room to be placed at your disposal so my mother can ease some of your suffering."

"Some?" Anna bit out with irritation as she continued to take in shallow breaths. "Are you laughing at me again?"

"No. I can see you're miserable." Sebastian's expression was one of empathy as his fingers flicked in a gesture for her to place her hand in his. "I have no desire to see anyone as uncomfortable as you clearly are."

"Thank you," she breathed. "When you aren't being so pompous, you really are quite nice."

"I am *not* pompous."

Anna ignored his growl of protest as she placed her hand in his. The moment his fingers closed around hers, heat pulsed its way through the gloves into her hand. She drew in a sharp breath as the touch sent a trail of fire racing across her skin. The corset made it difficult to exhale easily, and she experienced another moment of lightheadedness. Sebastian's fingers tightened around hers as he leaned into her.

"If you intend to faint, do it now." He paused for a brief moment before his lips quirked up in a small smile. "Unless, of course, you wish for me to carry you out of the ballroom in what will most definitely be fodder for the gossip columns tomorrow."

Sebastian's warning was filled with a wicked note of laughter as he met her gaze. For a brief second, Anna contemplated the thought of being carried by Sebastian again.

It heightened the fiery sensation still tingling her skin. The sudden memory of Alexander stating that her dark angel was preparing to offer marriage to Lady Margaret doused the fire his touch had ignited.

Their gazes locked and the amusement in Sebastian's eyes faded into puzzlement as they stared at each other. Panic spiraled through Anna the moment he narrowed his gaze at her, as if he were trying to read her thoughts. She swallowed hard and shook her head.

"I'll be fine," she said coolly as she accepted his help to exit the vehicle. The moment she was out of the carriage, she tugged her hand free of his and turned toward Lady Harding, who was standing a few feet away, eyeing her with worry. Anna offered the woman a weak smile and allowed Lady Harding to guide her into Sheringham House.

Less than fifteen minutes later, Anna breathed a sigh of relief as Sebastian's mother finished relacing Anna's corset. The older woman quickly closed the back of Anna's gown, then brushed her hand over the material to smooth out the wrinkles.

"There, I think you'll find it much easier to survive the evening. I should have supervised Lucy dressing you to begin with. She's a sweet girl, but she's never been a lady's maid before." Lady Harding turned Anna around to inspect her appearance. "I think I'll need to secure the services of someone more experienced."

"*Oh no,*" Anna exclaimed softly. "I like Lucy very much, and she's constantly poring over the fashion books you gave me. She's eager to try out one or two new hair styles she saw in one."

"Well, if you're certain that's what you want," Lady Harding said with more than a hint of reservation. Anna smiled.

"I do. Everyone deserves a second chance, and we all have to start somewhere when it comes to learning new things."

"All right, but we'll need to make certain she doesn't lace you so tightly tomorrow night."

Lady Harding nodded her acceptance of Anna's wishes, then quickly guided her out into the hallway. Sebastian was waiting for them and strode forward as they emerged from the small room.

"You look as if you can breathe again." At his quiet observation, Anna nodded.

"Yes, I'm much better."

"Shall we?" Sebastian offered his arm to her, and for a heartbeat Anna hesitated before she slowly slid her hand into the crook of his elbow. At her reluctance, Sebastian arched his eyebrow. "That can't be fear I see in Anna Sawyer's eyes?"

Anna jerked slightly at his words, but her only response was a brief shake of her head. If the man saw fear, it wasn't from the thought of facing the Marlborough Set. She quickly ignored the voice in the back of her head trying to capture her attention. Instead, she shoved it into a dark corner of her mind and quickly closed the door.

Fear was simply an obstacle to overcome. There were a great many things to fear in life, losing herself and becoming someone she didn't recognize was one of them, and Anna refused to be something she wasn't. A tremor shot through her as they reached the entrance to the ballroom, and Sebastian bent his head.

"It might feel as if you're about to be fed to the lions, Anna, but I won't let that happen."

The quiet words sent another shiver skimming through her. Anna jerked her gaze up to him. At the silent promise in his gaze, she nodded, and he continued forward to lead her into the ballroom. The moment they stepped through the doorway into the large room, an oppressive wave of heat hit her in the face. It was as if she'd stepped into the hot Egyptian sun.

A moment later, Sebastian was introducing her to their hosts, who eyed her with nothing more than a kind, polite interest. Their obligations done, Sebastian escorted her deeper into the ballroom, with Lady Harding close behind. The orchestra was coming to the end of a sedate polka, and Anna watched with fascination as the dancers whirled around the dance floor.

"Oh, Anna. It didn't even occur to me to ask if you needed a dance instructor." Lady Harding's mortification was evident in her voice, and Anna quickly touched the woman's arm in a gesture of reassurance.

"Uncle Charles and Céleste taught me," she said with a smile. "Although it was only to the sound of a fiddle."

"Thank goodness." Lady Harding's expression was one of immense relief. Before Anna could say anything else, Sebastian offered his hand to her.

"Then if you'll give me the honor of this dance, we'll see how apt a pupil you were." Although his expression was polite, she saw the amusement in his dark eyes, and she glared at him.

"You're doing it again," she snapped softly as her hand slid into his. With determination, she steeled herself to ignore the electricity pulsing its way through her the moment he wrapped his fingers around hers.

"And what, pray tell, is that?" The quiet, deep note of his voice whispered across her skin in an intangible caress as they reached the dance floor. He pulled her into his arms, then guided her across the floor to the sound of a Strauss waltz.

"You're making fun of me." Anna heard the breathless note in her voice and swallowed hard as she realized her entire body was suddenly on fire.

"I'm not making fun of you." Sebastian shook his head as he stared down at her. "I'm teasing you, and for some reason, you're acting as prickly as a hedgehog."

"Don't be absurd," she bit out through clenched teeth. "I am not acting like a hedgehog."

"You just did." The laughter in his voice made Anna glare at him again. Her harsh look made him laugh. "If looks could mortally wound me, that one would."

"It would be better than you deserve, my lord."

"My lord?" He arched his eyebrows at her. "Earlier it was Sebastian."

"I wasn't annoyed with you then."

"And you're irritated with me now?"

"Yes," she muttered with another glare at him before she glanced behind her to see how close they were to the edge of the dance floor as she debated whether she could free herself and flee. No sooner had she considered pushing herself from his arms and leaving him on the dance floor, he pulled her closer. The warm male scent of him over ran her senses, threatening to steal every bit of air from her lungs. He smelled delicious, and every part of her tingled with heat.

"Don't even consider it. Leaving me on the dance floor is not the proper thing to do." The warning was laced with amusement, and again his voice was an intangible touch that sent her heart pounding out a frantic beat in her chest.

"And I know it's improper for you to hold me so close."

"Is it? I don't think I'm holding you too closely." The wicked laughter she'd seen earlier in his gaze returned as a small smile curved his tantalizing mouth. With a smooth movement, he spun her away from a couple they'd almost collided with.

"You know you are," she said breathlessly.

"Does that mean you're not enjoying yourself?"

"Why are you doing this?" Anna stared up at him in bewilderment. "Why are you deliberately antagonizing me?"

"You're avoiding answering my question by posing two of your own." A quiet laugh rumbled out of Sebastian.

"Then, my answer is no. I'm not enjoying myself one

bit."

Anna's jaw clenched. In the span of just an hour, he'd transformed himself into a man who had the power to reduce her to a quivering mass. It terrified and excited her in equal measure.

"A pity, as I'm enjoying myself a great deal." Sebastian pulled her even closer to skirt another couple.

"Oh, that's quite obvious," she snapped. "But clearly, you're oblivious to the fact that other people are beginning to take quite an interest in us. Everyone is staring."

"Are they? I hadn't noticed." The smile curving his lips made her grit her teeth.

"Well, they *are*."

"Hmm, perhaps you're right. I see quite a number of young men scowling at me for dancing with the loveliest woman in the room." Sebastian's gaze swept around the room, while Anna tried to assimilate the fact that he thought her lovely.

"Don't be *ridiculous*."

"Then don't underestimate the power of your charm and beauty."

"That's an exaggeration, and you know it. So, stop being a horse's arse," she muttered fiercely. The disapproval flaring in his dark eyes was replaced almost instantly with laughter and something else that made her pulse flutter out of control.

"I never exaggerate, Anna, but that mouth of yours could be your undoing."

The words were almost a caress, and heat washed over her as their gazes locked. Air became a prized resource as she struggled to keep breathing, while the echo of something seductive in his voice teased her senses until every inch of her hummed and tingled with sensation. Fire singed her cheeks as she fought to control her reaction to her dark angel's voice, his words, and everything else about him that was delicious and enticing.

Almost as if Sebastian knew what she was feeling, one corner of his mouth tipped upward. Bloody hell, he enjoyed seeing her befuddled. It was one thing to find herself unsettled by the man, but knowing he was aware of how badly he affected her was far worse. Quickly looking away from him, she struggled to control her anger.

Anna had no idea why the man had done nothing but tease and flirt with her all evening, but he was clearly savoring her reaction. The realization angered her, and before she realized what she was doing, she allowed a slow smile to touch her lips.

"My undoing or a man's?" she whispered huskily as she moved her hand a fraction of an inch to lightly stroke the back of his neck with her fingertips. "I've heard there are numerous ways for a woman to please a man with her mouth. Do you have anyone in mind I might kiss to prove or disprove your assertion?"

Anna wanted to immediately swallow her tongue the instant the words slipped past her lips. It didn't matter that her dark angel's entire demeanor this evening had thrown her off kilter and incited her anger. She'd just crossed a line that, even by her standards, was a step too far. If it had been anyone else who'd heard her remark, she'd be drowning in a sea far more dangerous than those the Falcon occasionally sailed.

Instinctively, she'd known the words were a double entendre, and the knotted shoulder muscles beneath her hand were a clear sign Sebastian understood the underlying meaning in her reply. The question was, would her dark angel realize she understood exactly what her words inferred? Would he realize how much she knew about the intimacies between a man and woman, or would he interpret the veiled meaning as unintentional?

Anna wasn't sure she wanted to know the answer. The moment strong fingers pressed deeply into her waist without pulling her closer, she trembled at the touch. Deliberately schooling her features to reflect an innocence she didn't possess, she looked up at him. Anna didn't know what she had expected, but Sebastian's expression stole her breath from her lungs in one gasp.

Never in her life had a man looked at her the way Sebastian was at this precise moment. Not even the morning after she arrived in Starling House had his eyes glittered with such raw, earthy emotion. Unable to look away, the fire in his gaze created a small tremor that sent a white-hot frisson skimming downward to the apex of her thighs. As a ripple of heat raced across her skin, Anna's blood thickened until it flowed lethargically through her veins.

If they'd been alone, she had no doubt he would be kissing her passionately. For the first time in her life, Anna understood what Céleste had meant when she'd said a woman could be as powerful as a man, but in a different way. Exhilaration streaked through her as she realized she'd ignited the flame in Sebastian's dark eyes with her suggestive remark.

The silence stretched out between them until it was a taut thread, and all she could hear was her heart thundering in her ears. Unable to look away from his intense gaze, she watched as the fire in his eyes slowly died, and his features relaxed into an expression that bordered on ennui.

"Tread lightly, Anna. Most men wouldn't hesitate to take advantage of such a challenge."

"What? To let them kiss me?" Her eyebrows shot up as if surprised that a simple kiss required her to take care. "Surely one kiss is quite harmless?"

The lust she'd witnessed a moment ago had vanished, and she realized he'd decided her innuendo was an innocent one. It was impossible not to experience a small amount of relief, that he'd concluded she'd unwittingly incited lustful images in him. Still, she couldn't deny she was somewhat disappointed as well.

"A simple kiss might be quite harmless, but even one kiss can lead to things much more dangerous."

"I see. I take it you have practical experience in the more dangerous aspects of a kiss?" She smiled as his mouth tightened with irritation.

"Are you asking me to instruct you in such matters?" The question was a vibration against her senses as she heard the low rumble in his chest.

"What makes you think I have need of instruction when it comes to a kiss?"

"And what makes you think you've been instructed properly?"

The soft question sent her senses reeling. Although he appeared to be completely unmoved by their exchange, the strength with which his fingers pressed deep into her waist again made her think differently. There was something possessive in the gesture that made her believe he wasn't happy with the thought of another man kissing her. The thought sent a shiver down her spine that was a trail of fire and ice combined, as he studied her intently.

Anna remembered their visit to the museum, and his words about his ability to inflict punishment. She'd known what he'd meant that day, and the same electric current of excitement that had sped through her then did so once more. Whatever he was thinking, she was certain he was considering the possibility of demanding a penance from her that wouldn't be a punishment at all.

"There are few people to be trusted in this world, Anna," he said in a voice devoid of emotion as the hand against her back relaxed. "And in most cases, you won't discover it until it's too late. Never forget that."

Before she could question him, the orchestra carried the Strauss tune to an electrifying conclusion. Seconds later, Sebastian released her, and with his hand cupping her elbow, he led her back toward his mother.

Chapter 15

As the music died away, Sebastian quickly released Anna from his embrace and guided her back to where his mother was conversing with one of her friends. The moment Anna was safely in his mother's custody, he bowed sharply to the both of them.

"If you'll excuse me, I saw the Duke of Sanderling a moment ago, and there's a matter I need to discuss with him."

Lady Harding's astonishment didn't surprise him, any more than Anna's troubled frown. Without waiting for either of them to say anything, he quickly turned away and headed toward the last place he'd seen Sanderling. He had nothing to discuss with the duke. He'd merely needed an excuse to avoid arousing his mother's curiosity as to why he was suddenly so eager to put space between him and Anna.

With a glance over his shoulder, he saw Anna and his mother had been quickly surrounded by a small crowd of young men. Sebastian released a low growl of irritation as he walked out into the darkness of Sheringham's prized gardens. His stride long and fast, Sebastian quickly reached the brick wall that enclosed the ornamental landscape, then turned left along the pathway.

In seconds, he reached one of the benches he remembered Sheringham had placed at different intervals along the stone barrier. As he flung himself down onto the stone seat, he leaned back and rested his head against the brick behind him. Eyes closed, Sebastian released a harsh sound of disgust.

Christ almighty, what the hell had he been thinking to tease Anna from the moment they'd left home? When he'd seen her descending the stairs tonight, she'd taken his breath away. Her gown didn't just emphasize her lush curves, it was a reflection of Anna herself in its simplicity and elegance.

Vibrant, yet soft and regal, the blue silk fabric made her chestnut-colored eyes gleam in the gaslight, while enhancing the warmth of her sun-kissed skin. Everything about her was exquisite, right down to the bodice that sculpted her breasts in the same way he'd often imagined his hand doing.

He should have known better than to dance that damn waltz with her. But the thought of holding her in his arms had been too tempting to resist. Anna had been right that he'd been holding her too close. While it was unlikely the gossips would vilify her for his behavior, he was certain his actions had raised eyebrows. He had no excuse other than madness and a lapse in decorum.

If he'd realized the direction their conversation was about to take, he would never have taken her onto the dance floor. He released another low groan. What had begun as a light-hearted exchange had quickly erupted into something much more volatile. Just the two sentences whispered huskily between them, had him making the leap between shock and full-blown lust in the blink of an eye.

Sebastian still didn't fully understand how he'd thwarted disaster as tantalizing images of Anna at his feet with her mouth wrapped around his cock had filled his head. Even now, he wasn't sure whether her comment had been a deliberate double entendre or simply an innocent reference to how a woman's kisses could please a man.

If he were being honest, he didn't want to know, because a part of him believed she'd known exactly what she was saying. The problem was, he would wager money that she was an innocent, which made her even more alluring. A woman with carnal knowledge, but no clear understanding of the actual experience.

Worst of all, he was supposed to be considering Lady Margaret as a prospective wife, and he'd done little to forward that plan of action since Anna had arrived at Starling House. Why was he hesitating to move forward with his courtship with Margaret? The memory of Anna blushing so sweetly as he teased her earlier made him stiffen. Was Anna the reason he'd not sought out Margaret's company in over a month?

Sebastian dragged in a harsh breath as a voice in the back of his head answered the question. Damnation. Anna Sawyer was unsuitable for the role of Viscountess of Starling. Completely unsuitable. That he'd unconsciously contemplated the question appalled him. Marriage was a duty.

One did not marry for any reason other than securing an heir—not even if it meant one's marriage bed would be filled with passion and lust. Marriage was meant to secure one's lineage, and that meant marrying a woman from a respectable family. A woman such as Lady Margaret. Anyone else was out of the question. It was time he put things in order and continued with his courtship of Lady Margaret.

With a grunt, Sebastian sprang to his feet and headed back toward the ballroom. In the back of his head, he heard a shout of angry protest. The voice tried to argue that Anna was just as suitable as Lady Margaret. He snorted with disbelief and banished the protests into the darkest recesses of his mind.

Aware that he'd been neglecting his duties as Anna's escort for the evening, Sebastian made his way through the crush toward where his mother was standing alone. He glanced out at the dancers circling the floor and saw Anna dancing with the Earl of Thorpe's heir. His jaw tightened. The young viscount had already earned a reputation for his wild ways, and he was surprised his mother hadn't tried to dissuade Anna from dancing with Monckton.

"Should she be dancing with Thorpe's eldest?" he said quietly as he reached his mother's side.

"I had little choice. The earl is here tonight, and Monckton was quite persistent." Sebastian glanced at his mother to see her frowning with curiosity at him. "It would be a good match."

"The man's reckless, and he's always at the center of one scandal or another," he muttered.

The moment he spoke, he regretted it. Out of the corner of his eye, he saw Lady Harding turn toward him, eyebrows arched in astonishment. Sebastian's jaw tightened as he continued to stare out at the dancers. After a brief moment, his mother returned her attention to the dance floor.

"Is that why you offered to serve as our escort this evening?" She paused for a fraction of an instant. "Do you think to determine the suitability of whomever asks for her hand?"

Sebastian stiffened. Is that what he was doing? He didn't like the answer that whispered through his head. Aware that his mother was waiting for his reply, he shot her a brief glance before his gaze searched for Anna again. Sebastian's mouth tightened as he saw the viscount and Anna laughing. Sebastian's muscles knotted as he fought the wild urge to cut in and take Anna back into his arms.

"It was merely an observation."

"Well, if you think either of us will have any sway over the man Anna chooses to marry, you are suffering from delusions." His mother's suggestion that he was delusional caused Sebastian's mouth to tighten. Lady Harding apparently sensed his annoyance, and she laughed quietly. "Anna is of age and free to marry whomever she wishes. Even if she wasn't, I doubt anyone could make her marry someone she didn't want to."

"According to Alexander, she has no intention of marrying anyone." At his reply, his mother jerked her head toward him.

"No intention—" Appalled, Lady Harding stared at him in dismay. "Are you certain you heard Alexander correctly?"

"I did. It seems Miss Trafford has set her mind to finding Anna a husband."

"Good heavens," the viscountess slowly turned back toward the dance floor. "Charles and Céleste never mentioned anything about her intentions."

"I would imagine Anna hasn't informed them. I know she doesn't really want to be here." Sebastian recalled the tears on her lashes as she darted out of the salon the day her friends had called on her.

"What do you mean, she doesn't want to be here?" Lady Harding exclaimed with rising dismay. "Did she tell you that?"

"Not directly." Sebastian's jaw locked with tension as he remembered Anna gesturing at him as if he were the hangman's noose. "I overheard her berating her friends from the Falcon, that she didn't want to be in London. She made her feelings in the matter quite clear."

"Her friends—oh, Sebastian, I did you an injustice by accusing you of having upset Anna that day. I'm terribly sorry." The light touch of his mother's hand on his arm made Sebastian look downward, and Lady Harding immediately pulled her hand away. "Forgive…forgive me for assuming you were responsible for upsetting Anna. I'm sorry."

Tension spread a fine web between the two of them, and he cleared his throat before nodding his head.

"It was an understandable reaction as I am guilty of having a sharp tongue where you're concerned. An apology is unnecessary." His throat closed up as a voice in his head urged him to mend the breach between the two of them.

Lady Harding's mouth was agape as she stared up at

him, but he ignored her astonishment to focus on the dancers. The orchestra was bringing the current piece of music to a close, and the moment Sebastian heard his best friend's voice behind them, he uttered a silent prayer of gratitude.

"Good evening, Lady Harding. Sebastian."

The tension in his muscles relaxed slightly as he turned to face Nicholas. Smiling with delight, Sebastian greeted the tall, dark-haired man with a firm handshake.

"Nicholas, this is a pleasant surprise. I didn't expect to see you here this evening," Sebastian said.

"When you mentioned tonight was Miss Sawyer's first introduction to the Marlborough Set, I decided it was time you introduced me to the young lady." Nicholas bowed to Sebastian's mother as he brushed his lips across the back of her hand. "Lady Harding, as beautiful as always."

"You are a rogue, Nicholas." Sebastian's mother laughed as she waved his compliment away, a light blush rising in her cheeks as she shook her head. "But thank you."

The sound of laughter echoed behind him, and Sebastian turned slightly to see Viscount Monckton escorting Anna back to his mother. The two had their heads together, and when Anna murmured something, the viscount threw back his head and laughed enthusiastically. Sebastian barely managed to suppress a savage noise of irritation as he glared at the young man.

Monckton looked in his direction, and the man's smile died swiftly beneath Sebastian's harsh scrutiny. Thorpe's heir politely thanked Anna for their dance and murmured something about seeing her soon before he quickly made his departure. As if realizing Monckton had left because of Sebastian's scowl, Anna's displeasure flashed in her brown eyes as she looked at him. Swallowing another sound of aggravation, he gestured toward Nicholas.

"Anna, I'd like to introduce you to one of my oldest

friends, Nicholas Thornhill, Earl of Guilford. Nicholas, this is Anna Sawyer."

Nicholas turned away from Lady Harding to face Anna with a smile. Instantly, the flush in her cheeks ebbed away, and she stared transfixed at his friend as if she'd seen a ghost. In fact, it was similar to the look she'd had when she'd been standing in front of the grandfather clock in his study a few weeks ago.

"Miss Sawyer," Nicholas said with a smile as he took her hand in his and brushed her knuckles with his lips. "It's said I have a terrible scowl, but I didn't realize it was quite so horrifying as to make a woman tremble."

"I…forgive me, my lord. This evening is slightly overwhelming for me."

The strained note in Anna's voice only emphasized the pale sheen of her cheeks. Puzzled by Anna's distraught manner, Sebastian bent his head toward her.

"Are you feeling all right?"

The moment his mouth brushed over her ear, a tremor rippled through her and it vibrated against his mouth. Anna met his gaze, then bobbed her head in a silent reply. The color returned to her cheeks as Sebastian heard his mother finish her explanation as to how Anna had come to stay with them. Nicholas turned back to Anna.

"You're in the most capable of hands," the earl said with a smile before he leaned toward her in an exaggerated whisper. "But I *would* like to know what you said to convince Sebastian to be your escort this evening."

"I doubt there's anything I could say to convince Sebastian to do anything at all." Anna cast a quick glance in his direction as the hint of a smile touched her luscious mouth. "However, I admit to being surprised as well. Despite our short acquaintance, he is acting quite outside the norm this evening. Until tonight, his usual demeanor has been rather stuffy and pompous."

"Exactly how *long* have you known each other, Sebastian?" Nicholas laughed as he eyed Sebastian with more than a hint of curiosity. "Miss Sawyer appears to know you quite well."

"Our acquaintance is a little less than two months." Sebastian heard the annoyance in his voice, and Nicholas's reaction said he'd heard it as well.

"Not quite two months. Interesting." Nicholas arched an eyebrow as he studied Sebastian for a brief moment. His friend smiled slyly at him, then turned to Anna and gave her a slight bow. "Then perhaps Miss Sawyer will grant me the honor of a dance, and I'll happily tout your best qualities, Sebastian, which most *definitely* offset your *sometimes* pompous air."

The last part of his invitation was riddled with amusement, and Nicholas's mouth twitched, making it clear his friend was fighting not to laugh out loud. Despite his best intentions not to appear affected by his friend's jests, Sebastian released a soft sound of umbrage. This time, his friend grinned at him, making it clear Nicholas had seen through Sebastian's attempt to remain detached from the teasing.

"What about your leg?"

Sebastian immediately regretted his words as Nicholas narrowed his gaze to study Sebastian with amused curiosity. The earl darted a glance toward Anna and smiled with pleasure before looking back at Sebastian.

"When it comes to dancing with a beautiful woman, I'm always willing to pay a price later."

Antipathy rolled through Sebastian as he remembered Nicholas had been a notorious seducer of more than one widow before his unhappy marriage. Honor and duty had made his friend remain faithful to a woman that cuckolded him, but no one would blame Nicholas if he were to find happiness elsewhere.

"If you're injured, my lord, I have no wish to be the cause of any undue pain." Dismay made Anna shake her head. "I'm perfectly happy to forego a dance."

"It's an old injury that flares up from time to time, but I have never allowed it to interfere in my enjoying the pleasure of a lovely woman's company."

Never in his life had Sebastian ever wanted to land a blow to someone's jaw so badly. The thought of Anna falling under his friend's spell tightened his body with a possessiveness that alarmed him. Not even the knowledge that his friend's honor would never allow him to seduce an unmarried woman, alleviated Sebastian's desire to lunge at his oldest and dearest friend.

Alarm bells rang loudly in the back of his head as he fought to destroy the urge to keep Anna out of Nicholas's arms. What the devil did it matter who the woman danced with? Sebastian obliterated the suggestion his brain offered him. Instead, he put his reaction down to lust. Desire was not a reason to marry, and he'd already deemed Anna completely unsuitable for the role of Viscountess Starling.

The fact didn't stop his brain from trying to think of another reason to keep his friend away from Anna. As Sebastian glared at his friend, he suddenly caught the calculating gleam in his friend's gaze. Nicholas was testing him, and Sebastian knew he'd revealed far more than he should have to someone who knew him as well as Nicholas did. Sebastian forced himself to relax and shrug nonchalantly.

"Far be it from me to question the extent of your endurance, Nicholas." The insouciant attempt to dismiss his friend's suspicions only made the earl's grin broaden as he returned his attention to Anna.

"Perhaps Sebastian is right, Miss Sawyer. However, I wouldn't mind a short stroll out to the garden patio." Nicholas smiled at Sebastian's mother. "Considering I'm a family friend, I doubt the gossips could make too much of that."

"I agree." Lady Harding nodded her head with a smile. "Anna isn't a debutante and is more than capable of making good decisions."

"I would love to take a walk with you, my lord. I'm eager to hear what you consider Lord Starling's best qualities are. As you can tell, his lordship does not take well to teasing, despite his proclivity to hand it out himself." Anna laughed as she glanced at Sebastian before offering Nicholas a radiant smile.

"Then if Lady Harding and Sebastian will excuse us." Clearly enjoying himself at his friend's expense, Nicholas nodded at Sebastian, then with a bow in the viscountess's direction, he offered his arm to Anna. "Shall we?"

Anna smiled up at Sebastian, and he narrowed his gaze at her as she placed her hand in the crook of Nicholas's arm. Another wave of possessiveness lashed out at him, and he saw her eyes widen with surprise and her smile falter. A second later, she eyed him with what he could only define as a sultry look of daring. It was an expression that said she'd seen his desire to keep Nicholas away from her. The small smile curving her lips was further confirmation she understood his internal struggle.

Sebastian wished they were alone as he had the sudden urge to turn her over his knee and spank her. But before he did so, he'd take his time teasing her and making her guess what his intentions were. His throat suddenly closed off at the image of his fingers leisurely caressing their way up the back of her legs to her lush thighs.

It was easy to imagine her soft whimper as his hand reached the plump, rounded curve of her bottom. That soft cry would become a gasp of surprise as he administered a single, hard smack to her buttocks as punishment for her teasing. Then he'd flip her over to kiss her hard.

The thought of teaching her a lesson, for her poking fun

at him, made Sebastian arch an eyebrow as he offered her a small smile of retribution. He should have known it wouldn't alarm her as her smile became one of triumph. As Nicholas guided her toward the patio doors, Anna's fingertips glided across the back of Sebastian's hand as she walked past him.

Caught off guard, Sebastian couldn't suppress his flinch, as electricity surged through him with the strength of a lightning bolt. Anyone who might have seen the gesture would have simply viewed it as an inadvertent touch. He might have thought the same if he'd not caught her mischievous smile as she walked away. The light caress was anything *but* accidental, and he could only pray she didn't realize just how badly it affected and alarmed him.

Sebastian swallowed hard as he struggled with the emotions pounding against him. Instead, he acknowledged her amusement with a slight nod. As Nicholas led Anna out of earshot, Sebastian glanced at his mother, steeling himself for either a silent look of curiosity or even a question.

To his relief, one of his mother's friends had caught her attention the moment Nicholas walked away with Anna. Based on his reaction just now, it was clear he'd underestimated the strength of his attraction to Anna. Worse, he was unprepared to answer his mother's or anyone else's questions. The one thing Sebastian was certain of, was that unless he wanted to find his heart ensnared by the woman and betrayed as his father had been, he needed to act quickly. The alternative would be a hell of his own making.

Chapter 16

Butterflies took flight in Anna's stomach as she felt Sebastian jerk the moment her fingers trailed across his hand. Lord, what was she doing playing such a dangerous game with a man who disapproved of her so deeply? She didn't want the man to think she was enamored with him.

The voice she'd shut away in the back of her head earlier tried to force its way into the open, but she quickly silenced it as the earl guided her toward the terrace doors. Just as Nicholas had promised, he proceeded to highlight Sebastian's best qualities as they walked out onto the patio. Anna enjoyed his dry sense of humor, but it was his loyalty to her dark angel that impressed her the most.

She understood that kind of friendship and recognized it for the valuable thing it was. Something told her it was a rare quality and difficult to come by among the Marlborough Set. Most of Sebastian's traits, she'd already seen for herself, but it was Nicholas's concern that his friend was headed toward a life of misery that took Anna by surprise.

"I fear he'll realize too late the extent of what an unhappy marriage will cost him."

"I don't understand," she said quietly at Nicholas's troubled frown. "Why do you think Sebastian will be unhappy when he marries?"

"Sebastian believes his mother was unfaithful to his father, and it has soured him on the idea of marriage for anything other than securing an heir." Nicholas's statement made Anna gasp in surprise.

"Why in heaven's name would he think such a thing about his mother? Lady Harding speaks of Lord Starling often and with such fondness. I cannot imagine her capable of such a betrayal."

"I agree. I'm convinced their marriage was one of deep love and friendship. But Sebastian's conviction as to his mother's betrayal is unshakeable." They came to a halt at the balustrade running the length of the patio that overlooked a large garden. Withdrawing her hand from Nicholas's arm, Anna watched several couples strolling through the moonlit gardens before she looked at Sebastian's friend with curiosity.

"Has he ever explained why he's convinced his mother would do such a thing?"

"The little he *has* told me was revealed only after we'd imbibed several glasses of brandy. We'd been drinking heavily, and the most that I can remember is that something he saw or overheard as a boy convinced him that Lady Harding had been unfaithful to his father." Nicholas winced with something close to regret. "When we were sober the next day, it almost destroyed our friendship when I pressed him for more details."

"It certainly explains why he's always so abrasive and cold toward Lady Harding, which I know pains her deeply," Anna mused as the sudden need to ease Sebastian's pain streaked through her.

"I have no doubt of her ladyship's sorrow. While Sebastian is the dutiful, polite, and considerate son in public, his cold treatment of her in private has always troubled me. Whatever Sebastian saw or heard, it's clear he'll not change his mind." Nicholas turned his head toward the garden. "But if Sebastian is correct in his belief, I can easily understand his hostility. He was close to his father. There was a deep affection and respect between the two of them. Sebastian was almost inconsolable when his father died."

Anna's heart ached for Sebastian's loss. She remembered how devastated she and her mother had been when Uncle Augustus had died so quickly. She looked back into the ballroom to where Sebastian had been standing with his mother. When she didn't see him, her gaze swept the dance floor.

She regretted doing so the moment she saw him dancing with Lady Margaret. The sight pulled the air from her lungs, and her heart twisted painfully in her chest. As the woman smiled up at Sebastian with a look of adoration, Anna experienced the urge to scratch the woman's eyes out. It wasn't until she turned away and saw Nicholas staring at her in surprise that she realized she'd uttered a soft cry of dismay.

Puzzlement swept across the earl's face as he touched her arm in a gesture of concern. When she remained silent, Nicholas turned his head toward the interior of the house and the crowd of guests circling the dance floor. Seconds later, his concern became a dark scowl, and Anna was certain he'd seen Sebastian dancing with the petite, dark-haired beauty.

"You'd think he would have seen through her by now."

The disgust in Nicholas's barely audible words emphasized his displeasure at seeing Sebastian dancing with Lady Margaret. Silently, she agreed with the earl. The memory of the cloud of darkness she'd seen swirling around the woman when she'd touched Lady Margaret's hand that day in the museum still haunted her. The woman was a viper, and Sebastian's inability to see it made Anna want to shake some sense into him.

"We are in agreement."

"My apologies, Miss Sawyer. I didn't mean for my observation to be heard."

"There's no need. I think your assessment is more than

accurate. For an intelligent man, Sebastian's inability to recognize her lack of sincerity baffles me."

"Hopefully my friend will come to his senses in time. I'm beginning to see you understand Sebastian far better than either he or I realized, Miss Sawyer." The dry note of humor in his voice made her laugh.

"I am not so sure I completely understand him, but I am beginning too, and please, call me Anna," she said with a smile. "I'm certain Sebastian will think it *improper* to do so, but as you're his friend, it seems more than appropriate to me. Besides, as Lady Harding said, I'm capable of making good decisions, and I confess to being at my wit's end with all this stuffiness and rigid protocol."

"Ah, there it is. An explanation as to why Sebastian was scowling at the two of us a few minutes ago." There was a speculative gleam in the earl's eyes as he met Anna's gaze. The astute look said he'd observed the tension between her and Sebastian. "He must find you quite the challenge."

"I think nuisance might be a better word. I seem to have a propensity to irritate him when it comes to almost anything I say or do."

"Then continue to challenge and irritate him, Anna. It will do him good."

"That is something I shall have no problem accomplishing," Anna said with a laugh. "My language alone is enough to horrify him."

"Your language?" The earl stared at her in surprised puzzlement.

"I have lived with my uncle onboard his merchant ship for the past fifteen some years. My schooling has been quite extensive in all things, including languages. I'm fluent in French, Italian, and Latin, but I am also fluent in a fourth language that is deemed most unsuitable for polite society, let alone a woman."

"*Good God.*" Nicholas stared at her in astonished

amusement.

"Poseidon's balls happens to be my favorite when it comes to being surprised by something," she said softly as she offered him an audacious wink.

Anna winced as she took in the earl's stunned expression. It had been a risk to share the coarse oath, but she had thought Nicholas would find it amusing. Now, she wasn't quite so sure. She bit down on her lip as she found herself regretting her impulsiveness. Suddenly, Nicholas threw back his head and laughed heartily. Relieved, Anna offered him a mischievous smile, and he laughed again.

"If anyone can teach Sebastian to be less rigid in his manner, it is you, Anna."

"I'm not sure I want that particular role," she said, laughing.

"Perhaps not, but in my experience, I think you are one of the few people I know who has the audacity to stand up to my friend."

The earl grinned broadly at her as the orchestra ended its waltz with a flourish and dancers on the floor came to a halt. Offering his arm to her, Nicholas led her back into the ballroom. As they passed through the open doorway, she saw Sebastian and Lady Margaret join a small group of people on the edge of the dance floor.

"In fact, I think someone needs to show him exactly what kind of woman he's considering introducing as the future Viscountess Starling."

Startled, she jerked her gaze away from Sebastian to look up at his friend. The challenge in the earl's gaze made Anna swallow the knot that suddenly lodged in her throat. She quickly looked away as he guided her back to where Lady Harding was standing. At his quiet chuckle, Anna darted a glance at him. He was watching her with amusement, but there was a glint in Nicholas's green eyes that dared her to take up his challenge.

As they reached Lady Harding, Nicholas bowed and briefly kissed her hand, then lifted his head slightly to give her a discreet wink. Heat flooded her cheeks as he straightened to say goodbye to her and Lady Harding. But before he left, Anna saw the gleam in his eyes that declared he wouldn't hesitate to challenge her again the next time they met.

Even if she'd been able to find her voice, Anna would not have been able to say a word as several men her age appeared in front of her and Lady Harding with requests for an introduction. In seconds, Anna was on the dance floor with a young viscount guiding her energetically around the dance floor.

It was a repetitive scene for the next three hours. Just as Lady Harding had promised, Anna was inundated with requests to escort her onto the dance floor. By the time supper was announced, Anna didn't think she could bear to accept one more dance. As the young man she'd been dancing with led her back to Lady Harding, Anna drew in a breath of anticipation as she saw Sebastian's tall figure facing his mother. He would rescue her just as he had promised before they left Starling House.

The fluttering in her stomach vanished as he shifted his position, and she saw Lady Margaret, who'd been hidden from view. When Anna and her partner reached Lady Harding, the young man she'd been dancing with bowed and said goodbye after indicating he would call on her in the near future. Anna forced a smile to her lips as she turned to greet the petite woman at Sebastian's side.

"Good evening, Lady Margaret."

"How lovely you look, Miss Sawyer. Such a...remarkable transformation since our last meeting." The other woman slipped her arm through Sebastian's as she eyed Anna with condescension. "You looked quite charming dancing with *young* Lord Hayling."

The woman reminded her of a vine clinging to a tree as

it slowly devoured its victim, while the tree remained completely unaware of the danger it was in. Anna quietly murmured her thanks at the compliment, even though the calculating gleam in Lady Margaret's eyes said it had been a subtle reference to Anna's age. Suppressing the urge to say something deeply offensive, she turned toward Lady Harding.

"Is it possible we could go home now?" she asked softly.

"Of course, are you feeling unwell again?" The viscountess eyed her with concern.

"No, I'm simply tired, and my feet hurt."

Anna smiled at Lady Harding as she realized it was the truth. Her feet really did hurt, and she was exhausted from the strain of small talk with the men she had danced with over the last three hours. There had only been two or three of them who possessed any brains at all. Lord Monckton was one of them. The memory of their conversation and his promise to help her enter his club disguised as a man lifted Anna's spirits slightly.

"I'll have the carriage summoned so we can leave as soon as I escort Lady Margaret back to her friends." Sebastian's immediate reaction made Anna glance over her shoulder and shake her head vehemently.

"That won't be necessary. They've just announced supper, and I have no wish to pull you away from Lady Margaret. Your mother and I can manage without you having to leave."

It was difficult to keep her voice neutral and polite when what she really wanted to do was call the man an idiot for not seeing through Lady Margaret. If he were to accompany them home, it meant she would have to guard her tongue the entire ride back to Starling House. It was something she was certain she would fail at, given how tired she suddenly was. She turned her head to look at Lady Harding in a silent plea for the older woman to agree with her. With a nod, the viscountess smiled at Anna, then turned her attention to Sebastian.

"Anna's right. There's no need for you to accompany us home, Sebastian. If you'll simply request the carriage be sent around, then you can take Lady Margaret into supper."

"Oh, do say you'll stay, Sebastian."

The woman's soft plea was delivered with a beseeching smile, and Anna once again experienced the urge to scratch the woman's eyes out. Just in the nick of time, she managed to avoid giving an exaggerated impersonation of the woman's simpering behavior. Sebastian looked from Anna to his mother, then back again as if uncertain as to whether to argue with them.

"*Christ Almighty, Sebastian.* Just order the bloody carriage," she whispered in a waspish tone. He jerked at her harsh command before glaring his disapproval at her. Beside him, Lady Margaret stared at her in shock.

"Go, Sebastian. Lady Margaret can stay with us until you return."

Lady Harding gave him a look that said not to argue with her. With a grunt of irritation and puzzlement, Sebastian nodded his agreement to do as he was asked. Anna tipped her chin up at a defiant angle as he sent her another dark look before he excused himself and walked away from the three women.

A scandalous expression still on her beautiful face, Lady Margaret pressed her hand to the base of her throat as if debating whether to say anything. Anna met the woman's gaze and smiled slightly.

"Forgive me, Lady Margaret. I'm impatient by nature and can't abide people taking forever to make up their mind."

"Of course, I'm simply unaccustomed to hearing language of that sort, even from a gentleman."

"You should try it sometime," Anna said with a sudden sense of spiteful pleasure as she took in the woman's shocked expression. "I'd be happy to share one or two of my favorite phrases. You'd be surprised how much better you'll feel when you use the phrase, Poseidon's balls, during a moment of anger or frustration."

"I couldn't possibly." Lady Margaret gasped in shock. Anna smiled at the woman's appalled reaction as she heard Lady Harding coughing hard in an effort to cover up her laughter.

"That's quite understandable. It takes a great deal of confidence not to care what others think."

"I don't think it's a lack of confidence at all." The woman released a haughty sniff of disagreement as her gaze skimmed over Anna with an air of distaste. "I think it's the difference between a refined lady and a fishwife."

"What an interesting comparison. I've never been called a fishwife before."

Anna hid her anger as she smiled mockingly at the woman. Lady Margaret's reaction was designed to resemble dismay as she shook her head in protest. To most people, the woman's regret would have seemed genuine, but Anna saw the contempt in Lady Margaret's eyes.

"Forgive me, Miss Sawyer. It wasn't my intent to suggest—"

"Of course, it was." Anna studied the woman with an amusement she didn't feel. What she really felt was a growing antipathy that was threatening to get the best of her.

"You must believe me, Miss Sawyer. I truly am sorry if my words injured you. They were not meant to do so."

Lady Margaret's apology sounded so sincere that if the woman hadn't darted a look over Anna's shoulder or if the back of Anna's neck hadn't begun to tingle at Sebastian's close proximity, it would have been difficult to doubt the woman's sincerity. But the glitter of scorn in Lady Margaret's eyes made it clear her apology was solely for Sebastian's benefit. Anna arched her eyebrows and smiled at the woman with derision and disbelief.

"As any good fishwife will tell you, apologies made solely for the sake of appearances are meaningless. As a *refined* lady, you mistakenly confuse vulgar language for what is actually blunt honesty. Honesty is the sign of an independent woman who speaks her mind and doesn't give a damn what others think. I find honesty an admirable quality in someone. It is by far more preferable than a *refined* lady's contrived efforts to hide her true nature. A talent you possess and wield with great skill, much in the same way a spider spins its web for its unsuspecting, chowder-head victim."

The fiery anger in Lady Margaret's gaze filled Anna with a small amount of satisfaction, and she smiled coldly at the woman. Eager to escape the vile woman's company, Anna turned around and looked up at Sebastian with more than a hint of disgust. For a man as intelligent as he was, the fact that he was completely blind to who Lady Margaret really was behind that beautiful face made Anna angry as hell. Worse, she didn't like how much it made her heart hurt that Sebastian couldn't see the truth about who Lady Margaret was. That she didn't like one bit.

"Your carriage is waiting." Sebastian studied her with a look of puzzlement, and with her anger still simmering beneath the surface, Anna acknowledged his words with a mere jerk of her head.

"Goodnight."

Anna didn't even try to make her tone pleasant as she quickly skirted Sebastian on her way toward the exit. Behind her, Lady Margaret said Sebastian's name in a plaintive voice that indicated she was upset by Anna's refusal to say goodnight to her. Although she didn't hear Sebastian reply, she was convinced the man would try to console the woman's so-called hurt feelings. The man was an utter idiot to be taken in by the woman, and the two deserved each other. No sooner had the thought rushed through her head than Anna's heart clenched painfully in her breast. *She* was a fool.

Chapter 17

Anna accepted the footman's hand and followed Lady Harding into the carriage. The door closed, and a second later, the vehicle rocked forward. Silence hung in the air for several minutes until the viscountess released a soft breath of amusement.

"I don't like her either." At Lady Harding's confession, Anna jerked her head away from the window to stare in astonishment at the viscountess. The woman laughed at Anna's reaction. "Did you really think you were hiding your dislike for the woman?"

"No, I suppose not," Anna admitted with a reluctant shake of her head.

"I confess I thoroughly enjoyed your exchange while Sebastian was gone." Lady Harding laughed again. "But Poseidon's balls?"

"It was the least offensive curse I could think of in the heat of the moment." Anna sighed in disgust at the unpleasant conversation. "There's just something about her that I find terribly irritating. She's so...so..."

"Disingenuous?"

"Yes, that's the word." Anna didn't mention the other words she could apply to Lady Margaret. Those words needed evidence before they could be spoken.

"I agree. I honestly don't know what Sebastian sees in

her or why he's even considering making an offer for her hand."

"I would imagine it's because she acts exactly as he thinks a proper, *refined* woman should act."

"She'll never make him happy." The note of sadness in the viscountess's voice made Anna lean forward to squeeze the woman's hand in an empathetic gesture.

"Maybe he'll realize that before he makes the mistake of marrying her."

"Perhaps, but I don't really believe that's possible."

Silence fell between them once more, and Lady Harding stared out the window, lost in thought. After several moments, Lady Harding uttered a soft sound, as if remembering a happy moment.

"You're more like Augustus than your mother." The older woman turned her head and smiled. "Your uncle could be just as fiery as you when provoked."

"For you to see Uncle Augustus in me is a compliment I shall cherish, my lady."

The viscountess's words warmed Anna's heart, and an image of her uncle laughing as he teased her over something silly filled her head. Uncle Augustus had been even more handsome than Uncle Charles, and she had fond memories of him. He'd always spoiled her and her mother whenever they visited him. He would shower both of them with love and attention.

When she turned eight, the two of them had gone into the village, where Uncle Augustus had allowed her to pick out a toy for her birthday. Several people had been vulgar and hostile when they'd been forced to speak to him, while others had looked at him in disgust. The way the villagers had treated her uncle had made Anna angry and indignant that anyone would try to make her uncle feel bad. She still remembered telling him how rude she thought the villagers were. He'd smiled sadly and shook his head.

"People are often afraid of anything they don't understand, my pet."

"You mean because you're different from other people?" At her blunt, matter-of-fact question, her uncle looked at her in surprise. She shrugged her shoulders insouciantly. "I overheard Papa fighting with Mama. He said he didn't like her bringing me to see you. He called you a name, but I didn't know what it meant, and when I asked Mama about it, she said I didn't need to know."

"I don't know what word your father used, but I can guess, and your Mama was right. You don't need to know."

"Well, Papa was wrong to call you a name. Mama says you're kind, funny, and love us very much. She said that just because you're different doesn't make you a bad person."

"I see." Her uncle's response was accompanied by an odd expression crossing his handsome face. "You're right, I do love both of you very much. However, I think perhaps I need to have a talk with your mother."

"Oh no, Uncle Augustus, please don't. Mama made me promise not to tell you or Papa what I heard."

"Did she now?" Her uncle's voice sounded like a frog croaking. "What else did your mother say?"

"She said it would hurt you to find out she knows your secret. She said she'll always love you, no matter what. She said she doesn't care if you're different from other people."

"Your mother knows me better than I realized." A resigned smile curved his mouth.

"Mama says all that matters is how kind and good you are. And I don't care that you're different either. I'm different too." Anna grinned up at him before she grew somber and frowned with trepidation. "You won't tell Mama that I broke my promise, will you? It will upset her."

"No, I won't tell her. It will be our secret."

"Just like Levi is a secret?"

"Levi?" Alarm echoed loudly in her uncle's exclamation

as he jerked his head to look down at her. "Who told you about Levi?"

"Papa said he knew about Levi, but Mama said he was wrong, and that Levi was simply your friend. But I think she said it because she was afraid for you. She made me promise never to tell anyone that you and Levi were best friends."

"Your Mama is right." The sternness in his voice surprised her as she met his gaze. "That is one secret you must never tell anyone because someone might hurt Levi or me."

"Why would someone want to hurt you?" Anna stared up at her uncle as a wave of fear swept through her.

"It's complicated, my pet. I just need you to remember not to tell anyone." The serious note in Uncle Augustus's voice made Anna nod her head solemnly.

"I won't."

The memory slowly faded from Anna's mind, and an overwhelming sadness swept through her. It had been years later when she'd learned the meaning of the word her father had used in reference to her uncle. Her father had called Uncle Augustus a sodomite, and she'd once asked Céleste about it. When her friend had explained the meaning of the word, everything suddenly made sense.

Uncle Augustus truly had been different, but like her mother, it changed nothing about the fact that Anna had loved him deeply. In her eyes, just like her Uncle Charles, her uncle could do no wrong. Uncle Augustus had died suddenly from cancer a few months before her mother had thrown herself off the bridge into the Thet river. When her mother took her own life, Anna had viewed her uncle's death as a small blessing.

It would have devastated Uncle Augustus to know how terrible his sister's life had been. Her mother had hidden her miserable existence from both her brothers. Anna still remembered how Uncle Charles had reacted when he'd learned the truth as to how Anna's father had beaten his wife. Guilt had weighed down on him as heavily as his grief.

Uncle Augustus would have felt the same way, but Anna's mother had been determined not to cause her brothers pain. She knew they would have blamed themselves for not stopping their father from marrying her off to Anna's father. As the painful memories slowly faded, Anna sighed softly and turned her head toward Lady Harding.

"Did you know my uncle and mother well?"

"Oh yes, quite well. Both of your uncles and your mother were very dear to me. They were the siblings I never had." A happy smile curved Lady Harding's lips as she leaned back and rested her head on the squabs of the carriage seat. "But I loved your Uncle Augustus and Levi the most. The three of us were joined at the hip in a manner of speaking."

"Levi?"

Anna stiffened as she stared at Lady Harding in surprise and remembered her uncle's best friend had been called Levi. It was an unusual name, and she'd never forgotten it, nor her uncle's insistence that she never tell anyone the two men were such good friends. The viscountess's brow furrowed as if puzzled by Anna's amazement, before her expression relaxed and her smile returned.

"Levi was Sebastian's father. Other than your Uncle Augustus, he was the kindest, sweetest soul I've ever known."

"It sounds as if the two of you were very happy together."

"We *were* happy. We both had everything we wanted, even though that happiness came with some sacrifices, but I never regretted marrying Levi. Not even after I met James."

"James? Do you mean Lord Harding?"

"Yes, James and I met shortly after Levi and I celebrated our fourth anniversary. If I hadn't married Levi, things would have turned out quite differently."

"In what way?" Anna pressed gently. It was obvious the

viscountess was lost in her memories, and she found the woman's story fascinating.

"I would have been married to the man my parents had chosen for me. Darrenton's still alive, so James and I would never have enjoyed the few years we had. While I'll never know, I think if I'd been married to Darrenton when I met James, the man might have gone so far as to arrange for James or me to meet our end in some type of accident. He's a cruel man."

The viscountess's voice echoed with horror, and she grew pale for a moment. A small shudder shook Lady Harding's body, and Anna was certain it was a tremor of fear. A moment later, a small smile curved the older woman's mouth as her fear vanished.

"I have Levi and Augustus to thank for saving me from Darrenton."

"Saving you?" Anna's question caused Lady Harding to straighten in her seat.

"My parents had been trying to convince me to marry Darrenton, but I had refused. My father threatened to force me to accept the man's offer, and I was terrified. The rumors I'd heard about Darrenton were horrifying, but all my parents cared about was that the man was rich. Your uncles, Serena, and Levi all tried to reassure me, but I was beside myself."

Tears filled Lady Harding's voice as she stared into space. Suddenly, a look of shame and regret made her squeeze her eyes tightly shut as if fighting to keep tears from spilling down her cheeks. The viscountess's throat moved violently as she struggled to control the dark emotions Anna could see were threatening to overtake the woman. She was about to interrupt the viscountess when the older woman bit down on her lower lip before taking a deep breath and continuing with her tale.

"When Augustus caught me with a bottle of poison, he was horrified. It was then that all four of my friends understood my desperation. We all tried to think of a solution that would save me from marrying Darrenton, but nothing anyone proposed could guarantee I wouldn't have to marry the man. That is until Augustus decided Levi and I should marry." A small smile touched the viscountess's lips as they looked at each other, and Anna smiled back at the older woman.

"Uncle Augustus always seemed to have a good solution for every problem once he thought about it for a while."

"Yes, he did. Your uncle was quite brilliant, even when it came down to figuring out how to build a tree house that could hold all five of us at the same time. He was also quite handy with carpentry tools." Sebastian's mother laughed softly before she continued. "Augustus was certain his solution would work, and he was right. Levi's grandfather had been pressuring Levi to marry and produce an heir. He also had a title and was far wealthier than Darrenton. It was the perfect solution for all three of us. Not once did I ever regret marrying Levi. Not even when I met James four years later did I suffer a moment's remorse for what I did. Levi and I had saved each other, and Augustus as well."

The viscountess's voice dropped to a mere whisper as she murmured the last part of her story, and something about the woman's words made Anna frown. How had three people been saved by Lady Harding marrying Sebastian's father? She fiddled with her closed silk fan as she contemplated what the woman had meant. Lady Harding sighed and offered Anna an apologetic smile.

"I apologize, my dear. I can't believe how I was rambling on. I've not talked about those early days in a very long time." Worry furrowed the woman's forehead as she met Anna's gaze. "I trust you'll keep my confidence?"

"Of course, my lady. I would never willingly do anything to injure you." Anna leaned forward and squeezed the other woman's hand in a reassuring gesture. The viscountess smiled with relief.

"As I said, you're very much like Augustus. He was a good listener and confidante too, and my heart clearly saw that in you, just as I did in him."

"I consider it the highest of compliments that you think I'm like Uncle Augustus. I loved him very much."

"I miss him greatly. If he hadn't died, then maybe Levi…" The woman's voice trailed off as an odd look crossed her features. "But I confess sharing my story with you is a great comfort. In fact, other than James and Alexander, I've never told another soul about that time, and if Alexander had not found those old letters, he would still know nothing."

The moment Lady Harding mentioned old letters, Anna remembered the vision she'd had at the British Museum. In it, she'd seen Alexander holding sheets of paper as he demanded Sebastian be told the truth. But Lady Harding had refused, convinced Sebastian would see it as one more betrayal. But what kind of betrayal? Why had Alexander been so insistent Sebastian see the letters?

Suddenly, it was as if someone had given her a map to use when charting a course for the Falcon. Each longitude and latitude line fell into place, starting with the promise she'd made as a child never to tell anyone Levi was her uncle's best friend.

Then there was Lady Harding's statement that marrying Sebastian's father had saved all three of them. Sebastian's mother hadn't just married Lord Starling to save herself, she'd done it to protect Levi's and her uncle's secret. Levi hadn't just been Uncle Augustus's best friend. Her uncle and Lord Starling had cared for each other in a way society viewed not only as a sin, but a crime as well. But what would have been in the letters—Anna drew in a sharp breath of understanding.

"They were letters Levi and Uncle Augustus wrote to each other. It's how Alexander learned that Lord Harding was his real father."

"Yes, Augustus and Levi were quite prolific in their—"

Lady Harding started violently, and Anna jerked up her head at the woman's loud gasp of horror. She looked at the viscountess, and her heart sank like a stone to the ocean floor as she realized she'd spoken her thoughts out loud. Fear and outrage suddenly contorted Lady Harding's face.

"How do you know about the letters? Did Alexander tell you?"

The ferocity of the viscountess's demand was emphasized by the way she leaned forward to close the distance between them. It was a threatening posture that made Anna flinch. It was understandable the woman would question whether her son had divulged her secret.

What else was the woman to think? How could Anna explain Alexander had not betrayed his mother without revealing her own secret? She couldn't, and the realization made her tremble in horror. Anna swallowed her fear as she met the other woman's gaze steadily.

"You shared your secrets with me, my lady, and it is time for me to share *my* secret," Anna said softly. "Do you remember the morning after I arrived at Starling House?"

"What does *that* have to do with my questions?"

Lady Harding's icy voice only intensified as the viscountess's anger filled the small space between them, and Anna forced herself to ignore the woman's menacing look.

"If you'll recall, I had a spell where you thought I was in a trance." Anna clasped the fan in her hand so tightly she thought it might break under the pressure of her grip. "I told you I had a mild form of epilepsy. That was the truth, but it was only a half-truth."

"What happened that morning has *nothing* to do with your revelation seconds ago. *How* do you know about the letters?"

"It is very relevant," Anna said firmly. "I have the ability to see things during most of my spells."

"See things?" Lady Harding's mouth tightened with a sneer as she scoffed at Anna's explanation. "Do *not* play me for a fool, Miss Sawyer, what sort of nonsense are you using to explain away Alexander's betrayal of my trust?"

"He *didn't* betray you, my lady. A vision I had recently showed the two of you arguing. Alexander was holding several letters and demanding you tell Sebastian the truth, but you refused."

"Do you *really* expect me to believe something so ludicrous?" Lady Harding's rebuke was scathing, but there was a growing note of fear running beneath the woman's words.

"I have no need to lie to you, my lady. In my vision, you told Alexander that Levi had wanted you and him to tell Sebastian the truth together. A truth you believed would have driven a wedge between a son and his father." At her quiet reply, Lady Harding jumped violently.

"Dear God." The viscountess's words were a mere whisper as she stared at Anna in stunned horror before anger replaced her fear. "My conversation with Alexander happened more than a year ago. How could you possibly know that unless my son told you?"

Anna desperately wanted to reach out to touch the viscountess's hand in a sympathetic gesture but was afraid the woman would reject the offer of comfort. The older woman's reaction was as Uncle Augustus had warned her, people who do not understand something fear it.

Despite the viscountess's alarm, Anna knew she had no choice but to continue if she was to make Lady Harding believe Alexander had not betrayed her. All she could do was be honest and tell the woman what she'd seen in her vision. Anna didn't look away from the viscountess as she continued.

"Sebastian has never hidden the discord between you and him. I never understood why, because I know how kind, thoughtful, and generous you are. My vision clarified so many things I didn't understand. It was your refusal to tell Sebastian the truth, despite Lord Starling's, and later, Alexander's urgings, that made me realize just now, how you have been protecting Sebastian, despite what it costs you. Only a mother who loves their child would willingly pay such a price."

Anna swallowed hard as she saw the deepening fear and shock in Lady Harding's wide eyes and the woman's features were white as chalk. Although the viscountess's mouth moved as if she were trying to speak, no words passed her lips. It was obvious Anna's words were inflicting pain on the woman. The knowledge made Anna hesitate, but she'd already passed the point of no return and needed to finish what she'd begun.

"I think Sebastian saw or overheard something as a child that convinced him you betrayed his father with Lord Harding. Letters confirming such a liaison or even that Lord Harding was Alexander's father wouldn't surprise Sebastian. It would simply confirm that his treatment of you is justified."

The torment on Lady Harding's pale features made Anna's heart ache even more. Tears of sympathy and understanding began to clog her throat, and she swallowed hard as she continued with her explanation.

"You said Sebastian would see the truth as one more betrayal, and you refused to damage his opinion of his father. I can think of only two things that might compel you to do that. The first is easily dismissed. There is no question that Lord Starling is Sebastian's father. Sebastian's resemblance to his father's portrait is undeniable."

"And this other possibility?" Lady Harding's voice was hoarse and vibrated with fear.

"My uncle and Lord Starling loved each other in a way society views as an abomination. What Alexander found were love letters between the two of them. You married Lord

Starling to save yourself and to protect Levi and Uncle Augustus. That is the truth you're hiding from Sebastian. You refused to administer a blow that would have damaged Sebastian's relationship with his father and later his opinion of Lord Starling. Even at the cost of enduring Sebastian's antipathy."

In the dim light of the carriage's interior, the viscountess's features were devoid of any color. The stark anguish and fear on Lady Harding's face as she met Anna's gaze made tears well up in Anna's eyes. Since coming to Starling House, she'd become quite fond of the woman. It pained her to know she was responsible for the woman's misery. Anna quickly leaned forward to catch the viscountess's hands in hers.

"Forgive me, my lady. I am so sorry. I didn't mean to speak my thoughts out loud. I never intended to cause you such pain. If I could take my words back, I would."

The viscountess closed her eyes and rested her head on the leather squabs of her seat. After a long moment of silence, Lady Harding pulled one of her hands free of Anna's grasp to pat her other hand lightly. With a slight shake of her head, the viscountess released a sigh.

"I know you meant no harm, Anna." Eyes shimmering with tears, the older woman offered Anna a weak smile. "Is there anything else this gift of yours showed you?"

"Only a vision of my uncle looking happier than I'd ever seen him when I was in Sebastian's study."

"You saw Augustus while you were in Sebastian's study?" Lady Harding's voice echoed with bewilderment as she stared at Anna in puzzlement.

"Yes, it was several weeks ago. Do you think it might mean something?"

"I'm not sure." The viscountess stared off into space as if trying to make sense of what Anna had told her. "Augustus visited us often. He and Levi spent a great deal of time together in the study."

The carriage suddenly rocked to a halt, and Anna saw through the window they'd arrived at Starling House. Lady Harding's hand touched hers, and Anna turned toward the woman.

"Thank you, my dear for convincing me that Alexander didn't betray me. It could not have been easy telling me your secret, any more than it was for me to tell you mine." The color had returned to the viscountess's face. Her smile was almost mischievous as she met Anna's gaze. "We are comrades in arms, now that we know each other's secrets."

"Yes, my lady, we are." Anna nodded and returned Lady Harding's smile as the door of the carriage opened, and the footman extended his hand to assist them out of the vehicle.

Chapter 18

With a small grunt, Anna managed to push the small settee a few inches across the rug. Yesterday, Lady Harding had given her blessing for Anna to move the couch closer to the front windows to take advantage of the afternoon light while reading. Although Anna preferred the window seat overlooking the garden, the afternoon light wasn't as strong there as it was in the mornings.

Drawing in another deep breath, Anna pushed the couch a few inches closer to the window. On board the Falcon, she'd worked with the ship's sails quite often, much to Céleste's dismay, but she had enjoyed the exercise. The couch wasn't much heavier than the heavy canvas sails, but then she hadn't been handicapped on the Falcon, like she was here. Straightening upright, Anna glared down at her gown and muttered an oath.

"*Hells bells*, it wouldn't be so damn difficult to move this bloody couch if I didn't have to wear a torture device under this dress."

"Your language skills seem to have improved somewhat."

Sebastian's quiet words drifted over her shoulder, and she spun around to see her dark angel standing just inside the salon doorway. Other than a brief greeting when their paths crossed, it was the first time he'd said more than two words to her since the Sheringham ball more than three weeks ago.

Not once since then had Sebastian ventured near her. She was certain he'd been deliberately ignoring her. He always ate lunch in his study or at his club and dined with friends in the evening. Even if their paths crossed when she and Lady Harding attended the theater or some soirée, he would simply nod his head at them from across the room. The only time he approached them was when Lady Margaret was on his arm.

Anna wasn't sure if it was Sebastian's attempt to emphasize his intentions where the woman was concerned, or if Lady Margaret had insisted they greet Anna. She had concluded it was the latter, as whenever the couple greeted her and Lady Harding, Sebastian was clearly uncomfortable.

Every time their gazes had met, he would stare at her with such intensity it was as if they were the only two people in the room. A moment later, the emotion would vanish, and his eyes would grow shuttered as he focused his attention on Lady Margaret.

Worse, Lady Margaret fawned over Sebastian with a cloying sweetness Anna found nauseating. She wavered between wanting to punch the man or shout at him for being so blind about the woman's duplicitous character.

The only thing that had prevented Anna from using her tongue to scathingly insult the woman was Viscountess Harding's fingers pressing firmly into Anna's forearm. The older woman would quickly break the tense atmosphere with an excuse she and Anna were needed elsewhere. Every time they walked away from the couple, Lady Harding would look at her with sympathy before offering Anna a commiserating sigh.

All of it had created a growing resentment of his behavior. She didn't understand why he'd been avoiding her, any more than she understood the anger and resentment it aroused in her. Already frustrated by her inability to easily move the couch, Anna's resentment at his avoidance of her and his continued association with Lady Margaret combined to become bitter outrage. With a baleful scowl in his direction, she drew in a breath.

"I am not in the mood for any lectures, my lord."

"Did I say I was going to lecture you?"

"Despite you rarely deigning to be in my presence, the moments we do encounter each other, you always manage to point out at least *one* of my many flaws," she snapped. Hands pressed into her waist, she exhaled a puff of air in an effort to blow a strand of hair off her face as she glared at him. Surprise sent his eyebrows upward, and she immediately regretted giving the impression she'd noticed his absence.

"Then what would you like me to lecture you on?" The question was devoid of anything except polite curiosity, but his dark eyes revealed his amusement.

"Have I ever told you that you're a horse's arse?" she spat out fiercely.

"I don't recall, and I'm afraid to ask how many times you have, when I've been out of earshot." Although he acted as if they were simply engaging in small talk, his mouth twitched with amusement.

"*Cocky bastard,*" she muttered beneath her breath. A second later, the air left her lungs as Sebastian walked toward her. With each step that closed the distance between them, Anna's heartbeat accelerated proportionately.

"And just a moment ago, I complimented you on how you'd improved your language skills." Amusement filled Sebastian's words more than disapproval or any other emotion. Ignoring any thought of impending danger, her mouth tightened with irritation.

"I'm rather busy at the moment, is there something you wanted?"

Sebastian halted in front of her and reached out to tuck

another stray lock of hair behind her ear. Warm fingertips glided along the edge of her jaw as his gaze locked with hers. The touch was barely tangible, but it sent a white-hot heat spreading across her skin until it engulfed every inch of her.

For a moment, she stopped breathing as she saw the raw hunger burning in his dark eyes. Mesmerized by the desire smoldering in his gaze, she drew in a deep breath. Instantly, his scent cascaded over her. Sandalwood, patchouli, and a subtle hint of cinnamon flooded her senses. Unable to look away, the wild pounding of her heart was a soft roar in her ears as her blood flowed hot through her limbs.

Lost in his fiery gaze, she saw the promise of sinful pleasures and something so dangerous she knew it could easily consume her, heart and soul. Just like she had several weeks ago, she ached for him to pull her close and kiss her. The thought made her swallow hard as she unconsciously wet her lips with her tongue. A dark, low sound whispered out of him. The fingers of one hand dug pleasurably into her waist, while his other hand cupped her chin. Anna didn't think as she pressed her body into his and tilted her head upward in anticipation of his kiss.

Suddenly, he uttered a fierce growl as he shoved her away and spun around as if poised to stride quickly out of the room. When he didn't move, a spider web of tension hovered in the air between them. Its invisible strands held her motionless as she stared at his back in frustration. With just one look, he'd thrown her body into a state of fiery need, then turned away, unwilling to quench her thirst for his kiss and something more. The man was beyond exasperating.

Anna drew in a deep breath and tried to calm herself in the way Uncle Charles had taught her. As she exhaled, she knew it wasn't possible at the moment. She was too agitated by the feelings Sebastian stirred inside her, and she was angry. Whether her anger was because he'd refused to fulfill the promise his eyes had made or because she'd allowed herself to feel anything at all, she didn't know. All she understood was that he had toyed with her emotions just now, and she didn't like it. She didn't like it one bit.

"Other than to taunt me, did you come into the salon for a specific reason, Sebastian?" At her icy question, she saw his back stiffen before he slowly turned to face her.

"I came to tell you that Scotland Yard has arrested another member of the Hatshepsut cult. They still don't know how many there are, but they're working to find the leaders of the cult."

"The High Priest and Priestess." At her statement, Sebastian confirmed her suspicions with a look of surprise. Anna ignored his startled expression as she frowned in concentration. "I doubt they'll find them. They're most likely members of the Marlborough Set. It will be next to impossible to discover who they are unless one of those arrested tells the police."

"What do you mean you think they're members of the Set?"

At the tightly spoken question, she winced. Anna and her friends had agreed not to speak of their investigations until they had something definitive they could present to Scotland Yard. At least she'd managed not to reveal Sarah's or Alexander's involvement in her search for answers. Sebastian would have Alexander's head for agreeing to even research the cult.

"If you'll recall, I've been reading about Hatshepsut because I was curious about the cult. I was hoping to find something I could use to find those who escaped that night."

"*Good God.*" Sebastian's low, forceful words of anger darkened the air between them. "Have you lost your mind?"

"*No*, I am *quite sane*," she snapped. "But I'm of the opinion that learning more about Hatshepsut might prove helpful."

"*Christ Jesus*, you almost lost your life to these fanatics more than two months ago. Don't you understand how dangerous these people are?" Sebastian didn't allow her to reply as he viciously waved his hand in the air. "Don't answer that. You know. You're simply determined to find them, even if it gets you killed."

"*Of course*, I know how dangerous they are." Infuriated by his dismissive gesture, she narrowed her eyes at him. "I'd be a fool not to realize that. All I'm doing is reading everything I can find on Hatshepsut, nothing more."

"By nothing more, you really mean not yet, because you've not found something of use to date." The heavy sarcasm in his voice made her begin to protest, but he raised his hand to silence her objections. "Don't deny it."

"I'm not denying *anything*, you arrogant *jackass*. I'm telling you the truth. I'm reading everything I can find on Hatshepsut to try and find a lead that hasn't been explored yet."

It was the truth. Just not the whole truth, and if Alexander were here, he'd be the first one to point that out. Ever since they'd discovered information about the rubbings Farthington's father had made at Hatshepsut's tomb, they'd focused their attention on the viscount's activities. For the past several weeks, Alexander and Sarah had also been doing a great deal of reading. But not even Alexander knew about the most recent evidence she and Sarah had stumbled upon two days ago.

When Lady Harding had visited the dressmaker's shop for a new gown, Sarah had joined Anna in accompanying the viscountess. While Sebastian's mother was being measured for her new gown, Anna and Sarah had sat down near the fitting rooms to chat.

They'd barely settled in their chairs when they'd overheard Lady Farthington bemoaning her husband's obsession with an ancient Egyptian pharaoh. The woman had complained that he was even planning on hosting a party to unwrap a mummy he'd recently acquired.

Another woman had murmured words of comfort as Lady Farthington continued with her lament about Lord Cookham and '*that woman*' of leading her husband astray. But it was the mention of the unnamed woman she and Anna had found so intriguing.

Lady Farthington's contemptuous tone had emphasized her intense dislike of the woman, which might signal the viscount was possibly involved in a liaison. Although it didn't prove Farthington was the high priest in the cult, it was a start. Her gaze met Sebastian's again as she considered telling him about Lady Farthington's remarks. Anna chose not to as the scowl on his face made her realize expanding on the extent of her investigation would only incense him that much more.

§ § §

"And if you *did* find something worth investigating, who would you tell?" The harsh, brutal note in his voice dangled in the air between them as they glared at each other. Anna shrugged.

"Since most things need to be followed up with more research, there wouldn't be anything to tell anyone." Her reply was as nonchalant as her shrug, and it only fed the angry tension between them.

"You're dodging the question, which is *far* from reassuring," Sebastian snarled as something close to fear surged through him. The woman seemed oblivious to the danger she was in. As she narrowed her gaze on him, her glare became one of condemnation and fury.

"Why? Because you think I'm a fool, or because you think a woman isn't capable of understanding something so complicated as a police investigation?"

"I did *not* say that," he bit out between clenched teeth.

Sebastian stared at Anna with increasing frustration at her stubbornness. The woman confounded him. It was exactly why he'd not ventured near her for the past several weeks. One moment, she was inflicting mayhem on his senses. The next, she was the prosecution, grilling him as if he was a defendant on the witness stand. God help him if she ever found out he'd refused to allow the Home Secretary to use her as bait. He had no doubt she would be a tigress, ready to rip him to shreds for having made an arbitrary decision where she was concerned.

"But you're not denying it, you *pompous* ass." Her offensive language was compounded by one word, and Sebastian quickly closed the distance between them and leaned forward in a deliberate act of intimidation.

"I am *not* pompous," he bit out between clenched teeth as he scowled at her with indignation. "And someone needs to wash your mouth out with soap."

"Well, it *won't* be you, Lord Boringly *Pompous*."

This time, the insult she flung at him stung that much more. Sebastian immediately jerked back to straighten to his full height and remained frozen where he stood as he fought to control his fury at having been derided a second time. Suddenly, Anna uttered a wordless sound of disgust and turned away to stare out the window. Her shoulders slumped slightly as she bowed her head.

"I'm sorry. That was incredibly rude of me. You and your mother have been nothing but kind." The defeat in her voice made Sebastian's mouth tug to one side in a grimace of resignation.

"You're forgiven," he murmured. "And I do *not* believe you're a fool."

"But you *do* think it's improper and unbecoming for a woman to involve herself in a matter no one would question a man doing."

The quiet statement was flat and unemotional as she turned to face him. Sebastian frowned as he contemplated her question. It was one he'd never considered before, simply because he'd never met any other woman like Anna. They barely knew each other, and yet for some unknown reason, it was as if he'd known her a long time.

Her actions and words had already defined her as loyal, caring, determined, brave, well-educated, and more intelligent than most of the women he'd met in the Set. Everything about her declared her to be someone of excellent character. But she wasn't asking what he thought of her.

She wanted to know if he thought it proper for a woman to do a job reserved for men. Sebastian placed his hands behind his back, his fingers wrapping tightly around his wrist. It was a valid question, and he knew his answer would not make her happy—no matter what the reason.

"Well, my lord?"

"While I do not deny there are women who show a propensity to excel at jobs reserved for men, I do not believe all those roles are suitable for a woman." He eyed her steadily. "Some positions are dangerous enough for a man, let alone a woman, no matter how intelligent she is."

Disappointment suddenly darkened her brown eyes as she stared at him in silence. It was as if she'd tested him on an issue of great importance, and he'd failed. Sebastian didn't enjoy the way it made him feel. With a shake of her head, Anna inhaled and quickly exhaled a deep breath of air, then turned toward the couch she'd been moving when he'd first entered the salon.

The thick book lying on the sofa reminded him of the one she'd been reading several weeks ago. It was proof he wouldn't be able to convince her to stop reading more about the cult. Although she'd been emphatic in her statement that she wouldn't do something foolish, he was still worried for her safety. Deeply worried.

It was why Captain Wentworth and he had agreed to expand the number of men guarding Anna and Sarah. The problem was whether she would realize they'd increased security measures. He knew Anna well enough by now to believe she could easily lose someone tracking her movements. Sebastian drew in a deep breath.

"If you do find something of interest in your reading, will you give me your word that you'll tell me what you find *before* you think to act on it?"

At his quiet question, she jerked her head toward him. Their gazes locked, and as the silence stretched out between them, his hope that she would agree to his request began to fade. Suddenly, she released a heavy sigh.

"Yes." There was a great deal of reluctance in her voice, but her answer filled him with relief. Although he was certain she would likely regret her agreement, somehow he knew she would honor his request.

"Thank you," he said with relief. Sebastian turned to leave the room, then stopped. "And have George or John move the couch for you."

With that, he left the salon as quickly as he could. He was in deep water where Anna Sawyer was concerned, and he didn't know how to save himself.

Chapter 19

Anna turned her head to survey the packed ballroom. She'd seen sardines in nets that weren't packed together as tightly as the throng collected in the Farthington's ballroom tonight. It wasn't a small room by any means, which only made the crowded room feel even more overwhelming. It was as if everyone in the Marlborough Set had accepted the invitation to the ball.

She flinched as a woman standing nearby laughed at something her companion had said. It was a twittering sound she'd come to hate because Lady Margaret always laughed the same way. Anna gritted her teeth at the thought of the woman. Lately she'd been hearing rumors that Sebastian was on the verge of proposing to Lady Margaret, and she hated how it made her feel every time someone mentioned it.

Lady Harding was right, the woman would never make him happy. But she wasn't sure who could. The sudden sound of someone calling her name pushed through her thoughts, and Anna turned toward the voice. The sight of Charlotte Plummer pushing her way through the crowd made Anna smile.

The two of them had struck up a conversation about the Rosetta Stone the day Sebastian had taken her to the museum. When they'd crossed paths several weeks later at one of the soirée's she'd attended, Anna had been hesitant to say more than a couple of polite words to Charlotte, knowing she was Lady Margaret's niece.

But when the two of them had met by chance at the museum several days later, they'd struck up a conversation about Egyptian and Roman history. Charlotte was nothing like her aunt, which had been Anna's biggest concern. Since their second meeting, the two of them had become good friends.

Outgoing and quite pleasant, Charlotte's love of history was as avid as Anna's, and it made the young woman easy to talk to. Lady Margaret was never mentioned when the two of them spoke. A fact for which Anna was grateful because she was certain she'd not be able to keep from saying something rude about Charlotte's aunt.

While her friend had never said anything derogatory about her aunt, Anna had seen Charlotte's eyes flash with annoyance whenever Lady Margaret arrogantly gestured for her niece to remove herself from Anna's presence. A wide smile on her sweet face, Charlotte came to a halt in front of her and immediately kissed Anna on the cheek. She then stepped back to eye Anna with a mischievously critical glance before laughing.

"Perfect, as always. I so admire your ability to wear such rich colors." Charlotte stared down at her own gown with a woebegone look. "I hate wearing all these pastels Aunt Margaret insists I wear."

Anna winced at her friend's observation, and Charlotte shook her head with disgust.

"There's no need to say a word. I know exactly why Aunt Margaret makes me wear such unflattering dresses. She doesn't want anyone to know I'm much older than she says." Anger flared in the young woman's eyes as she looked across the room. With a shake of her head, Charlotte leaned forward and lowered her voice. "I know she's my aunt, but he's far too nice for her."

Following her friend's gaze, Anna glanced over her shoulder to see Sebastian and Lady Margaret standing with the usual group of friends the woman was always with. Anna rolled her eyes as she turned back to her friend, surprised to see Charlotte studying her with an assessment.

"What?" Anna arched her eyebrow in puzzlement.

"Nothing. Well, it's just that for a second you looked at Lord Starling as if you were upset he was with Aunt Margaret." The observation made Anna draw in a sharp breath of amazement as she stared at her friend in open-mouthed astonishment. Charlotte shrugged. "Don't look so surprised. I'm your friend. I notice things most people don't see, but there's something between the two of you."

"Don't be ridiculous," Anna scoffed with a laugh as she shook her head. "If anything, Lord Starling is constantly appalled by my lack of decorum. We aren't in the same room together for two minutes before we're arguing about something."

"I don't know," Charlotte's voice and expression revealed her deep skepticism. "I think you might not realize how you look at him."

The young woman's words made Anna stare at her in horror. Dear God, was that why Sebastian had stayed as far away from her as he could? Did he think she had feelings for him and was embarrassed by the fact? Anna's heart began to race as she remembered how on more than one occasion, she'd practically begged for him to kiss her.

"I think you're mistaking my irritation at his constant association with your aunt as something more than what it is. I agree your aunt won't make him happy. So does his mother and others. But there's nothing between us," Anna said firmly.

She wasn't sure who she was trying to convince, her friend or herself. In the back of her head, a small voice tried to suggest something different. She quickly pushed the thought into the deep recesses of her mind.

"Well, if I noticed it, someone else might too." Charlotte said with a concerned look before she glanced over Anna's shoulder again, and her mouth tightened with annoyance. "Oh for heaven's sake, must she always make me dance with that decrepit old man?"

"Who?"

"Farthington." Charlotte expelled a harsh breath of disgust. "He thinks himself a connoisseur when it comes to ancient Egypt and Roman cultures. If I have to listen to one more minute of his plans to visit some tomb in Egypt at the end of the season, I think I will be ill."

"He's going to Egypt?" Anna's eyes widened at Charlotte's statement, and excitement rushed through her.

"Yes, he has some special map he's using to plan his expedition. I think he mentioned something about a place called the Northern Monastery." Charlotte released a soft snort of antipathy. "At least he won't be here to ask me to dance. If he wasn't already married, I think he'd make an offer."

"Then it's fortunate the man is most definitely unavailable," Anna said with a grin as she struggled to suppress her exhilaration. She'd been right. The rubbings had to be here, and she was determined to find them.

"You're correct. I really must go, or there will be the devil to pay on the way home." Charlotte squeezed Anna's hands and started to move away, then paused in mid-step. "Are we still meeting at the museum tomorrow night for Professor Stanley's presentation on how the Romans conquered Egypt?"

"I wouldn't miss it. Sarah and Alexander asked to join us as well." A smile of delight curved Charlotte's lips.

"Oh yes, I would love for them to come with us. I enjoyed meeting them last week while riding in the park, and I would love to become better acquainted." Another glance in Lady Margaret's direction made Charlotte release an incoherent sound of irritation. "Until tomorrow evening, then."

With another squeeze of her hand, Charlotte disappeared into the crowd. Across the ballroom, Anna spotted Sarah standing beside her mother, while Alexander was engaged in a cheerful conversation with her father. Careful not to act overly excited, she waved to her friend, but Sarah didn't see her. With a noise of frustration, Anna rapidly tapped her fan against her palm as she tried to relax. Supper would be announced soon, and she needed to keep her wits about her.

After almost two weeks of cajoling, Sarah had finally agreed to Anna's plan to search Farthington's study tonight. Several days ago, her friend had bribed one of Farthington's maids to tell her where all the rooms were in the house. The maid had done better than that. The woman had drawn a crude outline of the house's interior.

When they'd had a moment to review the map, she and Sarah had put their heads together to plan when Anna would leave the ballroom to search the viscount's study. The study was on the second floor of the house, and the maid had told Sarah two of the study's windows overlooked a small garden with a tall hedge separating the grounds and the mews.

Anna had insisted she search the viscount's study alone while Sarah waited below in the garden as a precautionary measure. When Sarah had protested, Anna reminded her there was a reason they'd not told Alexander about their plan, because they knew he would do whatever it took to stop them.

She'd also stressed that if Sarah did anything other than wait for Anna in the garden, it could easily cause a rift between her and Alexander. If Anna was caught, then only one of them would be involved in the scandal that would surely follow. Anna had made it clear she had nothing to lose, but Sarah did.

Her mind reviewed the map of the house she'd memorized. It had been a stroke of luck to learn that the ladies retiring chamber was on the second floor, which would make leaving the ballroom that much easier. Anna tipped her head to one side to see if she could catch Sarah's attention again, but she was laughing at something her father had said to Alexander.

Patience. She needed to have patience. If Uncle Charles was here, he would chastise her for allowing her excitement to control her actions. No, if her uncle was here, he'd be dragging her back to Starling House and locking her in her room. But he wasn't here, and Charlotte had just confirmed Farthington had the rubbings. She had to find them. Closing her eyes for a moment, she forced herself to take a deep breath, then slowly release it.

When she looked out at the ballroom again, her gaze involuntary shifted to where she'd last seen Sebastian. She saw Charlotte speaking with her aunt and the Farthingtons, with Sebastian standing off to Lady Margaret's side. Antipathy swept through her as she saw Charlotte's aunt turn and say something to Sebastian. He nodded and offered the woman a half-smile before Lady Margaret turned back to the Farthingtons.

Anna started to look away when Sebastian turned his head in her direction. The moment their eyes met, the world fell away as they stared at each other from across the room. Something pulsed through her, and she remembered Charlotte's observation. With a small gulp, Anna quickly turned away, terrified Sebastian would think she was languishing away over him.

The last thing she wanted was to be a source of amusement for the man. A moment later, Lady Harding caught her attention. With a relieved sigh, Anna joined the woman, who introduced her to a young man Anna had not met before. In less than a minute, he was escorting her out onto the dance floor. While he was a pleasant companion, she found herself bored by their conversation.

As they circled the floor, she saw Sebastian standing next to his mother. Startled that he'd left Lady Margaret and her friends, she met his gaze in surprise. Anna's dance partner asked her a question, and she was forced to turn her attention back to the young man. Moments later, her partner whirled her past Sebastian, and her heart skipped a beat when she saw his attention was still pinned on her.

The dance finally ended, and when her partner guided her back to where Lady Harding stood, she thanked the young man, and he walked away with a happy grin. The viscountess was deep in conversation with one of her friends, and Anna glanced in Sebastian's direction. He was still watching her, and with a sense of trepidation, she turned toward him, determined to hear his criticism and be done with it.

"If you're finding fault with me, please share your thoughts, then leave." At her fierce tone, his brows rose in surprise before he shook his head and smiled.

"I dare any man in the room to find fault with how beautiful you look this evening."

The sincerity in his voice combined with the fire flaring in his eyes caused her heart to plummet down toward her stomach, then back into her chest, where it began to pound wildly. She dragged a deep breath into her lungs as she tried to think of a response, but failed. Still held hostage by his penetrating gaze, she swallowed hard. A small smile tipped the corners of his mouth.

"Dance with me." His soft words were a seductive caress over every part of her as he extended his hand.

She trembled slightly as her hand slipped into his, and the warmth of his hand around hers sent a pulse of electricity sliding through her. As he pulled her into his arms, Anna avoided his gaze and tried to think of something witty to say as they began to dance. The instant he pulled her close to avoid another couple, she drew in a sharp gasp. Expecting him to relax his hold on her, butterflies took flight in her stomach when he didn't expand the space between them.

"I don't think I've ever known you to go so long without having something to say." There was just a trace of amusement in his gaze, but she saw another emotion that made her mouth go dry.

"I'm still too stunned by your invitation to dance to think of anything to say." It was the truth, and the moment he smiled complacently, she wanted to box his ears.

"I didn't realize you were longing to dance with me."

"I *wasn't*, you arrogant beast." The laugh that floated out of him made Anna wish he would laugh like that much more often. It was a happy sound.

"By the way, you didn't thank me."

"What am I supposed to thank you for now?"

"For saying how lovely you look this evening."

"A few moments ago, I was beautiful." She rolled her eyes and fought back the rising tide of excitement hovering close at hand. "Now I'm simply lovely. I think you toss compliments out like pieces of candy to a child."

"Perhaps the word I should use is exquisite."

His soft words were like silk brushing across her senses, and as their gazes locked, her breathing became unsteady. Mesmerized by the emotions she saw in his eyes, the butterflies in her stomach took flight once more. The sudden increased pressure of his fingers into her back made her heartbeat race, and the sound of it echoed in her ears until it drowned out everything except his voice. A tingling sensation spread a fine net of tension across her skin, causing a small tremor to speed through her. The shudder didn't escape Sebastian's notice.

"Am I that terrifying?" A small smile of amusement

touched his beautiful mouth, and she forced herself to not be affected by it.

"I don't find you frightening at all, but you do have a strong propensity to be…pompous, which I find incredibly annoying." She bit back a smile as his hand tightened around hers, and he pulled her even closer, his dark eyes growing darker with irritation. "But you do have your good traits too, so I always forgive you once I calm down."

"I see. Tell me, what were you and Margaret's niece discussing before the girl was summoned?"

"Nothing much," Anna said as she fought not to let her excitement get the best of her as she remembered what Charlotte had told her.

"Why do I think you're prevaricating?" Suspicion furrowed his brow as he studied her intently. "You've not forgotten your promise, have you?"

"Promise?" Her reply caused Sebastian to narrow his gaze at her, and she winced. "Oh, that one."

"Yes, that promise. Whatever the young lady said appeared to have caused a great deal of excitement in you."

"What on earth makes you think that?" Startled, Anna looked into a pair of eyes that held a calculating gleam.

"Do you honestly think you can hide it when you become excited about something? You looked as if the woman had just handed you the keys to Solomon's gold mines."

Anna nibbled at her bottom lip. If she told him the truth, he would automatically assume she would try to explore Farthington's study, and he'd stop her. She couldn't let that happen. With a sigh, she looked away from him.

"She said the man is planning a trip to Egypt."

"A fact almost everyone in the Set knows. Something tells me that Miss Plummer told you something else."

"She said the man had some kind of special map."

"A special map?" The odd note in his voice made Anna

look up to see him studying her carefully.

"Yes, that's what she said. A special map."

Anna averted her gaze and stared out at the other dancers on the floor. She was dangerously close to breaking her vow to Sebastian. The thought didn't make her happy. She'd never broken her word to anyone before, and she didn't want to start now—particularly with Sebastian. If her dark angel found out, he'd never forgive her. He would see her lying to him as evidence that she couldn't be trusted.

"What else?" The demand for more information made her scowl up at him.

"That's all. She said Farthington was planning on visiting Egypt with a special map, and she mentioned something about the Northern Monastery."

"The Northern Monastery." Sebastian's speculative expression aroused her suspicion that he might know something she didn't. His penetrating gaze captured hers again. "And that's *all* she said?"

"*Yes*, that's *all* she said." Anna huffed a breath of irritation past her lips.

"And?"

"And I think the man is a member of the Hatshepsut cult."

Exasperated by his persistent questioning, she stared up at him in anger. As their gazes locked, Anna realized Sebastian didn't appear surprised by anything she'd just told him. In fact, his expression was one of contemplation. When he didn't say anything, she narrowed her gaze at him.

"*Now* who's hiding something?"

"I didn't make any promises."

"Of course you didn't, you arrogant bastard." Anna gritted her teeth at his nonchalant reply.

"I thought you were beginning to learn how to control that mouth of yours." The rebuke made Anna utter a sarcastic sound of amusement.

"I have, it's just that there's this one *pompous* ass who brings out the worst in me." She smiled as his mouth tightened into a thin line, and the devil on her shoulder urged her on. "You know the one. The man who holds women to a higher standard than himself."

"That's unfair, Anna."

"Is it?" With a haughty tilt of her chin, Anna sniffed with disdain. "All I know, my lord, is that you have done nothing but find fault with me since the day we first met."

"If I've found fault with anyone, I've found it in me." The ferocity of his statement mixed with a dark sound that rumbled out of him, startled her. "It's why I've tried everything I can think of to stay as far away from you as possible."

As his words faded, Anna stared up at him, slack jawed. Had the man just said he was attracted to her? For the briefest of moments, she thought she saw panic flash in his eyes before it vanished beneath an unreadable façade. Stunned by the revelation, she was unable to speak, and Sebastian glanced away from her.

The silence hanging between them was raw with tension, and the shoulder beneath her palm was rigid and inflexible. Despite his detached appearance, an emotion similar to jubilation unfurled inside her. Was it possible her dark angel cared for her? She tried to squelch the thought but failed. Studying his face, she silently willed him to look at her.

It did her little good, and the moment the music ended, he released Anna as if he'd been burned. Without looking at her, he offered his arm and escorted her back to Lady Harding. As they stopped on the edge of the dance floor, he bowed slightly, then wheeled about and left her staring after him as the crowd opened up and swallowed him from view.

"Anna. *Anna,* are you all right?" Sarah's voice drifted past her ears like a gentle breeze. Still dazed by Sebastian's revelation, Anna slowly turned toward her friend.

"What?" she whispered as she struggled to comprehend what had just happened.

"Whatever is the matter with you?" At Sarah's scolding, Anna stared at her friend in confusion, which made Sarah eye her with exasperation. "They're about to announce supper, and Alexander hasn't let me out of his sight most of the night. It's almost as if he knows we're up to something."

"Your intended is a smart man, because we are." Anna nodded as her wits slowly began to return.

"You can still back out. I'd not think any less of you." Sarah winced as she studied Anna with concern.

"Back—absolutely not," she said with a gasp as she remembered what Charlotte had told her. "I intend to find those rubbings."

"But we don't even know if they're real."

"They're real. Charlotte said Farthington is using them for the trip to Egypt he's planning."

"Good heavens." Sarah's soft exclamation accompanied the look of wonder on her face just as the sound of the supper gong echoed through the ballroom.

"It's time." Anna squeezed the other woman's hand. "Go now, before Alexander finds you. If he does, simply insist the two of you take a walk in the garden because it's so hot in here."

"It wouldn't be a lie." Sarah waved her fan in front of her face in obvious discomfort.

With another squeeze of her hand, Anna watched her friend make her way toward the patio doors. Looking around the room, she tried to see Sebastian or Alexander, and the fact she couldn't see them eased her mind. At least they wouldn't be able to stop her.

From a short distance away, Lady Harding waved to her, and Anna smiled in return. In silent gestures, she told the viscountess she'd join her in a moment. The supper gong sounded again, and she made her way toward the stairs.

Several people greeted her, but she merely offered a small response and continued on her way.

Anna slowly made her way through the crowd toward the house's main corridor. A glance over her shoulder revealed no sign of Sebastian or Alexander, and a small wave of relief skimmed through her. Once she was out of the ballroom and heading up the stairs, Anna drew in a deep breath of cool, fresh air. She hadn't realized until now just how hot it had been in the ballroom.

She'd visited the ladies room earlier with Sarah, simply to gain a small amount of familiarity with her surroundings. Two women emerged from the room set aside for female guests, and Anna smiled as she made a pretense of going into the refreshing room. The moment the women had their backs to her, she bypassed the room and headed toward the end of the corridor.

With a glance over her shoulder to ensure she wasn't seen, Anna turned left and hurried along the empty corridor toward her destination. When she reached the study, she paused and looked behind her before slowly opening the door just a small crack. Only a small glimmer of light illuminated the inside of the study, and no sound filled the air, reassuring her the room was unoccupied. Dragging in a deep breath, Anna quickly slipped into the room and closed the door behind her.

For a moment, she simply stood where she was as she struggled to calm her nerves. She'd expected to be nervous, but she was experiencing more than her usual share of trepidation. The low light she'd seen the moment she opened the study's door was from a fire in the hearth and gas lights that had been turned down until their flames could be extinguished with a simple breath.

"Get moving, Anna Sawyer. You don't know how much time you have," she whispered to herself.

As she bolstered her courage with her words, she moved

quickly toward the room's window. With fumbling fingers, she flipped the latch and pushed it open. Bending over the sill, she tried to see Sarah in the darkness.

"Sarah, are you there?" Anna kept her voice as quiet as she could, afraid someone else might be in the garden and look upward to see her hanging out of the window.

When her friend didn't answer, her heart sank. She was about to call out to her friend again when she heard the sound of a nightingale. Leaning out of the window a little further, she saw Sarah step out from behind a large tree and wave at her. Relief surged through her, and Anna sagged against the window's ledge.

Sarah made a vicious gesture for her to hurry, and with a grin, Anna nodded. Pulling the window inward until it was brushing against the latch, she turned and looked around the room. If she were Farthington, where would she keep delicate stone rubbings?

The man was planning an expedition. They had to be with the maps. A quick glance around the room revealed a large table that had papers scattered across the surface. Hurrying forward, she stared down at the documents that varied in size. Some were notes and drawings, while beneath the smaller papers were several navigational charts and land maps.

It only took a cursory review of a few notes to confirm Lord Farthington's destination was that of Hatshepsut's tomb. A shiver of excitement streaked down her spine. The viscount must have deciphered one of the rubbings from the woman's tomb. The question was, what had the rubbings revealed? A treasure or something far worse? Possibly a new ritual that involved more sacrifices?

Carefully sifting through the maps on top of the table, Anna made certain not to disturb their placement. When she peeked under the last chart, all she found was a brightly polished table-top.

"*Damn it*," she muttered in frustration.

All too aware she needed to work more quickly, she turned her attention to the bookshelves. Would the man have been so stupid as to have folded up the rubbings? Tonight was the first time she'd met the man. He'd seemed far from being an idiot, but she would never consider anyone who believed killing could bring them everlasting life, as exceptionally bright. Perhaps he'd rolled them up and laid them on one of the bookshelves to prevent any creases.

Hurrying toward the shelves lining the walls, she searched for anything that might have been rolled up and placed on top of a row of books. When she reached the last shelf only to find nothing, she wondered if Charlotte had heard the viscount correctly. No, the man was planning a trip to Hatshepsut's tomb. She was certain the rubbings existed, they just didn't seem to be here in the viscount's study.

Dejected at coming up empty-handed, Anna headed toward the window to alert Sarah to return to the ballroom. Her leg bumped against the side of the desk as she walked past it, and out of the corner of her eye, she saw something jutting out from beneath the furniture. In the dim light, it was difficult to make out what it was, and she hesitated to explore further.

She'd already been absent from the ballroom longer than she should have. If Sarah was gone too long, Alexander would suspect what they were up to, and he'd not hesitate to find Sebastian. There'd be hell to pay in one form or another if Sebastian were to learn what she'd done. Anna shoved the thought aside and moved quickly to where a chair had been carelessly pushed back from the large piece of furniture.

The moment she saw the leather map case leaning against the inside panel of the desk, she inhaled a quick breath of excitement. Her heart pounding madly, Anna's hands shook as she reached for the long leather tube. It almost slipped from her fingers as she pulled it out from beneath the desk.

She gasped in fear and fumbled with the case until it was clutched tightly to her breast to keep from dropping it. Even the smallest thud on the floor might cause someone in the corridor to investigate. Desperate not to alert anyone as to her presence in the study, Anna closed her eyes.

If the rubbings were in the case, now was not the time to make a mistake and be caught. She worked hard to slow her breathing, and as her tremors slowly abated, Anna examined the long container. It was identical to the map case her uncle kept his charts and maps in, and with great care, Anna popped open the latch on the case and lifted the cap from the tube.

The dim light made it impossible to see if anything was in the leather container, and she uttered an inaudible curse. Carefully tilting the tube downward, she tapped on it to dislodge any contents. The moment the thin parchment slid halfway out of the tube, a rush of exhilaration surged through her.

Holding the case up, she angled the parchment toward the firelight. If she could avoid unrolling the case's contents, it would save time. The moment she saw the ancient markings, she quickly pushed the parchment back into the container. Now she could only hope Sarah hadn't been caught and forced to leave her position.

Anna skirted the desk and hurried toward the window. Pushing it open, she looked down into the garden below. She didn't even have to call out her friend's name as Sarah stepped out from behind the tree.

With a grin of triumph, Anna held up the map case. Excitement lit up her friend's face as she hurried to stand below the window. Anna never had a chance to drop the case, as a strong hand covered her mouth, and she was tugged backward into a hard, muscular body. Fear whipped through her, and a sickening lurch took hold in her stomach. Dear

God, how was she going to explain why she was in Farthington's study, in the dark, at an open window with the map case?

"Have you *lost* your mind?"

The harsh whisper filling her ear made Anna sag in relief. Sebastian. With a vicious tug, he pulled the case from her hand and dropped it onto the desk. His grip on her arm tightened as he roughly pulled her toward a ladder-back chair a few feet from the window. In seconds, he'd sent her toppling over his hard thighs and yanked the skirt of her gown up to her waist. Breasts pinned against the outer edge of his leg and her stomach pressed deep into his lap, she struggled to comprehend what he was doing.

Was he so angry with her that he'd lost all sense of his highly prized propriety? If someone were to come in and see them like this, it would ruin her. Not that she cared— she'd be overjoyed to return to the Falcon. But for Sebastian, it would be humiliating. Worse, he might even be forced to do something far more devastating. Propose marriage. The thought of sealing her cage forever sent fear spiraling through her.

"Sebastian, please," she whispered, still cognizant of the fact that being caught in the study was dangerous for two different reasons.

Embarrassed, she wiggled against him as she tried to break free, only to have his arm press down hard into her back to hold her firmly in place. In the next breath, he tugged her drawers down off her buttocks and issued a hard smack to her bottom. Stunned, Anna stiffened with disbelief at his action. Fire settled on her buttocks, and she'd barely absorbed the fact he'd spanked her before his hand connected with her flesh again.

"*Bloody hell,*" she bit out between clenched teeth. Sebastian's hand massaged her burning flesh as he bent his head toward her.

"I ought to beat you until you can't sit down for a week." The hoarse words in her ear sent her pulse spiraling out of control as she enjoyed the way his fingers lightly massaged the spot where he'd spanked her.

It eased the burning sensation, and she relaxed slightly against him. As his fingers stopped massaging her flesh, she murmured a protest that became a sharp inhalation as his hand slid down toward her inner thighs before he stopped.

With a guttural sound, he yanked her drawers back over her bottom, dropped her skirts, then flipped her over in his lap. His expression startled her. He looked almost as if he was in pain. His eyes were closed, and his throat bobbed as if he was having difficulty swallowing. The instant he met her gaze, her heart slammed to a halt in her chest at the desire blazing in his dark eyes. Another rumble of sound rolled past his lips as he pulled her toward him and kissed her.

Chapter 20

Anna's lips were hot and sweet against his. Christ Jesus, he'd never wanted to devour a woman before, like he did her. He wanted to explore every inch of her with his mouth. He wanted to savor the sweet heat of her skin against his as he taught her what the ultimate pleasure felt like. Need barreled through him as his cock stiffened beneath her bottom. He wanted to drive his body into hers until they were both spent.

Even then, he knew he would need to take her over and over again, if he thought to free himself of this invisible hold she had on him. The instant her teeth gently tugged at his bottom lip, he grunted with surprise. Her tongue quickly slipped into his mouth and swirled around his. Teasing and tantalizing, she was a seductress wrapped in innocence as she responded to him with an eagerness that sent his heart crashing into his chest.

The soft scent of jasmine filled his nostrils. Caught up in the delicious heat of her tongue against his, he plundered her mouth with a need he feared would be his undoing. Her arms wrapped around his neck, and her fingertips stroked his neck with the same light finesse she'd done at Sheringham's ball. It sent a shudder through him.

God help him. What was he doing? With a jerk, he lifted his head and stared down at her. The smile curving Anna's lips as she met his gaze, tightened his insides. It was the call of a siren. For a moment, his body tried to control his brain as he considered answering the call, then sanity returned. He was a fool for allowing himself to lose control.

An alarm sounded in the back of his head. Voices. They were close. If someone caught them together, especially in Anna's state of déshabillé, her reputation would be destroyed. In the back of his head, a voice urged him to simply let it happen, but he ignored the whisper threatening to destroy the plan he'd mapped out for his future. Roughly setting her on her feet, he remembered the map case he'd dropped on top of the desk.

"Where did you find this?" His harsh whisper made her eyes widen.

"Under the desk, but we need to take—"

"*Don't* be a fool."

Obviously stunned by his savage response, she stared at him with her mouth parted in surprise. He quickly placed the cylindrical case back underneath the desk. The voices were growing louder now, and Anna glanced over her shoulder.

"*Bloody hell.* We'll have to jump." Panic echoed in her soft whisper as she rushed to the window that was still open. She leaned over the sill and made a gesture as if shooing someone away. Sebastian pulled her back from the window and looked out to see Sarah hurrying away into the darkness. As he assessed the distance to the ground, Sebastian drew in a sharp hiss of air as he realized Anna might get hurt if he made her jump from the window.

Sebastian turned his head to see her frantically pulling her skirts up over her hips. Anna glanced over her shoulder at the door once more, then stepped toward the window. Even if he'd not already realized they had no choice but to jump, Anna had already made the decision for him. One hand holding her skirts high off her legs, she accepted the hand he offered her. Lithe and supple in her movements, Anna jumped up onto the windowsill with his help. Her hand still in his, she tugged him toward her.

"You're coming too, aren't you?"

Fear swept across her lovely face as she studied him with a look of deep concern. Her worry for his safety, shot a bolt of exultation through him before he shoved it aside. Once again, his brain argued with his body. She looked delightfully kissable. It would be so easy to damn the consequences, tug her off the windowsill, and kiss her without caring who found them together. With a grunt of anger at his inability to stay focused on the approaching danger, he glared at her.

"I *can't* do that if you're *standing* in the way," he snarled. "Now *jump*."

Anna turned away from him and did as he ordered. Leaning over the windowsill, Sebastian watched as she came upright and lifted her head to stare at him. Why it didn't surprise him that she managed to land like a cat, he didn't know. Behind him, the voices were right outside the study, and he quickly jumped up onto the windowsill.

He was about to jump when he realized the open window would be a problem. Without hesitating, he sidled to the left of the window and closed it gently until he heard the soft snap of the latch falling into place.

Sebastian heard Farthington's voice through the glass panes of the window, followed by a softer, feminine voice. There was something familiar about it, but he couldn't place it. Sebastian remained still for a moment as he waited for the woman to speak again. The silence didn't last for long as Farthington began boasting as the man always did.

"*Poseidon's balls*, will you please jump." The urgency in Anna's whisper drifted upward.

It wasn't a plea he intended to ignore, and a second later, he landed hard on the ground a few feet away from her. The moment Sebastian stood up, he swallowed a cry of pain and almost fell to the ground as a ring of fire wrapped itself around his ankle.

"*Sweet mother of God*," he rasped softly. Anna was immediately at his side, and with her arm wrapped around his waist, she helped him stand up.

"Lean on me."

The quiet command filtered its way through his pain, and he jerked his head in a sharp nod. In seconds, Anna had helped him limp into the shadows, and the two of them pushed their way through the tall hedge that separated the garden from the stable yard. The yard was dark, with only a single light shining out of the stable. Inside, there was the low sound of laughter and voices. Sebastian hobbled to a halt before Anna pointed to a hitching post.

"I don't see a bench, but the hitching post will be easier than you leaning against a tree." Without waiting for his agreement, Anna urged him to hop to the long rail used to tie horses to. As his hips pressed into the hard pole, Anna touched his arm.

"Stay here." As she began to turn away from him, Sebastian's hand shot out to grab her arm and tug her into his side.

"Where the devil do you think you're going?"

"To find Sarah."

"Looking like that?" he bit out between clenched teeth as he looked her up and down. "What if someone sees you?"

Even despite the fiery throb of his ankle, it was impossible to miss how disheveled she looked. He grimaced as he noted the heightened color in her cheeks, and the way her lips were plump and rosy from his kisses. She had the appearance of a woman who'd just been seduced by a scoundrel. Sebastian almost groaned at the thought. In every respect but one, it was exactly what had happened. He'd seduced her.

It didn't matter that he'd not completed his seduction by embedding himself inside her. And God help him, he'd wanted desperately to have her straddle him. His entire body had ached to have her sheath his cock and ride him until she shattered around him. The memory of how he'd smacked her sweetly curved bottom, then almost stroked her sex made him grit his teeth. Anna glared back at him.

"I am not a complete fool. Sarah and I agreed to meet up at the garden entrance if something went wrong, which clearly it did." For the first time, her low voice held a hard note of anger. "Besides, I wouldn't *look* like this if you hadn't taken it upon yourself to *hunt* me down in Farthington's study."

"Be grateful I *did* hunt you down. Where would you be right now if I'd not caught you?"

"I'd be on my way down to supper." Anna broke free of his grip and planted her hands on her hips. "Instead, I'm standing in Farthington's stable yard with a man who's as hardheaded as a plank of wood."

"And I wouldn't be half-sitting on a hitching post in pain if you'd not decided to venture into harm's way," he snarled. Regret darkened her gaze as she stepped into him.

"I'm sorry you're hurt, Sebastian."

Her whisper was a warm sultry breeze across his face as Anna's hands cupped his face. Before he could stop her, she kissed him. It was a light caress that wasn't meant to arouse him, but it ignited a fire that demanded to be quenched. Without thinking, he pulled her into his arms and deepened their kiss. As their tongues tangled in an erotic dance, he heard the small mewl she made, and his cock was hard in seconds.

She pressed her body deeper into his, and he welcomed her without even considering the ramifications. One hand slid up over her waist to cup her breast, and beneath his thumb he felt her hard nipple. Circling the stiff peak, he broke off their kiss, and his lips glided across her silky skin, then down the side of her throat. The moment his tongue found the valley between her breasts, she drew in a soft breath of surprise, then released it in a low moan of delight.

A soft arm wrapped its way around his neck, and the moment her hand brushed across his erection, he jerked. There wasn't the slightest hesitation in her movements as she stroked him through his trousers. He knew he should stop her, but he couldn't.

Instead, his hands moved up over her back to the top of her gown, where he undid the first few buttons. The moment her bodice was loose, he roughly tugged it downward to reach the nipple jutting out over the top of her corset. Taking her into his mouth, he heard her sharp gasp of pleasure.

Lost in the exotic scent and taste of her, his teeth abraded the hard peak of her breast. A low cry escaped her, and the sound made him tend to the other breast. His tongue circled and flicked over a hard nipple while his fingers gently tweaked and pulled on the other.

He didn't know how or when she'd undone his trousers, but the moment his cock was in her hand, he shuddered at the sensation of her fingers wrapped firmly around him. Need pulled a groan out of him as the white-hot heat of her touch brought him to the edge of something he didn't want to acknowledge. With a skill that surprised him, she tightened her fingers to slide her hand up and down the length of him in leisurely strokes.

Desire crashed through him like a raging bull, and as he continued to nip at her breasts, he tugged her skirt upward. Blind to everything except the urgent need to touch her, his hand slid across her thigh to part the soft linen of her underwear. Just as he'd imagined almost every night in his bed as he'd pumped his cock with his hand, she was slick with a silky, wet heat.

Another gasp escaped her as his fingers parted her slick folds to find the small bud at the heart of her. The soft sound of pleasure she released heightened the strength of his need for her, and he pressed one, then two fingers up into her while thrumming the plump nub of flesh with his thumb. Small sobs rolled past her lips as he teased and played with her. Exhilaration pounded its way through him at her response.

Christ Jesus, he wanted to drive his body into hers. The muscles of her snug, slick passage flexed against his fingers, while a small shudder rocked her body as she moaned and jerked against his hand. Another hard tremor shook her, and her soft cry began to grow in strength. With his free hand, he caught her by the back of her neck and tugged her head downward to drive his tongue into the heat of her mouth, smothering the wild cry of her climax.

Even despite experiencing her own pleasure, her hand continued to stroke his cock with increased speed, and he knew he was close. He jerked against her caress as her fingers tightened around him. In the back of his mind, he tried to remember where his handkerchief was to contain his seed.

Soft linen brushed against his cock as her hand pumped him even harder. Somewhere in the back of his mind, he noted how she milked him with the practiced ease of a courtesan. She was the consummate mixture of innocence and carnal knowledge.

It was a fleeting thought as her hot strokes around his cock drove every thought from his head. Suddenly, his body stiffened, and with a hard jerk, he spilled his seed into the linen of her undergarments. Just as he had her, she swallowed his shout of release with her mouth, as he throbbed violently in her hand. Slowly, her fingers eased their pressure until she released him completely. Her mouth left his, and her head fell forward until her forehead was pressed into his shoulder. Harsh, ragged breathing echoed out of her to mix with his own deep breaths of release.

Slowly, his mind began to clear, and with a growing lucidity, he realized the depth of his error in judgement. He'd sullied her. He'd lost control, and touched her in a way no man except her husband should. Sebastian yanked his hand away from her, then savagely tugged her skirt downward.

In silence, he pushed her away from him to adjust her bodice. Soft fingers brushed across his as she finished restoring her appearance. What the devil had he been thinking? Why in hell hadn't he stopped things from going so far? Thank God, he'd not lifted her up and thrust into her while lost in the blind haze of lust.

The realization that he'd also given her the expectation of something more than he could ever feel or even offer made his gut twist with a sickening violence. Deep in his brain, a whisper condemned him for the lie. Grimly, he turned her around, his fingers fumbling slightly as he buttoned her gown. When he dropped his hands, she faced him with a shy smile before she quickly bent her head and kissed him deeply. It held the same power as a hard punch from a sparring partner delivered in the ring. Frozen in place, he didn't move as she lifted her head.

"That was wonderful."

Soft and sweet, a siren's voice could not have sounded any more sultry as she smiled at him. Even the look she gave him echoed with a power of a seductress. Sebastian cleared his throat, but before he could say anything. Anna squeezed his hand.

"Sarah is waiting for me, and I'm sure she's worried sick. She can get Alexander to send the carriage to the mews. I'll be right back."

Anna studied him with a worried frown as his only reply was a hard nod of understanding. When she didn't move, he eyed her fiercely and jerked his head hard in a silent order for her to go find his future sister-in-law. With one last look at him, Anna turned and hurried away. The moment she vanished into the darkness, Sebastian bowed his head. Angered by his stupidity, a fierce growl of self-disgust rolled out of him.

"*Fuck*," he snarled as he slammed the bottom of his fist into the hitching post.

The irony of his verbal expression of anger didn't escape him. If Anna had heard him, she would have used it against him every time he chastised her for cursing. Slumping forward, Sebastian braced his hands against his knees. Eyes closed, he released a groan of self-disgust. Anna hadn't lost her mind. He had. Never in his life had he ever made such an egregious error as he had a moment ago.

A mistake that had implications so damning, he wasn't sure what to do. He'd allowed his desire for Anna to throw his well-ordered plans for his future into a complete state of disarray. It was an intolerable situation, and he couldn't let it continue. He had to find a way out of this mess. The problem was, he didn't know where to start. He'd only compounded his mistake by bringing her to a climax moments ago.

Now, he didn't know how to explain that what had happened between them wasn't a declaration of anything except lust. Nothing more. The voices in his head cackled madly at his rationale. Objecting to the sound, Sebastian grunted in anger and silenced the mocking laughter with a crushing blow. Damnation, he'd made a mess of things.

After his dance with Anna, he'd made it a priority to keep an eye on her. There had been something about her responses when he'd queried her that had made him believe she'd not told him everything she knew.

From a distance, he'd seen her talking excitedly with Sarah. Her excitement had been restrained, but it was the animated expression on her lovely face that had made him certain she'd not told him everything when they'd danced.

When his future sister-in-law had left Anna's side and headed toward the doors leading out into the gardens, Sebastian had been puzzled as to what the two women were up to. He'd been distracted enough by Sarah's departure that when he'd turned back to where Anna had been, she was gone. It was at that moment he'd realized Anna had deduced the special map Farthington had was really the rubbings.

In the three months since Sebastian and Nicholas had begun working with the commissioner, with Lord Asquith's agreement, Farthington had become the center of their investigation. Neither Sebastian nor Nicholas had an extensive knowledge about Egyptology, and they'd gone to Budge at the British Museum with their questions. As Keeper of Egyptian Antiquities, the man had been happy to help.

Budge had provided them with a plethora of information for them to plow through. There was little about Hatshepsut in the documents, but they'd stumbled onto a report that had detailed an expedition Farthington's father had taken with the Earl of Cookham to Hatshepsut's tomb.

As they'd continued to devote more time to tracking the viscount's movements, he and Nicholas had made it a point to always take a seat near wherever Farthington was seated in the club. Two weeks ago, they'd heard the man bragging to friends about a collection of rubbings his father had made at the ancient pharaoh's tomb.

The fact that the viscount was planning an expedition to Hatshepsut's tomb in the next six months, along with his boasts about a great treasure, had strengthened their suspicions about the man. The problem was, it wasn't until tonight that he'd realized Anna knew just as much about Farthington as he and Nicholas did.

If he'd not stopped Anna from dropping that map case to Sarah, things would be even worse than they were at the moment. Either the man wasn't a cult member, or he believed himself free of any suspicion. The likely answer was that Farthington believed himself untouchable. But Sebastian found it difficult to see the man as a leader of the cult. As Anna had said more than a week ago, it would be difficult to link a peer to the human sacrifices uncovered by Alexander's bride-to-be.

Farthington wasn't without a brain, but the viscount didn't have the amount of cunning one would expect the cult's leader to have. The man was a follower, not a leader. But as a member of the cult, Farthington would know who Anna and Sarah were. He wouldn't hesitate to suspect the two when he discovered the rubbings had gone missing.

According to police reports and Alexander's confirmation, any follower of Hatshepsut would recognize them from that night they'd escaped certain death. The minute Farthington had discovered the rubbings were missing, the viscount would have immediately suspected the two women.

Sebastian released a harsh breath of anger at Anna's failure to think things through. It wasn't like her to make that kind of mistake. He should have kept a closer eye on her. Instead, he'd stayed away from her as far as he could. The memory of what had happened in Farthington's study a short time ago was the perfect example of his reasons for keeping his distance from her.

He'd been right that he should have paddled Anna until she couldn't sit for a week. Another oath of disgust escaped him as he remembered the way he'd exposed her beautiful, plump buttocks to spank her. He'd barely managed to keep from delving into her heat. The only thing that had prevented him, had been the knowledge that they might have been caught, but God help him, he'd ached to explore her heat. It was why he'd been unable to resist her when she'd kissed him.

He'd needed to ease some of his hunger for her, but it hadn't. It had simply intensified his desire. A passion that had exploded out of control only a few moments ago as he'd touched her in a way only her husband should.

The quiet echo of voices fluttered out of the darkness, and Sebastian jerked his head up. He had no idea what he was going to say if another guest were to stride into the stable yard. The sudden sight of Anna hurrying toward him with Nicholas close on her heels sent relief surging through him. Anna reached him first, and she offered him a smile of encouragement.

"Alexander saw Nicholas and sent him with me, while he and Sarah come around in the carriage." Her fingertips lightly brushed across his cheek in a tender gesture, and he stiffened as his friend's eyebrows shot upward in surprise.

"We need to get you into the mews before Alexander arrives with the carriage," Nicholas's voice was quiet as he moved forward to help Sebastian to his feet. "The last thing we need is for a stable hand to be able to identify any of us."

Sebastian nodded with understanding as he accepted Nicholas's assistance in crossing the stable yard. They had just reached the mews when he saw his carriage rolling toward them, with his brother seated next to the coachman. Alexander said something to the driver, and the vehicle halted a short distance from where Farthington's stable yard opened into the narrow alley. Nicholas instructed Sebastian's brother and the two women to enter the vehicle first.

"I had Alexander summon my carriage. I'll follow shortly."

Sebastian's mouth tightened as he bobbed his head in an abrupt acknowledgement of his friend's explanation. In silence, Nicholas cupped Sebastian's elbow to assist him into the carriage. To his dismay, the only seat available was the one next to Anna. With a grunt, he threw himself down into the seat next to her. Instantly, his body was on fire, and his jaw clenched at his inability to control the desire surging through him.

"Aren't you coming, Nicholas?"

At Anna's question, Sebastian slowly turned his head toward her. Since when had she become on a first-name basis with his friend? As he scowled at her, a flush filled her cheeks before an almost shy smile curved her tempting lips. God almighty, she'd assumed he was jealous. A second later, he realized she was right as he fought back the urge to leap out of the carriage and pummel Nicholas to the ground for even looking at Anna.

"Someone needs to offer up an explanation to Lady Harding. I'll make your excuses to her and anyone else who questions your whereabouts."

Sebastian turned back to his friend as Nicholas closed the door. A small smile tugged at the other man's mouth as he met Sebastian's glare. Slapping his hand on the side of the carriage, Nicholas ordered the driver to move on. The moment the carriage rocked forward, Sebastian released a quiet sigh of relief. At least they'd managed to avoid a major scandal tonight, but it changed nothing about his current situation. Across from him, Alexander eyed him with curiosity.

"How did you hurt your ankle, Bash?"

"I jumped out of a window to avoid being caught by Farthington in his study."

Sebastian didn't look at Anna for fear of lashing out at her. If there was one thing he was willing to admit, it was that he shouldered much of the blame for not dragging Anna out of the study the instant he pulled her back from the window.

"*Farthington's study*. What the devil were you doing in there?" Alexander stared at his brother in amazement.

"I was trying to prevent *someone* from being caught red-handed by the viscount." Sebastian didn't look in Anna's direction, but he heard her make a small sound of irritation. Alexander's gaze jumped back and forth between Sebastian and Anna before he abruptly jerked his head toward his bride-to-be.

"Did you know about this, Sarah Elizabeth Trafford?" The anger in Alexander's voice made his betrothed flinch.

"She had nothing to do with it. It was my idea to search the viscount's study." At Anna's defense of his future sister-in-law, Sebastian's jaw clenched in anger. Across from him, Alexander leaned toward Anna, his face harsh with anger.

"An idea we all concurred was *far* too risky. You agreed to simply encourage him to talk in the hope he'd reveal something. Even Sarah knew searching the man's study was too dangerous." Alexander's comment sent a jolt through Sebastian. He uttered a sound of anger as he narrowed his gaze at his brother.

"Do you mean to tell me you *knew* what she'd proposed to do? You *knew*, and you didn't think it wise to inform me. And what the devil do you mean by we?"

This time, it was Alexander's turn to look uncomfortable. Clearing his throat, his brother shot a look in first Sarah's direction and then Anna's.

"We've been searching for clues that might lead us to the leaders of the Hatshepsut cult."

"*Christ Almighty*," he snarled with outrage at his brother's actions. "You let the two of them convince you to do that?"

"What would you have suggested?" Alexander bit out in a defensive tone. "Let them do it on their own without knowing what they were doing—"

"Did you know about Anna's plans this evening?"

"*No*, and if I had, I would have put an end to it before she could follow through with her ill-advised plan." Alexander scowled at the two women.

"I am not a child, and I took precautions." Anna's reaction was swift, and anger made her words fierce and sharp. "I would not have searched Lord Farthington's study if I had thought I would be discovered."

"But you *were* discovered." Sebastian jerked his head toward her and narrowed his gaze at her with restrained fury.

"And if you'd not stopped me, I would have been able to show you the rubbings."

"*Stolen* rubbings. If Farthington had learned you'd taken them, either he would have seen to it you were arrested or worse. If the man *is* one of the cult's leaders, he might have killed you in his study, citing he thought you were a thief. Did you even factor *that* possibility into your plan?"

"No." Guilt and remorse made her soft, single word reply all the more alarming.

"What happened tonight would *never* have happened if you'd not searched Farthington's study. *None* of it. Worse than that, you gave me your word you would tell me if you found something. But you didn't do that, did you?"

Even Sebastian heard the brutally caustic note in his voice as he eyed her with severity. Beneath his icy look, she paled, and Sebastian was certain she understood his reference to what had happened between them in Farthington's study and stable yard. Whatever she'd been poised to say never crossed her lips.

With a chastened look, she turned away to stare out the window. Sebastian looked at his brother, who was studying him in bewilderment. Sebastian ignored his brother's expression as he rested his head back against the squabs of the seat and closed his eyes. Damnation.

While her plan might have been reasonably sound, she'd not planned for every contingency. The thought scared the hell out of him. He needed time to think, and he couldn't do that with Anna in the same house.

No matter how badly his ankle hurt, he was leaving for Birchwood first thing in the morning. He'd already made one disastrous miscalculation where Anna was concerned. He couldn't afford to make another, and God help him, he wanted to make one mistake after another with her. The more distance between them, the better. Any further delay would be far too dangerous.

Chapter 21

Anna stood in the foyer beside Lady Harding as the two of them watched Nicholas and Alexander help Sebastian into the house. They tried to take him upstairs to his room, but he adamantly declared he would spend the night in his study. Guilt swept through her as she realized she was responsible for his injury.

He'd followed her to Lord Farthington's study to keep her from being discovered by the viscount. The end result was his being forced to jump from a second-story window. If she wasn't fully aware of her folly, she might have blamed their near discovery on Sebastian. Anna bent her head at the memory of Sebastian spanking her, then turning her over in his lap and kissing her until she was incapable of clear thought. Heat spun its way through her at the memory, and she shivered as her gaze focused on her dark angel's tall figure.

As the three men slowly made their way into Sebastian's private sanctuary, Hodgekiss answered the doorbell. The moment Dr. Johnson entered the foyer, Lady Harding swept forward and led him into Sebastian's study. Stunned, Anna watched her enter the room without any hesitation.

It was the first time she'd ever seen Sebastian's mother enter his study. Off to the side, she heard a small sound escape Hodgekiss. Surprise arched the man's eyebrows as he stared after the mistress of the house. An instant later, his usual imperturbable expression settled on his face again.

"What the hell are you doing in here?" Sebastian's snarl was loud enough to reach the foyer, and Anna hurried forward to stand just inside the doorway of his study.

"I summoned Dr. Johnson to examine—"

"It's a bad sprain, *and* I don't need your mothering, my lady." The vicious note in Sebastian's voice didn't even make his mother flinch.

"Do *not* argue with me, Lord Starling," Lady Harding's reply was just as sharp and strident as her son's. "You *will* allow Dr. Johnson to examine you to ensure you've not broken something. Do I *make* myself clear?"

An odd expression darkened Sebastian's face before he turned his head away from her. After a brief second of hesitation, he jerked his head in agreement to her instructions. Amazed by his acquiescence, Anna watched Nicholas and Alexander look at each other with disbelief.

"I will be in the salon, Dr. Johnson. I expect a full report—" The sound Sebastian made as he scowled up at her caused Lady Harding's mouth to thin into a stubborn and unyielding line. The intimidating expression on her face was one Anna had seen on Sebastian's features many times. It dared him to challenge his mother's edict. When he remained silent, the viscountess turned to the doctor. "I will be waiting in the salon for a report as to my son's injury when you're finished, Dr. Johnson."

Without another word, Sebastian's mother turned and walked out of the study. Sebastian's unreadable gaze followed his mother's figure as she disappeared through the doorway. A second later, Sebastian's eyes narrowed as his gaze fell on Anna.

"*Go*, Anna. There's *no need* for you to be here."

"I'm here because I want to ensure you're going to be all right."

"I *said* leave. Do your hovering with my mother. The last thing I want right now is a woman buzzing about me like a busy bee." Sebastian's snarl became a loud grunt of pain as Dr. Johnson removed the stocking from his swollen ankle. "*Christ Jesus, man.*"

"My apologies, my lord."

Tension made Anna stiffen as she met Sebastian's cold gaze. His antagonism alarmed her. What had happened to the man who'd held her in his arms such a short time ago? Was he in so much pain he couldn't bear the sight of her because his injury was her fault?

Anna remained frozen in place, staring at him in dismay. When she didn't move, his mouth thinned with anger, and an icy challenge reflected in his gaze. Instinctively, she knew she would pay a high price if she ignored his command. With difficulty, she swallowed the knot that had formed in her throat. He'd never eyed her with such antipathy or contempt.

For a moment, she considered the possibility he might not be as scornful as his outward appearance suggested. As much as she wanted to believe that was true, the cold, unemotional way he was watching her made Anna dismiss the possibility. Nicholas took a step in her direction but halted at a sharp sound of objection from Sebastian.

She saw Nicholas scowl at Sebastian before his friend's attention returned to her, but she avoided his concerned gaze. Out of the corner of her eye, she saw Alexander dart a look toward his brother, then back to her in obvious puzzlement and concern. It was obvious the two men could sense the underlying currents flowing between her and Sebastian but were uncertain what to do about it.

Anna held back a cry of pain as she turned and left Sebastian's study. In the foyer, she could hear the quiet rumble of male voices behind her but couldn't make out what they were saying. Nicholas seemed particularly angry based on the tone of his voice. Unable to hear what Sebastian's friend was saying, Anna stared at the salon doorway just a few feet away.

The last thing she wanted to do was sit in the salon with Lady Harding. The viscountess would know something was wrong. Worse, she knew she was incapable of concealing her misery. If the woman suspected even the smallest hint of what had happened tonight, there would be questions. Questions she didn't want to answer. Her senses were still too raw.

Instead of crossing the foyer to the salon, she made her way up the stairs. When she reached her bedroom, she began to undress. Lucy arrived as she was halfway done, and the girl gasped in dismay that Anna had tried to disrobe without help. Anna didn't protest as Lucy quickly set about helping her prepare for bed.

The lady's maid seemed to understand Anna had no wish to talk and worked in silence. A fact for which Anna was grateful, and several moments later the maid turned down the bedsheets, gathered the clothing resting on the floor, then left the room with a soft good night.

Sinking down onto the edge of the bed's mattress, Anna stared at the floor, trying to understand Sebastian's cold manner. Her stomach roiled as she remembered the glacial scowl, he'd pinned her with in the study. He had every right to be angry with her. She was at fault, and she'd acted foolishly, despite having planned things out.

Anna released a soft sigh of regret at her mistakes this evening. Her biggest folly had been her failure to consider all the possible outcomes when Farthington discovered the rubbings had been stolen. She'd also withheld information when she'd given Sebastian her word to tell him if she discovered something of importance. While she'd not broken her promise outright, withholding everything she knew did little to make him see her as someone he could trust.

Tomorrow she would ask his forgiveness and tell him

everything she knew. It was more than likely he would try to forbid her to continue her search for the truth. But she would make it clear that she had no intention of giving up her investigation. This time, she would promise to tell him everything before she took any actions at all.

At least he would know what her intentions were and not be forced into stopping her from acting without all points of her plan evaluated. But would she be able to help him reconcile what had happened between them tonight?

Sebastian had admitted he desired her during their dance, then proven it in Farthington's stable yard when they'd both achieved a climax simply by touching each other. The intensity of her emotions had left her shaken to the core. It had been easy to see that Sebastian had been equally shaken, but his reaction had been much different.

Her dark angel had struggled hard with the strength of his response to her and his behavior. It was the same struggle she'd seen on his face in Farthington's study just before he'd kissed her so passionately. Despite believing he needed to behave according to the rules of proper behavior, he'd done something society would deem unacceptable.

In his mind, he'd crossed a line he never should have. It didn't matter that she believed differently, what mattered was how Sebastian perceived his actions. Charlotte had been right. There *was* something between them. Sebastian had revealed that tonight while they were dancing. She had no doubts that he desired her with a craving that matched her own.

She also knew his desire was an emotion he saw as a threat to his beliefs and the proper, respectable life he'd planned out so meticulously. Anna understood some of what he had been feeling. The last few months had illustrated how she could never spend the rest of her life in London. On the Falcon she had her freedom, something she didn't have here.

Bit by bit, the constraints of propriety and expectations

of acceptable behavior were tightening the bars of her cage. Already she found herself acting with restraint when in the company of others. Whenever she was out in public, she was always careful of what she said and to act as everyone thought a lady should behave.

The idea of spending the rest of her life surrendering to the propriety Sebastian and society prized so highly was an unpleasant one. It would be impossible to live under the weight of so many rules unless Sebastian was a part of that life. Being with him would make society's expectations easier to endure. Anna inhaled a breath of horror.

Dear God, she was in love with Sebastian. How could she have been so blind as to what was happening? How could she have fallen in love with a man who disapproved of her inability to act properly? The how didn't matter.

It was a truth she couldn't deny. She'd fallen hopelessly in love with her dark angel. The realization brought with it an agony that surpassed the pain inflicted by the knife that had almost taken her life. A tear slid down her cheek as her stomach roiled from the hell she'd fallen into.

Numb with pain and shock, she began to shiver uncontrollably. It was as if someone had thrown her off the Falcon into a stormy ocean at the height of winter, leaving her to drown. Part of her wished that was true as she crawled beneath the covers and pulled them up over her.

Despite the bed coverings, Anna's shivers intensified. She felt so sick to her stomach she was afraid she might throw up what little she'd had to eat during the day. God, how she wished she'd never agreed to her uncle's request to remain at Starling House. She should have fought tooth and nail to return to the Falcon. She would have been happy there.

Desperation streaked through Anna as she wondered how much longer it would be before she received word the Falcon had docked in London again. It was impossible to do so when she could barely think straight. The one thing she was certain of now was her determination to leave Starling House as quickly as possible.

She had nowhere else to go other than Georgina's, and that would be almost as bad as her current situation. No, when the Falcon docked in London again, she would go home. She'd fulfilled her uncle's request at a cost higher than she could ever have imagined. Her only goal now was her determination to leave Starling House.

Anna prayed the Falcon would return soon, because the torment she was experiencing now was worse than the grief she'd endured at the loss of her mother or Uncle Augustus. A tear slid down her cheek, accompanied by a pain-filled sob. It was followed by another soft cry of agony, and then another. Devastated at the reality of her situation, Anna buried her face in her pillow and cried until her headrest was soaked with tears.

Hours later, the first light of dawn peeked its way through the drapes over the windows. She'd slept little as tears had kept her awake or exhaustion had failed to keep Sebastian out of her dreams. Dreams that were more like nightmares. Lucy arrived with her breakfast, and the moment she saw the tray, Anna became nauseated. With a sharp command, she'd ordered the maid to remove it immediately.

A short time later, a quiet knock whispered through the air before Lady Harding entered the bedroom and closed the door behind her. The worried look on the viscountess's face made Anna look away from her. She would have to tell Lucy never to reveal the secrets of her next mistress if she wanted to remain a lady's maid. Almost as if the viscountess had read her mind, Lady Harding sat on the edge of the mattress and took Anna's hand in hers.

"Lucy did not tell me anything, my dear girl. I saw her enter your room, then leave barely a moment later, still carrying your breakfast tray." Lady Harding squeezed her hand gently. "If not from your puffy eyes, I would think you were coming down with something, but you've been crying. Why?"

"I miss my family." The quiet words pleased Anna as she succeeded in not allowing her voice to tremble or reveal the state of her misery.

"But why? What has happened to make you so unhappy?"

"I miss the Falcon. I'm homesick."

"I understand that my dear girl, but I think something else is troubling you. Troubling you deeply, I think."

"I'm fine."

"No, you're not. Anyone with half a brain could see that you're terribly upset. What happened last night?"

"Nothing."

"*Poppycock*, when the Earl of Guildford appears at my side at a ball with word that Sebastian has been hurt, and you, Sarah, and Alexander have left with him for Starling House, that does *not* sound like nothing happened." The note of frustration in Lady Harding's voice made Anna's eyes widen in surprise. The viscountess sniffed with disgust. "Sebastian disobeyed Dr. Johnson's orders to rest and left for Birchwood at first light, while Alexander is nowhere to be found. Now I discover you lying in bed from what I suspect is a night of crying, and I demand to know what happened."

Anna averted her gaze from the woman and tried to find a way to explain the events of last night without revealing what had happened between her and Sebastian. Another sound of exasperation escaped Lady Harding. Anna turned her head back toward the woman.

The expression on the viscountess's face was one she'd seen on Sebastian's features numerous times. For all his physical features that declared him the true son of the last Lord Starling, his mother could still be seen in his face.

"*Now*, Anna. Do *not* prevaricate." The firm note in the viscountess's voice made Anna flinch, knowing she had no choice but to share her folly and Sebastian's rescue.

"Sebastian caught me searching Lord Farthington's study last night." At her soft statement, Lady Harding's mouth fell open as she stared at Anna in appalled horror.

"You did *what*?"

"Alexander, Sarah, and I have been trying to find out who the leaders of the Hatshepsut cult are. We're convinced they're members of the peerage, and we believe Lord Farthington is one of them, possibly even a leader." Anna winced as she saw the other woman's horrified disapproval. "We learned the viscount had some documents in his possession that might provide the police with evidence of the man's involvement in the cult."

"Dear God," Lady Harding gasped before her mouth tightened with anger. "And what possessed you to search the Farthington's study? Did Sebastian put you up to it? Did Alexander?"

"*No*." Anna shook her head. "Neither one of them knew what I was doing. At least not until Sebastian figured it out last night, and he followed me to the viscount's study to stop me."

"And *how* did Sebastian come to be injured?" Lady Harding's anger was growing by the second, and Anna swallowed hard. She deserved to be the target of the woman's ire.

"We heard someone coming toward the study and were forced to jump out of a window into the garden. Sebastian landed wrong and injured his ankle." Anna looked away from the viscountess as her misery returned. "I'm responsible for his injury. He was simply trying to save me from being caught, and he was hurt in the process."

"But that doesn't explain what sent my eldest son rushing off to Birchwood without a word, when he's clearly unable to fend well for himself."

"He's gone?" For the first time, Anna grasped the fact

that it was the second time the woman had mentioned Sebastian had left Starling House. The realization made her heart tighten painfully in her chest. The viscountess gave a sharp nod.

"According to Hodgekiss, Sebastian was helped into a carriage before it was barely light out." Lady Harding narrowed her gaze at her. "What I want to know is why?"

"I don't know why he left." Anna barely managed to choke her reply out as her throat tried to close up with tears. She turned her head away from Lady Harding, unwilling to continue. Anna knew why Sebastian had left. He'd left because of what had happened between them. It was a problem he didn't know how to deal with.

"Anna, are you in love with my son?" The soft question made her heart slam into her chest as she jerked her head toward the viscountess.

"*No*," she exclaimed fiercely, then tried to reinforce her denial by hiding behind Alexander. "I'm exceedingly fond of Alexander, but I am not in love with him."

"I am not referring to Alexander, and you know it. I am asking you if you're in love with Sebastian." The woman's gaze narrowed and pinned Anna beneath a familiar penetrating stare. When she shook her head in her second denial, Lady Harding arched an eyebrow. "I have eyes, my dear. I see the way you look at him and the way he looks at you."

"He doesn't love me," Anna said quietly in an effort to avoid revealing her feelings.

"I'm not so certain of that." Lady Harding shook her head as a look of conviction swept across her features. "My son is as stubborn as his mother. Admitting he loves you comes at a cost. The question is whether he's willing to pay that price."

"Please, I would like to be alone now," she whispered as she crushed the small bud of hope that had leapt to life at

Lady Harding's words. "I didn't sleep well, and I'm very tired."

"Of course," the viscountess murmured. Standing up, Lady Harding bent and brushed her lips across Anna's forehead. "All will be well, Anna. You must believe that."

Anna didn't answer the woman, she simply rolled away from Sebastian's mother to lie on her side, staring at the blue sky beyond the window. The only way anything would be well again, was when she was back home on the Falcon. There she would be able to forget, and she'd learn to live without Sebastian.

Chapter 22

Anna tried to relax against the back of the cab's seat as it rolled toward the Beefsteak Club. When Sebastian had left almost two weeks ago for his country estate, she'd chosen to spend most of her evenings in the salon reading, and she'd refused callers. Nothing held her interest anymore, and with each passing day, Anna tried to chip away at the bars of her gilded cage.

Lady Harding had tried to persuade her to go out with her, but Anna had only relented twice. Last night, for the first time in almost a week, she'd found something to excite her.

When the Viscount Monckton had sought her out last night at the theater, he'd teased her about not accepting any callers, especially when he'd wanted to discuss her entering the Beefsteak Club disguised as a man. The idea had been even more appealing than when she'd first proposed it to Alexander, because she knew how appalled Sebastian would be when he heard how she'd stormed a male fortress.

In fact, she was looking forward to defiantly regaling Sebastian with the story of her escapade. She'd make it perfectly clear she didn't give a damn about his rules of propriety, decorum, or what the Marlborough Set might think of her if she was discovered. Anna had no doubt as to the scandal her behavior would cause, but she didn't care. Soon the Falcon would return to London, and she would be done with society for good.

The hack rolled to a halt in front of the Beefsteak Club, and Anna offered the driver the fare before stepping out of the cab. Viscount Monckton stood at the foot of the steps leading into the club, and she walked past him and started to climb the steps to the club's entrance. Monckton nodded at her as she passed him, but it was obvious he didn't recognize her.

When she reached the club door, she glanced over her shoulder to see her coconspirator pull his pocket watch out to look at the time. He snapped it closed, then turned his head to look up and down the street. Clearly, the man thought she was late. Biting back a smile, she adjusted her vocal pitch to make it lower than normal.

"Excuse me, my lord, the lady has already arrived. Did you look for her inside?"

"*Damnation*, how the devil did she get past—*Good God*."

Thunderstruck, Monckton stared up at her with his mouth agape. Anna grinned as she brushed her finger beneath the waxed mustache she'd bought the other day to wear for the evening. Anna flicked an imaginary fleck of lint off the lapel of her jacket. It had been necessary to let Lucy in on her adventure, and the maid had eagerly agreed to help her with the sworn promise not to tell anyone.

Earlier in the afternoon, she'd had Lucy sneak a set of Alexander's evening clothes out of his room along with a pair of his shoes. His shoes had been too small for her, and Lucy had been forced to steal a pair from Sebastian's room. Where Alexander's shoes had been too small, Sebastian's were too large, and she'd been forced to stuff the toes of the shoes with stockings, until they were manageable. The wig she was wearing she'd found in the same theatrical costume shop where she'd bought her mustache. Now, as Monckton stared at her in amazement, she winked at him.

"I believe you promised I would be able to find a game

of Brag this evening, my lord." At her challenge, the viscount grinned and climbed the steps. Before he could open it for her, she stepped in front of him and pushed the club door inward. The last thing she needed was for Monckton to treat her like a woman out of habit. The interior of the club was noisy, and she glanced over her shoulder at the viscount.

"Are you sure they're here?"

"Yes, I asked Reddington if he and Eastcote would be here this evening, but just to be sure, I waited across the street and saw them arrive a short time ago." Monckton stepped closer and bent his head until his warm breath brushed against her ear. "Let me get you registered in the book as my guest."

The viscount started toward a narrow reception desk before he stopped and came back to her side.

"I'll need a name." The man's words made her smile. She would use the name she'd been using since the first time she'd followed Hamish and Smitty into the Cat and Hound tavern.

"Mr. Alfred Sawyer, known to his friends as Alfie."

"Well then, Alfie. You're to call me George." Monckton grinned broadly before he made his way to the reception desk. The viscount was back in less than a minute, and he nodded toward one of the rooms off the main entryway.

"That's the card room. If you're as good as you say you are, then a winning streak will bring half the club in to watch."

"I'm ready," she said quietly as she patted the pound notes she'd placed in her inside pocket. Anna saw Monckton arch his eyebrows as he stared at her jacket. She smiled, knowing the man was wondering how she'd hidden her breasts.

"Bindings." The single word sent color flying into the viscount's cheeks, and she laughed. "Come on, I'm feeling quite lucky tonight."

Pushing him forward, Anna followed Monckton into

the card room, where she quickly found a game to join. Over the next hour, her winnings began to grow, and a small crowd had formed behind her when she saw Alexander and Eastcote studying the game in a group across from her. As she included her stake with the other three players, she waited for the hand to be dealt. Carefully lifting cards just enough to see her hand, Anna allowed them to fall.

"George," she called out over her shoulder to where the viscount had started a pool as to how long before his guest at the table would lose handily.

"What do you need, Alfie?"

"I'm parched, old man. Might we order a bottle of champagne?" The viscount laughed and patted her shoulder.

"Done."

As the game started, the betting began to weed out players, and Anna noted the one player who was as good as she was, tapped his finger on his cards before he raised the bet. With a smile, Anna folded and watched as her opponent scooped up his winnings. The man waved the pound notes in front of him as he began to rise from his chair.

"I think I'll bow out while I still have my shirt, Sawyer." The man extended his hand across the table. "It's been a pleasure."

Anna nodded sagely, and as the man stood up and stepped away from the table, she pinned her gaze on Alexander, whose eyes had widened the moment the man said her last name. His stunned expression made her smile with amusement, and she arched her eyebrow at him as she brushed one finger against the bottom of her mustache.

"Reddington. Care to try your luck?" At her challenge, Alexander frowned as if he were contemplating what to do. "Come now, sir, surely you're not worried I'll trounce you that easily."

Alexander jerked slightly, and she saw him clutch Eastcote's elbow as he whispered something into his friend's ear. The viscount met Alexander's gaze with skepticism as he turned his head toward Anna. The moment she arched her eyebrows at the two of them, Eastcote went rigid. Before anyone could speak up, Alexander stepped forward and took the empty seat across from her. With a grim expression, he opened his jacket and pulled out pound notes for the stake.

"Champagne?" Anna offered him the bottle, and he accepted a glass someone handed him and poured himself a drink. He downed the alcohol in one gulp, and she smiled.

"Another to bolster your courage, perhaps?" She lifted her glass and drank what was left of her champagne in one swallow. Alexander shook his head.

"I want to keep my wits about me."

"And so you should." With a grin, she poured herself another glass of the bubbly liquid, then smiled at him. "Shall we begin?"

The first hand they played, Anna folded without placing a bet. She took another drink of champagne and watched the other players at the table. It didn't take long for her to learn Alexander's tell. He always narrowed his eyes at his opponents when he had a strong hand. When it was a poor hand, he'd lean back in his chair with a confident air and try to win the pot by outlasting everyone at the table.

They'd been playing for more than an hour, with Anna winning two or three pots and Alexander winning about the same. As they started another game, the bets circled the table quickly several times before the first man folded. Two bets later, the second man folded, leaving Anna and Alexander. To her surprise, Alexander continued to raise the ante, and she frowned as she saw him lean back into his chair. Something was wrong. He wasn't just reclining back in his chair, he had narrowed his eyes at her. Either the man had a good hand, or he was bluffing. Alexander nodded toward the pound notes in the center of the table and grinned.

"Your bet, Sawyer."

As he arched his eyebrow in amusement, Anna lifted her cards slightly to peek at them. There was only one of two other hands that could beat hers, and she knew two of the aces had been played two hands back. She frowned as she tried to remember the last time she'd seen a king show up in someone's winning hand. When she couldn't remember, she sat still for a moment, then reached into her coat pocket and pulled out enough notes to equal two hundred pounds. Without smiling, she laid the stack of pound notes in the middle of the table. She heard a low rumble float around the table at her action, and Alexander stiffened and slowly straightened in his chair.

"That's a rather large sum of money, Sawyer. Are you sure you want to make that bet?"

"Are you worried I'm bluffing, Reddington?" Her voice was devoid of emotion as she met his gaze across the table. Alexander frowned as he took a quick peek at his cards, then at the money in the center of the table.

"I don't think you have the winning hand, Sawyer."

"Then pay to find out."

Alexander pulled a handful of notes from his coat and counted out four hundred pounds, then laid the money on top of Anna's. Her heart pounding, she smiled slowly, then turned over her first queen.

Alexander chuckled, and her heart slammed into her chest as she met his amused gaze across the table. Slowly, she turned over her second queen. This time Alexander started slightly. His gaze narrowed on her as her hand hovered over her last card.

With a quick flick of her wrist, she turned over the third queen. Alexander closed his eyes for a moment as he silently signaled his defeat. It was at that moment she knew she'd beaten her friend, and she watched him turn over a running flush, ace high. The crowd surrounding the table erupted in cheers, and Anna extended her hand to her friend.

"An excellent game. Thank you," she said with a small smile.

Alexander shook her hand as a number of men behind her were slapping her on the back and offering her their congratulations. Her friend tightened his grip on her hand and tugged on it slightly to ensure he had her attention.

"I think you and Monckton should join Eastcote and me for a round of drinks to celebrate your victory." His eyes narrowed in a stern look that was reminiscent of Sebastian, and Anna knew not to argue as Alexander looked at George. "Monckton, order more champagne, while Eastcote and I show our new friend the seat of honor in the Marshall room."

George laughed and went off to do as he'd been ordered, while Anna gathered her winnings, then rose to her feet to follow Alexander. As she pushed her way through the crowd of men who were continuing to slap her on the back, she saw Alexander pause at the card room's open doorway. She wasn't sure what he was thinking, and the moment she reached him, Alexander wrapped his arm around her shoulder in a time-honored male gesture.

"Do you have *any* idea what will happen if you're discovered?" Alexander's quiet chastisement was a harsh whisper in her ear as he guided her down the hall. "You and Monckton will both be thrown out, he'll lose his membership, and you'll be ruined, not to mention what Bash will say. He'll have my head for not having told him about your idea to begin with."

"I don't *give* a fuck what Sebastian has to say," she snapped bitterly. The startled look on Alexander's face made her wince before she eyed him with irritation. "I seem to recall telling you I knew several languages."

"Yes, you did." Her friend nodded, but she saw him eye her with an assessment she didn't like.

"So are you going to expose us," she asked quietly, eager to distract his attention from her bitter reaction to

Alexander's mention of his older brother.

She didn't care about what happened to her, but she liked George and didn't want him to suffer any repercussions from their adventure. Alexander studied her for a moment, before a laugh of surrender escaped him.

"No. You said you could do it, and I didn't believe you. My admiration is that of a student observing a master in action."

"Thank you." Anna breathed a sigh of relief. "I would hate for George to suffer on my account."

"The only stipulation I have is that you are never to make this suggestion to Sarah. I'll have your head if you do."

"I promise," Anna said solemnly.

As they entered what Alexander called the Marshall room, she saw Eastcote waiting for them in front of a fireplace with four chairs. George's cheerful voice announced his arrival, and she laughed as he raised two bottles of champagne over his head.

"Gentlemen, I believe we have several toasts to make this evening for young Sawyer here. He said he would do it, and he did." With a bow in her direction, the young viscount quickly poured champagne for the four of them. Raising his glass to her, he grinned. "To Sawyer, a damn fine Brag player, among other talents."

Alexander and Eastcote raised their glasses as well. Over the next two hours, the four of them finished the champagne, and Anna was beginning to feel tipsy. As a large portion of the bubbly alcohol spilled from the glass Monckton had just poured for her, she giggled. Alexander muttered something beneath his breath before he rose from his chair.

"That's it. We need to get you home before you make a mistake. Bash will blame me for this whole thing when he comes home and hears of this." The worry in his soft words made Anna wince.

"I'm sorry, Alexander. I didn't think—"she made a soft,

yet unladylike burp—"about that. He'll definitely be upset with you."

"I'll survive." Alexander grinned. "Come on, old man. Let's get you home."

Alexander helped her to her feet while Eastcote and Monckton followed, and the four of them staggered their way out of the club.

Chapter 23

Anna's side hurt from laughing so much as the hack she and Alexander were in rolled to a stop in front of Starling House. As the two of them lurched their way out of the vehicle, she couldn't stop giggling. One arm wrapped around her waist, Alexander guided Anna up the steps and into the house.

As she stumbled over the threshold into the main entryway, Anna forgot to compensate for the large male shoes she was wearing. The sound of Alexander's soft grunt as she stepped on his foot made her laugh.

"*Bloody hell*, will you be quiet. If someone hears us and comes to investigate, Bash will know about it the minute he returns from Birchwood." Alexander's warning whispered its way into her ear as he guided her through the front door of Starling Place. Despite the warning, she heard him suppress a laugh.

"I'm trying," she retorted with a giggle. "But these shoes are too big for me."

"What you mean is that your feet are bigger than most other ladies, or you would have stolen a pair of mine instead of stealing a pair from Bash."

"I did steal a pair from your room first," she whispered in disgust. Alexander snorted softly with laughter at her reply, then steadied her before leaving her swaying on her feet just inside the foyer for a brief instant as he closed the heavy wood door behind them.

"Oh, and if you keep telling me my feet are huge," she muttered as she wagged her finger at him. "I'm not going to play cards with you anymore."

"I don't think *anyone* is going to *want* to play cards with you ever again."

"I told you I was good, but you didn't believe me," Anna whispered loudly as she snorted with laughter.

"Come on, let's get you upstairs before—"

"What the devil is going on here, Alexander James Reddington?"

The sound of Sebastian's harsh voice behind her made Anna stiffen. Poseidon's balls, when had he arrived home? He hadn't been here when Lucy had helped her sneak out of the house to meet George. She stared at Alexander, who was looking over her shoulder with a look of confusion and a bit of unease.

Her friend's expression said he believed they'd landed in the fire. A part of her ached to whirl around and tell the bastard to go fuck off, but she remained frozen in place. The last thing she wanted was for Alexander to face his brother's sharp censure. She took comfort in knowing she wouldn't be denied the pleasure of telling Sebastian what she'd accomplished tonight when she was clear-headed. The sudden soft burp that escaped her made her throw her hand up to her mouth and cough in an effort not to laugh. As she met Alexander's gaze, she saw her friend struggle not to laugh.

"He used your full name," she mouthed the words at him and surreptitiously waved her finger in front of her chest in a sign he'd been a naughty boy. Alexander made a choking sound in an obvious effort not to laugh as he looked at his brother.

"Bash, when did you get back from Birchwood?"

"A couple of hours ago. I had planned on having dinner with Margaret and some friends but left the estate too late."

The moment Sebastian said Lady Margaret's name, Anna bit down on her tongue to keep from whirling around and saying something ugly about the woman. It made her angry as hell that the man could be so blind where Lady Margaret was concerned. The woman was insufferable, condescending, and a viper. Sebastian was an utter ass for not seeing through the woman. Even worse was the jealousy she experienced knowing he was going to marry the woman.

"Well, sorry your plans fell through."

Alexander's tone was almost too cheerful as he deliberately placed his body between her and Sebastian as he turned her toward the stairs in an effort to conceal her identity. Keeping her head down, Anna released an unintelligible sound of agreement as she leaned into Alexander, and he wrapped his arm around her waist to guide her toward the stairs.

"Where the devil do you think you're going?" Sebastian's anger hadn't ebbed one bit. If anything, it sounded as if he was growing more incensed by the moment, and it sent a small shiver of worry through her. She and Alexander needed to get upstairs right away.

"Alfie's in his cups, and he couldn't find the key to his lodgings. I decided to bring him home to sleep it off. We'll find his key in the morning. Come along, Alfie, old chap."

"Yep, lost my key," she mumbled. The effect was spoiled as she giggled softly.

"Good God."

The horror in Sebastian's voice was all the more strident because his exclamation was so soft. Christ, now they truly were in for it. Beside her, Alexander muttered an oath, and a second later a pair of black shoes came into view as Anna kept her head bent and her gaze focused on the foyer's marble floor.

"Anna Sawyer." There was enough condemnation in his voice to make Anna cringe before she straightened and lifted her head to defiantly meet his incredulous gaze.

"That's *Alfie* Sawyer to you, my lord," she said brashly as she used her finger to brush against the mustache in a swaggering move.

It failed dramatically, as the mustache fell to the floor. Beside her, a snort of laughter escaped Alexander. She grinned at the younger man before turning her head back to see Sebastian's grim disapproval. It was obvious her beautiful, dark prince from hell was livid. Satisfaction streaked through her. Good. The man was a priggish fuckwit. He'd walked away without one word to her about that night at Farthington's, and she was mad as hell about it.

"And exactly *why*, in the name of all the saints, are you dressed as a man?"

Sebastian's arm snaked out to tug the wig from her head. She yelped as hair pins scraped against her scalp. Her hair tumbled down over her shoulders in mad disarray the moment the wig was pulled off her head. With a small shake of her head, Anna used one hand to push the hair out of her eyes.

"Because the Beefsteak Club only allows men." Her scalp still stinging, Anna scowled at him for having caused her pain.

"Are *you* telling *me* that you *dressed* up in men's *clothing* and went into a *male-only* club?" The astonishment on Sebastian's face quickly became one of fury. Rebelliously, she met his furious gaze with a look of amusement and antipathy.

"Yes, and no one was the wiser. In fact, I was the toast of the club for my gambling skills, wasn't I, Alexander?" She flashed a brilliant smile at her friend before turning to meet Sebastian's outrage. "I won an obscene amount of money tonight, and I think I might just have to go back."

"And I told you no one was going to want to play cards

with you again."

Alexander's reminder went ignored as Anna watched Sebastian's face harden into a stony façade. The gaze he pinned on her said there would be hell to pay for tonight. Not if she could help it. Last week, she had paid one of the footmen to visit the docks for news of the Falcon. According to the footman, the ship had already returned to port at least three times during her stay at Starling House.

That piece of information had aroused resentment and fury inside her. It was a bone of contention she would address when she saw her uncle again. She knew she wouldn't have long to wait for that confrontation. The last time the Falcon had left port had been almost three weeks ago. It meant the ship had to be on her way back to London by now. Anna's eyes focused on his mouth that had thinned into a firm line of judgement.

Even when he was furious, he looked deliciously male, and her heart ached at how much she'd missed him these past two weeks. Why did he have to have such a beautiful mouth? Hell, why did he have to be so damn gorgeous to begin with?

"You're three sheets to the wind."

"Are you suggesting I'm drunk, Lord Pompous?" she snapped back.

At her insult, Alexander made a strangled sound as he smothered a laugh, while Sebastian stiffened. The man was wrong. She was *not* falling down drunk. Anna knew she was feeling good, but she was confident she could make it to her room without help. A snort of laughter echoed in her head.

All right, perhaps she wasn't as steady as she should be, but she was most definitely *not* in a drunken stupor. She was in complete control of her faculties. Correction. That wasn't true. This man made it impossible for her to think straight. He set her on edge in every way possible, and if she wasn't careful, she'd do something incredibly foolish.

The sudden appearance of a tic in Sebastian's cheek

indicated how tightly his jaw was clenched. Obviously, he didn't enjoy hearing how stodgy he was. Anna smiled at him in triumph, elated that her insult had hit its mark.

"That's exactly what I'm saying." The cloud of anger on his face didn't abate as he towered over her. She ignored the heat that suffused her body as he took a small step closer in an obvious attempt to intimidate her.

"Sorry to disappoint you, Lord Pompously—" Anna deliberately paused to cover her mouth and dramatically fake a wide yawn. Beside her, she heard Alexander choke back another laugh as she finished her insult. "—Boring. I am *not* three sheets to the wind as you call it. If I were, I'd be passed out somewhere. What do you think, Alexander? Do you think Terrence would have put me up for the night if I'd batted my eyes at him and promised to be good?"

Anna turned her head and fluttered her eyelids at Alexander in an imitation of Lady Margaret simpering over Sebastian. The snort of laughter that escaped Alexander became a laughing fit as he pressed his forehead into her shoulder. Her friend's convulsions of laughter made her grin.

Lord Starling be damned. She was feeling too good to let the jackass ruin the last bit of her evening. She'd had a wonderful time tonight at the Beefsteak Club. It was the first time since she had left the Falcon that she'd been able to truly relax without fear of being judged for some ridiculous misstep. Turning back to Sebastian, his look of fury made her heart skip a beat. Was that jealousy she saw in his dark eyes? She frowned, and whatever she thought she'd seen had vanished.

"It doesn't matter how many sheets to the wind you are, Anna. It's completely unacceptable, and you know it." Sebastian's condemnation infuriated her, but he didn't give her a chance to respond before he was raining hell's fire down on his brother's head. "And as for you, Alexander. Do you not know how to use the good sense God gave you? What if someone had recognized her dressed as she is?"

Tired of hearing him rattle on about all the restrictions that had been placed on her shoulders, Anna's anger grew. She could do, say, and think what she pleased. The man wasn't her guardian, and if she wanted to sneak into a male-only club and drink until she *was* three sheets in the wind, she would.

Anna opened her mouth to deliver a blistering insult, but stopped as she met Sebastian's eyes. The hunger and desire she saw there, as his gaze swept over her, made her mouth go dry. The memory of how they'd pleasured each other the night of Farthington's ball caused her body to tighten, and a charge of electricity zipped its way through her veins. Almost instantly, the spot between her legs throbbed, and she swallowed hard at the effect he was having on her senses.

For the first time, she realized he wasn't wearing a coat or vest. Without thinking, she ran her gaze over him as if he were a piece of cake that she couldn't wait to taste. The white high-neck shirt with its narrow strip of a tie around his neck emphasized his well-toned, muscular shape. She couldn't see beneath his shirt sleeves, but she remembered the power and strength of his arms. Angered by her reaction to him, she tilted her chin upward in defiance as he muttered something unintelligible, then continued.

"You've both imbibed far too much alcohol this evening."

"We are *not* drunk." She waved her hand in the air in a dismissive, cavalier gesture. Alexander snorted at her nonchalant reaction, and Anna looked at her friend. "Okay, Alexander and I might be a little tipsy, but—"

"I am not *any* sheets to the wind," Alexander said as he swayed into her side. Anna jerked her head in his direction to roll her eyes at him, and his feigned look of innocence evaporated. With a sheepish shrug, he corrected his statement. "Very well. I'm feeling pretty damn good at the moment, but you, my lad, are going to feel as if a hammer hit your head in the morning."

"I'm going to bed," she said with an icy condescension as she arched her eyebrows at Sebastian. She broke free of Alexander's hold and smiled at him. "Alexander, thank you for such a wonderful evening. It was the most fun I've had since I arrived at Starling House."

Aware her movements were anything but graceful, Anna took two unsteady steps around Sebastian and zigzagged her way toward the staircase. A low growl of displeasure buzzed close to her ear as the world became topsy-turvy. Strong arms lifted her up off the floor, pulling her snug against a hard male chest.

"Go to bed, Alexander. I'll deal with you in the morning." Sebastian's harsh command was issued in a scathing tone as he headed toward the staircase. "In the meantime, I'll see to it that Anna reaches her room without falling and breaking her damn neck."

"Put me down, you pompous ass. I'm perfectly capable of going to my room by myself," she bit out in a fierce protest. It was a half-truth as she knew managing the stairs would have been more of an exercise in how to use a bannister to pull herself up the staircase.

"*Shut up, Anna.*" The clipped command made her eyes widen as she stared up at him. Something in his voice made his order sound different from his usual form of reprimand. Recovering from her surprise, she scowled at his sharp jawline.

Sebastian barely spared her a glance as he strode across the foyer and up the stairs. The speed with which he moved was startling, and in less than a minute he was setting Anna on her feet in front of her room. With a sharp movement, he pushed the door open for her, then stepped aside. The moment the heat of him vanished, Anna wanted to cry out at being deprived of his warmth.

"I'll send Lucy up to help you undress." Something about his stilted tone skimmed across Anna's senses, but she couldn't identify why it sounded so different.

"*No.* I told her not to wait up for me, and she's asleep by now. I'll manage."

Suddenly feeling as if she were about to cry, Anna shook her head, then rushed through the open door. As she staggered forward, she stumbled over Sebastian's large shoes on her feet. In the next instant, her bumbling gait threw her sideways and into the tall wardrobe just inside the door. A crack filled the air as her head met the side of the heavy piece of furniture.

"*Fuck,*" she cried out as she bent over and clutched at her head.

"*Christ Jesus,* you'll wake the entire household with that mouth of yours." Sebastian moved quickly through the doorway and closed the door behind him. Still bent at the waist and holding the side of her head, Anna eyed him with scorn as he bent over to look at her.

"Oh, thank you for the sympathy," she said sarcastically. "But it *fucking* hurts."

Straightening upright until her posture was stiff and rigid, she eyed him with antipathy. Well it was probably more like a glare of pain at his less than compassionate response. For all he knew, she might have hurt herself badly.

Sebastian uttered a harsh sound of disapproval at her deliberate use of the curse, then he reached out to tilt her head to examine the side of her face. The minute his fingers touched her, fire streaked across her skin until her entire body was consumed in a firestorm. Angered by his disapproval and her reaction to him, she batted his hand away. His response was a harsh exclamation of frustration.

"You have to be the most *exasperating* creature I've ever met."

"Unlike your perfect Lady Margaret."

She wanted to bite her tongue off at the note of jealousy she heard in her voice. What the hell was wrong with her? She didn't give a damn that he was enamored with the woman. The lie set off wild, mocking laughter in the back of her mind.

"What the devil do you have against Margaret?"

"Nothing," she snapped. She could only hope he believed her lie.

The pain from her run-in with the wardrobe had ebbed, and she was suddenly all too aware of the fact that the two of them were alone in her room in the middle of the night. It was dangerous. Her emotions teetered on the tip of a sword, and if she slid off, she wasn't sure she'd survive the sharp edges of the blade. Worse, she might do something she would live to regret. The last thing she wanted was for him to pity her for having made the mistake of falling in love with him.

"Please leave."

"Hold on to the wardrobe while I help you get your shoes off to avoid any further injuries."

"*No*, I can do it myself." She waved her hand in a sharp gesture for him to leave the room.

"Not only will your tongue get you into trouble, but your stubborn, contrary manner doesn't help."

"I can do without the commentary on my negative qualities because it's obvious I don't have any good ones as far as you're concerned."

Sebastian ignored her angry retort and squatted in front of her to remove the offensive shoes off her feet. As his fingers gently wrapped around an ankle to lift her foot, it was as if a ring of fire encircled the area before it exploded and raced its way up her leg and into every inch of her body. The sensation took her by surprise, and she drew in a sharp breath.

The sound made Sebastian look up at her, and his gaze

narrowed as their eyes met. Whatever he was thinking, she couldn't determine what it was. Breaking free of his hypnotic gaze, she jerked her leg from his grasp, then hopped in place for a second to remove the shoe on her own. Slowly, he rose to tower over her and studied her in silence. Beneath his gaze, her nerves became raw with love, pain, and anger.

"Please go, Sebastian. I don't need or want your help." Anna heard the pain in her voice, and she prayed he couldn't. Suddenly bone weary, she turned away from him.

"Anna."

The instant his hand wrapped around her arm, Anna didn't stop to think. She reacted. Spinning her body away from his hand, the moment she was parallel to him, she hooked her foot under his lower leg and pulled it forward to throw him off balance and drop him to the floor. The amazement on his face as he stared up at her from where he lay at her feet, made Anna's mouth twist in a bitter smile of satisfaction.

"I told you I wasn't three sheets to the wind. I'm tipsy, which means I'm fully capable of undressing myself."

With a jerk, she tugged off Alexander's coat and threw it aside. Sebastian started to sit up and Anna quickly sank down to straddle his hips and pin his forearms against the floor. She slowly leaned forward until her face was inches from his. Immediately, her senses were enveloped by his unique spicy aroma, and she swallowed hard as she stared down at him.

"Anna." His breathing labored, Sebastian shook his head slightly. "I think—"

"Don't think, Sebastian," she whispered as she lowered her head and lightly brushed her mouth across his. "Feel."

Anna pressed her mouth against his, and the taste of him was as heady as the champagne she'd had at the club. Against her thighs, his muscles hardened and tensed, but he was little more than a statue as her lips tried to tease a response from him. After a few seconds, her heart twisted viciously in her chest as her brain jeered at her for thinking she could make the man respond to her advances.

Humiliation splintered its way through her, and she jerked her head up at her failure to illicit a reaction from him. Mortified that her behavior might have repulsed him, Anna braced her hands on the floor, intent on standing. The moment she pulled away from Sebastian, his hand curled around the back of her and tugged her roughly downward. The moment his mouth captured hers in a hard kiss, her heart dropped to the pit of her stomach, then back up to slam into her chest.

With a devastating skill that made her blood flow hot and fast, his lips crushed hers in a kiss that stole the air from her lungs. As his tongue slipped past her lips to swirl around hers, a tremor shook its way through every part of her. Another frisson skimmed its way along the length of her spine as his fingers drifted lazily across her cheek, then continued their downward path until he reached the hollow of her throat.

Heart beating with a wild fury, she wanted to explore everything about him. As his mouth continued to bruise hers with unrestrained passion, her fingers made short work of his narrow tie and the stiff, buttoned-up collar of his shirt. The moment the heat of his upper chest pressed on her fingers, she pulled her lips away from his to caress the side of his face.

He was a heady mixture of spice and leather, with the faint smell of the country still lingering on his skin. Eagerly, she drank him into her senses as the light layer of stubble on the edge of his jaw abraded her mouth. A dark growl rumbled out of his throat as she nibbled at his earlobe. It was a distinct sound of pleasure, and it encouraged her to be bolder.

Hot skin singed her mouth as she pushed aside the material of his shirt and grabbed a small section of skin with her lips to suck gently. Another sound of pleasure passed his lips, and it encouraged her to unbutton the rest of his shirt while caressing him with her mouth. He murmured something, and his hands threaded into her hair as if he intended to drag her upward to kiss her. She resisted and continued downward with each button that came undone.

Everything about him sent her senses reeling. He was beautiful and devastating in ways only a dark angel could be. With each kiss and beat of her heart, she bound herself to him. His shirt splayed open as she undid the last button, and she bent her head to explore his hard, masculine chest with her mouth.

Anna caught a rigid nipple between her teeth and gently tugged on it. The harsh intake of breath over her head made her smile against his skin, and she repeated the action. Another rough noise escaped him as she swirled her tongue around the hard peak.

Her mouth continued to explore his muscular chest as she slid her body downward to straddle his thighs. Fumbling slightly, her fingers undid the buttons of his trousers, only to encounter his drawers as she pushed his fly open. His erection was hard, thick, and solid under the material of his undergarment. Frustration swept through her. She wanted to touch him. No, taste him. The thought startled her.

Fellatio was the one thing Céleste had refused to explain to Anna, despite her pleas. The Frenchwoman had said that it was something a husband would teach her if he so desired. When Anna had failed to convince Céleste to explain it, she'd found a book inside a small shop the last time they'd visited Paris.

The description and techniques had amused her, but she'd found them arousing, too. Would Sebastian enjoy her exploring him so intimately? Fingers moving swiftly, she tugged his trousers down a little, along with his undergarments, to expose his hard body. Her mouth grew dry as she paused to stare down at him.

He was beautiful. Hard, raw, potent male, and she wanted him. She wanted him desperately. Suddenly aware he'd grown so still he seemed to be frozen in place, her gaze lifted to meet his. Desire slumbered in his eyes, and she wanted to melt beneath the hot, smoldering look. As they stared at each other, his expression suddenly changed, and she saw his desire start to fade. The moment he tried to sit up, she gently pressed her hand into his chest.

He froze again, and their gazes locked as she lowered her head to work her way down the thin line of hair to the tip of him. The instant her tongue flicked out to swirl around the mushroom cap at the tip of his erection, a guttural sound rolled past his lips.

"Sweet Jesus."

"Do you like this?" Her tongue swirled around him in the same way it did when she licked a spoon.

"*God Almighty, Anna.*" His voice was a mixture of desire, amazement, and a soft note of resistance.

"That's not an answer, Sebastian," she murmured. "Do you like this?"

She blew a slow steady breath down the length of him before dragging her tongue up from the base of his cock to the tip of him, where she licked off a hot, tangy bead of desire. Determined to make him lose all control of any sense of propriety and restraint, she steadily met his eyes and waited.

"*God, yes*, but you need to stop. I—"

She didn't allow him to finish as she slowly slid him into her mouth. The harsh groan that rolled out of him was one of surrender, and he sank back down to the floor. Sheer pleasure hardened his features, and he arched his hips upward slightly as she drew him deeper into her mouth.

Not looking away from him, she stroked him with her lips and tongue. He was hot, velvety steel in her mouth. She watched his face as she pleasured him. His eyes were closed, but she didn't have to see them to know how much he was enjoying her intimate caresses. A deep groan rolled out of him as his hips moved with every downward stroke of her mouth. The moment her fingers stroked the sacs at the base of his erection, a guttural sound escaped him.

Against her fingers, his sacs began to draw upward while his cock grew even harder. His hips jerked as he uttered a low cry, and he tried to wrench his body free of her grip, but she held him in place. Over her head, she heard him utter a strangled protest before he jerked hard and exploded inside her mouth. When his shudders began to ebb, her tongue swirled around the length of him one last time, then she sat back on her haunches to study his expression. His eyes were still closed, and his breathing was ragged, as if he'd run a long distance.

Even though her body was screaming with need, she ignored the silent cries and enjoyed the satiated look on his handsome face. Despite her lack of experience, she'd aroused and pleasured him. As if sensing her watching him, his eyelids fluttered open, and she found herself thinking it was unfair for a man to have such beautiful eyes. Sebastian stretched out his hand to cup her cheek with passion still smoldering in the depths of his dark gaze. She turned her head to press a kiss into the palm of his hand.

"So, you're not really pompous and stodgy after all, are you Lord Starling?" she teased softly as she smiled down at him.

The playful observation made him narrow his gaze at her. In the next breath, he took her by surprise as his hand wrapped around the nape of her neck, then tugged her downward to bruise her lips in a hard kiss.

It was a kiss meant to dominate and control. Filled with repressed passion, the kiss was a sign that she'd unleashed something inside him that she wouldn't be able to control, let alone resist. Hot and voracious, his mouth ravaged hers in a way that sent her heart skidding along.

A warm hand stroked its way across the base of her throat, down to the masculine shirt she was wearing. Long fingers wrapped around the soft linen where it parted in a vee. In one sharp, vicious tug, he ripped her shirt open. Buttons bounced against the wood floor, and she jerked upright and away from him in surprise.

Sebastian followed her in a blaze of speed she was unprepared for and rolled her onto her back. As he hovered over her, her heartbeat skidded out of control at the passion flaring in his eyes. Excitement spiraled through her, and she trailed the tips of her fingers across his hard chest, downward.

The instant her fingers brushed over the tip of him, he stiffened. Once more he moved with the speed of a jungle cat, only this time he was on his feet, and he caught her hand and pulled her up to stand in front of him.

Chapter 24

Sebastian had never seen a more beautiful woman in his life. Like a coward, he'd fled to Birchwood, and for the past two weeks he'd done everything he could to forget her and the pleasure they'd shared the night of the Farthington ball.

It had taken several days before his ankle had healed well enough to fend for himself, which had made it difficult to find things to do that would occupy his mind. When he was able to move about freely, he'd taken to doing chores with the servants.

Driving all thought of Anna from his head had been his sole purpose for the past two weeks. He'd done everything he could think of to push her out of his head. Whether it was cleaning stalls, grooming horses, or soaping and polishing tack, he'd buried himself in the task. It had worked until darkness set in.

Lying alone in his bed each night trying to fall asleep, he'd fought desperately to crush his need for her. But she was etched into his mind so deeply, he couldn't free himself from her. Not even his hand could satisfy the ache he knew she could fulfill. Sebastian swallowed hard at the memory as his gaze slowly moved over her.

He'd had more than his fair share of liaisons, but none of those women had been as alluring or enticing as Anna was.

The sight of her standing in front of him, half-dressed in men's clothing, so confident and without shame, left him speechless. And God help him, he'd never been so aroused in his life.

He was teetering on the edge of a passion that could hurt her and destroy him. He saw her tremble, but he knew it wasn't from fear. His Anna would never show fear. She faced it head on and dared the danger to do its worst.

Sebastian's gaze shifted down to the strips of linen she'd used to bind her breasts until they were pressed flat against her chest. In a sharp movement, he stepped forward and pulled her shirt off her completely, then flung it aside. Deliberately taking his time, his fingers traced a slow path across the curve of her shoulder, then downward to the top edge of the wrappings. Every part of him tightened with an emotion that threatened to take control of his senses as he ran the tip of one finger along the upper layer of the linen strips.

"Remove these."

The harshness of his command made her eyes widened. But she didn't object. Instead, she began to remove the strips of material from her chest. Barely able to breathe, Sebastian's blood pounded its way through his veins like a steam engine racing out of control. It thundered in his ears as he watched Anna slowly reach for the first layer of linen strips. As her fingers touched the top layer of cloth, she hesitated for the briefest of seconds.

The moment she faltered, Sebastian heard a voice in the back of his head tell him there was still time to leave. The voice was wrong. It was impossible to walk away from her now. He'd known that from the moment she'd knocked him off his feet and straddled his waist. Mesmerized by her, Sebastian watched her undo one cloth strip after another until the only one left was the linen that hid her nipples.

Their eyes met, and with a small smile, she stepped

forward until there were mere inches between them. With a flick of her wrist, the last strip of linen fell away, and Sebastian drew in a sharp hiss of air. She was even more beautiful than he'd imagined, every night, as he'd pumped his cock until his seed was spent.

"I've wanted you since the night Alexander brought you here," he rasped as his hand cupped her cheek. A fiery heat warmed his palm, and he saw pink color flood her cheeks before she smiled.

"And I've wanted you since the morning you found me in the hall and carried me back to my bed."

Her voice was the sweet call of a siren, and his hands caught her by her shoulders and tugged her forward. She came willingly, a sultry smile on her beautiful mouth. Sebastian's hand gently drifted across her skin before his fingertips brushed lightly over a stiff nipple. A shudder rippled through her as his thumb rubbed against the hard peak. Slowly, he lowered his head to close his mouth over the rigid nipple and cupped her full breast.

The exotic and tantalizing scent of jasmine filled his nostrils as he swirled his tongue around the stiff peak. As his teeth abraded and nipped at the hard tip of her breast, she uttered a soft cry of surprise. Fast on the heels of that cry was a moan of delight. As he suckled and nipped at first one breast and then the other, her hands pushed his shirt off his shoulders.

Heat spread its way across his skin as her palms explored him from the waist upward. The moment her fingers thrummed one of his nipples, a violent surge of hunger hammered its way through his blood. She was a siren he couldn't resist, and with each small moan that passed her lips, his need for her grew.

Sweeping her up into his arms, Sebastian carried her to the bed and set her down on the edge of the mattress. In seconds, he'd removed her clothing and stood staring down at her. Brown eyes met his in a steady gaze, and he saw her breasts rise and fall with agitation. The sound of her rapid breaths matched his own ragged breathing.

"You're far too fond of calling me pompous," he rasped as he knelt in front of her. "You've no idea how erotic my nightly fantasies are where you're concerned. They're anything *but* respectable."

Her eyes widened and color filled her cheeks at his words. His caresses unhurried, he slid his hands up over her calves. When he reached her knees, he lowered his head to gently bite on the plump inner flesh of her leg. The sharp breath she inhaled sent satisfaction crashing through him. Deliberate and slow, his mouth worked its way upward along her inner thigh. With one gentle nip after another, he punished her flesh, then quickly soothed each spot with his tongue.

Just before he reached the apex of her thighs, he turned his attention to the other leg. With a leisurely precision, he started at her knee and worked his way upward, inflicting the same penalty to her skin as he had on the opposite limb. When he reached the top part of her inner thigh, he lifted his head to meet her gaze. The fiery desire in her eyes made his heart slam into his chest.

Despite his body demanding it satisfy his hunger, an intense need to arouse her to a fevered pitch crashed through him. He wanted her to experience the same torment he'd suffered every night since the moment Alexander had placed her in his arms. A sudden resolve surged through him.

Tonight he would watch her reach the brink of satisfaction, only to snatch it from her. He would make her ache and throb with need, then just as she peaked on the edge of her release, he would deny her the ultimate pleasure until he was ready to satisfy his own need.

She stretched out her hand to touch his cheek, and he immediately wrapped his fingers around her wrist. Slowly, he guided her hand down to the apex of her thighs and smiled with satisfaction as her lips parted in a silent gasp of surprise.

"I want to watch you touch yourself." He heard his stark need in his voice as he met her gaze.

"But I don't under—"

"Do it." At his harsh command, she swallowed hard as her fingers parted her flesh. For a second time, a hint of color tinged her cheeks as she shook her head in a mute protest. "Stroke yourself. *now*. I want to see you pleasure yourself in the same way I've been forced to pleasure myself in the dead of night."

"Like this?"

The soft question echoed with uncertainty as she stared at him in wide-eyed surprise, but with a look of dawning realization as to the meaning of his confession. As she slowly began to pleasure herself beneath his gaze, his cock throbbed with a demand for satisfaction. He shoved the harsh summons aside and watched her expression slowly change as the rhythm of her strokes increased and her eyes fluttered closed. Massaging her thighs, he allowed himself to stroke the outside of her slick folds at the same time she played with herself.

Her sudden small tremor sent a pulse throbbing through her and into his hands. A split second later, her mouth parted in a quiet moan of pleasure. Just as she reached the edge of the cliff, he denied her satisfaction by tugging her hand away from her glistening sex.

Surprise and then frustration swept across her lovely face, and he smiled. Raising her hand to his lips, his tongue licked her wet fingers. Bright pink color flooded her cheeks, and her startled look made him smile. Methodically, he slid her finger in and out of his mouth until her eyelids fluttered shut.

Certain her arousal was rising fast, he guided her hand down to the apex of her thighs once more. A hard shudder pulsed through her as his fingers parted her folds, and he forced her finger to rub the small nub of flesh that had become swollen in reaction to stimulation.

"Again," he whispered hoarsely.

Leaning forward, his teeth abraded the nipple of each breast. Biting down harder than he had before, she jerked against his mouth as his tongue swirled around a stiff, rigid peak. The action tugged a small cry from her as he forced her to pleasure herself.

"Shall I tell you how erotic and decadent my thoughts of you are in the middle of the night as I ache for your body to be clutching my cock?"

She licked her lips as he spoke and began to touch herself at a fast pace in reaction to his words. He allowed her to continue for a few more seconds, and the moment she shuddered, he pulled her hand away to suck on her wet fingers. With a small cry of frustration, her eyes flew open, and she glared at him.

"Don't tease me like this." The husky sound of her voice didn't hide how much she was aching for her release.

"I'm not teasing you, sweetheart."

"You are, and you know it."

Her ragged breathing indicated her state of arousal, and he smiled as he made her dip her fingers into her wet heat for a brief stroke before pulling her hand upward. A small sob echoed out of her as his tongue swirled around her finger.

"Do you even know how good you taste? You're a creamy mixture of heat and a slightly tangy bite."

This time, it was he who slipped his fingers past the nub at the rim of her sex to slide into her hot channel. Gasping, she bit down on her bottom lip as he pressed three fingers deep into her and stroked her. Instantly, her body tightened around his fingers, and he quickly retreated. Quickly licking the thick, buttery cream of her desire off his fingers, he silenced her sob of vexation with a hot kiss.

As his tongue mated with hers, he knew she would taste her essence. The thought excited him to the point he almost forgot his resolve to drive her mad with need. He ended the kiss almost as quickly as it began and pulled back from her.

"Shall I tell you what I've imagined when I'm lying awake at night thinking of you? They're decadent, lustful images. I've imagined you lying beneath me as I drive my cock into that sweet, hot channel of yours." He heard the hunger in his voice as she trembled, and he began to play with her. The moment he pressed his fingers into her again, she moaned with delight. Passion and excitement darkened her eyes as he refused to let her look away from him.

"In my mind, I've taken you to the brink of the ultimate pleasure before denying you complete satisfaction. Lying awake at night, I've imagined tasting every inch of your body. I want to do that now. I want to explore *every* inch of you. I want to fill my mouth with your hot cream. I want you to writhe as my tongue goes where my fingers were just now."

"Oh, God." Anticipation and desire whispered out of her as she stared down at him with slumberous eyes shimmering with longing and passion.

Eager to taste her, he pushed her legs wide and lowered his head to nibble at her inner thigh. Another gasp escaped her, and she went rigid as his mouth brushed across her sex. The moment his tongue swirled its way into the part of her that he was certain no man had ever touched, she cried out in surprise.

"Oh, dear God."

The excitement in her voice sent a wave of triumph through him as she shuddered against his mouth. One hand slid up over her stomach to gently force her to lie back on the bed, while his teeth grazed across the sensitive nub of flesh between her legs. The tangy bite of her teased his tongue as he delved into the heart of her.

As his mouth and tongue explored her heat, his fingers

rubbed over a hard nipple. He gently pinched the rigid peak at the precise moment he nipped at the swollen nub of flesh inside her slick folds. A small cry of surprise and pleasure filled the air. The sound was followed by a small gush of tangy cream flowing across his tongue.

He tweaked her nipple again as he reveled in the slick heat of her. Another cry escaped her, and her buttocks lifted off the bed as her body shuddered with what he knew was intense pleasure on her part. The first tremor that rippled through her was accompanied by a low moan rising in her throat.

Her reaction made him delve into her with rapid flicks of his tongue against the small nub at her core. As her shudders increased, she softly cried out his name. In that instant, he knew he was unable to deny himself any longer. Desire and a blazing need to bury himself inside her made him lift his head and silently urge her to move back from the edge of the mattress.

As she scooted backward, he quickly removed the remainder of his clothes, then stood silently staring down at her, taking in her full, voluptuous legs and curves. She was exquisite, and his body shouted a roar of hunger he knew he needed to control if he was to cause her as little pain as possible. Slowly, he pressed her deeper into the mattress with his body, marveling at how her curves fit his. It was as if God had made her just for him. Hard and stiff, his cock pressed against the rim of her sex, and he hesitated.

"If you want me to stop, tell me now, because there will be no going back once it's done," he rasped. Her hands gripped his shoulders to pull him down and kiss him. The sweetness of her breath warmed his skin as her mouth brushed against his ear.

"I want this more than anything else in the world. I want you to be the only man who ever pleasures my body. I want you with every fiber of my being, my dark angel."

The reply made him stiffen as he heard a shout of warning in the deep recesses of his mind. He tried to hear what the voice was saying, but his mind lost the battle as she moved beneath him. As if sensing his hesitation, she thrust her hips forward and his cock slid a small way into her heat. Desire silenced the warning signals his mind was sending, and he began to press his body deeper into hers.

His jaw tightened with tension as he fought his base need to take her quickly. He moved slowly to allow her tight channel to adjust to him. As her body gave way to his possession, her muscles contracted in a tight, velvety vise that tugged a deep groan of pleasure out of him. It tested his will power to control the way he took her. When he reached the barrier that kept him from possessing her completely, he drank in a deep breath.

The soft whimper of ecstasy that escaped her as she shifted her body against him said she was unaware of what was to come. He lowered his head to suckle her breast, teasing her nipple until her hands gripped his shoulders, and she pleaded with him to fill her completely.

"This might hurt a little," he whispered in her ear before he kissed her deeply to distract her, and with one hard thrust, he filled her completely.

The cry of shock and discomfort that parted her lips was quickly silenced by his kiss, but he froze to give her time to adjust to his body. The strain of not moving caused his body to protest viciously, and he closed his eyes against the onslaught of desire and hunger that slammed into him.

After a moment, a soft hand touched his cheek, and he lifted his head to see her quirk an eyebrow at him in a silent demand that he continue. Beneath him, her hips moved impatiently against his. It tugged a deep groan out of him as he fought the urge to move fast and furious.

With what little will power he had left, he slowly withdrew from her then returned. As he retreated again, her body clutched at him in an effort to keep him from pulling away from her. The sharp inhalation that echoed out of her was accompanied by her fingers digging into his buttocks as she urged him to go faster.

Unable to deny her or himself any longer, he increased the pace of his thrusts. The friction assaulting his cock as he possessed her completely made him harder than he'd ever been. Christ Jesus, she was everything and more than he'd imagined. Hot silk wrapped around his cock as his body took control and sent him spinning into a mind-numbing haze. Caught up in a fog of passion and desire, all his brain could comprehend was how incredible she felt as her insides spasmed around him with each thrust he made into her hot core.

The intensity of their lovemaking became one burning stroke after another, until he lost all thought of where she ended and he began. The blood pounding through his veins caused his heart to beat with a savage fury that made him plunder her mouth with a passionate kiss as his body raged with a fire he couldn't control. Suddenly, she grew still beneath him, then in the next second, her hips jerked upward. The first spasm of her climax gripped his cock with a strength that made him groan with pleasure.

As she tightened around him with one hard flex of her body, his breathing became harsh and ragged as he barreled toward his own release. The soft keening cry of ecstasy that filled the air grew in strength, and he smothered her vocal response with his mouth as she writhed against his body. Fingers dug into his shoulders as she bucked violently against him.

With a surge of raging desire, he pumped his body into hers at an unrestrained pace that dragged him toward a release unlike anything he'd ever experienced before. The moment his cock throbbed inside her, it tugged a guttural noise out of his throat, and he spilled his seed in a blinding haze of passion. One shudder after another pummeled his body as they fed off each other's climax. Slowly, the tension drained from his limbs, and his brain slowly began to comprehend the gravity of what he'd done. Christ Jesus, he'd ruined her. Appalled by his loss of control, he rolled off her and draped an arm over his eyes, still reeling from where his desire and lust had taken him.

The memory of Alexander telling him that Anna had been emphatic about not marrying eased some of his tension, but not his guilt. He was a bastard for taking her innocence. It didn't matter that she'd consented and made her desire for him clear from the start. Beside him, Anna's breathing slowly returned to normal.

She rolled toward him and kissed him before he could stop her. He jerked hard at the light caress and abruptly pushed her away from him and moved to leave the bed. Her hand caught his wrist as she tugged hard on his arm in a clear effort to make him look at her, but he couldn't. Guilt became an invisible whip lashing at every part of him.

"What's wrong?"

"I should never have allowed this to happen," he snarled as he pulled free of her grasp and began to dress. "I should have stopped this madness sooner. No, I should never have entered this room to begin with."

As he pulled his trousers on, he grimaced at the way his fingers fumbled with the buttons of his fly. Behind him, he heard the rustle of the bed covers and before he could think straight, she was standing in front of him. Despite the voice of reason urging him to charge out of her room half-dressed before he lost control of his senses again, it was impossible not to let his gaze slide over her.

Sebastian had thought her beautiful before, but now there was a radiance about her that assaulted every inch of him. He'd awakened a woman who had the power to destroy him. It was a risk he refused to take. The instant she pressed her palm into his chest, it was as if he'd been struck by a bolt of lightning.

"I have no regrets, Sebastian. I'm not ashamed of what we just shared. It was wonderful. Glorious." Her fingers leisurely explored his chest as she continued. "From that first morning when you carried me back to my room, I saw a dark angel desperate not to show his true self. Even then I knew that dark angel, *my* dark angel, was the *only* man I would ever want to touch me."

Mere inches separated them as she stepped into him. Desperately, Sebastian struggled not to pull her close and taste every inch of her over and over again. He swallowed hard at the battle raging inside him. A war he knew he would lose if he gave way to the soft, passionate words that exposed her soul to him.

"Please Sebastian. Whatever this is between us, passion or something else, it isn't wrong. I gave myself to you of my own free will. Let me—don't shut me out."

The soft, lyrical notes in her voice struck a vicious blow to Sebastian's mid-section. The depth of emotion in her words held a power that urged him to sweep her up into his arms and never let her go. They possessed a strength to destroy every vow he'd ever made to himself since he was a boy.

Vows he could never break if he were to save himself from a life of misery the moment Anna betrayed him, just as his mother had his father. The emotions radiating off her were almost tangible, and they represented something he would never feel for her. In the back of Sebastian's mind, he heard a mocking laugh, and he silenced it with a savage blow.

Muscles taut with his struggle not to give way to her plea, he refused to surrender to the demons, trying to tear apart the meticulous plans he'd made for his future. He turned away from her to pick up his shirt and pull it on. Her hand touched his arm, and Sebastian closed his eyes as a shout of protest echoed in his head at what he was about to do.

Had he not done enough already by taking her innocence? The answer to the question made him realize he needed to end whatever this was before he did even more harm to her. And he would hurt her in the end. It was inevitable. It was why he needed to make her hate him. There was no other choice available. Voices in the back of his mind said he had a choice, but he crushed their protests in a savage blow. Steeling himself to hide any trace of emotion from his features, Sebastian slowly turned to face her.

"If we proceed with this passion you say we have for each other, you need to understand it will be as my mistress. It will *never* be anything more than that."

The moment he ground out the words with icy precision, Anna jerked back from him. The horror on her face eviscerated his insides with a brutality that threatened to drive him to his knees and beg her forgiveness. Guilt lashed at him as a shout of anguish rose in his throat. His gaze never left her face as he watched her horrified expression evolve into one of contempt.

"Get. Out."

The harsh and bitter note in her command struck another blow to his insides and opened a wound he knew would never heal. She whirled away from him and walked toward the chifforobe to retrieve a robe. The only sign of his cruelty she displayed was a small stumble as she walked away from him. Frozen in place, Sebastian tried to will his body to walk out of the room, but his brain refused to obey. Voices in the back of his head shouted at him for being a fool. They demanded he not leave her without making a different offer. As if realizing he'd not left, Anna spun around to glare at him with an antipathy that sliced through him.

"I told you to *get out*."

"I'll not make the offer again, Anna."

The moment the words spilled out into the air, Sebastian wished he could take them back. God help him. Alexander had called him cold-hearted, and he was forced to admit his younger brother knew him far better than Sebastian knew himself. Only a selfish, ruthless, unfeeling bastard was capable of making an obscene offer twice. An offer he desperately wanted her to say yes to. The knowledge made him hate himself all the more. Anna deserved better from him.

"And just like it is now, my answer wouldn't just be no, it would be *no fucking way in hell*, you sanctimonious bastard." Outrage made her beautiful mouth thin and tight, but it was the fury and pain blazing in her large brown eyes that made his insides twist into knots. "I am *not* some tart willing to be fucked occasionally in exchange for jewels and other gifts."

"Oh, it wouldn't be occasionally, Anna. I'd have you sobbing with delight every single night until I've had my fill of you." His sharp, vicious snarl made her jerk backward.

Sebastian blew out a harsh breath of self-disgust at the realization she believed he saw her as nothing but a whore. It couldn't be further from the truth. Worst of all, he knew he was lying to himself. He would never have enough of her. Whether she was in his arms, in another room, or far away from him, he would never be free of her. Guilt crashed through Sebastian at his cowardice for not making the one offer she deserved. The sudden image of his mother in Harding's arms pushed its way out of the dark recesses of his brain.

It was a vivid reminder of the pain his father had suffered at his wife's betrayal. A pain he refused to suffer as well. Sebastian lowered his gaze and continued to straighten his appearance. It shocked him how badly his hands were shaking as he tried to tug his tie into its proper position.

"Nightly? You seem to be forgetting Lady Margaret." Her scorn was an invisible scourge against his back, and the sudden thought of bedding Margaret made his mouth go sour.

"The sole purpose of my marriage to Margaret will be to secure an heir," he said in a flat voice without looking up from his necktie that he was struggling to tie into a knot.

It was the truth. He'd specifically chosen Margaret because she was no more interested in a marriage of emotional entanglements than he was. Once she'd given him a son, there would be nothing more between them. He also knew Margaret would never even come close to satisfying his carnal needs. Only one woman could do that, and she was unsuitable for his way of life.

"In other words, she'll be a brood mare." Anna flung the sneer at him with a disgust he knew he deserved. "I'd almost feel sorry for her, if the woman wasn't such an obnoxious, disingenuous bitch."

"As usual, your language belongs in the gutter." Sebastian cast a harsh look of disapproval in her direction. The instant his response echoed through the air, he knew she would fight back.

"No. It doesn't. My words say I'm an honest, forthright individual." Anna's voice emphasized her confidence and belief in herself. "I'm not a hypocrite hiding behind a façade of propriety. Like a man who's already decided to be unfaithful to the woman he intends to marry."

The cold accusation couldn't have stunned Sebastian more than if she'd slapped him. Beneath her gaze of disgust, he could feel the blood draining from his face, leaving an icy chill in its place. Invisible steel bands wrapped around his chest until it became difficult to breathe. Anna was right.

His decision to court Margaret had been nothing more than a cold, premeditated plan to secure the Starling title. It didn't matter that Margaret understood their marriage was nothing more than his providing for her in exchange for her providing him with an heir. Anna's gaze swept over him with a scorn that emphasized her disgust and contempt.

"But do you want to know what the worst part of this is? You actually have the ballocks and temerity to hold your mother to a higher standard than yourself." Her words were as volatile as a lightning bolt splitting the air above his head.

"You know *nothing* about my mother," he ground out with fury.

Enraged that she'd dared to mention the woman who'd given birth to him, Sebastian closed the distance between them in two quick strides. He halted to tower over her in a manner others would have found more than intimidating. In the next breath, he knew it wouldn't work. Anna wasn't easily intimidated, and he wasn't surprised to see her brown eyes harden with fury.

"I know enough to know just how wrong you are about her." She was as ferocious in her defense of his mother as a lioness protecting her cubs. "She doesn't deserve your hatred or contempt. If anything, you should crawl on your knees and grovel as you beg for her forgiveness."

Anna flung the words at him in a haphazard manner, and in the next breath, her features became ashen. She knew something. But what? Sebastian narrowed his eyes to study her carefully as he tried to determine if it was merely her affection for his mother that had prompted her remark, or if there was an unspoken truth in her words. Something Sebastian could only define as panic darkened her gaze. It only confirmed his suspicions that she was hiding something from him.

"Exactly *what*, do you think you know about my mother's behavior?" he asked in a menacing tone. His question sent a small shudder through her, and he saw her swallow hard and sway slightly on her feet.

"Suspicions. I have suspicions as to what happened between the two of you."

"No. Not suspicions. You were far too confident

flinging that accusation at me," Sebastian countered as he narrowed his gaze at her and realized she was trying to cover up what had clearly been a misstep on her part. "It sounded as if you know something I don't."

"You're wrong." Although her anger had returned, he heard panic whispering its way through her fierce denial. Her chin tilted upward in defiance as she met his gaze. "If I truly knew something, I'd use it to inflict as much pain on you as I could. Now *get out* of my room before I scream loud enough to rouse the house, and someone finds us together."

Anna reached up to push a lock of hair off her face, and he saw her hand tremble. Sebastian gritted his teeth as raw fury pounded its way through him. She was lying. He eyed her carefully for a long moment as he discarded one strategy after another to drag the truth out of her. For a fleeting instant, he considered ignoring her warning. A split second later, he knew it would be a mistake. The woman he'd fallen in love with didn't make idle threats or promises.

The thought stunned him as if someone had picked up a sledgehammer and delivered a savage blow to his chest. Sebastian recoiled from Anna as if he'd been burned. What in God's name had he done? Another invisible, vicious blow slammed into him as he realized the significance of his error. He'd broken the most sacred of all the vows he'd ever made to himself. His failure made Sebastian's gut twist violently.

Despite the stiff, knotted muscles in his body, he gave her a slight bow, and somehow managed to walk out of her room without revealing how badly shaken he was. As the latch of her bedroom door clicked quietly closed behind him, Sebastian braced himself against the doorjamb. The life of misery he'd vowed to avoid had become a grave he would never be able to crawl out of.

He'd lost the one thing that might have saved his soul. The only woman who could ever make him feel things he'd tried not to feel since childhood. He was a goddamn fool.

Anna was right. He *was* a dark angel, and his refusal to admit the truth had condemned him to eternal damnation.

Chapter 25

Anna shivered in front of her open bedroom window and pulled her shawl tighter around her shoulders. Although sunrise had been more than an hour ago, the morning air still held a snap to it, despite being the middle of June. One shoulder pressed into the window frame, she stared down at the garden below.

The sound of laughter made her lean forward slightly, and she saw two of the gardeners teasing one of the kitchen maids. A fraction of a minute later, she saw the maid scurry away toward the house. The sight of Sebastian's tall figure striding along the path that led to the stable yard gate made her suck in a breath of longing. It was the first time she'd seen him since the night he'd made love to her a week ago.

Anna watched him pause and speak with the gardeners, who laughed at something he said before he resumed walking toward the back of the garden. Hungrily, she watched him make his way along the path at a brisk pace. God, how she'd missed him. Tears choked her at the thought. A second later, he came to an abrupt halt and spun around.

Anna stiffened as he lifted his head to look up at her window. The moment their eyes met, her heart began to pound frantically in her breast. There was a haggard look about him that suggested he'd not been sleeping well. Still staring up at her, Sebastian took two steps toward the house as if he meant to speak to her, and the air left her lungs.

Leaning forward slightly, she stretched her hand out to him. The moment she did so, an unfathomable expression darkened his face. She watched him draw in a deep breath, then expel it harshly before he turned away and continued toward the stable yard. Her heart breaking, Anna watched Sebastian until he disappeared from view, then she slowly sank down to the floor and closed her eyes as she rested her head against the wall.

The morning after Sebastian had broken her heart, she'd been grateful for having imbibed copious amounts of champagne the night before. It had left her with a vicious, unrelenting headache that hid the real reason for her misery. Alexander had sent up a horrible potion said to cure all ills after a night of drinking, but she knew it wouldn't mend her heart.

Anna's misery hadn't ended with Sebastian's departure that night. Her adventure the night before had severely affected her relationship with Lady Harding. The woman had been shocked, angered, and deeply disappointed in Anna when the viscountess had demanded Alexander explain the false mustache and wig a servant had found in the foyer the following morning. The woman hadn't come to visit her at breakfast that morning as she often did most days, instead she'd sent a short, brusque note as to her displeasure with Anna's behavior.

Unable to hide how miserable she was, Anna had refused to accept any calls. Although when Viscount Monckton had called, she'd written George a note of apology with the promise she would see him soon. The remainder of the past week had been spent in her bedroom reading. The thought of carrying a book into the salon was a terrifying one because it meant she might see Sebastian.

Until now, she'd not known how either of them would react when they came face to face. Now she did. Sebastian had just walked away from her for a second time. The pain of his doing so only added to what she'd been suffering for the past week. For not the first time, she revisited those terrible moments after giving herself to Sebastian.

It had been like waking from a beautiful dream, only to have it turn into a horrifying nightmare. Her stomach lurched as she remembered Sebastian offering her the role of his mistress. It wasn't the role she objected to. God knows she'd seen for years how happy her uncle and Céleste had been in such a relationship.

What had made Sebastian's offer so heart wrenching, was how he'd made it clear his plans to marry Lady Margaret hadn't changed. Even his offer to make her his mistress had broken her heart, not because he'd made the offer, but because he'd extended his offer of patronage not once, but twice. Had he made his second offer because he'd been afraid to admit he might have feelings for her other than desire?

Was his fear of being betrayed so great that he refused to risk loving her? That she could understand. It hurt, but she understood it. The other possibility was much more devastating. Had she misjudged him? Was it possible he thought she was beneath his station, or worst of all, he simply saw her as a woman to discard once he'd grown weary of her?

Tears welled up in her throat. She could understand if he was afraid to love, but if his reason was the latter, then he wasn't the man she believed him to be. It made her chest tighten painfully until she could have sworn someone was holding her heart in their hands and squeezing the life out of her.

The quiet knock on her bedroom door made her scramble to her feet as Lucy entered the room with her breakfast tray. The young woman immediately eyed her with concern as she set the tray she carried on the table near the fireplace.

"Are you feeling better today, miss?"

"Yes, thank you, Lucy." The lie came easily as Anna moved toward the fireplace and sat down in the chair closest to the table.

"I'm not so sure I believe that, but maybe the note that arrived a few moments ago will pick your spirits up."

"Note?"

For a moment, Anna thought Sebastian had written a note to her, then rejected the idea as she reminded herself that he'd turned away from her only a few moments ago. Lucy smiled cheerfully as she pointed to the white parchment on the edge of the tray. Quickly picking up the folded note, Anna broke the seal and opened it to see Céleste's elegant handwriting.

Ma petite cherie,

> *The Falcon is moored at the west indies dock, berth ten. I have missed you, my darling anna, and so has Charles. The ship has not been the same without you. I am certain you know by now that the Falcon has returned to London several times since we left you at starling house, but Charles was insistent we do not visit as he wanted to give you time to acclimate yourself to London.*

> *He knows you stayed only because he asked it of you. I know he is hoping to hear that you have met someone during your stay who will make you as happy as he and I have been with each other. We are excited to see you, ma petite cherie and eager to hear all your news.*

Céleste

The moment she finished reading her friend's letter, Anna bit back a sob as a tear slid down her cheek. Immediately, Lucy was at her side to wrap her arm around Anna's shoulders.

"Now, now there, miss, don't you fret, whatever is wrong, it will right itself soon enough."

"No, it will never be right again, never." Anna shook her head and closed her eyes for a moment. Inhaling a deep breath, she released it, then patted Lucy's hand. "Thank you for your kindness, Lucy. I need you to start packing my trunks. I'll have my uncle make arrangements to retrieve them as soon as they're ready."

"You're leaving, miss?" The surprise and disappointment in Lucy's voice made Anna nod.

"Yes, it's time for me to go home."

"I'm sorry to hear that, miss. I had thought…thought you might have a reason to stay."

"No, there's nothing here for me."

Anna heard the misery in her voice as she stared down at her friend's handwriting. It was the truth, and the sooner she left Starling House, the sooner her heart would begin to heal. Mocking laughter filled her head, and she flinched at the sound. An image of the Falcon filled her head, and she quickly rose to her feet.

"Take my tray away, Lucy," she said quietly. "I'm not hungry."

"Oh but, miss, I—"

"Do *it*, Lucy." She eyed the young maid sternly until Lucy bobbed her head and picked up the tray. Anna didn't bother to watch the maid leave the room, instead, she walked toward the secretaire. There were letters she needed to write, and their delivery would need to be timed, so no one objected or tried to stop her from leaving. A mirthless laugh broke past her lips as her heart suggested Sebastian might object.

"You're a fool, Anna Sawyer," she muttered fiercely. "The man wants nothing to do with you unless it involves bedding you like a back street whore."

The words gave her a renewed sense of purpose, and she quickly sat down to write her goodbyes. More than an hour later, she'd finished all her letters but one. Sebastian's. She didn't know why it was so important to write a letter to him, but she forced herself to begin writing. The first note had only three lines on it when she wadded the paper into a ball and dropped it into the wastebasket next to the desk. She started again, and this time she had half a page written before she tore that message up as well. After several attempts, she slapped the top of the desk with her palm.

"For the *love of Christ*, Anna, just *write* the goddamn note. It doesn't matter what you say, it will mean nothing to him."

The quiet words hung in the air as she struggled to endure the pain lashing at her heart. If anything, the man would be more than happy to see her out the front door. Suppressing the tears threatening to spill down her cheeks, Anna wrote several lines thanking him for his generosity in letting her stay at Starling House. It made her stomach churn nauseatingly as she forced herself to add well wishes on his impending nuptials and her hope he would be blessed with the heirs Lady Margaret would give him.

With her letters ready for delivery, she set Lady Harding's and Sebastian's notes aside and placed the remainder of her correspondence in a small stack. Lucy had already begun to pack Anna's smaller possessions in the small trunks, and Anna indulged herself for the last time in the one thing the Falcon didn't have, a heavy, claw-foot bathtub.

The water was cool when Anna reluctantly emerged from her bath, and when she entered her bedroom, Lucy immediately busied herself helping Anna dress. By the time Anna was ready, her courage was slowly fading, and she pressed her palm against her stomach. Part of her wanted to simply pick up her purse and walk out of the house without saying goodbye to anyone, but her stubborn side refused to let her sneak away as if she had something to be ashamed of.

Lucy appeared to understand what Anna was feeling as she patted Anna's hand with a soft word of encouragement. Collecting her letter to Sebastian, she left her room and headed toward the main staircase. Earlier, she had asked Lucy to check to see whether Sebastian had returned as she had no desire to run into him while delivering her note. Although Anna knew she was being a coward for not speaking with him directly, she knew herself well enough to know she was incapable of maintaining control of her emotions if she were to come face-to-face with Sebastian.

She was halfway down the stairs when she experienced the onset of a spell. Panic made her grip the bannister with both hands, and Anna's heart sank as she considered the odds of reaching her room before the decision was made for her. Aware of how precarious her position was on the stairs, she barely had time to sit down before the familiar sensation of lethargy swept over her.

In the next instant, she found herself standing on the Falcon at the ship's bow. The waves were churning wildly, and behind her a loud crack split the air as a blast of wind filled the sails until they were straining against the ropes that held them fastened to the masts. Anna looked over her shoulder and opened her mouth in a silent scream at the darkness chasing the ship. The moment it engulfed the Falcon, she was hurtled forward at a speed faster than the ship had ever sailed until it suddenly jerked to a halt.

Unprepared for the abrupt stop, Anna fell forward and crashed into someone directly in front of her as she was thrust into a strangely lit room filled with furniture. The woman she'd stumbled into turned around and eyed her with irritation. Anna began to apologize, but when she tried to speak, nothing came out of her mouth. Silently, she tried to display her regret at having bumped into the woman, but her inability to speak made the woman eye her with disgust.

With one last look of displeasure, the woman turned away, leaving Anna standing in a wide aisle lined with various items of furniture. The brightness of the room was in direct contrast to the pleasant temperature of the room. Despite so many people in the large room, it was much cooler than any social function she had ever attended. She looked up and blinked at the bright lighting that was so odd looking, but didn't seem out of place in the large room.

Anna returned her attention to the aisle she was in, suddenly registering for the first time that everyone was wearing different types of historical costumes. A costume party? But where was the orchestra? And why couldn't she hear anything? She saw several people talking to each other, as they stopped to study a piece of furniture. They consulted a paper brochure they held, but the silence in the room was complete, and it frightened her.

As she stood staring around her, completely lost as to what to do, a young man dressed in a dark blue jacket and trousers walked toward her. He wore a shiny gold medal on his breast pocket, and with a smile he stopped and offered her one of the thin catalogues other people were holding. She nodded her thanks as he continued on his way.

The slickness of the paper against her fingers was unlike any piece of paper or book she'd ever held in her hand. The vivid colors on the cover were crisp and clear, and she marveled at how someone had managed to create such a pamphlet. She opened it and stared in amazement at the bright, colorful images on the pages inside.

Riffling quickly through the thin book, she noted every page was as colorful as the book's cover. Filled with different images of furniture and artifacts, each page had small paragraphs of text next to each item, but it was a language she didn't recognize. She started to close the booklet, when something caught her eye as the pages flipped back into place.

She grew rigid with fear, certain she was imagining things. Fingers slipping slightly on the slick pages, she searched for the image she'd barely glimpsed. She was wrong. She had to be. It wasn't possible. The moment she found the page she was looking for, Anna's heart slammed into her chest with trepidation.

Sebastian's clock.

It was here. But how? Had he sold it? No. He would never willingly sell the clock. She glanced around the room, trying to understand why the grandfather clock Sebastian treasured would be in this room. Anna looked down at the picture again and tried to convince herself she was wrong. It had to be another clock. But she knew it wasn't. How the tall piece of furniture had gotten here, she knew without a doubt that it was the clock from Sebastian's study.

Staring down at the image, she suddenly realized it meant only one of two things, and she was only willing to consider one of those possibilities. She was being shown something in the future, which meant her first fear wasn't true. At least not at her point in time. But if she was in the future, why was she here? The one thing she found ironic was that everything she saw seemed so foreign to her, yet familiar at the same time.

Anna slowly turned around, marveling at everything she saw. There were small black objects people held in their hands, while several had the object pressed against their ear. One young woman held a bright pink object in her hand that had thin white cords running up into her ears. As the older couple she was with stopped to examine a beautiful pair of Queen Anne chairs, the girl bobbed her head and did a small shuffle and spin as if dancing. The moment their eyes met, the young girl grinned sheepishly, then rolled her eyes and turned away from Anna.

As Anna's gaze swept across the rest of the wide, open space cluttered with furniture, paintings, and smaller objects, in the distance she saw a woman with auburn-hair. The woman didn't even have to turn around, and Anna knew who she was. Fear lodged in her throat as she tried to understand what was happening. Although she desperately wanted to believe this was some type of hallucination, she knew it wasn't.

It was too much like the experience she'd had when she'd first awoken in Starling House. But this was different. It was even more tangible. In her previous vision, the only part of her body she'd felt was her hand and the stranger squeezing it tightly. Now, every part of her was alive with sensation. The scent of polished wood, the strange sights all around her, the lighting, the cool air on her skin, the woman she'd bumped into.

The only thing different was the silence. Not the slightest whisper. Anna looked down at the open booklet once more to study the image of Sebastian's clock. She had to find it. Maybe someone could tell her what had happened. Although she had no idea how she would be able to understand if she couldn't hear or speak. Fear rose in her throat as Sebastian's face filled her head. Dear God, if something had happened to him…she immediately suppressed the thought.

This was a vision. A frighteningly real vision, but it was nothing more than that. She was being shown this for a reason, but instinct said it was all about Sebastian's clock. Uncertain where to look for it, she saw a young woman dressed similarly to the young man who'd given her the catalog. Anna quickly closed the distance between the two of them and pointed to the image of the clock.

The younger woman said something, but Anna couldn't hear her and shook her head as she pointed to her ear. In response, the woman made a number of hand gestures that might have meant something, but Anna had no idea what. Even more confused, she stared helplessly at the young lady. With a smile and a nod, the woman gently touched Anna's arm and guided her down an aisle lined with furniture, then along several more aisles filled with paintings, furniture, and other different items.

Suddenly, the young woman came to a halt and pointed at something off to Anna's left. The moment she turned around, she drew in a sharp breath. It was Sebastian's clock. It had to be. How had it gotten here? A woman about Anna's height stood in front of the clock, her hand lovingly caressing the wood. Beside her a small, old woman opened the front of the clock and tried to reach something inside, up above the brass chimes hanging in the interior.

Another woman in dark blue clothing suddenly hurried forward and appeared to be chastising the two women. As the tall woman turned around, Anna gasped in amazement and awe. It was as if she was looking at herself. Desperately she struggled to comprehend what she was seeing, when the lights above were extinguished, and she was left standing in pitch black darkness.

A savage gust of wind suddenly filled the air around her and hit her in the chest with a painful blow. The blast of air pushed her backward at an incredible speed until she experienced the sensation of tumbling downward, head over foot, without control. The gusts of wind blowing past her ears grew in pitch, then suddenly stopped.

Anna blinked as the darkness vanished, and her body jerked violently against the main staircase's bannister in Starling House. Disoriented, her heart pounded wildly out of control as she clung to the spindles of the bannister. Trembling in reaction to the vividness of the clairvoyant episode, she rested her forehead against the smooth wood of the bannister. Unable to move, she stared down at the foyer between the spindles. Was she truly back in Starling House, or was this a vision, too? Behind her, Anna heard a loud gasp, and she turned her head to see Lady Harding hurrying down the stairs to where Anna was huddled against the stairwell railing.

"*Dear Lord*, you've had another spell," the woman exclaimed with fear and horror. "You might have fallen and injured yourself."

"I'm all right," Anna whispered hoarsely.

"Can you walk?"

"Yes." Anna nodded. Images flashed through her head, and as she looked down at the foot of the stairs, another wave of lethargy washed over her.

But to her surprise, it abated quickly, and as her gaze focused on the marble floor at the foot of the steps, she saw Sebastian standing in front of his study watching her. He smiled up at her, then turned and walked into his study. Puzzled by his reaction, she drew in a quick breath of surprise. It wasn't Sebastian. It was his father. Pulling herself up, Anna slowly began to descend the steps. Lady Harding uttered a gasp of protest and touched her shoulder.

"What on earth are you doing, Anna? You need to be in bed."

"Not yet," she whispered. "There's something I have to do for Lord Starling."

"Lord Sta—do you mean Levi?"

The hoarsely spoken question made Anna nod her head as she continued down the stairs. With each step downward, the weakness and lethargy eased its way out of her limbs, and by the time she reached the open doorway of the study, she was steady on her feet.

Her strength beginning to return rapidly, she entered Sebastian's sanctuary. Anna looked around the study, confused when she didn't see any sign of Lord Starling. Had she imagined him? As she turned to face Lady Harding, she saw a shimmer of light out of the corner of her eye.

Immediately, her heart twisted painfully in her chest as she saw the transparent form of her uncle smiling at her. Beside him was Lord Starling, and Uncle Augustus's arm was draped over Lord Starling's shoulder as the other man pointed toward the grandfather clock. The moment her gaze fell on the tall clock, her uncle and Sebastian's father faded from view.

Once more, Anna's heart began to pound rapidly in her

chest, and she walked forward to stand in front of the clock. A strange warmth flooded through her, forcing her hands to press against the warm wood surrounding the glass door of the timepiece. The sudden memory of the little old woman from her vision trying to reach up inside the clock made Anna gently tug the glass door open.

"*Dear God*, Anna, what are you doing? *Stop, Anna. You mustn't. Anna, please.*" Fear vibrated through Lady Harding's voice, but Anna ignored the woman's anguished pleas.

Whatever she was about to find, Uncle Augustus and Levi wanted her to find it. Of that, she was certain. She had no idea what she was supposed to be looking for, but Anna slowly reached up inside the cabinet's interior. Her fingers brushed across a rough surface of wood but found nothing. There had to be something here. There had to be.

Everything centered around Sebastian's clock. Otherwise, she wouldn't have seen her uncle and Lord Starling standing in front of it. The memory of the old woman reaching up inside the clock filled her head. Whatever the woman had been reaching for had been much higher up in the clock. Rising up on her tiptoes, the tips of Anna's fingers brushed against a long metal handle. Anna stretched her arm even more until her shoulder ached from the strain, and as her hand wrapped around the lever, she heard a vicious oath echo behind her.

"*What* the *hell* are you doing?"

The fury in Sebastian's voice startled her, and she almost lost her grip on the handle before she pulled it downward. A quiet click filled the air down at her feet, and as she stepped backward, a hidden drawer popped open at the base of the clock.

"*Oh, God.*" Lady Harding's whisper echoed through the quiet with anguish and fear. "What have you done, Anna? What have you done?"

The woman suddenly took two quick steps toward the

clock and pulled the drawer open. The strength of the woman's hard tug threw the compartment off its tracks and it landed on the floor in front of the clock. The moment it was free, the contents of the drawer spilled out onto the carpet. Frantically, the viscountess tried to gather up the large quantity of letters scattered across the floor. She was muttering incoherent words as her hands scraped and clawed at the yellowing letters on the carpet at Anna's feet.

"Stop *now*, my lady."

The viciously sharp command made Lady Harding freeze where she was kneeling in front of the letters. Fear and remorse made Anna's heart rise in her mouth. They were letters. Correspondence, Anna knew Levi and Uncle Augustus had written to each other. Dear God, what had she done?

"Clearly, this is *your* doing, Miss Sawyer. Her ladyship knows *not* to enter this room or *touch* anything in here. Now tell me *what the hell* the two of you are doing in *my* study."

The rage darkening Sebastian's face made Anna take a quick step back. An undefinable emotion flitted across his face before his fury returned. The antipathy on his handsome face made her flinch with fear. When she didn't reply, he looked down at his mother, still kneeling in front of the clock, her head bent, and her shoulders slumped in a look of defeat.

"Since Miss Sawyer refuses to answer me, I'll ask you, Lady Harding. What are you doing in here, and what are you trying to hide?"

"The truth." Anna suddenly found her voice, and her quiet words broke through the tension hanging in the air. "The truth your father tried to convince your mother to tell you a long time ago, but she refused because she loved you too much to hurt you any more than you'd already been hurt."

Sebastian's anger was still evident, but there was a growing puzzlement and confusion on his face that only increased Anna's regret for her actions. She should never have opened the clock. Sebastian turned his attention back to the woman knelt in front of the clock. Slowly, he bent over to pick up one of the letters off the carpet.

"Mother? Did you know these letters were here?"

At Sebastian's question, a shudder rocked Lady Harding's frame, and Anna's sorrow and self-reproach deepened. Uncle Charles was right, she *was* too impetuous. Unable to watch the pain her actions would inflict on the man she loved and the woman she'd come to see as a beloved friend, Anna gave way to cowardice for the first time in her life. Sprinting toward the doorway, she managed to evade Sebastian's attempt to catch her arm and bring her to a halt. Sick to her stomach at what she'd done, Anna fled the study.

"*Anna, stop.*" Sebastian's sharp command scraped across her senses, but she ignored his order and raced up the stairs. Without thinking things through, she'd done the unforgivable, and she knew she'd destroyed any possibility of Sebastian ever loving her.

Chapter 26

Sebastian watched Anna disappear around the corner of the upstairs hall, then returned to the study. As he entered the room again, he saw his mother had already gathered most of the correspondence up off the floor. Not about to let her leave without an explanation, Sebastian pulled his mother to her feet, then tugged the thick stack of letters out of her hands. It took two good tugs before Lady Harding's grip gave way.

"Who do these letters belong to?" Sebastian frowned as he stared down at the handwriting in puzzlement.

"They're mine. Your father hid them for me." Lady Harding's sharp reply held the faint hint of tears, sorrow, and fear. Sebastian jerked his head up and narrowed his gaze at her.

"I know your handwriting, my lady, and these weren't written by you."

Suddenly growing still, his gaze returned to the top letter of the stack he held in his hands as he recognized his father's handwriting. Letters his father had addressed to an Augustus Wentworth. Frowning with puzzlement, he continued to sift through the letters. The correspondence was a mix of missives addressed to his father in an unfamiliar handwriting and letters that bore his father's familiar strong scrawl addressing the man Sebastian didn't know. Baffled, he shook his head as he continued to sort through the letters to the bottom of the stack.

"This is correspondence between father and a man by the name of Augustus…" Sebastian's head jerked up, and he stared at his mother in stunned bewilderment. "Is this Augustus Wentworth related to Anna?"

"Yes." Lady Harding's reply was a harsh whisper of sound. "Augustus was her uncle."

"Augustus Wentworth. Captain Wentworth's brother?"

"Yes. They were childhood friends of your father's and mine, as well as their sister Serena, Anna's mother."

"Did you know these letters were in the clock?" At his question, his mother paled significantly, and her expression became pinched as if she was in deep pain.

"*No.*"

"But you thought it a possibility." Sebastian eyed Lady Harding carefully, but she kept her gaze focused on the floor.

"Yes."

"Do you know what's in these letters?" Sebastian's body tightened with a sudden growing horror. "If I read these, will I learn my father isn't Levi Reddington?"

"*No.*" Dismay and horror filled the gasp that escaped his mother as she jerked her head up to stare at him in shock. Her appalled expression quickly transformed into one of anger. "You are most *definitely* Levi's and my son. All you need to do is look at the portrait of your father in the salon. You are the very image of your father when he was your age."

"But you *do* know what's in these letters." The statement was met with silence, and Sebastian's mouth tightened with anger. "Damn it, *answer me*, mother."

"*Yes.*" The steely demeanor he'd witnessed more and more since Anna's arrival had returned as she met his gaze steadily and with determination. "But they have nothing to do with you, and I would appreciate it if you would respect your father's and my privacy."

"Anna said they held the truth. The truth about what?" Sebastian frowned as his puzzlement returned. "What are you trying to hide, my lady?"

"I'll not answer any more questions, my lord. Give me the letters, and we shall not speak of it again." Lady Harding stretched out her hand in a silent demand that he comply with her wishes. For a brief instant, he almost obeyed her, then refused her demand with a fierce shake of his head.

"I'll return them after I've sorted through them." His words made his mother release a soft sound that resembled one an animal might make when wounded or terrified. Sebastian narrowed his gaze at her, then nodded his head toward the door. "As I recall, when you returned to Starling House, you swore never to enter this study again. This is the second time in a month you've broken that oath. I trust you'll leave and never enter this room again."

"Sebastian—" His mother's voice was almost inaudible as she abruptly halted in mid-speech. To his surprise, he saw tears form in his mother's eyes before she nodded and hurried out of the study.

With a frown of confusion, Sebastian stared at the empty doorway. What the hell was happening in his house, and how had Anna come to discover the clock had a hidden compartment? A secret drawer even *he* hadn't known about. Had his mother told her where it was? No, from Lady Harding's reaction, he knew it was a secret she would never have shared with anyone.

So how had Anna known the drawer was there or even how to open it? Slowly moving toward his favorite seat by the fire, he sank down into the leather, winged-back chair and set the stack of correspondence on the table beside him. Picking up the letter on top, he opened it and began to read.

November 12, 1871
My dearest Augustus,

You should see Sebastian. He's a spirited little chap. He has his mother's stubbornness, and my patience. He will be a formidable opponent to face in the house of lords, I think.

Lily and I both miss you very much. We are eagerly awaiting your return next month for the holidays. I have something special planned when you arrive. Lily will take Sebastian and Lydia to Birchwood a couple of days after the new year, and I intend to clear the Starling House with a well-earned holiday. We will have the house to ourselves for that time. You will be able to cook whatever you wish, provided you leave cook's kitchen as she left it before you return home. You know how fond I am of your early morning delights.

As always, my letters are far too short, but we both know that it is best they stay that way. Lily sends her love, as do I.

Levi

Sebastian folded the letter and laid it down on the table with a perplexed frown. It was obvious Augustus Wentworth had been a close friend of his parents. Why had his mother been so frantic to have the letters returned to her? It didn't make any sense. With a disgruntled twist of his mouth, he picked up the next piece of correspondence. Several letters later, his bafflement had only grown as he found nothing out of the ordinary in the writings that had been exchanged between his father and Augustus Wentworth.

The letters the two men exchanged were like those any man might write to a very good friend. He reached for the next letter and a glance at the date showed it to be four years after his parents had been married.

July 20, 1871
My dearest Augustus,

The most wonderful thing has happened. Lily has met someone. He's a delightful chap. I like him very much, and I've encouraged Lily to spend more time with him. He will be good for her, as I know she's been lonely, although she reassures me she hasn't.

I wish things had been different for the three of us. We both know the idea of living in paris would never have worked as I didn't have the heart to ignore my grandfather's wish for an heir before the old man died. It was a wonderful dream to have. The alternative was the best solution for the three of us. God knows your suggestion that she and I marry was her salvation, as well as an answer to my own prayers. I have offered several times over the past two years to ease her suffering, but you know how stubborn she can be. She has said it's difficult enough for me to become aroused whenever I share her bed while trying to make her with child. Still, I am well aware that women have needs, just as men do.

However, now that young Harding has entered her life, I think it quite likely she will be adequately satisfied for some time to come, and that she will find an immeasurable amount of pleasure in the young man's arms. Harding is ten years younger than us, and Lily has expressed doubts as to the age gap.

When I insisted on meeting the fellow, she objected with her usual inflexible will, but I took it upon myself to invite the man for dinner. She wasn't happy with me when I told her what I'd done, but the entire evening was quite pleasant. I cannot tell you how much I enjoyed seeing her blush like she did years ago, before the three of us began down the path we've followed for several years now.

It was obvious to me in the first few minutes that Harding is enthralled with our dear girl. I can tell she is trying to resist him, but I believe she's already halfway in love with the chap. She was concerned with the matter of our unusual marriage, but I addressed the situation directly and in a matter-of-fact way after dinner, when Lily retired to the salon and left Harding and me to enjoy a glass of cognac.

I confess I couldn't help being amused at his reaction when I asked him if he was hoping for a liaison with Lily. The poor chap stammered and stuttered as if he was fresh out of eton, but I quickly put him at ease and said he had my blessing to enjoy Lily's company as often and in whatever manner he wished provided he treated her with respect and kindness. I told the man point blank that if he were to hurt our dear girl, I would make him pay dearly for doing so.

Naturally, the man stared at me as if I were mad, but I explained I loved Lily as dearly as one would a sister, and that our marriage was a platonic one that we'd entered into for convenience. Lily had been worried as to how to explain our unique arrangement, but I indicated to the young man that I had certain physical limitations that prevented me from sharing Lily's bed anymore. The young man clearly didn't know how to respond when I gave him my blessing to be a regular visitor at starling house.

However, since that moment, Harding has become a familiar face in the house. With each day that passes, I see him falling deeper in love with our Lily. Our girl has put up somewhat of a fight as she believes herself too old for Harding. But for his young age, Harding is far from a callow youth. He's also learned how to bend her to his will. She seldom argues with him unless it is a matter she feels strongly about.

I cannot begin to tell you how much i've enjoyed the battle of wills between them. They remind me of another couple we know. Lily and I both believe the young man to be quite handsome, but fear not, I am not one to betray the one who holds my heart or the love I carry inside it. It is a love that I will never deny.

Promise me, Augustus, that you will come to starling house soon. I am eager for you to meet the young man and see how happy Lily is. She's positively radiant and even more beautiful than she's ever been. I know she would love to see

*you, and after a few nights, we can go to Birchwood, where
you know we will be safe to be ourselves.*

*With my fondest of wishes for your happiness,
Your Levi*

Sebastian allowed the letter to fall into his lap as he tried to understand how delighted his father was that his mother and Lord Harding had met. His father hadn't just been happy for his wife, he'd been thrilled. He'd even gone so far as to encourage Harding to feel free to bed Sebastian's mother. Sebastian grimaced as he lifted the letter and reread the part about his father's wish to ease Lady Harding's suffering. What suffering?

The answer to the question was immediate, and Sebastian winced at the idea of his father satisfying his mother in bed. While he understood his parents had clearly had sex before his mother had taken Harding as her lover, it wasn't an image he wanted to have floating around in his head. Suddenly stiffening in his chair, Sebastian picked up and reread the last few lines of the letter. What had his father meant by the words safe to be ourselves?

Had his father, Augustus Wentworth, and his mother been involved in a ménage à trois relationship? It wasn't unheard of, but he quickly dismissed the idea. Sebastian's father had mentioned his wife refusing to share his bed because she'd known how difficult it would be for Sebastian's father. So, what exactly had his father meant by the words *safe to be ourselves?*

Sebastian read the paragraph again and for the first time, he noted the unusual way his father had signed the letter. Something deep in the recesses of his brain stirred to life, but he quickly locked the door to keep it from emerging. Slowly, he picked up the next letter from Augustus Wentworth to Sebastian's father.

My glorious and beautiful Levi,

I cannot begin to tell you how happy our two weeks together made me. Every moment spent with you at Birchwood will be etched in my memory forever. If only we could have more moments like that in each other's company. I cannot express the depth of emotion I experienced waking up each morning to my lover's tender touch. My love reaches the depths of my soul, and I am certain I am loved with the same depth I feel as well.

I was delighted to see how radiant Lily looked. Young Harding, as you said, is good for her. I cannot bear to think what might have become of her if we'd not rescued her from Darrenton. Of equal dismay is the thought of the miserable future you would have faced by marrying someone other than our dear girl. It would have made it impossible for you and me to be together if you had married someone else. You were right to remind me at Birchwood that marrying Lily was the best thing that could have happened to the three of us.

At least you and I have been able to enjoy unfettered moments of joy and happiness, even though every moment we spend with each other is never enough. My heart is always full when we greet each other, and when we say goodbye, I cannot begin to describe the pain and anguish I feel. It is as if my heart is being ripped from my chest each time we part.

Yours, Augustus

The door Sebastian had locked in his mind rattled violently as the truth tried to push its way into his consciousness. Dropping the letter onto the table, he sprang to his feet and strode to the liquor cabinet. He poured himself a stiff glass of brandy and tossed it down his throat. His mind reeling, Sebastian poured himself another glass of liquor and dispatched it just as quickly as the first.

Slowly turning toward his chair, he stared at the stack of letters he was halfway through. His stomach lurched at the thought of continuing, but if these letters represented a truth his mother had withheld from him, Sebastian wanted to know what that truth was. In the back of his mind, a voice quietly reminded him that his mother wasn't the only one who had not shared the truth with him. Sebastian poured another strong portion of brandy and carried it back to his chair.

Picking up another letter, he noted the date, then briefly skimmed the missive before dropping it onto the growing stack of letters he'd already read. There were only a few letters left, and he picked up the next one. The moment he saw the date, his gut twisted viciously. The letter had been written only three days after Sebastian had caught his mother in James Harding's arms outside her bedroom. Dread slid through him as he picked up his brandy glass and tossed back the few fiery drops left in the crystal snifter. Steeling himself for yet another blow, Sebastian began to read his father's handwriting.

My dearest Augustus,

The worst has happened. Sebastian caught Lily and James in each other's arms. The boy was apparently quite brutal in his condemnation of her. Lily is beside herself, and she's convinced Sebastian will never forgive her. I have tried vigorously, and to no avail, to convince her that we tell the boy the truth. I think him old enough to hear it, but Lily, as stubborn as always, refuses to be reasonable.

She said it will be a cold day in hell before she ever comes between me and the boy. Lily says Sebastian idolizes me, and I told her that knowing his father has feet of clay would be good for the boy. His condemnation of Lily was beyond cruel from what little I've been able to pry from her. The thought of the two of them being estranged is breaking my heart, and I don't know how to fix it.

Like the fool I can be on occasion, I vowed not to tell the boy anything without her approval. Naturally, that tied my hands when I failed to convince Lily to sit beside me as we tell Sebastian the truth. The lad has a good head on his shoulders, and while I've no doubt the truth of who I am and who I love will be a shock, I think he will come to accept it in time. I have great faith in my son. He has always been stalwart and defended those who are defenseless. It is why I think he can handle the truth.

Help me, my beloved Augustus. What am I to do? How can I help Sebastian see his mother's happiness is of the utmost importance to me, just as his happiness is significant to me as well? How do I make him understand James is vital to Lily's happiness?

I need to see you. I need your calm and sage advice. I need you to comfort me as only you can. I am lost as to how I can help my son understand that his mother deserves happiness, even if she must hide the love she and James have for each other. How do I tell Sebastian that the three of us, and now James, have done what we had to do to grasp small moments of happiness, without condemning all of us to a hellish existence from the scandal? It is unbearable for me to think of Sebastian losing all his friends, Lydia and Caroline never making suitable matches, or Alexander and Francis losing the protection of my name. Neither of us are so selfish as to inflict such a terrible fate on those we love.

It is why all of us have taken great care to maintain the outward appearance of Lily's and my happy marriage within the Marlborough Set. We have simply explained Lily's relationship with James as that of her need of an escort to society events as I have never cared for society's function.

While there has been gossip, I have made it clear there is nothing to the rumors as James and I have become the best of friends. He is like the younger brother I have never had.

The world is unfair, and Sebastian will learn that soon enough, but I want my boy to be a compassionate man. I want him to understand that how we are made is not the total sum of us. I want Sebastian to know there are many kinds of love. But he also needs to understand that for some, a heart can only love once, no matter where that love might be found.

Please, my beloved, give me the words of wisdom that will help me convince Lily that Sebastian must be told the truth, or at least give him something that will help him open up to the awareness of what you and I mean to each other.

I want him to understand that our love for each other doesn't change my love for Lily, my love for him or the rest of the children. I have no regrets about what I've done, and I know Lily feels the same, but I'm afraid that in refusing to tell Sebastian the truth, Lily will be punished for protecting me. To say I am reeling, and grieving is a mild description of what I am experiencing at this moment. Help me, Augustus. Give me the words to make my world right again.

Yours, Levi

The letter his father had written slipped out of Sebastian's fingers and floated to the floor as he leaned back into his seat and rested his head against the padded leather of the high-back chair. Staring up at the ceiling, Sebastian tried to reconcile the secret life his father had lived. A life that if he'd been discovered and convicted, would have resulted in his father being sent to prison, just as Oscar Wilde had been only a couple of months ago.

The irony of his personal obsession of living a life that was proper and dignified was not lost upon Sebastian. That was something he'd learned from his father. From the moment he'd become Viscount Starling, he'd worked hard to ensure the family name remained free of scandal, just as his father had.

Now, he realized why his father had worked hard not to do anything that would bring attention to the Reddington name. A scandal of even the smallest size might have exposed the private world his father had built for himself. The entire family would have suffered if the names Augustus Wentworth and Levi Reddington had been linked together in any way other than that of good friends.

One hand rubbing his forehead, Sebastian wished his father were alive so that they could talk. His father had been a thoughtful man who had never shied away from explaining something to Sebastian in a way that he could understand. But Sebastian wasn't sure it was possible for him to ever understand his father's relationship with Wentworth.

Sebastian glanced around the study that had once been his father's. The hours he'd spent in here either learning about how to run an estate or how to fix a broken toy had been joyful ones. How could he stop loving a father he'd looked up to and admired for being a man of strong principles and exemplary character? A man who'd taught him how to be kind and considerate to others.

Levi Reddington had been an honorable man who'd never turned anyone away in need. Nor had his father shied from pointing out injustices wherever he saw them. That was the man Sebastian remembered and loved. Would any of that have changed if his parents had told him the truth about his father when he was twelve? How did someone act or feel when one discovered their father was in love with another man?

Numb. It was the only way he could describe how he felt at this moment. How could his mother even think Sebastian would have condemned his father for being who he was? The answer sliced through him with the sharpness of a blade. Sebastian's behavior and condemnation of his mother that morning long ago had to have made his mother conclude he would react the same way toward his father if Sebastian had been told the truth.

It was difficult to comprehend how his father could love another man in the same way a man and woman did. And yet, there had been a depth of emotion in the last few letters the two men had exchanged that Sebastian couldn't dismiss. Still, his parents had deceived everyone. His father had married his mother and used her to beget an heir. It didn't matter that his mother had willingly agreed to the arrangement. Did he approve of his father's choices? No. How could he? His father had been living a lie. He'd married Sebastian's mother to secure an heir. What kind of man would do such a thing?

Self-disgust burned its way through Sebastian. *He* was that kind of man. That he'd answered the question with his own name illustrated he was no less flawed than his parents. If he was being truly honest with himself, he was far worse. The memory of telling Anna that his marriage to Margaret was solely to secure a male heir sickened him. His offer to make Anna his mistress had been more than insulting, it had been cruel.

When she'd pointed out his intentions where Margaret was concerned, Sebastian had ruthlessly dismissed her words. He'd allowed Anna to believe he would have no regrets leaving Margaret's bed only to enter hers a short time later. The almost tangible sensation of a whip lashing across his back made Sebastian wish it was the real thing.

He deserved a much harsher sentence for what he'd done to Anna. He was a callous, soulless man without scruples or a conscience. If he had still been alive, Sebastian's father would be appalled and disgusted by him.

While Sebastian's mother and father had made their choices as a matter of survival, Sebastian's choices had been made from fear. A fear that the woman he loved would betray him in the same way he had believed his mother had his father. The choices Sebastian had made, and the life he'd plotted out for himself, reinforced what a cold-hearted bastard he truly was. Anna had been right when she'd accused him of hiding behind a façade of respectability and proper behavior.

The secret life his father had led was not for him to

judge. Sebastian couldn't condemn his parents for the choices they'd made or the things that made them who they were. At least they'd been honest with themselves as to why they'd made the decisions they had. Sebastian hadn't been honest with anyone as to who he was, least of all himself.

The numbness in his body strengthened as he remembered the terrible things he'd said to his mother the morning after seeing her with Harding. His mother had sacrificed a great deal by protecting his father's and Sebastian's relationship.

Guilt slammed into him as an image of his mother formed in his head. For years, he'd punished her for an offense she wasn't guilty of. He'd inflicted so many harsh, cruel words on his mother. Each time she'd simply turned away from him with a pain and sadness in her eyes that he'd never allowed to touch his heart.

Anna had been right to find him contemptible for the way he treated his mother. Lady Harding hadn't deserved his scorn or denunciation. The memory of Anna condemning him for his behavior made Sebastian sit up straight. Had his mother told her the truth or had his fiery, brave, loyal Anna simply put two and two together? He couldn't believe his mother would tell Anna about his father, unless Anna had known the entire time she'd been here.

"*Bash.*" The strident tone in Alexander's voice barely penetrated Sebastian's brain as he vaguely noted his brother had charged into his study in a state of raw fury. "I'm speaking to you, Lord Starling."

"*Go away, Alexander.* I'm not in the mood for whatever complaint you have regarding my pompous behavior," he snarled.

"I've no intention of leaving until I say what I've come to say." Alexander's words were filled with icy contempt. "I told you if you were ever cruel to our mother again, I would make you pay."

"And exactly how do you expect to make me pay, dear brother?" Sebastian sprang to his feet to eye his younger brother bitterly. "I doubt there's anything you can say that will surpass what I've just learned in the past two hours."

"*Christ Jesus*. You *know*." Alexander's observation was hoarse as he looked down at the yellowed letters on the table.

Alexander's reaction sent Sebastian reeling once more. His brain sluggishly tried to latch onto the fact that his younger brother knew about their father.

"Are you telling me you knew about this?" Sebastian asked hoarsely. Guilt made Alexander's mouth turn downward in a grimace of regret as he nodded.

"I stumbled on some correspondence that father exchanged with Anna's uncle." Alexander met Sebastian's furious gaze with commiseration. "I tried to convince Mother to tell you the truth, but she refused. I was just as shocked as you, but even more so because Father wasn't…"

The moment his brother's voice trailed off into silence, Sebastian saw pain twist its way across Alexander's face. Without saying anything, Sebastian moved to close his study door, then went to the liquor cabinet and poured two glasses of cognac. Returning to his brother's side, he handed the younger man a glass, then pointed toward the chair across from his.

"You learned Harding was your real father, didn't you?" His quiet statement made Alexander jerk his head up and stare at Sebastian in amazement.

"You knew that?"

"No, but I suspected it." He stared down at the amber liquid in his snifter.

"How did you find these?" Alexander nodded toward the open letters.

"Anna found them."

"Anna? But how…" Puzzlement furrowed his brother's brow. "Did mother tell her?"

"No, I don't think so," Sebastian mused quietly. "Before I entered the study, Mother seemed confused as to what Anna was doing. I heard her tell Anna to stop, and when I entered the study, the compartment at the base of the clock popped open. When the letters spilled out onto the carpet, Mother became distraught, and Anna stared down at them without any surprise at all."

"Then if Mother didn't tell her, who did?"

"I don't know, but I intend to find out," Sebastian said with quiet resolve.

In his head, he pictured the scene he'd witnessed only a couple of hours earlier when Anna had said the letters contained the truth his mother had refused to tell him. How could she have known the truth about his father? Had Augustus Wentworth told her?

Sebastian glanced toward the clock he'd inherited from his father as another memory filled his head. He frowned as he remembered the day Anna had stood staring at the clock with a look of bewilderment. Her face had been ashen, and when Sebastian had touched her shoulder, she'd jumped violently, as if he'd awakened her from a trance.

He had no idea why, but something about the memory made him believe Anna's knowledge of the letters had to do with that day here in the study. Sebastian turned his head to see Alexander staring into the fire. The pensive expression on his younger brother's face made Sebastian clear his throat.

"You asked not too long-ago what mother had done to make me treat her so poorly. Just before I turned twelve, I saw her and Harding together in a compromising position. What I didn't know at the time was that Father had given them his blessing."

"That's what mother said when I found the collection of letters in an old trunk. Mother insisted you wouldn't believe her if we showed you the letters."

"I probably wouldn't have," Sebastian sighed before

taking a swig of his brandy.

"And now?"

"Everything is here in the letters Father wrote to…to Wentworth." Sebastian tapped on the correspondence that he'd read, still grappling with his father's secret life. "I wouldn't blame her if she refuses to forgive me."

"She will. Mother loves you very much, Bash. I know she'll understand."

"And you? Have you forgiven her? She kept secrets from you as well. All of them did."

"From what mother tells me, your father—"

"*No*," Sebastian growled with a ferocity that made Alexander jerk in surprise. "My father was *your father* as well. He gave you his name, and you're my heir if I don't have a son. Father loved you. He loved all of us. I won't have anyone in this family thinking otherwise."

Alexander met Sebastian's gaze for a moment before he tossed down the cognac Sebastian had poured for him.

"I did love him, Bash. Losing him was devastating for me too, but I cared about James as well. He was very much like your—" His brother stopped as Sebastian glared at him, before he continued. "—our father in many ways. James was always patient and willing to listen. He became a second father to me when Father died. It wasn't until I learned the truth that I understood why James always gave Caroline, Francis, and me his full attention. It's all just so…so…"

"Fucked up."

The moment he filled in the blank for Alexander, his brother's eyes widened in shock. Without a word, Alexander rose to his feet and headed quickly across the room to pour himself another drink. Slowly turning to face Sebastian, his brother's eyebrows arched in surprised amusement, and a small smile touched his lips.

"Now *that* was a remark worthy of a man who's suddenly decided to forget about being pompous for a change." His brother's statement made Sebastian snort and take a drink of his own cognac.

"If you knew half the things I've done of late, you would call me something far worse." Sebastian closed his eyes as he remembered the joy of making love to Anna, then the anguish that had followed as he'd deliberately destroyed any feelings she had for him.

"You're in love with her." Alexander's solemn words quietly broke through the air as he returned to his seat. Sebastian opened his eyes in surprise. This time it was his brother's turn to snort. "Did you really think you were hiding how you feel about Anna? Hell, even mother knew it. She mentioned it the morning after you left for Birchwood."

"*Christ Jesus*," he muttered as he looked away from Alexander. "It wasn't until I...I was a fool, and I saw it too late."

"Bloody hell, Bash. I've always looked up to you, but I'm beginning to think I might have misplaced my admiration." The angry words made Sebastian jerk his head back in Alexander's direction as his brother glared at him in outrage. "If you don't get up off your ass and climb those stairs to tell her how you feel, I'll lose every bit of respect I've had for you since I was a boy."

"I doubt she'll listen to me."

"She will if you tell her you love her. I don't know what you did, but apologize. You won't regret it. She'll make you a damn good wife."

"That's the problem. I made her a different offer." Sebastian sucked in a breath of self-disgust as Alexander stared at him with a gamut of emotions flashing across his face. Seconds later, his younger brother leaned forward with a threatening look that suggested he was seriously considering the idea of thrashing Sebastian.

"Are you *telling* me you offered to make her your *mistress*?" Alexander's voice was quiet, but vicious. The condemnation in his brother's soft accusation was almost as brutal as his own mental evisceration. Sebastian turned his head away.

"Yes," he rasped hoarsely. "I realized I was in love with her, and I pushed her away in the only way I knew how."

Sebastian rose to his feet in an abrupt lunge and moved to stand at the window and study the traffic rolling past the front of the house. When had it become dusk? It was a trivial thought, and he knew it was his brain's attempt to ignore the confession he'd just made to his brother.

He'd just dealt a savage blow to his relationship with Alexander, and it cut deep. Almost as deep as when he'd destroyed Anna with his insulting offer. An offer that had cost him the only woman he would ever love, simply because he'd refused to give her the one thing she deserved. His heart.

"I'm only going to say this one time, Sebastian, and if you don't do what I tell you, then we're going to come to blows." Behind him, Alexander's antipathy echoed in the way his brother called Sebastian by his given name. The sensation of his back being flayed open with a cat-o'-nine-tails returned with a renewed vengeance. "Go upstairs and convince her you love her. *Now.*"

Sebastian hesitated, then slowly turned around. Outrage made Alexander's eyes appear hard as flint. Everything about his brother's stance said he would make good on the threat to hit Sebastian. With a nod, Sebastian headed out of the study. He had no idea what he was going to say to Anna, and he could only hope she'd believe him when he told her how much he loved her.

Each step up the stairs and down the second-floor hallway increased the dread and fear twisting his gut. What would he do if she refused to listen to him? A voice in his head scoffed at him. He'd make her listen. Sebastian was only a few feet from Anna's bedroom when he heard his mother's voice floating out of the open doorway.

"When did she leave?"

Lady Harding's sharp words held a note of panic, and they were like a knife skewering his belly. In two long strides he was standing in the doorway of Anna's room to see several trunks waiting to be filled, and the wardrobe doors wide open. As he stared around the room, he saw Anna's maid looking uncomfortable in the face of his mother's distress.

"She left almost two hours ago, my lady."

The maid's answer made him flinch. Anna must have left immediately after she found his father's letters. Sebastian remembered how furious he'd been to find Anna and his mother in his study. The memory of her reaction when he'd demanded answers made Sebastian's muscles grow taut with anguished regret. He'd frightened her. Anna never retreated, but she had when he'd confronted her about the letters she'd discovered.

"Where is she?" he asked quietly, despite wanting to shout the question.

"Miss Anna received a letter this morning, my lord." The maid gestured toward the letter his mother held in her hand. "She told me to pack her things and that her uncle would make arrangements for someone to pick them up. She also left a letter for you and her ladyship."

The maid reached into her apron pocket, then handed him and his mother separate letters. Slowly, he opened the one addressed to him.

Lord Starling

> *Please accept my sincere gratitude for your generosity in allowing me to stay at starling house these past few months. I apologize for the inconvenience my presence has brought to your household. I wish you all the best on the occasion of your upcoming nuptials. I hope your wish for an heir is granted swiftly.*

Anna Sawyer

The formality of Anna's note was a sickening blow to his gut. The words were devoid of emotion, and the missive read as if it was the type of note one might write to an acquaintance of no importance.

"*Dear God*, she's gone back to the Falcon." His mother's soft gasp was filled with dismay. Looking up from the second piece of paper in her hand, Lady Harding clutched his arm. "She's gone to the docks without an escort, Sebastian. You must go after her. What if something happens to her?"

"Does the letter say where the ship is docked?" His chest constricted until it was difficult to breathe.

"Céleste's note to Anna says the ship is moored in berth ten at the West Indies dock." Horror filled his mother's voice as she choked out the location of the Falcon.

"*Bloody hell*," he whispered hoarsely. "That's close to where she was kidnapped by Hatshepsut's followers."

The blood drained from his mother's face, and he quickly steadied her as she swayed on her feet. His mind raced along with panic, fear, and fury at what an imbecile he'd been. Scully's men had been guarding the house and the Trafford residence for almost four months. Over the past few weeks, Scully's daily accountings had become mundane as the man had nothing to report.

Sebastian had allowed his guard to slip. Until this morning, he'd slowly convinced himself Hatshepsut's followers had failed to recognize Anna. He should have known better, and he should have been more diligent in believing the cult would find a way to monitor Anna's whereabouts.

No one, not even himself, had thought to consider the young boy who'd been selling newspapers up and down the street as an information source for the cult. The lad had been a familiar sight, selling papers on the street for more than a year before Anna came into his life. He'd been an utter fool not to instruct Scully to investigate anyone.

This morning, Scully had informed him that over the past several weeks, several of his men had observed the same carriage pausing to purchase a paper from the boy. Occasionally, the lad would disappear for a few minutes, then be back at his post selling papers. When the carriage had stopped for a paper today and rolled out of sight, the child had disappeared down a side street a few moments later.

Scully's man had immediately followed the boy. The guard had observed the boy speaking with someone in the carriage, and when he'd walked past the vehicle, the man had heard a woman's voice murmuring to the boy.

Apparently recognizing the guard as one of Scully's men, the child had muttered something to whomever was in the carriage before he then darted away. Before the security guard had a chance to look inside the carriage, the woman passenger had ordered the vehicle to move on, which it did at a fast pace. If anything happened to Anna, he would have no one to blame but himself. He should have insisted Scully check out anyone loitering near the house. Even a child who was a familiar sight on the street every day.

Gently, Sebastian pulled his mother's hand from his arm and raised it to his lips. The startled look on her face wasn't unexpected, but her expression aroused a wave of emotion in Sebastian. Guilt tightened his muscles until they ached uncomfortably as he met Lady Harding's gaze.

"I'll find her, mother, and I'll do my damnedest to make her see that Starling House is where she belongs." Sebastian's words clearly stunned his mother, and his mouth twisted in a grimace of regret. Aware of Lucy standing nearby, he leaned forward and kissed his mother's cheek, then whispered in her ear. "I have wronged you deeply. Forgive me."

Tears formed in her eyes as Sebastian stepped back from her, and he swallowed the knot that had closed off his throat. With a jerk of his head, he left Anna's room and strode quickly down the hall. As he ran down the main stairs, he called for Alexander, and the moment he reached the last step, his brother emerged from the study.

"What's happened?"

"She's gone. Her maid said Anna received a message from Céleste Dubois this morning and instructed the maid to pack her things." Sebastian forced Alexander to step back as he entered the study and waved toward the grandfather clock. "She left shortly after I found her and mother in my study with the letters."

"She's gone back to the Falcon, then." Alexander's observation made Sebastian bob his head sharply.

"I'm going after her."

"If you'd said otherwise, I would have dropped you to the floor with one blow." Alexander's relief was evident as his brother eyed him with satisfaction.

Sebastian moved quickly toward his desk, where he retrieved a revolver from the locked drawer of his desk. His brother raised his eyebrows as he watched Sebastian quickly load the weapon.

"Is that necessary?"

"I received news this morning that I'd not had time to act upon. Hatshepsut's followers have been tracking Anna's whereabouts for weeks, maybe the entire time she's been here."

"*Fuck.*" Alexander's anger was quickly followed with a look of alarm. "And Sarah?"

"Scully said they'd not noticed anything out of place at the Trafford residence either, but he's reviewing notes his men have taken over the last several months to see if there's something that's been overlooked." Alexander's fear was evident, and it matched his own. "I ordered him to increase the number of men watching the Trafford's house and inform the baron as to what's happened with the instruction to keep Sarah at home this evening."

"Knowing my Sarah, her father's going to have a fight

on his hands."

"I know you want to go to her, but I need you to do something for me first."

"*Name it.*" His brother's expression was grim as he bobbed his head.

"I want you to go to Guildford House and find out where Nicholas is. Then find Pratt. Have both of them meet me at the West Indies dock, berth ten. It's where the Falcon is moored."

"You can't go alone, Bash. It's obviously not safe."

"I'll take one of Scully's men with me. Now, go."

Alexander nodded sharply at the command and hurried out of the study. Sebastian followed close on his brother's heels, and as the front door closed behind him, he grimaced as he realized he should have told Hodgekiss to secure a hack for him. His gaze scanned the street looking for one of Scully's men, when he saw a recognizable figure at the end of the street. He gestured for the man to join him, just as a carriage rolled to a halt in front of the house.

"Lord Starling, you must come quickly."

The urgency in the familiar female voice took him by surprise, and he turned his head to see Charlotte Plummer's face in the window of the carriage.

"I'm afraid—"

"It's Anna," the young woman said with sharp insistence, and Sebastian took a step toward the vehicle. "I overheard my aunt and Lord Farthington talking. They're part of the cult you've been hunting, and I fear they're plotting to kill Anna. Please, we must hurry. I'll explain on the way."

Without hesitating, Sebastian opened the door of the carriage and flung himself into the seat opposite the young woman. It wasn't until the vehicle rocked forward that Sebastian saw something move in the darkness of the corner. The cowled figure leaned forward in a move of blazing speed before Sebastian even registered it was a person or saw the blow dart.

A second later, the weapon landed its projectile into the side of his neck just as if he'd been stung by a bee. Aware he only had a minute or less to react, Sebastian lunged toward the carriage door handle only to have the faceless monk drag him into the middle of the seat.

"Good heavens, my lord have you lost your mind?" Charlotte Plummer made a chastising sound. "I wouldn't want you to fall out of the carriage when it's obvious you're unwell. Besides, we need you."

"Why?" he asked as he tried to fight off the effects of the dart taking hold of his body and mind.

"Why do we need you?" Charlotte laughed softly as a malicious smile curved her lips. "Because you're the bait for a much more valuable prize."

"Anna," he whispered helplessly as Charlotte Plummer's features grew fuzzy.

"I see you understand. The minute I tell my friend you're in danger, she'll race to your side. And then I can clean up this mess for good." The words were faint in his ears, and fear gripped his insides tightly as he slid helplessly into a black void.

Chapter 27

Anna pushed the small potatoes around with her fork as she stared down at her plate. She'd always enjoyed Finley's cooking, but tonight, everything tasted like sawdust.

"Are you sure you don't want Finley to fix you something else?" her uncle asked quietly. Without lifting her gaze, Anna rejected his offer with a shake of her head.

"No, thank you. I'm just not hungry for some reason."

"A young man perhaps." There was a worried note in her uncle's voice, and Anna straightened in her chair to meet her uncle's concerned, yet curious, gaze.

"How soon before we set sail?"

"*Ma petite cherie*," Céleste said softly. "Will you not tell us what's happened to make you so sad?"

"I'm fine," Anna said quietly, but with a firmness that hid the fact that she was absolutely miserable. "I'm tired. I've not been sleeping well these last few weeks."

At least, that was the truth. She was exhausted from everything, and her heart ached in a way that made her think someone had gutted her like a fish. Anna forced herself to take a bite of potatoes, all too aware of her uncle's and Céleste's curiosity and concern.

"You've changed." Captain Wentworth's voice held an odd note that barely touched her mind.

"Have I?" Anna shrugged. "I imagine all the rules have finally caught up with me. I noticed the other day that I tend to think before I speak. I didn't want my language to reflect poorly on Lady Harding."

"I would think Lily not sending an escort with you this evening far outweighs any poor reflections on her because of your earthy language."

"I told you, Lady Harding didn't know I was leaving. I left without saying goodbye because I knew she would plead with me to stay, but I simply wanted to come home."

"Why do I think there's more to it than that?" The resolute tone in her uncle's voice made Anna stiffen. She met his penetrating gaze. "Especially when it comes to *how* you've changed. There's something different about you, and it's not just your language. You've lost that air of naiveté about you."

"You thought me naïve?" she asked with a small amount of irritation.

"Perhaps innocent is a better word." An odd expression swept across his face as he glanced at Céleste, then returned his attention to Anna. "It's as if someone's broken your heart and your spirit."

"My heart is perfectly intact," she lied.

"There it is," her uncle exclaimed. "You're cynical, guarded even."

"I am neither cynical nor guarded," Anna snapped as she pushed her chair back and stood up. "But I'm no longer the girl who is willing to please others at the expense of my own happiness. I did what you asked. I spent time with the Marlborough Set. Now, I'm home, and I have no intention of going back. Is that clear?"

Captain Wentworth stared at her in astonishment, and out of the corner of her eye, Anna saw Céleste reach out to clutch his arm. When her uncle didn't reply, she nodded sharply.

"If you'll excuse me, I'm going to change out of this

ridiculous contraption I've been forced to wear every day for the past several months, and then I intend to see if one of the men wishes to play a game of Brag."

The stunned look didn't leave her uncle's face as Anna glanced at his paramour. Céleste was studying her with narrowed eyes, and she knew her friend was far more astute than her uncle was when it came to matters of the heart. Unable to meet the Frenchwoman's assessing gaze, Anna turned away and left the captain's dining cabin and made her way to her cabin one deck below.

Everything in her cabin was just as she'd left it, except for a wardrobe that had been bolted into the cabin wall. She was certain Céleste had arranged for it, as she saw her clothes trunks nearby. Pressing her back into the cabin door, she closed her eyes and fought back the tears. Uncle Charles had almost guessed what was wrong with her. He'd said she was no longer naïve or innocent. Anna knew he was referring to her attitude, but her uncle was a smart man. Eventually, he would realize that she was no longer innocent.

All she needed to do was to divert his attention from the fact until they were at sea. Then it wouldn't matter because London would slowly become a distant memory. Her memories of Sebastian would take much longer to dim, but with each passing day Anna would work to make herself forget, even though she knew that would be an impossible task.

Anna blew out a harsh breath. If she was going to forget, then she needed to occupy her time, and what better than to enjoy a game of Brag and drink until her pain was a dull ache? With a determined twist of her lips, she quickly changed into a familiar pair of trousers, pulled on a shirt, and a pair of shoes. When she was done, Anna threw open the door and hurried up the stairs leading to the main deck.

Near the bow, she saw a group of her friends sitting on small crates and barrels, enjoying a game of cards. Anna headed toward them when a flash of blue and gold caught her attention at the gang plank. She turned and stared at the sight of Charlotte Plummer looking around as if she was lost.

"Charlotte," she exclaimed. "What on earth are you doing here?"

"*Oh, thank God, Anna.* I've found you," her friend exclaimed. There was a note of panic in her friend's voice, but the woman paused long enough to stare at her in appalled dismay. "Good heavens, what *are* you wearing?"

"What I always wear when I'm aboard the Falcon." Anna smiled at the woman's askance look. "Now tell me what you're doing here."

"It's Lord Starling." The fear threading through Charlotte's words sent an icy fear spiraling through Anna as she stared at the other woman. "I overheard Aunt Margaret and Lord Farthington discussing the Hatshepsut cult. I'm convinced they're the high priest and priestess you've been looking for."

"But how—"

"Oh, *do* give me some credit, Anna. With all the visits you and Sarah have made to the museum, it didn't take much for me to put things together. I know you and Sarah have been trying to find the leaders of the cult for some time now. Well, I know who they are, and they have Lord Starling."

Panic swept through Anna at her friend's statement. If Lady Margaret or Farthington hurt Sebastian, she would bring down the fires of hell upon their heads.

"Do you know where they are?"

"Yes, they're in a warehouse near the Isle of Dogs."

"How do you know that?" Anna asked with a frown, her senses suddenly making her hesitate, although she wasn't sure why.

"I was on my way to tell you what Aunt Margaret and Farthington planned, and when I arrived at Starling House, I saw his lordship climbing into my aunt's carriage."

Charlotte pressed her hand to her breast and closed her eyes as if her words were so terrifying she could barely go on.

"*Dear God*," Anna whispered in horror. "Sebastian."

"Exactly." Charlotte nodded sharply. "But at least I had the good sense to find a hack and follow them to the warehouse where Aunt Margaret's carriage stopped. I probably shouldn't have done it, but I followed them into the warehouse."

"Poseidon's balls, Charlotte. Are you mad?"

"Well, I needed to know what they were doing so I could tell you, didn't I? The inside of the building was just like all the temples I've read about so many times."

"Let me get Smitty and Hamish, we'll—"

"There's no time for more explanations. I watched them tying his lordship onto something that looked like an altar. I'm afraid we might be too late already."

Anna hesitated as her panic and fear said to go with Charlotte immediately. But in the next second, she knew she would only get herself and Sebastian killed if she didn't have help. With a shake of her head, Anna turned away from Charlotte.

"Hamish. Smitty. Come quick—" Anna's cry was interrupted as she heard Charlotte mutter something beneath her breath.

"Damnation, I thought you might do that." A familiar prick on the side of her neck made Anna turn her head to stare at the other woman in horror. "I'm afraid your friends aren't invited to this particular party, Anna. It's just you, Sarah, and Lord Starling who are expected at this intimate affair."

Anna tried to call out again, but a heavy hand clapped across her mouth as she sank into the void she'd experienced in the past. Just as she passed out, someone tossed her over a shoulder as if she was a sack of flour and carried her off the ship.

Anna heard the soft sound of voices arguing, along with an odd chirping noise as she pushed her way up out of the dark void. Eyes fluttering open, she gasped with fear as she realized she was hovering in the air. Panic made her frantically reach out for something to hold on to, but there was nothing. Slowly realizing she wouldn't fall, she stared down at the bed surrounded by strange apparatuses.

"*Ballocks*," she uttered softly as the figure in the bed came into full focus.

She was staring down at herself. Anna couldn't tell if she was simply asleep or if she was unconscious. A tall man stood at her bedside, gently stroking her cheek. A second later, he turned around, and she cried out Sebastian's name.

In the next instant, her body jerked hard as the cold stone beneath her back sent a chill of horror through her. Blinking her eyes to make them open wide, she found herself staring at a dark wall with dancing shadows. Slowly regaining her bearings, she realized she was lying on her side with her hands tied behind her back. Anna looked around her, hoping to see Sebastian, but when she didn't, her heart sank.

It had been a ruse. Charlotte had known she cared for Sebastian, and the woman had used that against her. Wherever she was, it had to be a warehouse like the last one she'd been imprisoned in. This time she was on the outer perimeter of what was obviously serving as a temple, although it wasn't complete like the last one. It only had the rudimentary structure of an Egyptian temple. The sound of voices whispered through the air, and Anna lifted her head slightly to look over her shoulder.

A woman stood on the other side of the immense building, arguing vehemently with a tall, dark-haired man. The couple was too far away for Anna to identify them with any real certainty. Although she had no doubt the woman was Charlotte because of the woman's blonde hair. Dressed in the robes of a high priestess, Charlotte wasn't wearing a mask. The stranger had his back to Anna, and he was dressed in a costume similar to Charlotte's. He suddenly shook his head as if he objected to whatever she was saying. In the next breath, Charlotte tugged the man's head down to kiss him passionately.

"*Hell's fire and damnation,*" Anna murmured as she stared in stunned amazement at the couple.

If Farthington was the man Charlotte was kissing, the woman had hidden her passion for the man well. Anna had been convinced her onetime friend hated the viscount. Now, the woman was displaying anything *but* hatred. Locked in a passionate embrace, the couple made Anna realize it was likely Charlotte was the man's mistress.

Still staring at the couple in amazement, her brain suddenly pounced on the fact that she should be looking for a way out. The first thing she had to do was free herself. Moving slowly so she didn't attract attention, Anna slowly came up on her knees, then hunched down and moved her arms forward until her bound hands were under her buttocks.

With a small grunt, she sank back down to the floor, then bent her legs and pulled them into her chest. Slowly, she was able to wiggle her arms and hands up and over her feet and legs until she was staring down at her bindings. Breathing hard from the exertion, she quickly laid down on her side again so anyone glancing her way would think she was still unconscious.

She could only hope the light was dim enough to keep anyone from noticing her hands were no longer behind her back. Anna's gaze searched for something she could use to cut through the rope binding her hands but saw nothing. With nothing to cut through the rope, Anna lifted her hands and studied the knots holding the rope in place, and a wave of relief sped through her.

Whoever had tied her up had obviously counted on the drug and her hands being bound behind her back to keep her from escaping. Raising her hands up to her mouth, she caught one end of the rope with her teeth and tugged gently. The rope gave way slightly, and Anna knew she had the correct end of the rope to loosen the knot enough to wiggle her hands free.

She was almost free of restraints when a soft scraping noise echoed close by. The sound made Anna grow still. Fully expecting someone had come for her, Anna's heart raced as she waited for unfamiliar hands to pull her to her feet. When it didn't happen, she slowly rolled toward the makeshift temple's interior.

"Anna."

"*Sarah?*" she gasped softly as she peered into the shadows

"We must stop meeting like this," Sarah whispered. Her friend's words caused Anna's lips to twist in a small smile, but she heard the fear in the other woman's voice.

"Are you hurt?"

"No, but I'm tied up and can't move."

"Hold on, I'm almost free." Bending her head again, Anna grasped the end of the rope and pulled harder while pressing her wrists together to slip one hand out of the rope and then the other.

As quietly as possible, she slid across the floor toward the dark area Sarah's voice had floated out of. Anna's fingers fumbled with the knot in the dark.

"Wait," Sarah whispered. "I need to move out into the light so you can see what you're doing."

Anna's friend slowly scooted her way into the dim light. While her features were still hard to see, Sarah's hands were much more visible. As Anna worked to free her friend, Sarah sighed softly.

"Alexander will die a young man if I continue to make him worry so much."

"He'll be fine," Anna murmured, darting a look over her shoulder to ensure they'd not been seen. "After tonight, the cult will be finished."

"If we survive, you mean." Sarah's cynicism made Anna shake her head vigorously.

"I may walk out of here injured, but I *will* walk out of here." Anna gritted her teeth, then released a small exclamation of triumph as she removed Sarah's restraints.

"What do we do now?" Sarah asked the moment she was free.

"We go for help."

Anna hesitated as she saw Charlotte and the man had donned their ceremonial masks and were walking toward the altar. Puzzled, she watched the couple climb the steps to the platform that ran the width of the building. As the High Priest and Priestess reached the platform that raised them up above the altar in front of them, cowled figures lined up in front of the altar. Why hadn't someone come for her or Sarah yet? Not that she was eager to fight her way out of this situation. A moment later, she understood why.

From a dark corner of the building, two followers in monk apparel appeared, dragging someone between them toward the altar. As the trio entered the light, Anna inhaled a sharp breath of fear as she recognized Sebastian's lean, muscular body.

"Bloody hell," she choked out, her body tightening with a terror she'd never experienced before.

"Who is...*dear God*. Sebastian." The horror in Sarah's voice made Anna jerk her head in her friend's direction.

"Go for help. I'll hold them off for as long as possible."

"But, what—"

"I won't leave him," she said emphatically. Anna saw Sarah's wide-eyed surprise as she answered her friend's unspoken question. "I love him, and I won't leave without him. Now go."

Anna pointed to a door she could see, and Sarah nodded at the harsh command. Staying low, Sarah moved away from Anna toward the door. Anna watched as her friend slipped silently through the exit before she turned her attention back to where the monks had lifted Sebastian up onto the altar.

Sebastian appeared as though he were still unconscious, and she could only guess that whatever Charlotte and her lover had used in the blow dart poison, they must have increased the amount with Sebastian. It was the only explanation for why he was still unconscious. Unless—she shoved the thought aside. They wouldn't have placed Sebastian on the altar if he were dead. No, he was still alive.

As slowly as she could, Anna came up off the floor in a low crouch and looked around her for any sign of movement in the darkness. Carefully returning to the spot where she'd been left on the floor, Anna hugged the wall of the building. Sufficiently hidden in the shadows dancing off the wall, she considered her options. She wouldn't be able to save Sebastian if she tried to work her way through the monks at the altar.

There were more than fifteen followers taking part in the rituals. The odds weren't in her favor this time. Not that they had been last time, but the monks had been spread out over a much wider area then. But Sebastian's life was at stake this time. If she were fighting off the cult members, Charlotte or Farthington would kill him. There was only one way out of here that she could think of, and that was to take Charlotte hostage. It was obvious the woman she'd thought a friend was the one in charge. Based on the exchange she'd witnessed between her and Farthington, the viscount was unwilling or unable to refuse the woman whatever she wanted.

Holding their leader hostage would hopefully keep the monks at bay long enough for her to rouse Sebastian. She'd have to play it by ear from there. The question was, how much time did she have to run from the wall to the altar before being seen? She also didn't know if her element of surprise would be large enough in scope to throw everyone in the room off-guard.

There was only one way to find out. Her back pressed into the wall, Anna continued to sidle her way forward. Quickly climbing up onto the platform that ran between the side walls of the temple, Anna pressed herself into the wall and continued forward until she was parallel with Charlotte. The group had begun chanting, and Anna saw Charlotte take a dagger off the pedestal between her and Farthington. She lifted it high overhead while chanting and swaying where she stood. Realizing now was her chance, Anna sprinted across the platform toward Charlotte.

There was a break in the chanting, and the woman at the altar turned her head this way and that, trying to understand what had interrupted their ungodly ceremony. As Charlotte turned toward Anna, a howl of rage echoed out from behind her mask. The woman lifted the dagger high in preparation to strike, but Anna didn't give her the chance, as she darted past the high priestess, and planted a solid kick in Farthington's balls.

The man howled in pain and fell to his knees, while Anna spun around to stand behind Charlotte. With a vicious tug, she yanked the woman's mask off and wrapped one arm around Charlotte's waist to pin her arm in place. For once, Anna was happy to let some of her anger slip out of control as she savagely pressed her thumb into the most painful pressure point of Charlotte's wrist. The woman cried out in pain, and Anna easily wrenched the knife out of her hand, then pressed the tip of the ceremonial dagger against Charlotte's neck.

"*Don't* move, Charlotte. I *will* kill you if you try anything."

Anna's words vibrated with an unrestrained anger. The woman deserved to die for everything she and Farthington had done, and she was doing her best not to simply slit the woman's throat herself.

Tension and hatred vibrated off Charlotte, but the woman's emotions paled in comparison to those coursing through Anna. In front of them, Anna saw two monks beginning to move toward her and Charlotte.

"*Stop*, unless you wish to watch me slit her throat."

"She wouldn't dare." Charlotte's words were confident as she countered Anna's declaration.

The moment the woman cried out, Anna pressed the point of the dagger into her throat just enough to cut through her skin. In seconds, a small rivulet of blood ran down her throat and darkened the woman's white robes. As the blood stained Charlotte's bodice, Anna called out firmly.

"If anyone thinks I'm bluffing, know this. I'll have no regrets when it comes to slitting her throat."

"*Don't listen to her.* I am Hatshepsut reincarnate, and I command you to stop her."

This time Anna pressed the tip of the dagger a little deeper into the woman's throat, and Charlotte gasped in pain. Out of the corner of her eye, Anna saw the High Priest staggering to his feet. With a vicious tug, the man removed his mask, and Anna's eyes widened as she recognized the Earl of Cookham.

Stunned that she and Sarah had never even considered the Cookham as a suspect, Anna stared at the man in disbelief. Something flashed in the firelight, and Anna almost failed to avoid the serpent-shaped dagger.

"*Fuck,*" she exclaimed as Cookham lunged toward her.

Quickly stepping to one side, Anna dragged Charlotte with her. The man rushed forward, and as his blade descended toward her, Anna didn't think, she reacted. With a jerk, she took two more steps backward, dragging Charlotte with her. The blade missed Anna's shoulder, and with the cry of an angry boar, Cookham lunged forward again, trying to slash Anna's arm this time.

"Jerome, don't—"

Charlotte's cry made the man stumble as he tried to stop his forward momentum, but he failed. Another cry escaped Charlotte's lips as Cookham's blade sank deep into the woman's chest. Cookham released a howl that would have terrified even a soul damned to hell as Charlotte bent her arm in an effort to reached out and touch her lover's cheek.

"I love…you, Jerome."

"*Oh God, Charlotte.*" The man continued to sob Charlotte's name as he tried to stop the life's blood pouring out of his lover.

Anna knew it was a futile effort as the woman's blood loss was substantial given the flood of dark color quickly spreading its way across her chest. Charlotte's hand fell away from her lover's face, and her arm dropped to hang limply at her side. The woman gurgled softly, and Anna took a step back as Cookham pulled the woman into his arms.

"Charlotte, don't leave me. I can't live without you, Charlotte." The man's grief was almost a live entity as his hand stroked the woman's face. For a moment, Anna experienced a sense of compassion.

"Jerome."

Charlotte's whisper was barely audible as another gurgling sound escaped her. The instant the woman's head lolled to one side, Anna knew Charlotte was dead. Sobbing wildly, Cookham rocked his lover in his arms, calling out her name over and over again.

Over the man's wild cries, Anna suddenly heard Hamish's booming voice ordering the Hatshepsut followers not to move or they'd be shot dead. Other voices echoed through the air, but Anna ignored them as she ran down the steps to where Sebastian laid upon the altar. He was breathing naturally, and her hands trembled as she quickly pushed his coat open to ensure he wasn't bleeding from some unseen wound. Tears streaming down her cheeks, Anna pressed her forehead against his, shuddering violently at how close she'd come to losing him. Gently, she brushed his hair off his brow.

"I love you, Sebastian," she whispered as she pressed her mouth to his forehead. Still trembling, Anna jerked as Alexander appeared across the altar from her with a look of terror on his face.

"Is he…"

"No, he's been drugged." Anna shook her head as she brushed her fingertips across his brow, then looked at Alexander. "Sarah?"

"Safe. She's in the carriage, although I'm certain she's struggling hard to obey my order not to come back in here."

Unsteady on her feet, Anna looked down at Sebastian, then closed her eyes as she silently offered up a prayer of gratitude that he was alive and unharmed.

"You saved him, Anna." Alexander's voice was full of emotion. "Thank you. I don't know what any of us would do if you hadn't done what you did."

Someone approached her from the side, and Anna gasped and stumbled away until her uncle's arms wrapped around her in a tight hug. Charles Wentworth's warm embrace tugged a quiet sob from her, before her fingers clutched at the lapels of his coat, and she began to cry. Anna soaked his coat with tears as she released all the horror, fear, and anguish of the past several minutes. Captain Wentworth whispered words of reassurance and love over the top of her head that she didn't hear. The quiet sound of Nicholas's voice as he spoke to her uncle registered with her slightly, and a moment later, a warm hand pressed into her back. Anna lifted her head slightly as she met the concerned gaze of Sebastian's best friend.

"Well done, Anna." Nicholas's words were a quiet

murmur in her ear as he bent his head toward her. "Well done. Alexander and his family are not the only ones grateful for what you've done tonight."

Anna didn't respond, and she glanced over her shoulder to see Alexander gently shaking his brother in an attempt to wake him. Her heart twisting in her chest, Anna pushed herself away from her uncle in an effort to stand on her own.

"I want to go home, Uncle Charles. I want to go back to the Falcon," she whispered.

In response to her words, Captain Wentworth wrapped his arm around her waist and guided her away from the altar and the man who held her heart.

Chapter 28

Sebastian blinked several times as he slowly emerged from the black void he'd sunk into after climbing into Charlotte Plummer's carriage. Shadows from an oil lamp bounced off the walls, and his blurry vision made it difficult to recognize where he was. There was something familiar about the room, and he suddenly realized he was home. Starling House. He was in his bedroom at Starling House. A split-second later, Anna's face filled his head.

He closed his eyes as a wave of fear crashed over him. Sweet Jesus, was she dead? Had the bastards sacrificed her? The question was one he desperately wanted answered, but he was terrified at the thought of what he might hear. A quiet sound echoed nearby, and he slowly turned toward it with a grimace. Damnation, his head hurt.

"Oh, thank God."

His mother's warm hand wrapped around his and squeezed it tightly as something wet splashed against his hand. The room slowly came into focus, and he saw the woman he'd wronged so badly, sitting beside his bed with tears rolling down her cheeks. He squeezed her hand back.

"Anna, is she…" Sebastian stopped speaking, unable to complete the question for fear of what the answer would be. He closed his eyes again at the thought of losing her forever.

"Anna is going to be fine, Bash. Captain Wentworth

took her back to the Falcon." Alexander squeezed his shoulder in a gesture of reassurance. "She's shaken up by what happened, but Wentworth says she'll be fine."

"Sarah?"

"My wonderful fiancée is safe and well too, thanks to Anna's quick thinking. You have her to thank for your life."

Sebastian's eyes flickered open to stare up at his brother, leaning over him with a worried expression on his usually cheerful features. Closing his eyes again, Sebastian nodded his head slightly, then winced. Not even after a drinking bout with Nicholas had he ever experienced such a bad headache.

"Oh, Bash." Tears filled his sister Lydia's voice on the opposite side of the bed as she leaned over him and brushed her lips against his forehead. "We thought we might lose you."

"Yes, we've been so worried," Caroline said quietly.

The voices of his sisters filtered their way through his hazy thoughts. What the devil were they doing here? Was he on his deathbed? The way his head hurt, it wouldn't surprise him. At the foot of his bed, he saw his youngest brother.

"Francis?" he whispered in amazement. "You're supposed to be at Brighton."

"Mother sent for me as the doctor was concerned as to your condition." Francis eyed him with deep concern.

"*Bloody hell*, I'm not dying," he mumbled.

"No, you're not. But you came damn close to it. If not for Anna, you would be dead." At Alexander's statement, Sebastian closed his eyes for a brief moment, then opened them to meet Alexander's somber gaze.

"How long?"

"Judging by the time we left the house, I'd say more than nine hours. It's almost four in the morning." His brother hesitated, then cleared his throat. "The Falcon sails on the morning tide."

"*Christ Jesus*," he muttered.

How was he supposed to convince Anna how much he loved her if she was on the Falcon when it left the harbor, and he was here in Starling House? Worse, how could he make her understand he loved her more than life itself? The things he said to her that night after making love to her were enough to make her hate him. He wouldn't blame her if she did. He hated himself for his cruelty.

Even if he were able to convince her how much he loved her, would it be enough? Would she agree to marry him? Anna hated London and all the Marlborough Set's rules. She might refuse for that reason alone. The moment the idea popped into his head, he knew it was the only way she would believe he loved her beyond measure.

"Everyone out," he choked out in as harsh a tone as he could without exacerbating his throbbing head. Sebastian ignored the sound of his sisters sharp breaths of surprise at his command. "Alexander, stay. Mama, send Stafford in here."

Again, his sisters gasped, but this time they were quiet sounds of astonished bewilderment. He knew immediately it was because of the manner in which he'd addressed their mother. Ignoring his younger siblings' reaction, he tightened his grip on his mother's hand.

"We will talk before I leave."

"Leave?" His mother stared at him in shock before her mouth tightened into a thin line. "The doctor said you needed rest. The drug those monsters used on you—"

"I'm going after her, and I don't give a *damn* what the doctor said."

His vicious response made him wince with discomfort, and he saw the worried look on his mother's face. But Sebastian was certain he also saw a gleam of approval in her eyes. Nodding at his statement, she rose from her chair and kissed his forehead. With one last squeeze of his hand, Lady Harding quickly ushered his sisters and youngest brother out of the room. When he and Alexander were alone, Sebastian met his brother's gaze steadily.

"I intend to disclaim my title, which will make you, Viscount Starling." Sebastian slowly sat up, preparing himself for the movement to send pain slicing through his head. It hurt less than he expected.

"*What?*" His brother stared at him in horrified amazement.

"I plan to be on that ship before it sails." Sebastian swung his legs off the bed and pressed the heel of his palm against his forehead, hoping the pressure would ease the throbbing. "You're to send for Hawkins immediately. I don't care if he arrives in his night clothes. He needs to draw up papers for me to sign before I leave that gives you control of all the family holdings. While I'm gone, you'll need to have him start taking steps to submit my abdication to Parliament and your claim to the title as my heir."

"You can't be serious, Bash."

"It's the only way I'll be able to convince Anna that I love her. She needs to know I'm willing to sacrifice everything for her."

"I don't believe that." Alexander objected to his statement, and a stubborn expression darkened his features. "Anna loves you, and she would never expect you to give your title up for her."

"Just do it, Alexander. You'll need legal control of the family's holdings to manage everything. Though we'll need to invest in a merchant ship."

"A merchant ship?" Alexander's eyes widened.

"If I'm going to live on a ship with Anna, I'd prefer not to be obligated to Wentworth. I refuse to live off the man's generosity."

"*Dammit, Bash.* Don't ask me to do this. You know I don't want the title."

"Maybe not, but I'm not giving her up."

"Don't be a bloody fool. You can't get to the Falcon in your current condition. Let me go in your stead. She won't hesitate—"

"*No.* She needs to know I'm willing to go to hell and back for her." He glared up at his brother.

"Be reasonable, Bash."

"I've made up my mind, Alexander. Don't argue with me," Sebastian bit out between clenched teeth. A quiet knock on the door interrupted them. "Come in."

The door opened, and his valet, Stafford, entered the room. Before the man could speak, Sebastian ordered him to pack suitable clothing to wear on the Falcon. Alexander hadn't moved from Sebastian's bedside, and his expression reminded him of their mother's steel will.

"Go. *Now*, Alexander."

Sebastian glared at his brother, and after several seconds, Alexander uttered an oath, then turned around and left. The sound of running water echoed through the air, and Sebastian rose from the mattress and slowly walked toward the bathroom. The next couple of hours were not going to be pleasant, given the way his head hurt.

He'd been right when he'd told himself the past two hours would be hellish. It was only in the last half hour that his headache had begun to ease. As the carriage rolled to a halt in front of the Falcon, fear twisted Sebastian's gut. Would she believe him? He closed his eyes for a moment, and across from him, Alexander cleared his throat.

"You look like hell."

"I feel like it," Sebastian muttered.

"What are you going to do if Captain Wentworth doesn't let you onboard?"

"I don't intend to take no for an answer."

With a twist of his mouth, Sebastian stepped out of the vehicle then accepted the two satchels Alexander handed him. He'd specifically instructed Stafford to pack only the bare essentials, and the valet had done as Sebastian ordered.

"Well, I'm going to wait here until you signal all is well."

"There's no need—"

"I'll wait."

The stubborn look on his brother's face made Sebastian acquiesce with a slight nod. Turning around, he hesitated as he saw the darkened ship in front of him. Gritting his teeth, he walked up the Falcon's steeply angled gang plank. What was he going to say to Wentworth? The man clearly loved his niece. Would the master sailor allow him to stay? Sebastian's jaw tightened with determination. He would not take no for an answer. A figure appeared at the top of the ramp.

"State your business."

"I'm here to see Captain Wentworth."

"The cap'n is asleep."

"Then wake him, now. He'll want to hear what I have to say."

A disgruntled look crossed the man's face at Sebastian's order, and he appeared ready to refuse when another man appeared at the sailor's side. The moment his gaze met Smitty's, Sebastian flinched at the sailor's dark glare.

"What do *ye* want?"

"I've business with Captain Wentworth."

"He didn't say he was expecting visitors."

"I can assure you, he *will* want to see me," Sebastian said firmly. "Now let me on board and take me to Wentworth."

For a long moment, Smitty stared at him, then with a jerk of his head, he motioned Sebastian to come on board. As Sebastian stepped onto the deck of the Falcon, Smitty's eyebrows soared upward as he saw the satchels he carried. With a grunt, the sailor said something to the other man, then gestured for Sebastian to follow him. They crossed the deck and Smitty led him into a narrow corridor before he stopped and quietly instructed Sebastian to wait. The sailor disappeared through a door, and a few moments later, the door flew open to reveal Wentworth glaring at him.

"What do you want, Starling?" The man's tone was icy, and if he didn't know it was June, he would have sworn it was the middle of winter.

"May I have a word with you in private, Captain?"

"I've nothing to say to you, and neither does my niece. Now, get *off* my ship."

The man's harsh tone made Sebastian's gut knot. Had Anna told the man about the offensive offer he'd made to her? As he stared at the man, the captain began to shut the door. Without thinking, Sebastian put his shoulder to the door to keep it open.

"I told you to get off my ship, *Starling*." Captain Wentworth's gaze made it clear the man wanted to impale Sebastian to the wall. "Don't make me have you bound and gagged before I throw you overboard."

"I'm a desperate man, captain," Sebastian said quietly. "I'm capable of doing almost anything at the moment. You don't have to like me. All I ask is that you listen."

"*Mon amor*, at least let him speak to you. If you don't like what Lord Starling has to say, *then* you can throw him overboard."

Sebastian immediately recognized Céleste Dubois's voice. At least the woman was willing to have him be heard. Wentworth narrowed his gaze at Sebastian and stared at him with antipathy for what seemed like an eternity. Then, with a jerk of his head, the master sailor gestured for him to enter.

The man's private quarters had a woman's touch, and Sebastian was certain that was Céleste Dubois' doing. The cabin served as both a sitting room and dining room. Wentworth said something to Smitty, and the sailor made a sound of disgust before he nodded his compliance with whatever command his captain had given him.

Antagonism glittering in his eyes, Smitty made his way out of the cabin. As the sailor passed Sebastian, the man's shoulder slammed into his side in a deliberate act of aggressive anger. The sailor muttered something beneath his breath as he walked out of the cabin and shut the door behind him. The man's action emphasized he'd be happy to obey the captain's order to throw Sebastian overboard.

Captain Wentworth had moved to the center of the room. Arms folded across his chest, the master sailor's gaze swept over him with a look of extreme dislike. The man eyed the satchels Sebastian had set down on the floor with a hint of puzzlement, before Captain Wentworth's anger returned.

"*Well*, what is it you have to say, Starling?"

"I would like your blessing to make an offer of marriage to your niece."

"*You what?*" Wentworth stared at him slack jawed for a brief moment, before he recovered from his surprise. Antipathy on the man's face, he narrowed his gaze at Sebastian. "Do you *honestly* think I'd approve of such an arrangement? I'll see you in hell first."

"I'm—"

"If you don't get off my ship now, you bastard, I'll throw you off myself. I don't know what game you're playing, but I'm not about to let you anywhere near my niece. When she came back to us, she'd changed into someone we barely recognized." Wentworth's face was dark with fury. "Someone had broken her heart. She never said it was you, but I saw her face tonight, and if you think I'm going to let—"

"*Charles Wentworth.*" The sharp tone Céleste Dubois used as she entered the cabin made Sebastian and the captain turn their heads in the woman's direction. It was obvious the woman had dressed hastily as her hair was tousled and unbound.

"Stay out of this, Céleste." Captain Wentworth's sharp command made the Frenchwoman jerk in surprise before outrage clouded her features.

"*Non*, I will *not*. You forget I love Anna and care about her happiness, too." The woman glared at her lover as she expressed her anger in her native tongue. "However, if my opinion is of so little value—"

"You know that's not true. I have always valued your opinion."

"Apparently *not* in this matter."

"Dammit Céleste, that's not what I mean, *mon amour*."

"Then do *not* treat me as nothing more than your *paramour*."

"Damnation, Céleste, you know you mean more to me than that. *Je t'aime, ma belle*." Wentworth took a step toward the Frenchwoman, whose mouth was set with determination.

"Then you will *listen* to what Lord Starling has to say. I will *not* allow you to take away Anna's independence *or* her right to make her *own* choices." The Frenchwoman arched her eyebrows at him. "As I recall, *you* were the one who insisted we should *not* return to London too soon, hoping Anna would *not* want to return to the Falcon."

From across the room, something unspoken passed between the couple. With an audible sigh, Céleste crossed the cabin to slip her arm through Wentworth's. The Frenchwoman looked up at her lover and whispered something to him. Whatever Céleste said, it made the master sailor grimace before he yielded to her grudgingly. Captain Wentworth turned his head back to Sebastian and nodded sharply.

"Say what you have to say, Starling."

"I love Anna, and I'm willing to do whatever it takes to make her see that."

"And what makes you think Anna wants anything to do with you?" The question was filled with cold contempt.

"I don't. In fact, there's a distinct possibility she won't want anything to do with me." The moment the words rolled past his lips, Sebastian's gut clenched. He had no idea what he'd do if that happened.

"*Pardon*, my lord, but what is in the satchels?" Céleste Dubois nodded toward the leather baggage Sebastian held.

"My clothes. If she'll have me, I'll live wherever she's happiest." Sebastian saw Captain Wentworth's eyebrows shoot upward in a skeptical look. The man's doubt made Sebastian's jaw clench with anger, but he wanted the man's blessing to marry Anna.

"Am I to assume you plan on remaining on the Falcon?" The man narrowed his gaze at him, and it was clear the last thing he wanted was for Sebastian to live on his ship.

"As I said, if Anna will accept my offer, I'll live wherever she wants."

"A pretty speech, Starling, but I doubt your responsibilities as a member of the peerage will allow you to be gone for great lengths of time. Do you expect to clip her wings then?"

"I'm disclaiming my title, and I've already given my brother the means to manage all my legal and financial affairs." Sebastian's words pulled a gasp from Céleste as she stared at him in wide-eyed amazement.

"Declaiming your *title*." For the second time since he'd entered Wentworth's quarters, the captain was stunned into silence.

Sebastian drew in a harsh breath as he realized giving up his title might not be enough to prove to Anna he loved her above anything else in his life. Fear struck deep at the possibility she might refuse to forgive him. Even if she did forgive him, Sebastian knew he'd spend a lifetime paying for every cruel word he'd uttered that night more than a week ago.

"Anna needs to understand that I'm willing to give up everything I own to prove my love to her." Sebastian drew in a harsh breath. "In the past twenty-four hours, I've come to realize a great many things, including what an ass I've been.

I've watched the spirit in the Anna I fell in love with slowly dying. She needs her freedom, and I'll give it to her anyway I know how."

Anna's uncle remained silent for a long moment, his gaze assessing Sebastian. The man's expression slowly changed to one of acceptance, and he nodded.

"As you know, Anna is of age and has the right to make her own decisions. I'll not advise her on the matter." Captain Wentworth narrowed his eyes, his features hardening into an implacable look. "However, if you hurt her in any way, I *will* find a way to make you pay dearly."

"I understand. My brother said almost the exact same thing." Sebastian nodded at the man's protective attitude.

"She's asleep right now, and I have no intention of waking her. Last night's events took its toll on her." Wentworth released a sound of anger as he met Sebastian's gaze. "I've an extra cabin you can use. When Anna wakes, I'll send for you. Do not leave your cabin before one of my men comes for you, or I will make you regret it."

"Understood."

"Let me be clear, Starling. Expect to be viewed as the enemy by my crew. Anna is the younger sister they either left behind or never had. My men will give no quarter to you if my niece's reaction is not to their liking." A small smile of vengeful satisfaction tugged at Captain Wentworth's mouth. "In fact, I am uncertain what punishment they'll bring down on your head. If Anna refuses to speak with you, you'll be put off this ship when we reach Lisbon, and until then, you will eat and sleep with the crew."

The warning made Sebastian's jaw tighten. Something told him that Anna's uncle might be the one to put ideas of revenge into the crew's heads. The only reply he allowed himself was a nod of understanding. Satisfied he'd made his point, Captain Wentworth walked around Sebastian to the door. He opened it and spoke quietly to Smitty, who'd been waiting outside. Anna's uncle turned back to Sebastian.

"Smitty will show you to your cabin."

"Thank you."

"Don't thank me yet. You still have to convince Anna as to your intentions. And if you do *anything* to hurt her, an accident while at sea is easily explained away if there are several witnesses.

Wentworth's veiled threat was emphasized by his harsh, unforgiving glare. Sebastian nodded, picked up his baggage, and followed Smitty out of the captain's quarters and down the narrow hallway. He was just about to shut the door to his cabin when he remembered Alexander was waiting for him to signal he was staying on board. As he turned to go up to the deck, Smitty roughly shoved him into the room. Sebastian staggered backward, then straightened upright to glare at the man.

"Ye were told to stay in ye cabin, ye fuck-wit."

"I need to let my brother know Captain Wentworth isn't going to throw me off the ship."

"Not yet, ye mean." The sailor eyed him menacingly. "Stay in the cabin like ye were told. I'll see ye brother gets the message."

The cabin door closed behind the sailor, and Sebastian hoped the man was good at his word. Although the cabin was sparsely decorated, the bed was more comfortable than Sebastian expected. It did him little good as he laid awake, staring up at the cabin's ceiling.

He'd not been lying to Wentworth when he'd said he would do whatever it took to make Anna understand he loved her. But what if giving up his title wasn't enough to prove his love for her? What did he have left? Nothing, and the thought scared the hell out of him.

Sebastian closed his eyes for a moment as he remembered the conversation he'd had with his mother before he'd left Starling House less than an hour ago. Even despite his mother's willingness to forgive him, it had still been a difficult apology to make. The memory of his mother's tears shot a bolt of pain through him.

After he had made himself presentable, he'd instructed Stafford to have his mother meet him in his study. When Sebastian entered his personal sanctuary, his mother had been standing in front of the clock his father had loved so well. She'd turned her head and smiled.

"Do you want to know why your father loved this clock so much?" Her smile was almost mischievous as she met his gaze. "The green carnations on the clock face."

"What do they represent?" His question changed her amusement to sadness.

"That all love is beautiful and yet some kinds of love can never be brought into the light. A man wearing a green carnation is a way for other like-minded men to identify each other."

"Was it difficult for him?"

"More than you will ever know, Sebastian. Your father and Augustus loved each other with a depth few people are ever blessed to feel. Just being in the same room with each other made them happy. But the time they spent in each other's company was never enough."

"I will not lie, all of this is a concept I am struggling to grasp. I am in no position to judge given my own behavior." An image of Anna formed in Sebastian's head, and his jaw grew painfully tight with tension. His mother wasn't the only one he'd treated badly.

"I don't think anyone can fully understand unless you are different in the same way your father and Augustus were." His mother's eyes shimmered with tears as she looked at him.

"Did you know about the letters?" Lady Harding looked away from him and nodded.

"Yes. I had the drawer added to the clock so your father could hide his letters. Augustus had quite a few as well."

"Are there more?"

"No. After Augustus died, Levi collected all his possessions and brought them here. There were letters in one of Augustus's trunks in the attic, which your brother found. They've been destroyed, and I think the ones you read should be destroyed as well." His mother drew in a deep breath. "Sebastian, I'm sorry—"

"You have *nothing* to be sorry about," Sebastian said firmly, with a hard shake of his head. "I'm the one at fault. I should be flogged for my treatment of you."

"You were a child, Sebastian. Your father tried to convince me that the three of us should sit down to discuss the matter, but I couldn't."

"Would you have done so if I'd not condemned you so viciously the morning after I saw you and James in the hall?" Sebastian asked quietly, and his mother jumped slightly as she met his gaze.

"I…I don't know."

"I think my behavior that morning is why you refused to agree to go along with Father's plan. You were worried I would turn on Father in the same way I turned on you."

Sebastian's mother closed her eyes for a moment before she met his gaze again.

"You and your father had a very special bond, Sebastian. If we had told you and you'd rejected your father, it would have been my fault. I couldn't let that happen. The thought of Levi being deprived of the joy of being your father or robbing you of a father you loved and respected was abhorrent to me."

"I understand, and as much as I'd like to believe I would have handled the truth well as a boy, I'm not sure I would have. But the truth has not diminished my love or respect for Father." Sebastian cleared his throat as he tried to dislodge the knot that had formed there. "I am ashamed of my treatment of you. It was undeserved. While it is easy for me to say I'm sorry and express my regrets for my behavior, I'm all too aware of the inadequacy of such an apology. It leaves me at a loss as to how to make amends for my conduct."

"The night Anna first arrived here in Starling House, I told you a mother never stops loving her children." Lady Harding cupped his cheeks in her palms and a tear slid down her cheek. "Just as it was true then, it is true now. It is easy to forgive you simply because a mother's love is unconditional."

"The years I've wasted…blaming you for something that didn't exist," he choked out. "I've been a fool about so many things."

"But when a fool sees their mistakes, they are no longer a fool."

Lady Harding's voice was soft as she wrapped her arms around him and hugged him as if he were a boy again. He returned her embrace and kissed her cheek. After a long moment of silence, his mother pulled away from him to study him intently.

"Alexander told me your—"

"I'll not be swayed, Mama." At his abrupt response, a knowing smile touched her lips.

"If you would allow me to finish my thoughts, Sebastian." His mother arched an eyebrow as she waited for him to agree. With a restrained nod, he remained silent. "As I was saying, Alexander has told me of your plan, and I approve."

"You do?" Startled, he stared at his mother in amazement.

"I do. Declaiming your title for the woman you love is one of the strongest declarations of love I think a man could make. However, I do not believe it will come to that." Her statement made Sebastian stare at her in bewilderment. Lady Harding laughed softly as she slid her arm through his and guided him toward the door. "You truly are a blind man, my darling boy. Anna is in love with you. She has been for some time now."

"Then why would she leave?" he snapped with frustration.

"Because I believe someone did everything he could to push her away until she believed the lies he was telling her and himself."

"What the devil makes you think that?"

"Because I am not the only one who stumbles across lovers in the middle of the night."

Lady Harding's confession made him go rigid. Had his mother seen him emerging from Anna's room the night he'd made love to her? Uncertain what to say, or how much to confess, Sebastian tipped his head to one side and studied his mother intently. With another smile, Lady Harding nodded her head as she answered his silent question.

"It was obvious to me that you loved Anna, but I had to wait and see who would win, your demons or your heart. I am pleased it was your heart." As they entered the foyer, his mother gestured toward the two satchels Stafford had packed for him. "Go, and just remember that I am certain she loves you."

As his mother's face and voice faded away, and the sparse cabin came back into focus, Sebastian's heart tightened in his chest. He prayed his mother was right, because if she was wrong, he wasn't sure what he would do. Closing his eyes, he rubbed his head to ease the throbbing that had returned.

At the sudden sound of pounding, Sebastian jerked upright, trying to fathom where he was. The moment Sebastian put his feet on the floor, he remembered he was on the Falcon, and he was surprised that he'd actually fallen asleep.

The pounding resumed, and he moved quickly to answer the door. The sight of Hamish's tall, burly figure in the doorway made him stiffen. The man looked ready to kill him with his bare hands. Sebastian remained silent. The sailor narrowed his gaze at him.

"Miss Anna is on deck at the bow. Time to see what ye are really made of, my lord."

A second later, Hamish's fist hit Sebastian's jaw in a vicious blow. Staggering backward, he tried to clear the fog of pain from his brain with a shake of his head. His hand lightly touched his jaw as he met the sailor's gaze.

"I'll give you that, Hamish. But it's the last time you'll lay a hand on me without finding yourself on the floor."

The man didn't respond. Instead, he stepped backward and jerked his head in the direction of the stairs leading to the main deck in a silent command to move. Sebastian glared at the man as he moved past the sailor and climbed the stairs. As he stepped out onto the deck, he saw the sails fully billowed out to act in conjunction with the ship's steam engine to propel the ship faster across the water. From where he stood, Sebastian saw Anna standing at the front part of the ship, exactly where Hamish said she would be.

Sebastian froze for a moment, uncertain as to what he was going to say to her. He'd only gone a few steps when one of the crew working at the side of the ship dropped a heavy hemp rope in front of him. Sebastian heard the man mutter something before the man's fist slammed into his stomach. The blow tugged the air out of his lungs, and he tripped over the large rope in his path. Sebastian landed flat on his face with a grunt. A second later, the sailor pulled him to his feet.

"Keep moving, man."

The sailor's quiet words resounded with a wrath that made Sebastian study the path that led to Anna. Although it looked free of anything he might stumble over, he suddenly realized a number of the crew were working along the path that led to Anna. Glancing over his shoulder, he saw Captain Wentworth standing on the next deck level where the ship's wheel was. The man's gaze met his, and with a satisfied smile on his lips, the captain nodded at him.

Sebastian spit out an oath as he scowled back at the man before he turned and continued toward the bow. By the time he was halfway to where Anna stood staring out at the water, Sebastian was breathing heavily as he silently endured the blows the sailors along his path slammed into his sides and legs. He was only a few feet from Anna when he saw Smitty waiting for him.

The man's cheerful smile was offset by the glint of anger in the man's eyes, and Sebastian knew whatever the man had planned for him would not be pleasant. He was right. He'd been so focused on Smitty, he missed seeing one of his last tormentors. The air was sucked out of his lungs as someone on his left slammed a fist into his face. The blow made him stagger to the side, right into Smitty's path, and another blow was applied to his mid-section.

Bent over at the waist, Sebastian breathed heavily as he waited for the pain in his body to subside to a manageable level. After several moments, he lifted his head to study Anna's rounded curves covered in men's trousers. Fear dried his mouth as he closed the distance between them. When he was within an arm's length of her, Sebastian cleared his throat.

"Anna."

If he'd not seen her body go rigid, Sebastian would have thought she'd not heard him. He called out to her again.

"Anna, look at me."

For what seemed like an eternity, he waited for her to slowly turn around. Eyes wide and a dazed expression on her face, Anna studied him in disbelief.

"Sebastian…what are you…doing here?"

"I'm here because I need to tell you what a fuck-wit I was…am." The moment the curse passed his lips, Anna's eyes widened even more, this time in shock. Pain wracking every part of him, he took another step closer to her.

"Another moment when you're speechless. I hope you don't intend to make it a habit."

"I don't understand. How did you get here? When?"

"I'm here because I love you."

Sebastian's soft declaration made her draw in a sharp breath as she stared at him in stunned silence. When she didn't answer, he glanced over his shoulder and took in the darkening looks on the face of the crew. Sebastian swallowed hard as he looked back at the woman he'd go to hell and back for.

"I love you, Anna Sawyer. I love your earthy language. Your laugh. Your smile. I love that devilish gleam in your eye when you've done something completely improper. When you're fighting back tears, all I can think about is holding you in my arms until your tears dry."

Anna's expression hadn't changed. She simply stared at him in amazement, but it was her silence that worried him. Sebastian took another step forward and went down on one knee.

"I love how you tease me and call me pompous. I love the way your beautiful eyes sparkle with fire when you're angry. I love your quick mind and your blunt honesty. I love how you aren't afraid to take a leap into the unknown. I adore everything about you, Anna. I've already discovered how bleak and miserable my world is without you.

"I'm here because I want to give you the world, if you'll let me. God knows you deserve someone better than me, but I want to wake up each morning to your warm smile and beautiful eyes. I want to love you the way you deserve to be loved and adored. I can do that if you'll let me, sweetheart. There's nothing I won't sacrifice for your happiness. Not even my title."

"Oh, Sebastian."

There was a soft quiver in her voice that made him drop his head in defeat. It was a sound of regret and pity. Despair swept through him as he realized how dark his world was about to become. Fingers brushed against his temple in a gentle stroke, but he recoiled as if he'd been burned.

"I don't want your pity, Anna," he snarled.

"You know *what?* You truly *are* a fuck-wit, Lord Starling." Her exasperation clearly evident in her reply, Sebastian jerked his head up to see her staring down at him with the same emotion he'd seen in her eyes the night he'd claimed her as his. "I *don't* pity you, you *pompous* ass. I've loved you from the first moment I looked up and saw a dark angel at my bedside. A dark angel I was determined to save."

Ignoring the pain in his body, Sebastian was on his feet in one swift move, and his mouth crushed hers in a kiss of relief and exultation. Behind them a rousing cheer filled the air, but Sebastian barely heard the cry as he tasted the sweetness of her again, knowing this was the first of many more kisses.

A moment later, Anna cupped his face in her hands, he grunted in pain. She quickly broke their kiss to stare up at him in alarm. Suddenly, she reached out and gently turned his face away from her to view his profile. A sharp gasp escaped her.

"Who did—"

She stopped in mid-speech and stepped past Sebastian to stare down at the crew who were still clapping and laughing. Beneath her glare, several of the men shifted their stance as an uneasy expression settled on their features. Every muscle in Sebastian's body ached as he reached out to turn her around and pull her into his embrace.

"It was a test, my love. I deserved every single blow. Call it the first installment of my penance for the things I said to you that night. I allowed my head to overrule my heart, and I said things only a cold, heartless bastard would say."

"No, they were things a dark angel who was fighting his inner demons would say." At her reply, Sebastian shook his head with regret.

"I didn't have the courage to make the offer you deserved. My name. An offer I made a few minutes ago, but you've not answered it yet."

"I thought my reply was obvious when I called you a fuck-wit, Lord Starling. But if you need to hear it in concise words, then yes, I'll marry you."

"Why do I think you'll push boundaries because I said I love your earthy language?" Sebastian grimaced at her unrepentant smile.

"I suppose I can restrain myself when we're visiting Marlborough House or some soiree we must attend." The blithe comment made him shake his head.

"That's something you won't have to worry about in the future. I am declaiming my title. As my heir, Alexander will become the new Viscount—"

"You did *what?*"

"I'm giving up my title. I told you there's nothing I won't sacrifice for your happiness."

"Well, you will undo that sacrifice as soon as we reach Lisbon." Anna arched her eyebrows in annoyed disgust.

"I don't understand," Sebastian stared down at her in confusion. "You hate the Marlborough Set and their rules. You've always made it clear you wanted to be here, on the Falcon."

"I wanted to return to the Falcon, because I thought you didn't love me. I am *equally* capable of making sacrifices for you, too, my lord, and I cannot have you turn Alexander's and Sarah's lives upside down. Alexander would be miserable as the new Lord Starling."

"A point he made quite clear in the early morning hours."

"I'm certain he will be relieved to know you've changed your mind. All I ask of you is that we will go sailing more than most people. Besides, I shall enjoy smiling gleefully at Lady Margaret every time Lord and Lady Starling are announced."

Anna's mischievous smile tugged a laugh from him followed by another grunt of pain.

"That is one grunt too many for me. I want Dr. Sullivan to look at you."

"I'll be fine."

"To quote your mother, do *not* argue with me, Lord Starling. You *will* allow Dr. Sullivan to examine you, because I would like to spend the night in the arms of my dark angel."

The bewitching smile curving Anna's lips sent Sebastian's heart slamming into his chest as she slipped her hand into his. God, how he loved her. She'd helped him defeat his demons, and she'd provided the means with which to heal the breach between him and his mother. The thought reminded him that he still didn't know how Anna had known about the clock's secret compartment. Tonight they would talk, and he would ask her then. For now, he was content to follow her wherever she led.

Chapter 29

Happiness rolled over Anna like a gentle wave lapping against the shore. Curled up into Sebastian's side with her arm draped across his chest, she heard the soft sound of his breathing. She shifted slightly in Sebastian's arms so she could study his face while he slept. For almost two weeks, she'd spent the happiest days of her life on the Falcon.

The days had been filled with laughter, warm kisses, the wind against her face as she'd leaned back into Sebastian's chest, staring out to sea, simply grateful that they were together. Then there had been Sebastian's vigorous protests when he'd catch her scaling the masts. After a quiet word from Hamish not to torture the man, she'd agreed to stay on deck.

Then there were the heart-skipping moments when she'd caught Sebastian staring at her with a love so deep it made her think she might be dreaming. A yell from Smitty for Sebastian to move his arse had reassured her it wasn't a dream. But it was the passion-filled nights, followed by quiet conversation before they'd fallen asleep in each other's arms that she loved the most.

It had taken Uncle Charles more than two days, with a great deal of coaxing by Céleste, to be reassured Sebastian was devoted to her. Hamish and Smitty had taken a little longer. The two sailors had insisted Sebastian pull his weight by learning how the steam engine and sails worked together to maintain a fast pace and manage rough seas better.

Her two friends hadn't made it easy for him. She'd done her best not to laugh whenever he made a mistake and the sailors jostled him around like a cadet. He'd not complained once at the abuse. If Anna was nearby, he'd often grin at her with good-natured amusement, making it obvious he understood he was being tested.

But in the last couple of days, she'd seen the wariness in her friends growing into respect. The memory of Smitty chewing Sebastian out yesterday for using the wrong knot on one of the sail lines, and how Hamish had intervened on Sebastian's behalf, made her smile.

"Do you intend to watch me all morning, Miss Sawyer?" His question was a soft rumble in her ear as he opened one eye to look at her.

"I intend to watch you every moment you're near me, my dark angel." Anna smiled as she brushed her fingers over his lips.

"As do I, my love." A sinfully wicked grin curved his beautiful mouth. "Especially when I make you fall apart in my arms every time I make love to you."

"Then I shall insist you do so at least once a day."

Her words sent his eyebrows upward as he eyed her with amusement. A split-second later, his expression became one of such deep love and adoration it stole her breath away. Sebastian cupped her face with his hand and bent his head to kiss her.

"I love you, Anna," he said with a depth of emotion that made her heart clench tightly in her chest. "I won't ever stop loving you."

Anna reached up to trace the contours of his face. The bristles of his morning beard scraped the pads of her fingers as she contemplated how to tell him what she needed to tell him. She had little time left. The Falcon had made excellent time to Lisbon, and then Cairo with the goods in the hold. The ship had made even better time heading back to London with calm seas and sunny days.

She'd put off things long enough, and as much as she preferred to remain silent, she couldn't marry him without telling him the truth. Fear had been holding her back, but she knew she would lack the courage to tell him the truth if she waited any longer. What if he refused to believe her?

"Are you sure?" Anna eyed him warily. "Even if I tell you something outrageous and hard to believe?"

"Now *that* is outrageous." Sebastian eyed her with skepticism and pulled her tighter into his side and kissed her temple. "I've never met anyone as forthright and honest as you. What in God's name makes you think I would dismiss anything you say?"

With a quick move, Anna slipped out of his arms and scrambled out of bed. She quickly retrieved a thin wrapper out of the wardrobe bolted to the wall. Unable to move for a moment, Anna stared blindly at the floor.

"Anna, come back to bed." The quiet words made her shudder as she gathered her courage and turned to face him. She studied him for a moment, then with a shake of her head, she began to pace the floor. She stopped abruptly, then turned to stare at him

"Sebastian…I…I have something I need to tell you…but…I don't know how." Trepidation made it difficult to breathe, and she watched him slowly sit upright and frown with puzzlement.

"All right, what is it you're afraid to tell me?"

"I'm *not* afraid."

Anna waved off his unfinished question. She was lying. She wasn't just afraid. She was terrified. The thought of losing him sent panic spiraling through her. Other than Lady Harding and her Uncle Augustus, she'd never told anyone else about her visions. In telling Uncle Augustus, she'd known he would believe her, and not dismiss her words as a child's fabrication.

With Lady Harding, she'd had little choice. It had been a necessary risk to repair the damage she'd done to the woman's relationship with Alexander. This time, the stakes were much higher. What would she do if he didn't believe her? Fear made her pace the floor at an almost frenetic pace as she forced herself to admit the truth to him.

"No, that's not true. I *am* afraid. I'm afraid of losing you."

"You will not lose me, Anna." The moment Sebastian started to get out of bed, Anna inhaled a sharp breath and raised her hand to stop him.

"*No. Don't.* Please Sebastian, this is hard enough for me as it is, please don't make it harder."

Anna heard the panic and fear in her voice, and it was easy to see Sebastian's alarm escalate. She met his gaze for a brief moment, then resumed her pacing. God, how in the hell could she explain her gift to him in a way that would make him believe her? He'd already stretched the boundaries of his strong sense of propriety and proper deportment where she was concerned.

Sebastian had given up everything he believed in for her. Now she was about to ask him to take an even greater leap than when he'd asked her to be his wife. His actions had openly declared how much he loved her, but did he love her enough to take this one last leap?

"*Dammit, Anna.* Just tell me what's wrong." The harsh command made her whirl around to face him.

"I see things." The moment she blurted out the words, she held her breath as she watched his reaction.

"I don't understand." Puzzlement replaced his alarm as he stared at her in obvious confusion.

"I have the ability to see things others can't. Visions that show me things. It's how I knew where the lever was to open the secret compartment of your father's clock." The moment she spoke, her entire body tightened with fear and tension as Sebastian brushed aside her words.

"You have to be mistaken, Anna. My mother knew about the secret drawer. She had to have been the one who told you about the drawer."

"Did she tell you that, or is that what you assumed happened?" The quiet question made Sebastian rub the back of his neck, his features dark with concentration. A second later, he shook his head in denial.

"You must not remember her telling you, sweetheart, or maybe you simply overheard her talking about it. It's easy to forget something and not remember where you've heard it before."

Sebastian's attempt to explain away her words made her heart sink.

"She did *not* tell me the clock had a hidden compartment, and I *didn't* overhear your mother talking about the secret drawer *or* the letters," Anna said quietly before she drew in a deep breath. "Do you remember the day you took me to the museum, and what happened when I was standing in front of your father's clock?"

"Yes, I thought you were about to faint."

"And I said I was simply lost in thought, but that was a half-truth. I was experiencing a vision. I saw my Uncle Augustus at the clock with a letter that fell to the floor right in front of the secret drawer. I didn't know what it meant until the day I found the letters."

"You must be mistaken, Anna. It's not—"

"It *is* possible. The day I found the secret drawer, I had a vision of a woman who looked like me with an old woman who was showing her something high up inside the clock." Anna swallowed hard as she saw his growing skepticism. "A few minutes after the vision ended, I saw your father standing at the foot of the stairs, smiling at me before he walked into the study."

"You know as well as I do, no one can do that, Anna. What is it you're really trying to say?"

Despair streaked through her at Sebastian's disbelief. In telling him the truth, she'd exposed the most vulnerable part of herself, only to have him view her as a liar. Inside her chest, Anna's heart felt as if it was shattering into sharp shards of glass that sliced through her with each breath she took.

"The truth. I don't want any secrets between us. Without trust, we have nothing."

It had been a mistake to tell him. Her gamble had only created a chasm between her and her dark angel. As she met Sebastian's gaze, his anger and distrust vibrated off him. It scraped along her senses, striking one blow after another to her body. She'd destroyed everything.

§ § §

Narrowing his gaze at her, Sebastian tried to restrain the anger and pain threatening to overtake him. Did she take him for a fool? Spiritualists and mediums were widely popular, but he'd never met one who wasn't a charlatan. What kind of game was she playing? Was this some type of ruse to push him out of her life? Had she decided marrying him was a mistake?

"If you've changed your mind about marrying me, then just say so. Don't make up some story to walk away from me. Simply tell me to leave." Climbing out of bed, he quickly pulled on his trousers in sharp, jerky movements.

"I am *not* making up a story." Anna glared at him. "I'm telling you the truth.

"That you're a fortune-teller?" Suddenly, a terrible thought made Sebastian's gut twist so violently he threw out the accusation. "Or is this some sort of revenge for my brutal words the night you came home drunk with Alexander? Have you planned this from the moment I crawled back to you?"

"*What?*"

The horror in her voice was emphasized by the shock on her face as every bit of color drained from her face, and she swayed on her feet. Christ almighty, what the hell was wrong with him? Anna would never have come up with such a plan, let alone pull off the kind of vengeance he'd suggested. It wasn't a part of who she was.

Anna drew in a sharp hiss of air as she sprang forward and crashed into him like a battering ram. The unexpected force of her body slamming into him made him fall backward onto the bed, and to save her from injury, his arms wrapped around her to pull her with him. With a strength he knew could only be driven by fury, she pressed his arms deep into the mattress as she straddled him. Trembling with outrage, she stared down at him with an icy contempt.

"*You bastard.* If I was going to extract my pound of flesh from you, do you *honestly* think I'd let you *fuck* me until I'm begging for more, just like I've been doing since the morning you showed up on the deck and, how did you put it, *oh yes*, crawled back to me? Do you think I'd even let you touch me? You nearly destroyed me the night I first gave myself to you, and you're doing it again, because you can't allow yourself to trust me."

Every scathing, bitter word Anna flung at him felt as if she were driving a knife into his body over and over again. God help him, what was he doing? The woman had given her heart to him when he didn't deserve it. Anna had never tried to push him away. He was doing that all on his own.

When in the hell was he going to learn to trust her? Trust himself to believe she wouldn't betray him. He closed his eyes as his chest constricted his lungs. Anna released her grip on his arms, and when she began to retreat from him, he quickly sat up and pulled her close, burying his face in her neck.

"Let me go, Sebastian."

Resignation and defeat filled her soft whisper, and the

sound tore its way through his flesh, down into his heart and then into his soul. Anna's hands pressed against his bare shoulders as she tried to free herself.

"Don't."

Sebastian squeezed his eyes tightly shut as he uttered the hoarse, heartfelt plea. He'd never been so terrified in his life. If he let her go now, he'd lose her forever. Wentworth and his crew wouldn't have to forcibly shove him overboard, he'd beg them to do it. He'd welcome the conviction and sentence for his sins, because he had no reason to live without Anna. His existence would become an unbearable darkness.

"Please, Sebastian. Just let me go." The pain in her voice intensified his own, and he shuddered with fear.

"I can't. If I let you go, it will be the end of me." He choked out the words as he struggled to breathe. "Until you, I lived in total darkness. You're the light that pulled me out of that desolate existence, Anna. Don't condemn me back to that hell."

Another shudder ripped through him as his arms tightened around her, pulling her even closer. If it were possible, he would have made her a part of him. Something wet hit his cheek, and for a moment he thought they were her tears, but suddenly realized they were his. A soft sound escaped her.

"Sebastian?"

The plea made him lift his head to look at her. Another quiet gasp blew past her lips. Quickly bending her head, she brushed her fingers over his cheeks, kissing his face, eyelids, and the corner of each eye until they were dry.

"I love you, Anna. Without you, I'll fall so deep, I'll never find myself again."

"I won't let you fall, my dark angel." The moment she whispered her promise, every inch of Sebastian's body tightened as he held his emotions in check.

"You're going to need the patience of Job himself when

it comes to keeping me in line, sweetheart." His voice cracked slightly as he winced with pained resignation. "Trust isn't something I do well."

"No, it's *definitely not* one of your better attributes. You're lucky I didn't drop you to your knees like I wanted to a moment ago." Anna's eyes suddenly glittered with outrage once more as she narrowed her gaze at him. "I don't think I've ever been so *furious* in my entire life. I'm *still* angry. How could you even *think* I'd do something that vile, let alone *say it out loud?*"

"Because you're marrying a fuck-wit."

"*Oh, you're right about that,* and I must be crazy to do so."

Her angry indignation made his heart pound violently in his chest. Christ Jesus, was she having second thoughts about marrying him? What if she suddenly decided being his mistress was a better arrangement? If their relationship remained as it was, she would have the freedom to walk away from him the moment he was an ass again. Especially when he was certain it wouldn't take much for him to meet that bar in the future, no matter how hard he would try not to. Terrified he might say something that would make matters worse, Sebastian remained silent.

"*What?* You're not going to say anything?"

Her anger simmered just below the surface, and he knew he'd given her every reason in the world to walk away from him. Sebastian barely shook his head, unwilling to upset the delicate balance between them, which was still precariously teetering on the edge of the abyss. Anna glared at him for a long moment before her eyes widened then in shock.

"*Poseidon's balls.* Loving me scares the hell out of you, doesn't it?" When he remained silent, she punched him in the shoulder with visible restraint. "Answer me, Lord Starling."

"*Yes,*" he snarled defensively. "God knows I don't deserve you, and the thought of failing you scares the hell out of me."

"Then you'd better find a way to control that fear, and fast. I refuse to let you hide your heart from me, Sebastian Reddington. You're going to wear it on your sleeve, so the whole fucking world knows how much Lord Starling loves his wife."

A harsh puff of air blew past her lips as she suddenly bent her head and kissed him. It wasn't a soft, gentle, or seductively teasing kiss like ones she'd given him in the past. This kiss was a wild mix of anger, fiery passion, and a demand he surrender his heart to her completely. One arm wrapped around his neck, her palm pressed into the spot where his heart thundered in his chest.

Her teeth suddenly bit down on his lower lip with a savagery that didn't draw blood, but was hard enough to make him grunt with discomfort. In a split-second, her tongue was swirling around his with fierce strokes that stirred a wave of desire deep inside him. It crashed upward to spread its fire into every cell of his body. He'd never wanted her more than he did now. It was a need he knew would never be quenched.

Falling backward onto the mattress, he pulled her with him. Desire blinded him to everything except her as he took control of their kiss. In a swift move, he rolled them over on the mattress until she was pinned beneath him. As his mouth plundered hers with an untamed ferocity, she responded in kind. No quarter was given between them, and as he roughly pulled her thin robe open, he kissed his way down to her breasts.

His teeth pinched one stiff peak hard enough to tug a cry of surprise out of her before she pleaded for him to repeat the action. He ignored her plea as he took her into his mouth, and his tongue flicked and swirled over the tip of her. Her hands slid through his hair as small pants of pleasure escaped her, and a second later his teeth pinched her nipple again.

Sobbing with delight, she jerked beneath him before

arching upward in a silent plea for more. Never had he reveled so much in the way she responded to him. His mouth slid its way down to her stomach as his hands spread her legs wide until his mouth found her sex. She was wet, hot silk against his mouth, the tangy taste of her flooded his senses as his tongue dove deep into the heart of her. A second later, his teeth abraded the swollen nub of flesh at the rim of her core.

The cry of delight splintering the air above his head heightened his need and made his cock expand. She bucked against his mouth and moaned his name as wild tremors made her writhe on the bed. Aching for her, he swiftly pushed his trousers off, then slid his hands under her to cup her buttocks and lift her off the mattress slightly. In one fierce, hard thrust, he buried himself inside her.

White-hot heat engulfed him as her body flexed and gripped his cock like a velvet vise. With each savage stroke of his body into hers, she responded with a furious abandon that sent his heart slamming into his chest. Eyes closed, his head fell backward as there was only her and the wild passion between them that silently declared he was tied to her for eternity.

Suddenly, she jerked hard against his cock. A cry of ecstasy escaped her, before her body tightened around him. Immersed in the fire of her, a mind-numbing pleasure crashed over him as she clenched and throbbed around his cock. The hard, shuddering vibrations of her body against his made him pound his body into hers at a frenetic pace. Then, with one last hard thrust, he uttered her name in a guttural cry and spilled his seed inside her.

The intense joy and ecstasy of the culmination of their passionate love-making held him motionless for a moment, before he released her and fell onto the mattress beside her. Their harsh, ragged breathing was the only sound in the room. Sebastian caught her hand and entwined his fingers with hers, unwilling to let go of her completely.

After several long moments, he turned his head toward Anna to study her profile. Her eyes were closed, while her cheeks were flushed with color. There was a soft glow to her skin that made her even more beautiful than he'd ever seen. Almost as if she could see him looking at her, she smiled but didn't open her eyes.

"Well, my lord, if you choose to fuck me like that every time you make a mistake, I think I'll have to encourage you to make mistakes all the time."

"*Christ Jesus*. Your mouth is going to be the death of me." He closed his eyes at her bawdy language and released a groan of amused resignation. Anna immediately laughed and turned her head toward him.

"I thought you loved my earthy language."

Rolling onto his side, Sebastian carried her hand up to brush his lips over her fingers. When he didn't reply, Anna rolled toward him and frowned in puzzlement. He wasn't really ready to discuss everything that had led to their fiery lovemaking, but he couldn't simply push aside the subject either.

"Anna…"

He met her gaze as he struggled with how to broach the subject. A warm palm cupped his cheek. To his dismay, a shadow of disappointment darkened her beautiful brown eyes.

"It's all right, Sebastian. We don't have to talk about it."

"*Yes*, we do," he growled with frustration.

"I know you don't believe—"

"I *want* to." Sebastian blew out a harsh breath. "I want to believe, sweetheart. I'm just not sure how."

"Your mother was the same way, although I was able to provide her proof, which made it easier to convince her."

"What kind of proof?" Sebastian frowned, and she rolled away from him to stare up at the wood ceiling.

"It concerned your parents, my uncle, Alexander, and you."

"*Me?*"

"Yes." Anna winced, but kept her eyes centered on the ceiling. "I had a vision of your mother and Alexander arguing. He'd found some letters that revealed who his real father was."

"His real father?"

Tension crashed through him. Who the devil would have told her that? No one. Alexander would be no more willing to share such a detail any more than his mother would. They both knew one wrong word in the right circles would create a scandal that might do more than just reveal Harding was Alexander's father.

"Lord Harding is Alexander's father, but I think you knew that long before Alexander did because, when you were a child, you saw something that made you believe your mother betrayed your father."

"Who told you that?" he bit out between clenched teeth as his anger returned. Anna immediately turned her head toward him, a look of fear on her face. Without hesitating, Sebastian leaned forward and kissed her gently. "I am not angry with you, my love. It's just unsettling to hear you telling me things that…that my mother, Alexander, or I would never share willingly."

"No one told me anything, the cold, distant relationship you had with your mother made me suspect you'd seen something that had put a wall between the two of you. Nicholas confirmed that for me the night of the Sheringham ball."

"*Nicholas.*" His harsh exclamation made Anna turn her head toward him and touch his cheek.

"He's a loyal friend, Sebastian. He was simply sharing his concern for you. It's obvious to me Nicholas looks on you as he would a brother."

"He still had no right—"

"Whether he had told me or not, it would have made no difference. I would still have known the whole truth later that night."

"What do you *mean*?"

His anger eased as he studied her in confusion. Sebastian was slowly coming to realize that for the remainder of his life, Anna would confuse and unsettle him quite often. It was a sensation he knew he needed to accept if he was to make her happy and ensure she never left him. As if she couldn't look at him as she spoke, she turned her head away and closed her eyes as she continued.

"The night I was introduced to the Marlborough Set, your mother and I chatted on the way home. She said Uncle Augustus saved her, Levi, and himself. It was the first time I'd heard anyone call your father by his given name. Even as a child, I knew my uncle was different. I didn't care, because he was so kind, thoughtful, funny, and gentle. I loved him very much. I also knew how much he cared for a man named Levi."

Anna paused for a moment as he saw her throat bob, as if holding back tears. The look of grief on her face made him want to cradle her in his arms and let her cry if only to ease her pain somewhat. But he knew Anna wouldn't hesitate to seek out his embrace if she wanted comfort. Instead, he forced himself not to touch her.

"Your mother had also expressed no regrets about her relationship with Lord Harding while your father was still alive."

"*Christ Almighty*. My mother told you about Harding?"

"Not everything, but enough to make all the puzzle pieces fall into place. I knew from my vision, Alexander had learned something disturbing from the letters. It could have been only one of two things. Either Lord Harding was your father too, which I quickly dismissed, or Alexander had learned the truth as to who his father was. That told me Alexander had found love letters between my uncle and your father."

Anna raised her hand up to rub her forehead as if she had a headache. Quickly, Sebastian reached out and moved her hand out of the way to gently stroke his fingers across her brow. A soft sigh whispered out of her, and Sebastian realized it wasn't any easier for her to tell him everything any more than it was for him to hear it.

"Unfortunately, I didn't realize I was thinking my conclusion out loud. When your mother thought Alexander had told me about the letters, I had no choice but to convince her of my ability…I couldn't bear to see her relationship with Alexander become like the one you and she had."

Anna fell silent, and Sebastian rolled away from her onto his back. His thoughts raced along like a steam engine out of control. He knew he could ask his mother and Alexander to verify everything Anna had just told him, but he didn't have to. It was obvious she had some form of ability that allowed her to see things others couldn't.

Sebastian remembered how he'd originally dismissed her and winced at the thought. He should have had more faith in her, trusted her. It was something he would have to work hard at, because he was still reeling from what she'd just told him. Another sigh escaped her.

"You still don't believe me." Her voice was flat and unemotional, but he heard the disappointment running underneath. Quickly rolling onto his side, he pulled her toward him.

"I believe you, my darling. I'm simply trying to take it all in. You were right about the letters Alexander found, and the ones in the clock. But even with all that you've told me, I should never have doubted you.

"When I saw how distraught your mother was when I opened the clock's drawer, I thought you would hate me for revealing the truth. I'm far too impulsive."

"Then we are well-suited for each other. You will teach me how to trust, and I will do my best to help you control your spontaneous behaviors."

"If you are thinking to break me of my bawdy language, I must warn you, it will not work. Céleste has tried for years, and while I have become more discreet with my usage, I refuse to give up my ability to express my anger, frustration, or surprise."

The resolute note in her voice didn't surprise him, and with a wry twist of his lips, he released a noise of amused resignation.

"I yield, my love. I said I loved your earthy language, and I meant it. All I ask is that you not teach it to our children or use it in public."

"Does this mean I'm not allowed to whisper, I *need you to fuck me, my lord*, in your ear when we are at a ball?"

"God help me, *woman. No.*"

"Why ever not? You would be the only one to hear it." Pushing herself up to hover over him, she laughed. With a slow smile, he arched his eyebrows at her.

"Because at that point in the evening, I would be forced to find a private room and make love to you until your hair and gown were completely disheveled." His fingers cupped her chin, and Sebastian rubbed his thumb over her plump lips. She grinned at him and nipped at the tip of his thumb. Sebastian tapped her mouth with his forefinger. "And once I'd had my way with you, we would return to the ballroom, and the Set would know that Viscount Starling had just fucked his wife."

The moment her eyes grew round, and a gasp escaped her, he grinned broadly. Suddenly, Anna narrowed her gaze at him.

"Clearly, my lord, I shall be forced to milk your cock *before* we leave the house for any public outing." Fingers stroking his face, she laughed as he groaned with resigned despair, before he smiled teasingly.

"A most appropriate task for any dutiful wife to perform."

The appalled expression on her face made his smile become a grin. As irritation replaced her look of shock, she punched his shoulder. Unable to help himself, Sebastian laughed. As he met her gaze, he saw a glint of mischief sparkling in her warm brown eyes.

"I think, my lord, we will not be going out in public very often."

The moment his loud laughter filled the air, a smug smile of satisfaction curved her sweet mouth. He reached up and tugged her toward him and kissed her. When he released her, and she raised her head, the happiness in her eyes made his heart swell. There would never be a day when he wouldn't give thanks for this woman. If he was her dark angel, then she was the light that would always pull him from the brink of hell. A puzzled frown furrowed her forehead.

"Why are you looking at me like that?"

"Like what?" He arched an eyebrow at her.

"As if you suddenly realized something." The bewilderment on her lovely face made Sebastian capture her hand and carry it to his mouth.

"I was thinking about your nickname for me."

"You mean my calling you, my dark angel?"

"Is there another one you use more?" He laughed as she rolled her eyes at him. With a small shake of his head, his laughter faded as he cupped her cheek. "I was thinking how lucky I am to love a woman whose light will always show me the way home. A woman I'll never stop loving."

Tears formed in Anna's eyes as she stared down at him, the emotion on her face made his heart swell with a joy he'd never felt before. She lowered her head to kiss him gently, and Sebastian pulled her close as she snuggled her body into his.

"I love you, Anna."

"And I love you, Sebastian. I'll always be yours. Forever yours, no matter what."

Sebastian tightened his hold on her, and she released a quiet sound of happiness. It said he was home.

Chapter 30

Present Day

"Anna, come on, sweetheart. Don't let go, now. Stay with me."

Sebastian caught Anna's hand in his, while brushing her hair out of her face. God, she looked so damned pale. His gaze ran over her voluptuous form in search of blood, but he saw none.

Across from him, a man and woman were staring at him as if he was insane. He darted a glance in the man's direction and a vague memory stirred to life in his conscious mind. The man leaned forward over Anna.

"Who the hell are you? And how do you know Nora?"

"It's complicated."

Sirens wailed their approach, and Sebastian muttered a soft oath that they weren't here already. He saw the other man staring down at Anna with a look of agonized fear. Not about to give way to the same paralyzing emotion, Sebastian bent his head and pressed his mouth against Anna's ear.

"You were right, my darling. You were right all along. We've found each other again. But you need to stay with me, Anna. Don't let it end before it's even begun."

She moved her lips and Sebastian could have sworn she said his name. The sirens were close now, and he lifted his head to see an ambulance pulling up alongside the car that had hit Anna. A moment later, he and everyone else was shoved out of the way by the medical personnel. The paramedics worked quickly, and in minutes, they'd placed Anna onto a stretcher and placed her into the back of the ambulance.

"Where are you taking her?" Sebastian and the other man spoke simultaneously as the paramedics closed the back of the ambulance.

"St. Thomas's."

The other man stared at Sebastian for a brief moment before he turned and walked quickly back to the woman who was with him. The woman was pregnant, and he assumed the couple were married.

As his gaze met the woman's, an odd expression swept across her face. It was as if she'd recognized him. The woman started to take a step in his direction before the man wrapped his arm around her waist to pull her away, clearly in a hurry to follow the ambulance.

Sebastian turned around to search for his parents in the crowd, suddenly uncertain what to do next. In seconds, he saw them emerging from the ballroom lobby of the hotel, followed by Bethany and Jesse. Pushing his way through the spectators who'd gathered to gawk at the accident, he experienced an urge to rage at them all for their morbid curiosity. The ambulance's siren began to wail again as it pulled away from the scene.

"What happened? Someone said there was an accident." His mother's question made Sebastian run his fingers through his hair as he closed his eyes and shook his head.

"It's my fault. I'd crossed the street to get a better look at the building across from the hotel. When I saw her, I knew it was her, and I called out to her."

"Called out to who?" Levi Sebastian Bennington, Sr. frowned in puzzlement.

"Anna," he replied in a distracted voice.

"Who's Anna?"

Mrs. Bennington looked at her husband, then back at Sebastian, but all he could think about was how he'd called out to Anna and what had happened next. He rubbed the back of his head, trying to collect his thoughts. It wasn't like him to be so indecisive or agitated. Usually, he was the one to organize everything in a crisis. But at the moment, he couldn't think straight.

"She *heard* me. I *know* she did. Before I could get across the street, she stepped out in front of the car. *Christ.*" Sebastian shook his head, then blew out a harsh breath of fear. "I need to get to the hospital."

"But *who's* Anna?" His mother eyed him with bewilderment.

"Anna's the woman he's been drawing since he was a kid, Mom." Bethany stepped forward and touched Sebastian's arm. "It wasn't your fault, Bash. Jesse tried to keep her in the lobby, but the clock upset her a great deal."

"What clock? Never mind, you can tell me later." With a dismissive wave of his hand, Sebastian looked back at his parents, who were studying him with growing alarm. "I'll get a cab to the hospital. My nav system has my address plugged in. All you have to do is press home and it will give you directions."

"But Sebastian, why do you have to—"

"I'll explain in the car, Mom. Give me your keys to the car and apartment, Bash." Bethany barely glanced at their mother as she extended her hand to Sebastian. He dug into his pants pocket and handed his sister the keys.

"Go, I've got this," his sister urged, as if understanding he couldn't think straight at the moment.

With a sharp bob of his head, Sebastian kissed his kid sister on the cheek, then wheeled around and darted through the small crowd on the pavement toward the front of the hotel. In minutes, he was in a black cab on his way to St. Thomas's. Reaching into his back pocket, he pulled out his wallet and retrieved the miniature photograph he'd taken of his favorite portrait of Anna. The moment it was finished, he'd photographed it, then printed it out and placed it in his wallet.

Staring down at her image, a vicious remorse twisted its way through him. What the hell had he been thinking when he'd called out to her like that? It was unlike him to do something so impulsive. If anyone was impulsive, it was Anna. The small bit of new information made him shake his head slightly. All his life, he'd acquired tidbits about the Anna he'd known and loved in the past.

"I'm a fuck-wit. Why didn't I just cross the street back to the hotel, then call out to her?"

Sebastian closed his eyes as anger and self-disgust jolted his body. For the briefest of moments, he tried to remember where he'd come up with the term fuck-wit. He discarded the thought the instant he recalled Anna's pale features as she'd laid on the road. It made his stomach knot with a sickening misgiving.

Close on its heels, a vivid memory increased his fear. He'd been with her the last time she'd been injured. The image of Anna dressed in a white, almost transparent garment covered in blood made his heart crash into his chest. She'd been wearing a similar costume tonight. It wasn't the first time memories of a past life had filled his head.

Every time he put Anna's face on a piece of paper or a canvas, different images of the two of them together always filled his head. Now, the memory of her covered in blood as he carried her up a staircase sent a vicious surge of fear through him that made his heart twist painfully in his chest. He blew out a harsh breath.

"There wasn't any blood tonight, Bennington. That has to be a good sign," he muttered as he tried to reassure himself

Anna would be all right in an attempt to ease the tension assaulting his body.

Then there was the glimmer of recognition he could have sworn he'd seen in her brown eyes before her eyelids fluttered closed. God, he'd just found her again, only to face the possibility of losing her. Dread crashed through him.

"Damn it to hell."

The oath was a violent whisper as Sebastian slammed his fist against the seat cushion. It was one thing to consider the possibility the woman he knew only from his dreams and artwork might actually exist. Confronting the knowledge that Anna was real was a different matter altogether. Even though he'd dreamed of this moment, he'd never expected it to happen.

Suddenly, his body tightened with a different fear. What if she was married? Had the man at her side been her husband? No, he'd displayed more of a brotherly concern than that of a lover. Then there was the pregnant woman the other man had focused his attention on when Sebastian had watched him walk away. The odd thing was, the man had seemed so familiar.

It was as if the two of them had survived a similar incident in the past. An event that hadn't ended well for a man he instinctively knew had been a close friend somewhere in the past. The thought made his gut knot. Was it an omen of what was to come where Anna was concerned? He suddenly remembered the man had called her by a different name. Sebastian concentrated for a moment, trying to remember the name the man had used.

His memory failed him, just as it always did when he tried to remember the first time he'd started calling her Anna. For years he'd questioned his unshakeable certainty it was her name until he finally stopped and simply accepted it. Sebastian's earliest memories of Anna were a couple of years before he started high school. He'd woken from a nightmare filled with faceless monks in the ruins of an Egyptian temple.

In the dream, Anna had been lying on an altar, and he'd been fighting to reach her. The nightmare had replayed itself for the next two nights. The morning after the third dream, Sebastian had drawn Anna's face on a sketch pad he'd received for Christmas. That night, he'd slept peacefully. The dreams had been intermittent over the years.

Some had come weeks, even days apart. Then he would go months without any dreams of Anna. He had quickly learned to sketch her as soon as he woke up. If he didn't, the dream would repeat itself the next night. What puzzled him the most was the grandfather clock. The tall grandfather clock was a magnificent piece of furniture with its intricately carved wood on all sides of the clock.

Every time he drew or painted Anna, the clock was always in the background. It was never something he'd added deliberately, it was just always part of the background. His sister, and even his parents, had commented on it several times when they'd seen a work in progress. Sebastian had simply shrugged his inability to explain it, nor did he question why he always added it into the background.

Over the years, he'd done his best to forget Anna, but the moment he tried, his dreams would return en masse. It wasn't as if he'd never had a relationship or been celibate. He'd had two girlfriends during his high school years. Although four years of a tough curriculum studying architecture at Virginia Tech had made dating less of a priority. Ironically, during his college years, his dreams of Anna had been almost non-existent.

After graduation, his social life had expanded, and in the past seven years, he'd been on more blind dates than he could count. There had been several women he'd dated consistently for short periods of time. All those times Anna would appear in his dreams, and he'd wake up dissatisfied with the relationships. His most serious relationship had been disrupted on a regular basis with dreams of Anna. They had been even more vivid and persistent whenever he'd considered proposing to Nancy. It was as if someone was telling him to be patient and wait.

From almost the first time he'd dreamed of Anna, he'd read dozens of books about past life experiences. Over time, he'd slowly come to believe they'd been together over a hundred years ago. It was the only way he could explain how he knew her name, what she looked like, and the multiple pieces of information his mind threw at him in every dream he'd had of her. For the most part, they'd all been happy ones.

But the occasional nightmare that did push its way into his sleep was always far too vivid and terrifying for his liking. They always centered around two specific events. The Egyptian one with its flickering torches and an altar stained with blood was horrifying enough. But it was the dream where he was locked in a pitch-black room with Anna calling his name outside the door that terrified him even more.

Although he'd never admitted to his parents or Bee what he'd come to accept as truth, his extremely intuitive sister had once told him that she was certain he and Anna were soul mates who hadn't found each other yet.

Then two years ago, a recruiter had reached out to him about a job based in London. Sebastian had requested a week to think about the offer, but after three consecutive nights filled with dreams of Anna, he accepted the job. From the moment Sebastian had arrived in London, his drawings of Anna had begun to change.

The first one he'd started only a week after his arrival. He'd not even finished unpacking. The result was his far from organized unpacking, as he'd frantically rummaged through more than a dozen boxes until he found his oils, brushes, and canvas. The moment he started painting, he knew it was the best of any painting he'd ever done of her. Dressed in a vibrant, royal-blue gown, it clung to her full curves as if it were a second skin.

When he'd applied the final brushstroke and stepped back, he'd experienced a moment of déjà vu where he'd seen her descending a staircase. She'd taken his breath away. The smile on her lips was mischievous and seductive, but it was her eyes that he loved the most. They sparkled with life and energy, and the love he saw glowing in her gaze tugged at him as his heart ached for something he understood but wasn't willing to admit. He'd known then he needed a photograph of the painting to carry with him. He never showed it to anyone, it had been for him alone.

Since then, he'd done dozens of drawings, watercolors, and oils of Anna as well. There had been the one of her in a wedding gown, when she was pregnant, a portrait of her with a child on her lap, and then there was the one of her in what he believed to be mourning clothes. The grief and anguish on her lovely features in that portrait always made his chest tighten until it was hard to breathe. It was as if he'd failed her in some way, but he wasn't sure how.

But it was the most recent painting that had left Sebastian stunned. It was of Anna with four children and a man he had no doubt was her husband. The man's hand rested on her shoulder, and her arm was bent so her hand laid on top of his. As always, the grandfather clock had been prominent, but more than ever before. Not until the painting was finished did he realize the man in the portrait was him.

The love and happiness depicted on the canvas had created a visceral reaction in Sebastian. His connection to the painting had been so strong, he'd had the artwork framed. It hung in the living room of the house he'd bought about forty minutes from the city. He'd purchased the house a few weeks after realizing his stay in London would be for at least five years. It had become a weekend retreat for him when he wasn't renting it out to tourists. It also gave his family a place to stay when they flew over the Atlantic for visits.

With each consecutive painting and sketch he made of Anna, the more convinced Sebastian had become that he'd never be completely whole without her in his life. It had been an insane thought to have, but he knew it was one of the reasons why he'd dated infrequently since arriving in London. It was also why he wasn't married yet. Now he'd found her again, but he had a huge obstacle in his way. How was he supposed to explain all of it to Anna? The woman would think him insane, then have a restraining order slapped on him.

He could always show her the paintings, but Sebastian had no idea how she'd react to those. That he could understand. He'd had trouble grappling with his obsession for years. Suddenly, Sebastian stiffened and quickly replaced Anna's picture back in his wallet. Tugging his phone from his coat pocket, he entered his sister's cell phone number.

"We just got in the car, Bash. I need to concentrate on driving this thing on the wrong side of the road."

"You mentioned a clock, Bee. Something about Anna being upset about a clock."

"Umm…yeah. Hold on a second." In the background, he heard whispering before he heard his mother demand his sister hand over the phone.

"Sebastian, sweetheart?"

"I really need to talk to Bee, mom." Irritation blazed through him. He loved his mother, but motherly advice was the last thing he wanted at the moment.

"You're on speaker, Bash." The sound of his father's voice caused him to jerk slightly. Sebastian couldn't remember the last time his father had called him by his nickname. "We bought your birthday present today."

There was a note of excitement in the senior Bennington's voice that deepened Sebastian's confusion. Levi Bennington, Sr. had always been low key, and the gleeful note in his father's voice was unusual. Sebastian had inherited his father's calm, steady demeanor, as well as the man's name, and he rarely heard his father this jubilant. Happy, yes, but overly excited maybe once or twice in his life.

Then there was the fact his father had called him by his nickname. Named after his father, his parents had chosen to call him by his middle name rather than causing confusion with two Levis' in the same room. As a toddler, Bethany had only been able to say Bash, and the nickname had stuck. But to his parents, he had always been Sebastian.

"It's *your clock*, sweetheart." His mother's voice was filled with the same exultation as his father.

"My clock?"

"We bought *your clock*, son." The excitement in Levi Bennington's voice seemed to have escalated. "We were going to surprise you with it when we celebrate your birthday at the house this weekend. But after what Bethany and Jesse told us, we decided to tell you now."

"My clock?"

Something inside Sebastian tightened, uncertain if it was in a good way or a bad way.

"It's the *clock* you've been sketching in your drawings of Anna *ever since* high school, Bash."

"You found *the* clock?"

Stunned, he sat staring out the window, trying to comprehend what his sister was saying.

"*Yes*. But that's not all, Bash." Even his sister sounded thrilled and more than a little stunned with a strong dose of amazement. "Your Anna wanted to buy it. She asked if you might sell it, and I told her there was no fucking way in hell that you'd let it go—"

"*Bethany Diana Bennington*." His mother's disapproval almost made him smile. He rarely swore, but his sister had a mouth that would make a sailor proud.

"*Mom*." His sister's disgust at the interruption made her huff out a harsh breath before she continued.

"Your Anna was devastated, Bash. I mean, she looked ready to pass out." In the background, he could hear Bethany's friend saying something. "Jesse said when she followed Anna into the bathroom, the woman was throwing up as if she'd been on a drinking binge. *she recognized the clock, Bash. I'm sure of it.* It's the only explanation for her reaction."

The black cab rolled to a stop, and Sebastian didn't move for a moment. It wasn't just him. Even Bee was convinced the woman she'd met at the gala was the same Anna he'd been drawing all his life. The driver cleared his throat, and he gestured for the driver to give him a moment.

"Look, I just arrived at the hospital, and I need to figure out what's happening. I'll call you back in a little while."

"You'd better. Otherwise, I'm apt to throw a party for you to clean up."

Sebastian smiled slightly as he ended the call. Bee knew how meticulous he was about keeping things in their place. Quickly pulling some pound notes out of his wallet, he handed them to the driver while telling the cabbie to keep the change.

Sliding out of the car, he stood frozen outside the emergency room lobby. He still hadn't figured out what he was going to say to her. Fear slashed through him again, but he moved forward, determined to do his best to convince the woman he'd been in love with for years that they were meant to be together.

Chapter 31

As he entered the emergency room lobby, Sebastian suddenly realized he didn't know Anna's legal name. How in the hell was he supposed to find out anything about her condition? He took a step toward the registration desk, when a quiet voice called out to him.

"Sebastian?"

The woman's voice behind him made him stiffen. No one here could possibly know him. Slowly, he turned around and saw the woman who'd been at Anna's side at the accident. The woman was dressed as if she'd just stepped out of the late Victorian era. The same era as the clothing he'd always painted in Anna's portraits. As he met a brilliant sapphire gaze, he had the oddest feeling that he should recognize the woman studying him.

"My kid sister and friends call me Bash." A smile touched her lips at his reply before she nodded.

"You're American." The smile she directed at him was warm and friendly.

"Yes, I work for a New York based architecture firm. I'm in charge of a project we're doing here in London."

"I'm Victoria, and I'm from the states too." She extended her hand, and Sebastian had the strangest urge to bend over and kiss the back of her hand. He quickly dismissed the sensation as a reaction to her historical costume. Instead, he shook her hand as she smiled at him. "I remember your brothers and sisters calling you Bash when Nicholas and I were at Starling House for dinner over the holidays in…"

"Starling House? Brothers and sisters?" An elusive memory flickered in the back of his mind before it was gone.

"Umm, maybe I was wrong. It's just that you look so much like—"

"You mean I look like Anna's husband in the past? Was his name Sebastian?"

"Yes. Do you have memories of that time?" She eyed him in surprise.

"Yes, some are vivid, and some are more like flashes of insight about Anna when I'm drawing her. It's something I've been doing since I was a kid." Sebastian paused as he took out his picture of Anna and handed it to Victoria. "Although since I arrived in London a few months ago, I've painted several portraits of her that were life events." Sebastian's shrug indicated he was still bewildered by everything that had happened this evening. Not to mention that Victoria seemed quite comfortable believing he'd been Anna's husband in the past.

"It's a remarkable likeness." There was a look of delight and approval on Victoria's face as she studied the picture. A moment later, she looked up at him with a wry twist of her mouth. "Your memory of the past sounds a great deal like my husband's. He remembers bits and pieces, but it's hard for him to fill in the blanks. It's just enough to drive him crazy."

"Nicholas never liked it when something happened that he couldn't control." The moment he spoke, Sebastian frowned in puzzlement.

"Yes. Nicholas is no different now, than he was in the past when it comes to that particular trait." The smile of satisfaction on her face increased his confusion as she waved a hand to prevent him from speaking. "There will be time for all of this later, but right now, I imagine you're probably impatient to see Anna."

"Yes. How is she?"

"The doctor said she has a broken hip, which needs to be replaced. She also appears to have a concussion. They had to sedate her because she kept muttering something about a dark angel."

Sebastian flinched at her words as a vivid memory crashed its way forward into his head. He was in a room lit only by firelight, and Anna was pulling his head down to hers, all the while calling him her dark angel. The love and passion between them was almost tangible, and it stirred something deep inside him. Seconds later, the image was gone, and Victoria eyed him with concern as she quickly reached out to hold him steady.

"Are you all right?"

"Yes, it's nothing." His reply made Victoria roll her eyes and snort softly.

"You're as bad as Nicholas. Wait here. I'll be right back."

Victoria hurried away, and Sebastian stumbled slightly as he moved to press his back against the wall. The vivid memory of him and Anna had knocked the wind out of his sails. Not only that, but how in the hell did Victoria know him? He was certain they'd never met before.

Everything the woman had said made him think she knew things he didn't. And what the devil was Starling House? What had she meant when she'd mentioned his brothers and sisters? He didn't have any brothers. Bee was his only sibling. None of it made any sense at all.

"Sebastian."

He turned his head to see Victoria waving for him to join her as she stood holding a door open. It sounded odd to hear his middle name echoing in his ears. The only people who called him by his full name were his parents, everyone else called him Bash. Yet it seemed quite natural for Victoria to use his full name. Still feeling a little unsteady from all that had happened, Sebastian moved as quickly as he could to follow Victoria deeper into the trauma center.

They came to a stop outside a closed room, and Victoria urged him to go through the door. Slowly, he entered the room and drew in a ragged breath at the sight of Anna's still form in the bed. She was unconscious and didn't stir as he crossed the room to take her hand in his. The moment he touched her, it was as if he'd been struck by lightning, and his legs almost gave way beneath him.

Rather than letting go of her hand, Sebastian clung to the bed rail to keep himself upright as images flooded his head. Images of a past he recognized but didn't remember clearly. The pictures careening through his head abruptly stopped, and as he regained his equilibrium, he heard Anna murmur something. He didn't catch what she said, and Sebastian leaned over her.

"What are you trying to say, sweetheart?"

"My dark angel. Where are you?"

Her whisper was barely audible, and the air disappeared from his lungs as he stared down at her. Gently, he kissed her forehead, then pressed his mouth against her ear.

"I'm right here, my love. You were right. You said you would find me again." A small wave of amusement crested through him. "But it was the other way around, I found you."

Behind him, the sound of the door opening made Sebastian glance over his shoulder. The moment he saw the man who'd been at Anna's side at the accident, Sebastian realized he was looking at Nicholas. The knowing was instantaneous, and when Nicholas jerked his head toward the door, Sebastian nodded. He kissed Anna's forehead again, then followed Nicholas out of Anna's room. The moment the door closed behind him, Sebastian studied the man intently.

"You're Anna's brother, Nicholas, right?" The question made the man bob his head sharply.

"Yes, I'm *Nora's* brother, Nick Barrows. Who are you? And why are you calling my sister, Anna?"

"I'm Sebastian Bennington."

"Tell me how you know my sister." The man's gaze narrowed at him with suspicion.

"I don't." The reply made Nicholas's eyes narrow with anger and suspicion. Clearly the wrong choice of words. Sebastian shoved a hand through his hair as he tried to come up with a rational explanation but failed. "I mean…it's complicated."

How was he supposed to explain his feelings or how he'd been dreaming and drawing pictures of Anna for years without knowing she wasn't a figment of his imagination?

"You said that at the accident. Exactly *how* complicated is it to tell me where you and *Nora* met?"

"*Nicholas*." The sound of Victoria's exasperation was evident as she hurried to her husband's side. "*Stop* interrogating the man. I leave for one minute, and you forget everything I said. Now I want you to look at Sebastian. Look at him closely."

"Sebastian? Who the hell is Sebastian?"

"It's my middle name. Levi *Sebastian* Bennington, Jr. And I'm almost as confused as you are."

"Do you *know* this man, Victoria?"

Nicholas Barrows glared at his wife, but she didn't answer him. Instead, she narrowed her gaze at him in a silent command to do as she said. With a low sound of anger, Nicholas turned back to face Sebastian. The look of assessment in the man's eyes was intense. After a long moment, Nicholas shook his head and turned his head toward his wife.

"Exactly what am I supposed to be seeing?" The question said he expected an answer from her.

"Do you remember one of the entries in your journals as to how you and someone at Andrew's and Jane's engagement party drank too much?"

For a long moment, Nicholas stared at his wife before he slowly turned to face Sebastian. As the man studied him in silence, Sebastian grimaced as the name Jane stirred a memory in his head of a young girl.

"*Christ Almighty*. Sebastian." Amazement, disbelief, and a hint of pleasure filled Nicholas's quiet words. "I don't believe it. It's really you."

When Sebastian remained silent, Nicholas chuckled, and he turned his head toward Victoria.

"Do you want to explain, sweet witch? I'm afraid I'll make a mess of it."

Before Victoria could say anything, a physician approached them, and two nurses entered Anna's room.

"The surgeon is almost ready for your sister, Mr. Barrows. She's in excellent hands. Dr. Merrick is considered the best orthopedic surgeon in London."

"How long will she be in surgery?" Sebastian's throat closed up at the thought of Anna lying on an operating table.

"Several hours. Dr. Merrick is doing a complete hip replacement, and there might be other damage that will need repair, but she's in excellent hands. The cafeteria has closed for the evening, but if you're hungry, several of the local restaurants deliver."

Sebastian turned around as he heard Anna being rolled out of the trauma room. Without thinking, he closed the distance between the two of them. Bending over her, Sebastian kissed her forehead.

"I'll be right here, my love."

At his soft words, she stirred, and her hand lifted as if trying to touch him. He caught her warm hand in his, and to his surprise, her eyes fluttered open. As she stared up at him, Sebastian's heart crashed into his chest. The love shining in her eyes was just like the emotion he'd seen in the picture of her that he carried in his wallet.

"My dark angel."

The whisper barely reached his ears as her eyes fluttered closed, and he was gently pushed out of the way. A strong hand clasped his shoulder.

"She's going to be okay, Sebastian. She's healthy and quite strong." Nicholas squeezed Sebastian's shoulder. "Right now, we need to talk. We have some planning to do, and I'm afraid you aren't going to like what I have to say."

An hour later, Sebastian was pacing the floor of the waiting lounge. Nicholas had been right. He didn't like what Anna's brother was telling him. He stopped and turned to face the man who'd been his best friend in the past.

"What you're telling me is that you don't want me to see her for six to eight weeks."

"Yes," Nicholas replied quietly. "I think the shock will be too much for her. I know from experience what Victoria and I went through the day she came out of her coma. It took some time for us to adjust to being together again. It won't be as easy a transition as you think."

"She recognized me." Sebastian glared at Nicholas. "She looked right at me and knew who I was."

"Maybe, but I'm more inclined to think my sister was seeing what the drugs were telling her. I also know that if she falls anytime during her recovery, it could do serious damage to her new hip. What happens if you startle her and she falls?"

"You've waited this long, Sebastian." Victoria studied him with a sympathetic gaze. "A few more weeks isn't a lot when it comes to giving her a chance to recover before she receives another shock to her system."

"And I'm convinced it's definitely going to be a shock to her, Sebastian. My sister, for all her...beliefs, isn't going to just fall into your arms. Anna—" His old friend stopped speaking with a confounded expression.

"I think you're going to have to get used to calling your sister, Anna, my darling." His wife's amusement made her husband scowl at her. With a sharp bob of his head, Nicholas turned back to Sebastian.

"As I was saying, Anna might believe in reincarnation, but whenever Victoria tells my sister how much she's like the Anna we knew in the past, I've seen her face. I'm not so sure she believes she was Anna, even if she can pass as an identical twin of the woman we knew."

"So, you believe me when I say she's my Anna?" The question caused an uncomfortable expression to cross Nicholas's face before he nodded abruptly.

"Yes, I believe you, but it's not me you have to convince, it's Nora—Anna." Nicholas directed a silent warning at his wife, Victoria just lifted her eyebrows, but her sapphire eyes sparkled with laughter. "Anna is fond of telling me there are no coincidences, and I'd say the picture in your wallet is definitely *not* a coincidence, especially if it's one of many you've done since you were a kid. But believing is one thing. Facing the reality of it is a different matter altogether. It took me several months to completely adjust to the fact that Victoria and I had been married in the past. I imagine Nor— Anna will make the transition more quickly, but she'll still have doubts."

"Nicholas is right, Sebastian. You need to be patient."

Everything Victoria and Nicholas were saying was true. He'd been waiting for years for this moment, even though he'd never known what he'd been waiting for. Would a few more weeks hurt, other than his impatient need to see Anna? Rubbing the back of his neck, Sebastian closed his eyes for a brief moment. Finally, with a sharp nod, he turned to face the couple.

"Fine."

"Thank you, old friend. Now then, our next step is to figure out the best way to bring the two of you together again, without traumatizing my sister."

Sebastian nodded as he met Nicholas's gaze, then took a seat next to his friend to make plans.

Sebastian stood in front of the tall grandfather clock he'd been drawing all his life. The fact that it was as real as Anna still had the ability to make him think he was dreaming. Nicholas still called his sister, Nora, although he would occasionally slip and refer to her as Anna. For Sebastian, he knew she would always be Anna to him.

Over the past five weeks, he and Nicholas had renewed their friendship. The camaraderie they'd enjoyed more than a hundred years ago had quickly reasserted itself, and they'd spent a great deal of time trying to piece together memories of their past lives.

Sebastian had seen firsthand how Nicholas was still adjusting to the memories of his past life. Even now, his old friend appeared surprised when he would remember something the two of them had done.

As for him, his memories had returned in a tsunami of images the moment he'd taken Anna's hand in his. He was grateful it hadn't happened at the scene of the accident. It had been difficult enough processing so many memories of a past life when he'd been with Anna in the trauma room.

Nicholas gave him daily reports as to how well Anna was doing. Without his friend's reassurances, he wasn't sure he would have been able to stay away from her. According to her brother, Anna had endured a lot of pain after the surgery. It had left her emotionally exhausted and prone to not working as hard on her exercises for fear of more pain. What troubled him was Nicholas's recent remarks that Anna didn't seem herself. She was putting up a good front, but Nicholas could tell his sister was hiding something from him. No matter how much he pressured her for the truth, Anna always denied anything was wrong.

Although Sebastian hadn't mentioned it to Nicholas, *his* hypothesis was that Anna still had memories of the night she'd been hit by the car. It gave him hope that when they finally met in a few days that she would remember him. Nicholas continued to warn Sebastian it might be a difficult transition for Anna, even though she believed in past lives.

Sebastian was inclined to disagree with his old friend as he'd come to grips with his new reality the night of Anna's accident in less than two hours. But time would tell, and that moment was quickly approaching. Nicholas and Victoria had suggested he come for dinner next week, and they'd ensure Anna was there. It would give her a safe environment in case she didn't recognize him, while helping him and his friends monitor her reactions.

He'd been hoping they could end his waiting this coming week, but Anna had informed Nicholas at the last minute she was spending the next few days in the country. Sebastian's friend had tried to learn where Anna was staying, but she'd simply said she was going to throw a dart at the board and go where it landed. Nicholas wasn't wild about her response, but she'd said she needed time to herself, and promised to let him know where she ended up.

The grandfather clock came into focus once more, and he contemplated it with puzzlement. Why was the clock so important? Did it mean something to Anna? A vague wisp of a memory floated through his head. It was an image of Anna reaching up inside the clock and tugging on something.

Slowly, he opened the front of the cabinet, then reached up inside the clock, uncertain what he was looking for. The moment Sebastian's fingers brushed over cool metal, he froze. Pulling his phone from his pocket, he activated the flashlight app and directed the light up into the clock while peering up inside. The moment his gaze settled on the lever, his heart slammed into his chest.

Fingers wrapped around the handle, Sebastian gently pulled it downward. He heard a soft pop echo from the base of the clock, and he took a step backward to watch a secret compartment open.

Squatting in front of the clock, he pulled the drawer all the way open to study its contents. They appeared to be letters, and on top of all of them was one addressed to Anna. When he picked it up, he saw it had been opened. He stared at it for a moment, and while part of him was tempted to pull out the letter, he decided to set it aside. The next piece of paper was a yellowed pamphlet that detailed how the clock was to be set and properly maintained.

Sebastian stood up, and following the document's directions, he set the clock and adjusted the chimes. Glancing down at the open drawer again, his gaze fell on an envelope with his name. Slowly, he bent over and picked up the letter then walked over to the couch to sit down and stare at the writing. It was Anna's handwriting, he was certain of it, but it wasn't the flowing script he remembered as being hers. This handwriting was shaky in the way someone ill or quite elderly might write. The gummed seal had given way, and the flap was brown from dried glue. Pulling the letter from the envelope, he carefully opened it.

October 11, 1966
My beloved dark angel,

How I've missed you. The night you left me, a large piece of my heart went with you. I deeply regret my anger when you finally told me you were dying. Your letter made me realize how well you know me. You knew I would fuss and fret over you, rather than experiencing the joy we had over those last four months of your life.

I know you did the right thing. although I wish you had told me sooner, so that I could have savored those moments even more than I did when you were helping me create new memories to sustain me after you were gone.

The years since you were taken from me have sometimes been quite difficult. I have often lain awake in the dark, longing for you to be lying beside me. But when I reach out to touch you and only feel the cold sheets where you once laid, it feels as if my heart is being ripped from my breast.

Then there are the mornings when I've slowly awakened to the unseen warmth of your arms wrapped around me as you hold me close. I think those times are when you know how badly I am missing you. I think you must sense my need for you, and you come to remind me that your soul and mine are still entwined and always shall be. at least that is what I tell myself, because I have doubts, my dearest dark angel.

As my time draws near, I am forced to face a terrible truth. I'm afraid, Sebastian. Terribly afraid. What if I am wrong? What if it has simply been my imagination at work and not the truth of how things are beyond the veil? What if there is nothing beyond this? What if I never see you again? I do not think my soul could bear it.

Even though I'm afraid I might have been wrong all these years, I hear your voice whisper in my head that I am not wrong. Your voice gives me the strength to face my fears in the same way I forced you to face yours all those years ago. I am ready to leave this world, because I am tired. My body is tired, and I am praying with all my heart and soul that we will be together again. I will have Sarah Jane place this letter in your clock's secret drawer. Despite my fears, I hope and pray you will one day read this in a new life with me at your side. I love you my dearest of dark angels.

Forever yours, Anna

Sebastian swallowed the knot in his throat as he slowly folded the letter and placed it back in its envelope. Jaw clenched with emotion, he closed his eyes as he processed Anna's words. Even though he believed things had happened the way they were supposed to, it did not lessen the impact of the emotions in Anna's letter.

The fear and loneliness she'd experienced at his death in the distant past had vibrated off the parchment. For the first time in his life, he wished he'd never added the clock to his drawings and paintings. It represented a pain that tore at him in the worst possible way.

A bolt of fear suddenly shot through him. What if she didn't recognize him when they met again at Nicholas's and Victoria's house? Sebastian winced as he realized the fear he was experiencing was different, and yet the same as what Anna had felt at the end of her previous life. There was also the possibility that he was wrong to think Nicholas's sister was his Anna. That in itself was a yawning hole that would send him to hell if he was wrong.

Sebastian's gaze fell on the clock again. If he was wrong, he knew he would have to sell the clock. Otherwise, it would be a constant reminder of the great happiness and love he'd been blessed with in his previous life, only to be alone in the present. His gaze dropped to the letter in his hand. The pain of it still made his heart ache. Launching himself off the couch, Sebastian quickly returned the letter to the hidden compartment, then closed it with a forceful push.

As he turned away from the clock, the portrait over the fireplace caught his eye. If the worst happened, and Anna didn't recognize him, then he would remove the painting as well. He knew he would also need to rid himself of every drawing and painting of Anna he'd ever done. If he was wrong about Anna, Sebastian wanted nothing to remind him of how he'd spent the majority of his life yearning for a woman who didn't exist.

Suddenly eager to leave the house, Sebastian made a quick sweep of all the rooms to make sure everything was ready for the guest arriving tomorrow for their week's rental. Satisfied Mrs. Harris, the housekeeper he used on a regular basis, hadn't missed anything, Sebastian walked through the living room without looking at the clock or the portrait. As he pulled the side door of the house closed, a wave of darkness crashed down over Sebastian. It was as if he had just cut out a piece of his soul.

Chapter 32

The nav system in Nora's car dinged, and the computer voice told her to take the next left. A few moments later, the computer announced she'd arrived. She parked her car in a space on the street and climbed out of the vehicle.

In minutes, Nora was stepping through the door of the realtor's office. An older woman speaking on the phone smiled at her and gestured for Nora to wait a moment. In less than two minutes, the woman ended the call then turned toward Nora.

"Good afternoon, how may I help you?"

"I'm Nora Barrows. I'm renting Green Lane House for the week."

"Oh, dear." The woman looked at her in surprise, then shook her head. "I think there must be a mistake."

"Mistake?" Nora directed a questioning look at the realtor.

The troubled look on the woman's face wasn't reassuring. Turning away, the realtor hurried toward her desk and picked up a leather binder. Fingers flicking the pages quickly, the realtor reached the spot she was looking for, and the woman shook her head in dismay.

"We weren't expecting you until tomorrow, Ms. Barrows."

"*Tomorrow*. I made arrangements more than a week ago for my rental to begin today." The older woman nodded in understanding.

"I *am* sorry for the mix up, Ms. Barrows. Fortunately, Mr. Bennington left the keys with me a little more than a half-hour ago, so the house is ready for you. I can simply add one night to your rental."

"Thank you."

Nora sighed as the woman began to process her rental paperwork. At least she didn't have to stay in a hotel tonight, then up and move to the rental tomorrow morning. Several minutes later, she was walking out of the realtor's office with the keys and directions to Green Lane House in her hand.

Quickly programming the property's location into the computer, Nora did a quick search on her phone for a grocery on the way to her rental. She found one close by and made a quick stop for fresh produce and milk. A short time later, she was driving along Green Lane to where the narrow lane ended in a roundabout and the small, cozy-looking house she'd seen on the internet came into view.

As Nora pulled into the drive and shut off the car, she leaned back and closed her eyes for a long moment. She was long overdue for a vacation away from the sounds and busy energy of London. The accident had taken its toll on her, physically as well as emotionally, over the past six weeks.

Nora's pain tolerance was on the low end of the charts, and it had been a struggle to walk and do the exercises the doctor had instructed her to do, without pain. There was the occasional twinge now and then when she moved about, but the more she walked, the less she hurt.

It was one of the reasons she'd chosen to rent Green Lane House when she'd seen it on the internet. The pictures had shown it nestled inside a landscape of forests and pastures. It was the perfect place to do some short ramblings across the countryside. The fresh air would also help her process some of the things troubling her about the night of the accident.

Expelling a forceful puff of air past her lips, Nora grabbed the two canvas bags of groceries, her laptop case, and headed toward the cottage's side door. From the video she'd watched online, she knew the door led straight into a small kitchen. Fumbling with the keys, she finally managed to unlock the door and entered the small kitchen. Nora set everything down on the countertop, then returned to the car to get her luggage and a box of dry goods. With everything in the house, she locked the door behind her. Just as she was about to go exploring, her mobile phone went off with Nicholas's ring tone, and she pulled it from her purse.

"Why do I get the feeling my big brother is checking up on me?" She tried to keep her voice light and cheerful, but wasn't sure she'd managed to do it successfully.

"I *am* checking up on you."

She visualized her brother's dark scowl in her head as she released a noise of exasperation and closed her eyes for a second.

"Okay, what do you want to know?" Nora shook her head slightly as she began to unload her groceries and put cold foods in the fridge.

"Where are you?" At his question, she hesitated. When she didn't answer, Nicholas cleared his throat. "Nora, I asked you—"

"I rented a small cottage outside of Guildford for the week." The silence on the other end of the phone drew out for several seconds, and she thought she'd lost the signal. "Nick, are you still there?"

"Yes, I'm here."

"I thought I'd lost the signal."

"What in the hell made you decide to go to Guildford?" The note of amazement in her brother's voice made Nora smile.

"I don't know, I was just looking for something in the country so I could go out on a couple of short ramblings through the countryside. I figured it would help limber up my hip a little more. I want to start doing martial arts again with Tanaka-sensei in a couple of weeks."

"Is that wise?"

"This from the man who pestered me to go walking all the time when I was in pain?"

"Forget I said it." Silence once again stretched out between them. "So, you didn't go to Guildford for any other reason?"

"No, I saw the cottage, and I really liked the looks of it. In fact, I was just about to go exploring when you called."

"Exploring?"

"Yes, I've been putting up the groceries while we've been talking." Nora pulled the phone away from her ear to glare at it before pressing it to her ear again. "What the hell is wrong with you? You're acting as if this is the first time I've ever traveled."

"No, I'm not."

"*Yes*. You *are*." Nora rolled her eyes.

"Well, I'm worried about you."

"Oh for fuck's sake, Nick. I'm a big girl. I'm perfectly capable of taking care of myself, and asking for help *if* I need it, and I *don't*."

"You know I'm here for you, right? No matter what you need?" The deep note of concern in her older brother's voice made her sigh.

"Yes, and you know I love you for it. But stop worrying about me. I'll be fine. I'll be back in the shop first of the week."

"Don't forget you're coming for dinner next Tuesday."

"I won't forget. And just so you won't jump off the deep end, I'm turning my phone off. I loaded my eReader and I'm going to exercise my hip and read for the next seven days.

Undisturbed. Now, goodbye."

"Goodbye."

The disgruntled note in her brother's voice made her snort with laughter as she ended the call. With a shake of her head, she grabbed her luggage and rolled it toward the narrow staircase she could see from the doorway leading into the living room. She'd just reached the foot of the stairs when the deep, sonorous notes of a clock's chimes rang out to announce the hour. Unprepared for the sound, Nora gave a violent start and grabbed the bannister to keep from falling.

"*Christ Almighty,*" she breathed as her heart raced wildly in her chest. "They should warn people about stuff like that. That's a fucking toll bell."

Nora threw a quick glance over her shoulder at the clock before she reached for her luggage. In the next breath, she froze. It couldn't be. Hesitant to turn around, she remained where she was, one hand gripping the bannister as if her life depended on it. After several seconds, she turned around, then sagged back against the spindles and bannister of the staircase. It was her clock.

How in the hell had it wound up here? Still unsteady on her feet, she moved forward at a slow pace. Put your foot forward, Nora. Now the other one. When she reached the clock, she stretched out her hand, fully expecting it to disappear because she was clearly delusional. The instant her fingers stroked the delicate panels of wildflowers, a pulse of energy jolted her body.

Images flooded her head as if she were watching a movie on fast forward, and she swayed as if drunk. Unsteady on her feet, she braced her palms against the hardwood surrounding the glass front of the clock. After what seemed like an eternity, but could only have been a minute or two, the movie in her head suddenly came to an abrupt stop, leaving her dizzy. Eyes closed, she bowed her head and waited for the queasy sensation to pass.

After several long moments, Nora dragged in a deep breath and straightened upright as she tried to process what had just happened, and the wide range of emotions still careening through her. The memory of the man whose features had been so prominent in her head a minute ago made tears well up in her eyes. Her dark angel. Fingertips caressing the dark wood of the massive clock, she swallowed hard. Sebastian had loved this clock. The unexpected thought sent a shiver through her.

There was only one man she knew by that name, and he was dead and buried. Nora swallowed hard. Now she understood what her brother must have felt when grappling with his visceral reaction to Victoria. But she wasn't her brother staring at a comatose soul mate in a hospital room. Nora closed her eyes again. Maybe not, but a small piece of her heart said her dark angel had been with her the night of the accident.

Nora hadn't seen him, but her memory of him was vivid and distinct. The warmth of his hand clasped around hers, the strong, authoritative sound of his voice when he'd commanded her not to leave him. She'd felt and heard him again at her bedside in the trauma room. But in the days following the accident, neither Nicholas nor Victoria had mentioned the man.

Although he'd seemed so real, she'd concluded her brain had conjured him up out of her imagination to deal with the shock of her trauma. It was a logical explanation. Especially when she'd been in so much pain. Nora winced at the memory of how badly her entire body had hurt. The problem was, a part of her still believed the stranger had been real. His features were nothing more than shadows in her mind, but Nora could have sworn he'd called her Anna.

Stepping back from the grandfather clock, she stared at it for a long moment. What were the odds she'd rent a house from the same person who'd bought her clock? A shiver streaked down her spine. No, it was Sebastian's clock. She needed to remember that.

The sudden memory of the old woman at the gala telling her about the secret compartment made Nora move forward. She carefully opened the front of the clock. Stretching her arm up inside the cabinetry, her fingers slid over a curved metal handle. Carefully, she pulled it downward.

The handle moved smoothly, and she heard a soft click, then looked down to see a drawer that had popped open at the base of the furniture. Nora slowly sank down to the floor to sit in front of the clock and stare at the drawer's contents. A small voice in the back of her head said she shouldn't be going through someone else's personal belongings.

It was easy to counter the warning with the observation that the new owner of the clock couldn't possibly know the drawer existed when they'd just bought the piece of furniture. Leaning forward, she picked up a pamphlet that contained directions on how to operate the clock. Nora set it aside and stared down at the envelope laying on top of several bundles of letters inside the drawer.

For Anna, the light of my life

Nora inhaled a sharp breath as she read the strong handwriting. She stared at the letter for a long moment before she picked it up. Carefully pulling the letter out of the envelope, she stared down at a handwriting she'd never seen before, and yet it was familiar at the same time.

My darling Anna,

I know how devastated and angry you were tonight when I told you what Dr. Newstrom had informed me of four months ago. You wanted to know why I kept the news from you, but I need for you to understand my reasons for not telling you until now, my love. I wanted to spend the remaining weeks and days of my life showing you how much I love you. I know you have looked at me in recent weeks with astonishment when I've insisted we go sailing on the channel or picnicking at Birchwood as the sun is setting, after which I made love to you under the stars.

Those evening hours in particular still make me smile because, for the first time in our lives, I managed to shock you. As I have changed in loving you, so have you, beautiful light of my heart. I think a tiny modicum of my love of propriety has rubbed off on you. I know you will deny it, but I believe it is true.

We have never been too old to express our love for one another by enjoying the pleasure and passion our bonding has always brought us. Doing so under the stars for the first time seemed appropriate for a man who has learned from his beloved wife that there are moments when one should put aside propriety and simply take pleasure in the caress of my lover, no matter where we are.

I only wish I had, at least once, pulled you into a dark corner at some soirée to make love to you. then when we rejoined the party, everyone would know Viscount Starling had just fucked and pleasured his wife, thereby ensuring every man in the room knew you were mine. See, my love, that I regret not having done so, is an example of how loving you has broadened my perspective.

My life would have been empty if I'd not taken the risk of loving you, my darling wife. And God, how I have loved you. Whether it was simply a smile across the room, hearing your laughter outside my study door, holding you in my arms, wishing I could ease your heartbreak as you sobbed the day we learned your Uncle Charles had died. I cannot begin to explain the depth of my helplessness to ease your sorrow that day.

Then there was the night James died. Losing our son aroused the darkest part of your dark angel. My cruelty and anger in the months that followed James's death were unforgiveable. Yet your love never wavered, and you forgave me nonetheless. But I have never forgiven myself for having pushed you away and almost losing you in those dark times.

My days have been filled with more laughter than sorrow, more joy than fear. there has not been one day when I did not thank God for allowing me to love you, even in those darkest and bleakest of moments when I know you thought I no longer loved you. That has never been true, my darling light of my heart. I have loved you more than life itself. Perhaps even more when I hid my heart from you.

Your dark angel has apologized to you so many times, my beloved, and you forgave me each time, but only after repeatedly calling me a fuck-wit with every apology. A name that I most heartily agree I deserved. Yet every time, you were the light that pulled me out of the abyss. You were and always will be my home.

You have shared your life with me. The nights I've spent in your arms, making love to you, holding you simply to keep you close, or watching you when you sleep, have given me glimpses of heaven. A heaven that will be lonely without you when I leave you in such a short time. You must know I do not wish to leave you, my love. My heart will never be whole without you, even in whatever place that is beyond the veil, as you call it.

I wanted to fill our last days and hours together with joy and laughter so you will know and remember the depth of love I feel for you. It's the only gift I had to give you before I leave you, my love. I wanted to give you new memories that were fresh in your mind in hopes they would sustain you for what is to come in the weeks and months ahead.

Your beliefs have always made you the stronger of the two of us, even though we have suffered the same loss and deep sorrow. I need you to be strong now, light of my soul. I need you to know that I believe we will be together again, otherwise I would not have been able to give you this last gift of love. I love you, my darling light of my heart. I cannot put into words how deeply I love you. But know this Anna, my love, I am forever yours, no matter where we are. You took a man who had nothing and gave him the world simply by loving him. I love you, my darling. We will see each other again. I believe that because I believe in you.

Forever and always yours,
Your dark angel, Sebastian

Nora could barely make out the last two sentences of the letter as tears blurred her vision. The depths of Sebastian's love flowing so poignantly from his letter made her shoulders sag, and she didn't try to stop the tears streaming down her cheeks. Inside her chest, it was as if someone was squeezing her heart until she could barely breathe from the pain.

For the first time since reading Victoria's journals, she realized that deep down inside she'd been holding out hope Sebastian would find her in this life. That wish had been granted, but not in the way she'd hoped. Wiping the tears from her cheeks, Nora slowly returned the yellowing letter to its envelope. She set it aside, then dragged in a deep breath and stared down at the other letters. There were five bundles of neatly stacked letters in the drawer.

Leaning forward, she picked up a bundle of correspondence and carefully untied the ribbon holding the letters together. From the way the envelopes were addressed, they appeared to be an exchange of correspondence between her and Sebastian. Nora reached out to pick up one of the other bundles of correspondence. They were more letters she and Sebastian had exchanged during their lives together in the past.

The thought made her shake her head slightly. Even with her firm belief in past lives, it was still a shock to realize the letters she held in her hand now had been held by her in the past. On top of the stack she'd undone, she recognized Sebastian's strong handwriting on the letter with its broken wax seal. It was addressed to Viscountess Starling, Birchwood, Surrey. Taking care, she unfolded the parchment to read the contents.

January 5, 1896
My beautiful darling wife,

As always, the opening session of parliament is chaotic and brimming with energy. Nicholas and I are enjoying the debates if only for the heated exchange of barbs delivered by one side or another.

I miss you, my beloved. It worries me that you are ill. I know my mother will take excellent care of you, as will the staff, but I do not like being away from you when you are feeling so poorly. I wish you had not fought me so vehemently about my remaining at Birchwood until you were feeling well enough to come with me to London. Despite your belief that my presence in parliament is a necessity, I would not be shirking my duties if I had delayed my appearance until after you were well.

I have spent the past two nights with Nicholas, playing cards at the club. While I hold my friend in the highest of regard, I confess there are other things I would prefer to do in the evenings. If you were here, I would be content to sit with you in the salon at Starling House with a good book in my hand, and you curled up on the settee next to me enjoying your current choice of read.

When we retired for the evening, I would remind you several times how much I adore and worship you. afterward, we would fall asleep in each other's arms until dawn broke. then, as the first rays of sunlight drifted across your lovely, sun-kissed body, I would take delight in kissing every fragrant part of you. I am counting the hours until Friday afternoon when I can return to you and your loving arms.

Forever yours, Sebastian

Nora folded the letter, set it aside, then picked up the next one that was addressed to Viscount Starling.

January 7, 1896
My cherished dark angel,

> *I am feeling much better than I was a few days ago.*
> *please do not worry about me, my darling. I am being well-*
> *cared for by mama. She asked that I send you her love.*
> *Although you know I enjoy being at Birchwood, it is a crypt*
> *when you are not here. But then, no matter where I am, if*
> *you are not with me, I am confined to exist in a mausoleum.*
>
> *Time passes so slowly without you near me. I find*
> *myself unable to think of anything but you and how much I*
> *miss you. I long for your touch, my love. I will never grow*
> *tired of your caresses or the tenderness of your kisses. come*
> *home to me soon, my most darling of dark angels. I need to*
> *breathe in your warmth, see and taste your hardness, hear*
> *your voice whispering words of love in my ear, but most of*
> *all, I crave your touch. I need it as a garden needs sunlight*
> *and water to flourish.*
>
> *Forever and always, your Anna*

One after another, Nora read letters filled with words of love, passion, and desire. Several of them made her smile, while others made her eyes water with unshed tears. She'd just finished reading a letter, when she heard the scraping of a key in the side door leading into the kitchen. Before she realized someone was entering the house, the door creaked open.

"Mrs. Harris, it's Bash. I forgot my chalks and oils."

The deep male voice sent a vibration through her that wasn't fear so much as it was surprise. Suddenly aware that the owner of the house was about to catch her red-handed with the clock's open drawer, panic streaked through Nora. As a heavy male tread crossed the kitchen floor toward the living room, she scrambled to her feet. She had no idea how she was going to explain the drawer with its letters, but she had no intention of attempting to do so sitting on the floor. Nora started to turn in the direction of the kitchen, then froze as her gaze settled on the painting over the fireplace.

"*Oh, my God,*" she whispered. Stunned, she stared at the portrait of her and her dark angel with their four children.

"What the hell are you—" The harsh words made her turn sharply toward the stranger, and shock made her sway slightly as she fought to remain standing.

"*Sebastian.*" Her voice was barely a whisper as she stared in disbelief at the man who was studying her with equal shock.

"Anna."

Neither one of them moved for a long moment, and the only sound in the room was the loud ticking of the clock. The moment he took a step toward her, Nora inhaled a quick breath. He immediately stopped.

"You're real."

"You're here."

They spoke simultaneously as they stared at each other across the small space between them. He started forward again, then stopped as she retreated a step. An emotion flashed across his face that she thought might be pain, and he froze where he was standing.

"You were there. At the accident." Her statement made him nod.

"Yes."

"And the hospital?"

"You remember me being there?" There was a note of hope in his voice that made her heart skip a beat.

"Yes…no, it's more like a dream than a memory. I was on some heavy-duty drugs." Confused, she shook her head in bewilderment. "But you weren't there when I woke up. I thought I'd imagined you."

"Nicholas thought it best not to give you another shock so soon on the heels of the accident."

"Since *when* in the *hell* did you start *listening* to him?" Anger streaked through her that Sebastian had taken her brother's advice, while experiencing resentment at her brother's interference. A second later, she realized her question had sounded as if Sebastian had known Nicholas a long time.

"I've always listened to him, although there were numerous times when I ignored his advice."

"Well, you *sure* as hell didn't when it came to Margaret. We all knew she wouldn't make you happy."

"Still jealous after more than a hundred years, my love?" The corner of his mouth twitched as if he were struggling hard not to laugh.

"*Don't* be ridiculous," she snapped.

So help her, if he laughed at her—the next breath she dragged into her lungs snuffed out her irritation. Christ, had he just said he was in love with her in a roundabout way? It threw her off-balance, but at the same time, it didn't sound ominous or creepy. If anything, the intimate term of affection he'd just used sounded as comfortable as an old t-shirt she might wear. It made her insides feel warm and fuzzy. It felt right. His dark eyes gleamed with amusement, his eyebrow quirking upward.

"You don't remember Margaret?"

"*No*. Her name just *popped* into my head."

Sebastian's quiet chuckle floating through the air earned him a sharp glare of annoyance from her. Who in the hell was Margaret? Suddenly, an intense emotion she couldn't define replaced his amusement.

"She was the woman I'd thought about marrying until I fell in love with you."

The depth of emotion vibrating in Sebastian's voice set off a tingling sensation across her skin. Sebastian's eyes suddenly darkened with a fire that sent her heart skidding out of control. God help her. Whenever he had looked at her like that in the past, she'd been willing to surrender completely to whatever he demanded of her. The sudden memory of the two of them locked in a passionate kiss warmed her blood until every cell in her body was reveling in a deliciously pleasurable heat. Nora immediately swallowed the knot threatening to close off her throat.

In the next instant, she realized he'd just admitted to being in love with her in the past on top of using the endearment, my love. Did that mean he had feelings for her in the here and now? Was that even possible? A snort of self-disgust reverberated in her head. Hadn't she seen her brother fall in love with Victoria in the space of hours because he'd loved her in the past? Not yet ready to confront the truth of what was happening, she took in a deep breath. Desperate to keep the topic from going down a path she wasn't quite prepared for, she nodded toward the portrait.

"Where did the painting come from?"

"I painted it." The matter-of-fact statement made her jerk her gaze back to him to stare at him in astonishment. The emotion in his gaze made her quickly turn back to the painting.

"It's very good."

"I have dozens more." Once more, she stared at him in amazement, and he smiled. "I've been drawing and painting you since I was a kid. Every time I dreamed about you, I put my memories of you on paper or canvas."

"Oh." Nora knew it was an inadequate response, but she wasn't quite sure what to make of his confession. Sebastian's mouth curled into a complacent grin, and she narrowed her eyes at him. "You don't need to look so *damn* smug."

"Smug?" Sebastian shook his head as he rejected her fierce comment. "I'm simply remembering another point in time when you were almost, if not completely, at a loss for words."

"I've never been stumped for words."

"Are you asking me to prove you wrong?" The laughter in his eyes held a hint of a challenge, too. "Because I think a kiss would definitely leave you speechless."

"That's an absurd idea. We don't even know each other." Nora suppressed a groan as she realized it was a lie. She *did* know him.

"*That* is completely unlike you, Anna. You were always bluntly honest. Has that changed?" Tension radiated off him as he eyed her with disappointment and a small amount of worry.

It was as if they'd been apart for a long time and were struggling to adapt. No, *she* was the one struggling. He seemed completely comfortable with the idea that they'd been lovers as well as husband and wife in the past. The irony of it all was that she'd always believed in past lives. Now she was questioning all of it. But she couldn't deny the effect he was inflicting on her senses. Not to mention how the thought of him kissing her had her heart racing out of control. The memory of other emotions he'd aroused in her in the distant past filled her head. Love, passion, joy, and sometimes a deep fear that she would lose him.

"Well, *answer* me, Anna." The demand in his voice reminded her of how arrogant and annoying he could be.

"*No.* I've never had a problem speaking my mind."

"Then what are you afraid of, sweetheart?" The arrogance was gone, and in its place was a note of tenderness.

"I'm not—" Nora immediately stopped speaking as he narrowed his gaze at her. "I'm uncertain as to what all this means. It's unsettling."

"I remember a time when you told me not to think, just feel."

The low, velvety smooth sound of his voice made her heart lurch. God, the man's voice still had the power to reduce her to a hot mess. It was as if she was riding a roller coaster and enjoying the air time that came with each downward plunge. But the sensation was quickly becoming a continuous, prolonged, exhilarating experience.

The realization made her mouth go dry as she met his gaze. The memory of her straddling his hips and exploring the hot steel of his chest with her mouth made her suck in a quick breath. Fire flared in his dark gaze at the sound.

She had always snorted with laughter every time she read about a hero's smoldering gaze in a romance book. The phrase had always seemed a little too cliché, overused, and unrealistic. Never had she been so wrong about something in her life. The way Sebastian was studying her now easily surpassed anything Mr. Darcy or Edward Rochester had been capable of.

It made her remember other moments when he'd looked at her like this. Moments when she'd barely been able to breathe as she'd anticipated his touch. Moments filled with an exquisite passion and love that she'd known would never die, even across the barriers of time. The images in her head were so striking, it was as if they'd just taken place days ago.

Legs wobbling beneath her, Nora's heartbeat quickened even more until her pulse was raging out of control. Needing something to keep her from sliding to the floor, she reached out for the solid wood mantel of the fireplace to brace herself. A small smile tipped the corners of his mouth as he studied her in silence. It was almost as if he could read her mind, and she suddenly realized that if she was able to remember passionate kisses and more of their lives in the past, he could too.

Breathing became difficult, and with an almost imperceptible shake of her head, she watched him take a step toward her. When she didn't retreat, he continued to close the distance between them.

"Sebastian…"

"Just feel, my love." His voice was a soft caress against her senses as he gently pulled her into his arms.

The moment his mouth met hers, a white-hot heat streaked through her. The years they'd been apart collapsed into mere minutes until it was as if they'd said goodbye only a few hours ago, and were together again, welcoming each other home with a passionate kiss. Her lips parted beneath his, and as her tongue danced with his, the emotions cascading through her made her heart ache in a way that was almost overwhelming.

Until now, she'd simply been existing. Being in his arms again opened a floodgate of memories. They were memories that said she was home. With just one kiss, she remembered all the joy, love, and passion that had always been a part of them loving each other.

Hands sliding up over his solid chest and shoulders, she clung to him, reveling in the crisp taste of mint flowing off his tongue. Everything about him teased her senses. From his hard muscles to his male scent. She breathed him in, and her nose tingled with the delicious scent of spice and pine. God, he smelled good. No, not good—wonderful. She trembled as his hand slid up over her waist until it came to rest just below her breast.

The moment his thumb pressed gently into the underside of her breast, she shuddered. It ignited a craving inside her that was wickedly sinful. A second later, he lifted his head. Disappointment shot through her, and she murmured a protest. It was answered with a low, dangerous growl that rumbled in his chest as he pressed his forehead against hers.

"*Christ*, you go to my head, Anna, but I want us to wait."

"*Wait?*" She stiffened in his arms and leaned back so she could see his face fully. "What the *fuck* do you *mean*, wait? First you kiss me until I'm ready to have an orgasm, then you stop and say you want us to *wait?*"

"I see your colorful language hasn't changed." An ironic smile twisted his lips.

"Oh, that's *nothing*, you sorry ass, fuck-wit. What sort of game are you playing, right now?"

"I'm not playing games, Anna. God only knows what this is costing me, right now." Sebastian closed his eyes for a moment before he met her gaze again. "You have no idea how badly I want to drag you up those stairs and make love to you. But I want us to wait, sweetheart, because I want you to be sure."

"Sure of *what?*" She narrowed her gaze at him.

"I've had years to come to grips with the life I lived before this one, and I still find it confusing and jarring from time to time." A rueful smile tilted Sebastian's mouth. "You've had all of what? Twenty minutes? Nicholas said you might find it hard to accept we were together in a past life, and I think he was right. I can tell you're struggling with all of this."

"*Oh*, is *that* so?" she exclaimed through clenched teeth.

Without hesitating, she hooked her leg behind his calve and tugged hard. In two seconds, he landed on the carpet with a grunt, his expression one of surprise and irritation as he met her gaze with an angry scowl. She followed him to the floor and straddle his waist as she had decades ago.

"*Dammit, Anna.* Listen to me."

She glared down at him and began to unbutton his shirt. When he tried to stop her, she batted his hand away with a hard smack. When his shirt was undone, she tugged her t-shirt up over her head in a quick, abrupt movement.

"Anna. Sweetheart. You need to listen—"

"*No. You* listen to *me*. The only thing I'm struggling with right now is the fact that my dark angel, the man I've loved in two lifetimes, just sent my body into overdrive, then pulled the plug."

Angry that he'd set her on fire, then arbitrarily decided she needed time to figure things out, she narrowed her eyes at him. Her gaze locked with his, she smiled slowly as she reached behind her and unhooked her bra. Passion and excitement flared in his eyes as she took her time removing the lacy undergarment. Sebastian's throat bobbed as he swallowed hard the moment she tossed it aside.

"Now then, isn't it time you showed me how much you love and missed me?"

"Who am I to say no to you, my love?"

A wicked smile touched Sebastian's mouth as he reached up to pull her downward. Satisfied she'd gotten her way, Anna sank into him, and her heart swelled with happiness. She was home for a second time.

Epilogue

August 1895

Sebastian stood quietly at the altar with the reverend and Nicholas as he waited for Anna to enter the chapel. Six months ago, if anyone had told him that he would marry a woman he'd deemed unsuitable, he would have scoffed at them. The thought of how close he'd come to losing his bride was enough to make his gut twist until it was a hard knot inside him.

Even now, a small part of him worried Anna might change her mind about marrying him. She would be giving up a great deal when she became Viscountess Starling. The knowledge had made him vow to do everything in his power to ensure her happiness, so she never regretted her decision to marry him. His gaze met his mother's as Alexander escorted her down the aisle, and her happy smile made him smile in return as he offered her a slight bow.

In the next breath, he saw Anna at the entrance to the chapel on her uncle's arm. Beside him, Nicholas chuckled softly, and Sebastian's mouth twitched with amusement. Defiant as always, his bride had foregone the now traditional white dress the queen had made so popular years ago. Instead, Anna was wearing the gown she'd worn the night she'd been introduced to the Marlborough Set.

Her flaunting convention was one of the reasons he

loved her, and with each step Anna took toward him, Sebastian's heart swelled in his chest. He'd never seen her so radiant. That this extraordinary, brave woman had agreed to be his wife humbled him in a way he'd never experienced until today.

Anna had asked that they have a simple ceremony inviting no one other than family and close friends. It was a request he'd agreed to without hesitation. Not because he was ashamed of his wife-to-be, but because he'd not wanted to share today with anyone outside their family. If he were being completely honest, he would have preferred to share this moment only with her.

Sebastian stretched out his hand as Captain Wentworth placed Anna's hand in his. The small quiver that rippled through her vibrated against his palm, and another twinge of fear and guilt slashed through him. For the past several days, he'd noticed there had been moments when he'd caught her staring off into space with a pensive expression on her exquisite features.

She'd been unaware that he'd seen her almost melancholy air, and he'd been afraid to ask her what was troubling her. The possibility that she might be having second thoughts about marrying him had haunted Sebastian in the dark every night since they'd returned to London. Now, as they looked at each other, he squeezed her hand and leaned forward to brush his mouth against her ear.

"If you're having doubts about marrying this fuckwit, my love, there's still time to back out," Sebastian whispered for her ears alone. "I know what you're giving up, and I don't want you to regret it. Ever."

Anna's eyes widened for an instant before she narrowed her gaze to study him with a piercing intensity. Annoyance flared in the brown depths of her gaze, causing the knot in his gut to tighten more viciously. She leaned forward, and he bent his head so only he could hear her reply.

"You are the most hard-headed, exasperating man I've ever met. Do you think I've not considered the possibility *you* might be thinking you made a mistake asking me to marry you?" She snorted softly with indignation, but her gaze softened as she stared up at him with a look of love that tightened his chest. Anna suddenly smiled at him. "Now shut up and marry me, before I prove just *how* unsuitable I am to be your viscountess."

With a nod, he carried her hand to his lips, and their gazes locked for a brief moment. Fingers entwined with hers, Sebastian turned back to the reverend. It was evident the man was put out for having been kept waiting, but when Sebastian narrowed his eyes at the man, the officiate cleared his throat and began the ceremony.

In short order, the reverend pronounced them husband and wife, then led them into a small room next to the vestibule to sign the marriage register along with Sarah's and Nicholas's signatures as witnesses. The legalities completed, Nicholas shook his hand, then gave him a brotherly hug.

"You're a lucky man, Sebastian. Never forget that." Nicholas stepped back, and Sebastian nodded his agreement.

"Luckier than I had ever hoped to be."

Sebastian turned to see Sarah smiling at his wife. The thought made his heart swelled with happiness. *His* wife. Nicholas had no idea just how fortunate Sebastian was. Anna had given her heart to a dark angel she'd pulled back from the brink of hell. She was the light that had saved him from a life that would have made him a shell of a man.

He vowed he would cherish her to the end of his days. The instant she turned toward him, the air disappeared from his lungs at the radiant expression on her sweet features. She stretched out her hand to him, and he caught it in his. The quiver that pulsed through her pierced his palm to spread a warm heat throughout his body.

"Shall we, Lady Starling? I believe our guests are

awaiting our appearance."

"I am yours to command, my lord." The mischievous smile on her lips made him laugh.

"Am I to assume you have finally decided to act like the proper wife of a viscount?" Sebastian teased, and Anna eyed him with a playful glare. Entwining her arm in his, she pressed herself into his side.

"As I recall, I warned you several times before today I was unsuitable to be your viscountess."

"So you did, but I wouldn't have you any other way, my love."

His words made her draw in a sharp breath, while her eyes suddenly shimmered with unshed tears. Sebastian gently stroked her cheek, then pressed his hand over the one resting on his arm and led her out to where their family and friends were waiting for them.

Hours later, Sebastian stood at the bow of the Falcon, his arms resting on the rounded wood rail. It was a full moon, and the stars glittered in the sky like tiny jewels so far away and yet so close. It had been after dark when he'd led Anna out of Starling House to their carriage. Once inside, he'd blindfolded her and laughingly refused to answer her as she demanded to know what he was up to.

Certain the sounds and smells of the docks would alert her to their destination, Sebastian had done the only thing he could think of that might distract her enough to ensure her surprise. His planned seduction had worked better than he'd hoped.

They'd been halfway to the river when he'd pulled the shades shut and brought his wife to her first climax. Anna had shuddered in his arms until she was sobbing for him to satisfy her completely. Sebastian had thought he would be able to resist taking Anna in the carriage, but he'd found the sight of his wife blinded by a black silk scarf just as arousing as when she wore men's clothing.

To his surprise and delight, their lovemaking had disoriented Anna enough that she'd been confused as to where when they'd arrived at the berth where the Falcon was docked. As he'd helped her out of the carriage and removed her blindfold, she'd stared at the ship and then back at him in amazement.

The moment he explained the Falcon was their means of travel for their wedding trip, Anna's happiness had been worth all the secret plans he made with Captain Wentworth. But it was her reaction when he told her they were traveling to Cairo and then to Greece he treasured the most.

She'd immediately burst into tears, then flung herself into his arms and began kissing him with excitement. Startled by her tears, his surprise had lasted only a second as he realized they were joyful ones. The memory made his mouth curve in a satisfied smile. He had several other surprises in store for his wife on their trip. Sebastian jumped as a pair of arms wrapped around his waist, and the sweet sound of Anna's voice echoed in his ear.

"Well, husband, I think you need to explain why you left our bed on our wedding night." Anna pressed her cheek into his back, and he laughed softly.

"I came up on deck to avoid waking you. You fell asleep so quickly after our earlier exertions, I didn't have the heart to interrupt your sleep." Sebastian reached behind him to pull his wife around to face him, then captured her mouth in a brief kiss. She tilted her head backward to eye him with mock disapproval before she smiled.

"I'm not sure whether to berate you for being so cruel in depriving me of your touch or to adore you even more than I already do for your thoughtfulness."

"I think I'll settle for adoration."

"Then adoration it shall be," Anna laughed.

She snuggled against him and turned her head to look out at the water shimmering in the moonlight as the ship sped along. They stood in silence for a long time, and Sebastian was content simply to hold her close with the knowledge that she was his and he was hers. The fact that his adorable, loving wife had rescued him from a bleak existence was something he would always be grateful for.

"I can't believe Hamish left the Falcon." Anna sighed as she looked up at him. "Uncle Charles wouldn't tell me what happened between the two of them. All he would tell me was that Hamish received an offer that was too good to say no to."

"You can't fault the man for wanting to improve his lot in life, Anna."

"I don't, but the horse's arse didn't even say goodbye."

"Perhaps he thought it would be too hard." Sebastian struggled to avoid laughing out loud.

"No. Hamish isn't a coward. There's something more to this than meets the eye. I'm going to speak to Uncle Charles in the morning."

"I don't think that will be necessary, my darling."

"Why not?" She tipped her head back to stare at him in surprise.

"Because Hamish is now the captain of his own ship."

"*Poseidon's balls*, his *own ship*?" Anna stared up at him, slack jawed. A moment later, she narrowed her gaze at him. "How do you know that?"

"Because I own the ship, he's captain of." Sebastian grinned at the flabbergasted look on his wife's sweet features.

"Since when do you own a ship?"

"I bought it shortly after we returned to port almost two months ago. One of the terms of your accepting my proposal was that I would take you sailing as often as possible."

"But I…you bought a ship just to take me sailing?"

The question was almost inaudible over the quiet sound of the sea slapping against the bow of the ship. Happiness streaked through Sebastian like a bolt of lightning at the stunned expression on Anna's face, and he smiled.

A single teardrop rolled down her cheek, and a knot of emotion became lodged in his throat. Not only had he surprised his wife, he'd given her a gift that was one more installment in his determination to atone for the pain he'd caused her in the past. Gently brushing the tear off her cheek, he bent slightly to press his forehead against hers.

"I told you I would make amends for my cruelty, light of my life. Greece and the Day Dream are the first of many installments to account for my transgressions."

"But…*bloody hell, Sebastian,* a ship? I meant sailing on the Falcon, you fuck-wit." She cupped the sides of his face, a scowl furrowing her brow. "It's a wonderful gift, my dark angel, but you need to sell it right away. If you keep spending money so freely, the future Viscount Starling will be penniless when he inherits his title."

"I am not a complete fool, my love. It's a three-masted schooner I acquired for a reasonable sum, and she'll pay for itself. When we're not using it, the ship will transport passengers on holiday to France, Spain, and the Mediterranean, along with a small amount of cargo in the hold." Sebastian grinned at her look of incredulity. It was unusual to see Anna speechless, and he reveled in her stunned reaction. Her inability to speak didn't last long, as skepticism touched her lovely face.

"I know you're not a fool…it's just that, and I'm sorry to doubt you, my dark angel," she added hurriedly as he stiffened. "But you know little about running a shipping business."

"True, but I have a great deal of wisdom and advice at my disposal. Your uncle helped me select the right ship, and he reassures me the Day Dream will be sea-worthy for years to come. He's also introduced me to a number of his contacts that Alexander and I can do business with. Once Hamish finishes overseeing the refitting, the Day Dream will easily accommodate at least fifteen passengers at a time. So this is most likely your last voyage on the Falcon."

"Oh, Sebastian," she breathed as she pulled his head down to brush her lips gently across his. "It's a wonderful gift, my dark angel."

"Only one of many to come, my love." Once more, they stood together in silence, watching the Falcon skim across the water under the rays of the moon.

"Sebastian." The love in her voice made his chest tighten.

"Umm," he murmured as he pressed his mouth into her silk hair on the top of her head.

"You remember me telling you this morning how unsuitable I was to be your viscountess?" Her words made him smile as he remembered her impertinent remark before and after they'd exchanged vows.

"I do."

"Well, I think you should know that although we've been married less than a day, I've already managed to create a scandal."

"A scandal? I don't see how that's possible, Anna." Puzzled, he turned her around to face him. The instant she eyed him with a disagreeable scowl, he shook his head. "All right, it's not impossible where you're concern, but I find it hard to believe you've managed such a feat in the last twenty-four hours."

"All right, maybe not in the past twenty-four hours, but the moment the Marlborough Set hears about it, I fully expect I'll be ostracized."

"Ostracized? I think that highly unlikely, Anna."

"Well, not you of course, you'll be offered sympathy from everyone, but I am certain to be persona non grata in almost every London household."

"Now, I'm certain you're exaggerating the situation."

"No, I'm not. I have no doubt at all that everyone will

think you were forced to marry me."

"Forced to…why would they think that?" he demanded, his mind already strategizing what he intended to do to protect his wife from false lies and gossip.

"Because they'll all know I shared your bed before we were married."

"How the devil would—" Dumbstruck, Sebastian stared at Anna in disbelief. "You're with child? But how—"

"Well, it does take two, and you were there, my darling dark angel." Laughter and joy danced in his wife's beautiful brown eyes, clearly enjoying his stunned reaction. He shook his head in a pointless gesture to clear his thoughts.

"Are you *certain*?"

"Yes, it's been two and a half months since the first time we made love." She nibbled nervously at her bottom lip, and trepidation suddenly darkened her features. "I know how much you hate scandal—"

With a jubilant shout of happiness, Sebastian picked Anna up and spun her around in a circle, and she laughed with obvious relief at his enthusiasm. Suddenly his gut snarled into knots. Setting her down, he kissed her then pulled her tight against his chest. No sooner had he done so, than she pushed herself back slightly to study him with her uncannily perceptive nature.

"I know what you're thinking," she said quietly.

"The child was conceived the night—" Sebastian flinched as he abruptly ended his reply. The memory of his cruelty slashed through him.

"Sebastian. Do you honestly think you could have made love to me that night if you didn't love me?"

It was an honest question, and he knew the answer was no. He would never have taken what she'd offered so freely and with such love and passion if he hadn't loved her in return.

"I didn't realize it until afterward. I —"

"*Dammit to hell,* Sebastian. I've forgiven you. I forgave you, because I understand *why* you said the things you did that night." Her irritation was in full force as she glared up at him. "When are you going to forgive yourself, my dark angel?"

"Never," he said softly.

"I'm beginning to think you enjoy being an idiot," she snapped. "If I—"

"*But,* I *will* try, light of my heart. I will work hard to be the man you believe I am. I will spend the rest of my life striving to be worthy of such a beautiful, strong, and courageous woman." A knot formed in his throat, and he swallowed hard to dislodge it. "A woman who dares to love a man so flawed he is humbled every time she tells him that she loves him."

Anna narrowed her gaze at him, then cupped his face with her hands. With a small smile of resignation, she pulled his head down to kiss him gently. As she pulled away from him, she nodded.

"That's a start, and I shall do my best to follow your example, my dark angel. I will work equally hard not to cause a scandal." The solemn note in her voice made his lips quirk in a small smile.

"Not too hard, my love. I fell in love with the woman who isn't afraid to speak her mind and challenges my pompous behavior."

The moment he said the word pompous, she laughed the full-bodied, rich sound that no matter when or where he heard it would make him ache to hold her close.

"Then at the next soiree we attend, when I say, 'I need you to fuck me this very minute, Lord Starling,' I expect you to immediately find a secluded corner and satisfy me as only you can."

Sebastian released a groan that was a mixture of laughter, desire, and the knowledge that one day he might actually risk doing as she demanded. Her eyebrows shot up in a silent demand that he agreed to her expectation. He shook his head.

"I'll not make a promise I can't keep, but at the very least, I will promptly make our excuses to our hostess and proceed to satisfy your needs in the carriage on our way home, and for the remainder of the night."

"That in and of itself is a remarkable concession, my dark angel." She laughed, while her dark brown eyes held a mischievous sparkle that said she intended to test him in the future.

"In fact, if you ask me now, I shall willingly comply with your wishes," he chuckled. Anna's gaze softened as she reached up to brush her finger tips across his cheek.

"Then I want you to make love to me right now, Lord Starling." The sweet, tender note in her voice emphasized the word love, and his chest tightened at her unbridled look of adoration. Emotion surged through him, and he kissed her quickly.

"I love you, Anna," he whispered as he caught her hand in his and led her back to their cabin, determined to demonstrate tonight and for the rest of their lives how much he loved her.

Present Day

Nora jerked upright in bed with a cry of anguish. The room was almost as dark as her dream, with only the light of the full moon streaming in through the window illuminating the room. A shudder wracked her body at the memory of the nightmare. It wasn't the first time she'd experienced it, but it had never been so black and foreboding before. The hard, male arm wrapping around her waist made her start violently.

"Hey, it's all right, sweetheart. It was just a dream."

Sebastian's steady, soothing voice tugged at her turbulent emotions, and she closed her eyes the moment they began to water, willing the tears not to fall. The strength and warmth of her husband's chest pressed into her back. The sensation of his solid muscles cradling her body would never grow old, and she cherished every moment they were together.

Nora's head fell backward to rest on his shoulder as he placed a tender kiss on the side of her neck. As her hand rubbed over her enlarged stomach, the familiar cold wave of fear sped through her. Another tremor rippled through her, and Sebastian's arm tightened around her.

"Want to talk about it?"

"Not really."

Nora rejected his offer with a sharp shake of her head. If she were to tell Sebastian she'd been dreaming about James again, it would only upset him. Pulling free of his embrace, she reclined back into the mattress and closed her eyes. When he didn't lie back down beside her, she peeked a glance up at him. The intensity with which he was studying her made her swallow hard.

"Another dream about James?" His quiet observation held a note of concern, and the sound tugged a sigh from her.

"Yes."

"It's just a memory from the past, sweetheart." Sebastian leaned forward and kissed her forehead. "The doctor told you yesterday the baby is fine, and that it's not unusual for a first-time mother to go a couple of weeks past her due date."

"I know," she murmured half-heartedly.

"*Anna*. Look at me." When she hesitated, he repeated the stern command. This time, the authoritative note in his voice made Nora obey him. Sebastian shook his head. "Things are different now. Modern medicine can perform what would have been deemed miraculous in the late nineteenth century."

"I know that," she said as a bleak emotion swept over her. "But this wasn't just about the baby. It was about you and me, too."

"What do you mean, you and me?"

"It was dark, and you weren't there, or if you were, you were so far away I couldn't reach you."

"Have you had this dream before?" Sebastian frowned with puzzlement and an odd look of emotion she couldn't define. Nora stared up at her dark angel, trying to figure out whether or not to tell him the truth. When she remained silent, his mouth thinned with irritation. "I *asked* you a *question*, Nora *Annabelle* Bennington."

"Yes."

"How many times?"

"I've lost count," she sighed as she averted her gaze. "They started when I was about five months pregnant."

"*Christ Almighty*. Are you telling me this has been happening for the past four months, and you've not said a word?" The moonlight illuminated the shock on Sebastian's face as he stared down at her. Nora flinched at the silent accusation in his expression.

"I didn't want to worry you."

It was the truth, but it was also because she couldn't make heads or tails out of the dream. It wasn't a nightmare with people or action. It was more like being thrown into a pit of emotions that were tangible physical sensations. Pain, anguish, and grief that clawed at her body like razors slicing through her skin.

The grief was the most visceral of the three emotions. It was like a rabid animal, snarling and gnawing at her. It was one of the most terrifying things she'd ever encountered in a dream. Instinct told her the dream was connected to their past life and the events that followed the death of their son,

James. She didn't know why, but the dream scared the hell out of her. All she understood was that the darkness had been almost absolute.

"*Damn it, Anna,*" Sebastian said with a quiet fury that made her wince. "I'm your husband. This is the sort of thing you're supposed to share with me. Stop being so goddamn independent."

"I'm sorry." This time she didn't stop the tears from flowing down her cheeks, and Sebastian uttered a quiet sound as he quickly laid down and pulled her close, gently wiping the wetness off her cheeks.

"Between your obsession with those damn journal entries Nicholas wrote about us, and these crazy mood swings of yours, I'm not surprised you're having nightmares."

"I'm not obsessed with the journals," she sniffed with annoyance as she pushed him away and cast a baleful glance in his direction before rolling onto her back and closing her eyes once more. "And my hormones are *not* causing my nightmares."

"I didn't say your hormones were the reason for these bad dreams, but I *do* think they're making them worse than they would be at any other time." When she didn't answer, Sebastian muttered something incoherent, and she turned her head to glare at him.

"If you have something to say, then say it loud and clear, Mr. Bennington."

"I said, whatever happened between us more than a hundred years ago after James's death won't happen again." The moment her eyes widened, Sebastian scowled at her. "Do you really think I don't understand you and how your mind works, Anna?"

Nora stared at her husband in amazement, and Sebastian expelled a harsh breath of exasperation. Elbow denting his pillow, he cradled his head in the palm of his hand, then quirked an eyebrow upward and silently dared her to reply.

"No, I know how well you know me," she said softly. "You know me just as well as I know you, but I didn't even tell you what I was —"

"You didn't have too, the letters—" The guilt she saw fly across his face was so fleeting, she wasn't really sure she saw it. The minute he rolled away to lie staring up at the ceiling, Nora frowned.

"I don't understand. Do you mean our letters to each other when we were Lord and Lady Starling?"

"Yes." His terse reply only increased her confusion.

"But there aren't any letters from those eighteen months between James's death and when William was born," Nora said in bewilderment, but he didn't say anything.

Baffled by his obvious reluctance to continue with his explanation, Nora's oversized belly made her feel like an ungainly cow as she struggled to sit up. In a clumsy, awkward movement, she sat upright and stared down at him with a perplexed look. When he didn't speak, she scowled at him in a silent demand for an explanation. Something in her expression must have warned him not to test her patience, and his jaw hardened with tension.

"The letters I'm talking about weren't in the clock."

"Not in the—" She stiffened, and her head jerked backward a fraction of an inch in astonishment. "Where did you find them?"

"They were delivered to my parents' home when they returned to the states, shortly after your accident at the Dorchester."

"Delivered to your parents? Why didn't you have them forward the letters to us?"

"I did."

His brief, uninformative reply escalated her exasperation from Defcon five to Defcon three in a split second. But she was rapidly closing in on Defcon two, which involved inflicting bodily harm if she didn't get an explanation from him fast. Nora pressed her fingertips to her forehead, then threw her hands up in the air in a gesture of bewilderment.

"Then *where* are the letters, Sebastian?"

"Nicholas and Victoria have them."

"*Okay.* Now, I'm *totally* confused. Not to *mention* feeling like I'm trying to wrestle a *bone* out of a pit bull's locked *jaw* with these short, cryptic answers of yours." Nora pinned a look of fierce irritation on him. "Why haven't you told me about these letters before now, and *why* do my brother and sister-in-law have them?"

"Because I wanted to protect you."

"Protect me? From *what*? And *what the fuck* happened to the 'this is something you share' philosophy, or is that only applicable to information *I'm* not sharing with *you*?"

"The letters are…they're…I was savagely cruel, Anna," he said in a flat voice.

The disgust and sickening horror reflected in Sebastian's beautiful dark eyes made her draw in a sharp breath. The correspondence from the clock they'd exchanged in their past lives together as members of the nobility had depicted a life filled with great love and happiness. All the letters she'd read had been filled with tender, passionate words of love between them.

While Sebastian's letters had periodically mentioned his need to atone for his treatment of her, the letters had never clarified what his sin had been. As for her, she'd clearly forgiven him many times for small and large transgressions, just as he'd managed to accept and forgive her sins as well, too.

Now, the pain and guilt Nora saw flit across her husband's handsome features indicated he'd discovered what sin or sins he'd committed when they'd been married in the late eighteen hundreds. The emotion in his piercing dark eyes indicated Sebastian believed his transgressions were far worse than anything the two of them had ever imagined. Whatever he'd learned when he'd read the newly discovered correspondence, it didn't matter.

As far as she was concerned, she'd forgiven him in the past, and she wouldn't hesitate to do so again. Nora stretched out her hand to touch his cheek in a silent gesture of understanding. The instant he jerked his head away, she leaned forward and quickly cupped his face with both hands.

"Whatever you did is in the past, my dark angel. I forgave you then, and I know I would forgive you now. My love for you is unshakeable."

"I didn't deserve you then. You had faith in me—in us—you never gave up on me."

"And I wouldn't give up on you or us, now," she said with a smile.

Sebastian came upright in bed at her quiet words and kissed her. It was a caress that stirred her soul. Sweet and tender, the kiss was infused with all the emotional strength and power of his love for her. After a long moment, Sebastian lifted his head. His forehead pressed against hers, he drew in a deep breath.

"Promise me you'll tell me the next time you have the dream again where you're alone in the dark." Once again, guilt darkened his features, and she nodded her agreement to do as he asked.

"I promise."

She wished there was something she could do to assuage whatever emotion he was feeling about his actions in the past. But she knew pressing him on the matter would make him clam up. Sebastian would explain things in his own good time. It was how he'd always been. He needed to work through the emotions internally before he was willing to openly confront and discuss them with her.

Nora leaned forward and kissed him. Her lips has just touched Sebastian's when Baby Bennington kicked her left side with the strength of a budding martial arts student. Unprepared for the blow, she grunted and quickly sank back into the mattress to lie still.

Sebastian's warm hand caressed her large belly. The moment his hand touched her, the baby kicked hard for a second time. Surprise crossed his face.

"Damn, he's going to love marital arts just like his mother." The lighthearted note in Sebastian's voice made her laugh. He grinned at her, and the baby kicked again. This time, it caused her to gasp out loud. Sebastian's smile faded into a look of concern.

"What?"

"Your *daughter* knows exactly what spot to kick to inflict the most discomfort." The moment she stressed the word daughter, he scowled at her. She laughed at his disgruntled expression. "I keep telling you, he is a she."

"We should have gone ahead and had the doctor tell us the sex when she asked us."

His grumbled reply made her start to laugh when a sharp pain lashed around her large girth as if she'd been roped by a lasso of fire. Gasping loudly at the sudden spasm slicing through her midsection, Nora closed her eyes as she tried to keep her body relaxed in an effort to minimize the pain.

"Anna?"

A small note of panic threaded its way into Sebastian's voice. Unable to answer him, she drank in a deep breath as his fingers wrapped around hers. This contraction seemed to last an eternity, and as the pain faded, she relaxed her grip on Sebastian's hand.

"Well?"

"What?" Nora smiled knowingly at him.

"You know damn good and well what." At his exasperation, she laughed.

"My water hasn't even broken yet. Let's wait an hour and see what happens."

"Fine," he said grumpily, eyeing her with annoyance at being thwarted in his unspoken attempt to whisk her off to the hospital. "But just in case, I'm going to make sure everything is in the suitcase and that our phones are charged. Although, I know there's something I'm probably forgetting."

No longer displaying any signs of panic, the calm, quiet, meticulous planner Sebastian had always been, past and present, was once more in complete control. He leaned over her and kissed her deeply, then slid out of bed and strode out the door. As he disappeared on his way to where he'd set the suitcase at the foot of the stairs, Nora closed her eyes and released a sigh of happiness.

Sebastian had always excelled at planning for any contingency. What he excelled at even more was how he loved her. Not a day went by without some unexpected gesture of love and affection. It was as if he had a monthly plan of action he followed to ensure she could never doubt how much he loved her. The memory of the letter he'd written her shortly before his death in their past life filled her head.

While the letter had detailed some things Sebastian had done for her in those last weeks of his life, there were other wisps of memories that would occasionally filter through from the past that would bring a happy smile to her lips. No sooner had the smiled curved her mouth than her heart twisted viciously in her chest.

Dear God, had she misunderstood her dream? Was the darkness she experienced in the nightmare not related to James's death at all? Could it have been the intense grief and pain she'd suffered when Sebastian had died? Was her dream telling her something about her life with Sebastian now? All the small, unexpected demonstrations of his love for her, was it because——an image from the distant past formed in her head, and she dragged in a silent cry of horror.

In her mind's eye, she saw herself sitting at Sebastian's bedside, their gazes locked as she watched the life flicker out of his eyes. Terrified, she screamed his name. The instant her cry filled the bedroom, she heard her husband's feet pounding their way up the stairs. He was at her side in seconds, and Nora flung her arms around his neck to cling to him as wild sobs fell past her lips.

"*Christ Almighty, Anna*, tell me what's wrong, sweetheart. What is it? Are you in pain?"

Fear filled Sebastian's words as he whispered her name soothingly, but she couldn't speak. When she didn't respond, his arms tightened even more around her as he stroked her hair in a calming gesture. Sebastian continued to murmur comforting words of love in her ear as her sobs slowly ebbed.

When she was no longer sobbing hysterically, Sebastian pushed her away from him, his fingers drying her tears off her cheeks as he met her gaze. Before he could speak, Nora's fingers dug into his shoulders as she stared at him terrified what his answer to her question would be.

"Are you dying?"

"*What?*" Sebastian's eyes widened in astonishment, as an incredulous expression settled on his handsome features. "What the hell makes you think that?"

"Because you're behaving exactly like you did in the weeks before you died in the past."

"*Anna*. I am *not* dying." Sebastian said firmly. "I just had my annual physical three months ago, and Dr. Lawrence said I'm in perfect health. And exactly *what* am I doing that would make you think I'm sick."

Relief sailed through her at his reassurance that he didn't have some terrible disease he was hiding from her. Deep inside, the darkness threatening to engulf her heart receded, and she sagged slightly. Her head fell forward to rest against his shoulder, and her heart rate began to resume a normal beat. God, her nightmares were fucking with her emotions worse than she'd realized.

"I asked you a question, Anna."

The steely note in his voice made her lift her head. The way he was studying her said her outburst had upset him deeply. She shook her head slightly at how she'd allowed herself to leap from one thought to another to imagine the worst. Sebastian was right. Her hormones were *definitely* out of control, and her brain wasn't functioning properly.

"It's all these thoughtful little gifts, messages, and activities you've been doing of late." At her reply, he shook his head in stunned disbelief.

"You think I'm dying because I enjoy doing things for you? Because I want to *show* you, not just tell you, how much I love you?"

"Yes," she bobbed her head and drew in a shuddering breath. "I remembered the letter you wrote to me…when you explained your reasons for all those spontaneous moments of happiness you created for us in the weeks before you…I thought…"

"God help me, woman." Sebastian blew out a harsh breath of relief and closed his eyes as he shoved a hand through his hair. Beneath her fingers, his taut shoulder muscles flexed and relaxed. She hated herself for upsetting him.

"Oh, Sebastian, I'm so sorry." Nora winced as tears welled in her eyes again. "It's these fucking nightmares and my hormones. I feel like I'm going crazy."

"Sweetheart, you're killing me here," he said softly as he brushed the hair at her temple away from her face.

"*Don't say that,*" she snapped fiercely. "Don't you *ever* say that again."

"I'm sorry," Sebastian said with a look of remorse. She nodded her acceptance of his soft apology and lifted his hand to stare down at the ring on his finger.

"No, *I'm* the one who's sorry. I've been a *fuckwit* for the past two or three months, and you've done nothing but act like a hero out of some romance novel. Always comforting me, loving me, and being so supportive, and in exchange, all I do is whine and complain."

"You seem to forget we've gone through this before."

"What?" Startled, Nora jumped slightly at the amusement she heard threading its way through his words.

"I've remembered a few things here and there from when you were pregnant with Jane all those years ago." Sebastian shrugged. "But that's not why I've been saying I love you with all the small gifts, notes, and surprises."

"Then why?" At her question, he caught her hand in his, and like she had a moment ago, he studied the wedding rings she wore.

"Your emotions have been all over the map in recent months." Sebastian paused for a moment and eyed her sternly. "Now that I know you've been dreaming about our life together in another time, your behavior makes a lot more sense now."

"I promised I'd tell you when I had another one, didn't I?" Nora quirked her lips to one side with irritation at his words.

"If you don't, there'll be hell to pay, Anna," he said grimly. It wasn't a threat, but a guarantee that he'd extract some form of punishment if she held anything back. Sebastian shook his head slightly. "But my reason for doing all these little surprises over the past three months is because things at work have been…chaotic."

"More red tape? I thought you guys were able to resolve the issues the environmental people demanded you fix."

"No, it has nothing to do with the project. I've not said anything before now because it was all just rumors."

"Rumors? Are you going to lose your job?" she exclaimed softly.

Nora's brain immediately jumped the tracks as she

began considering the possibility of moving to the states. Did she really want to go back? Sebastian's hand squeezed hers hard, and she gasped as the discomfort jerked her out of the thoughts careening wildly in her head.

"*Christ Jesus*, will you focus on what I'm saying, please? This is precisely *why* I haven't mentioned it before." The annoyance vibrating off of him made Nora nod slowly, willing her mind to stop rushing around like a mad woman. When she didn't look away from him, Sebastian nodded with satisfaction.

"About four months ago, rumors started circulating that the firm was going to be sold to another company." The moment her eyes widened with concern, Sebastian narrowed his gaze at her. With a small wave of her hand, she indicated she was still focused on what he was saying.

"The chaos those rumors created around the office made me realize that change was impossible to avoid. The only constant thing in my life was you and our love for each other. I know how lucky we are to have found each other again. So, I decided that I needed to do more than just tell you every day how much I love you. I wanted to show you on a daily basis how much you mean to me."

Sebastian's dark eyes studied her intently, and Nora's throat closed at the depth of emotion she saw reflected there. Eyes watering, she drew in a shuddering breath. Gentle fingers brushed across her cheek.

"I love you, Anna. Whether it's bringing you a single rose or a dozen, surprising you at the shop to take you to lunch, leaving a love note in your briefcase, or buying you *just one* chocolate truffle, because I know how guilty you feel when you go through a dozen in one hour, I plan on doing those little things for the rest of our lives together. I'll never stop saying I love you, Anna. I'm just doubling down on it by showing you in small ways how much you mean to me."

Unable to speak, she stared at him. Joy. It was the only

word she could think of to describe how his words made her feel. It had been the most heartfelt declaration of love she'd ever heard. Not even the richest person on the face of the earth could buy the kind of pure happiness and joy Sebastian's words had created inside her. Tears lodging in Nora's throat, she lifted his hand to her lips, then pressed it against her heart.

"I adore you, Sebastian Levi Bennington. I'll love you until the day I die, and then I'll love you even more in our next life together."

Sebastian bent his head to kiss her deeply, and her heart swelled in her breast at the emotion he conveyed in the sweet caress. When he lifted his head, he smiled with a hint of devilment glittering in his dark gaze.

"Just so we're clear, you understand completely how much I love you."

"Yes, my dark angel. I understand. I'll never doubt your love for me." Something flickered in his gaze for a moment, but it was gone so quickly, she thought she might have imagined it. In the next breath, she realized her hormones were trying to make problems where none existed. Nora wrapped her arms around Sebastian, and laid her head on her shoulder. The baby chose at that moment to kick her, and she grunted softly.

"He's active tonight."

"*She's* just eager to meet the amazing man who's going to her dad," she said softly as an image of Sebastian holding their daughter in his arms filled her head. Happiness warmed her from the inside out. She had it all, but the best thing she had in her life was Sebastian. Almost as if he could read her mind, his fingers tipped her chin upward, and he stared down into her eyes.

"I love you, Anna."

"I love you, too," she whispered. "I'll never stop loving you, Sebastian. I'll always be yours."

Author's Note

APEP AND HATSHEPSUT

Apep, also known as Apophis, was the Egyptian God of Chaos. The Cult of Hatshepsut in the story is completely fictitious and was used as a plot device for the story.

As for Hatshepsut herself, she was the second historically recorded pharaoh who was a woman. Hatshepsut's reign brought an era of great prosperity to her kingdom during her some twenty-year reign. To rule for more than twenty years in a world that was dominated by men is a tribute to her intellect and critical thinking capabilities.

She was a prolific builder, and the temple that was built to hold her remains is considered one of the most beautiful architectural wonders of the ancient world. It was designed with gardens, water pools, and other ornamental designs. She is also the pharaoh who built the two obelisks at the Temple of Karnak. One of which is still standing today.

Additionally, historians have examined and sync'd dates of the reigns of numerous pharaohs and other rulers during the New Kingdom era in Egypt. These synchronized dates strongly suggest Hatshepsut is the Queen of Sheba, who is said to have visited Solomon.

HOMOSEXUAL ACTS LEGISLATION

In 1791, France adopted a new penal code that no longer criminalized homosexual acts between consenting adults. France was the first country in Europe to do this. The United Kingdom did not decriminalize homosexuality acts until 1967.

Oscar Wilde, who was convicted of homosexual acts, was incarcerated from 25 May 1895 to 18 May 1897. He first entered Newgate Prison in London for processing, then was moved to Pentonville Prison, where the "hard labour" to which he had been sentenced consisted of many hours of walking a treadmill and picking oakum (separating the fibers in scraps of old navy ropes).

EPILEPSY, LONG QT SYNDROME, AND ANNA'S VISIONS

"Epilepsy is a neurological condition that affects the nervous system. Epilepsy is also known as a seizure disorder." — *Epilepsy Foundation*

The diagnosis of epilepsy Anna is given in the book is the same one I received at nineteen. After two or three unexplained fainting spells, an EKG (brain wave monitoring) showed abnormal spikes of electrical activity in my brain, and I was diagnosed epileptic.

Like me, Anna never had any seizures, which is why she refers to it as a mild form of the neurological disorder of epilepsy. There are four general types, and for more information visit the Epilepsy Foundation's website. While I fainted a time or two in my teens and early 20s, the most prevalent symptoms I experienced were the type of incidents/spells I gave to Anna. Those I had quite often, although I didn't have visions like Anna does.

The descriptions in the book are based on personal experience. My spells were a temporary cessation of movement or speech. Some might call it a catatonic state, but for me, it was more like an out-of-body experience, and the incidents only lasted a moment or two. I cannot call it a true catatonic state for a specific reason. It turns out that I'm not epileptic (although no one has yet to explain the warped signals they found on my EEG many moons ago when they diagnosed me as epileptic).

As with everything in the human body, there is so much interconnectivity between different functions in our bodies, it's sometimes hard to see where one disorder ends and another begins. So, more than thirty years after my epileptic diagnosis, and some gene testing, my lifelong symptoms were attributed to Long QT Syndrome.

"Long QT syndrome (LQTS) is an abnormal feature of the heart's electrical system that can lead to a potentially life-threatening arrhythmia called *torsades de pointes* (pronounced torsad de pwant). *Torsades de pointes* may result in syncope (fainting) or sudden cardiac death." — *John Hopkins Medicine, www.hopkinsmedicine.org*

Epilepsy and Long QT disorders are electrical in nature, so the fact that they present similar symptoms doesn't seem all that surprising. I should also point out that I've not had any spells since 2007 when I had a defibrillator implanted into my chest as a precautionary act. To date, my device has recorded several minor incidents, but nothing major.

Although I don't state it in the book (I couldn't since it's an undiscovered medical condition in 1895), I wrote Anna as if she has Long QT, using epilepsy as a cover, because I needed an explanation for when someone sees her fall into a trancelike state, and mild cases of epilepsy can mimic her symptoms (based on personal experience).

However, as I am planning on writing their second book, I wanted this specific info in my author note well in advance in the event there were reader questions (of course, there will always be those *smile*). And yes, it took me eight years to gain the courage to write this book, because with Forever Mine being so loved by readers, it's hard to raise the bar at that point. Anna's and Sebastian's second book, tentatively titled Always Yours, will be a second chance romance as it takes place after the death of their oldest son. I do not have a time frame yet.

Since Long QT wasn't discovered until 1988, I obviously couldn't name that disorder as a source for Anna's spells. However, epilepsy has been used for centuries as a catch-all diagnosis, and ironically as I pointed out above, other disorders mimic epileptic symptoms.

With so many documented reports of NDEs (near-death experiences) where the heart stops and people leave their bodies for a short period of time before they're resuscitated, that provided me with a loose connection to prognostication and psychic abilities.

Finally, while I've written many heroes and heroines with psychic abilities (my Reckless Rockwoods series), their physical reactions were not detailed in the same way as Anna's are, so I felt the need to label Anna's spells where I didn't in my other characters. In fact, Constance, from Dangerous in the Reckless Rockwoods series, is the only character who comes close to having similar traits to Anna when having a psychic experience.

Long QT is primarily a genetic disorder. I inherited the gene from my father, who died of unexpected, unexplained heart failure the same year the Long QT gene was discovered. However, his unexplained death prompted genetic testing of my niece and nephew when they began to exhibit Long QT symptoms in the mid-2000s.

Between my siblings, nieces, nephews, aunts and first cousins, we have jokingly been referred to as the motherload of research subjects for the clinical staff at the University of Rochester (UR) as approximately 25 of us are part of their research tracking program of people with the gene defect. About half of those 25 have defibrillators in place. Back in 2007 or 2008, we were the largest group of family members in UR's genetic clinical tracking program. I don't know if that's still true, although their database still has a small, select group of data points of around 7,100 people who have the gene being monitored, so it's more than possible (I come from a very large family).

JULIUS GAIUS CAESAR AND EPILEPSY

It is also a widely held belief among academics and historians that Julius Gaius Caesar had epilepsy. As Anna explains, it was called the falling sickness in ancient Rome, and Caesar hid his disorder because Romans would have viewed him as being cursed by the Gods. However, just recently, another possibility has been put forth that deserves notation. A new report suggests Caesar didn't have epilepsy, but possibly suffered from mini-strokes. — *History.com https://www.history.com/news/julius-caesar-suffered-from-strokes-not-epilepsy-new-study-says*

Other Titles by Monica Burns

THE RECKLESS ROCKWOODS SERIES

Obsession #1
Dangerous #2,
The Highlander's Woman #3
Redemption #4
The Beastly Earl #5

THE RECKLESS ROCKWOODS
The Next Generation

Scandalous #6 (Jul 2023)
Masquerade #7 (Dec 2023)
Brazen #8 (Jul 2024)
Reckless #9 (Dec 2024)

THE RECKLESS ROCKWOODS NOVELS
The Reluctant Rogues

The Rogue's Offer #1
The Rogue's Countess #2

FOREVERMORE SERIES (TIME TRAVEL)

Forever Mine #1
Forever Yours #2
Forever My Lass #3
Always Yours, #4 (TBA)

SELF-MADE MEN SERIES

His To Command #1 (Novella)
His Mistress #2

STAND ALONE TITLES

Kismet

Mirage

Pleasure Me

A Bluestocking Christmas

Love's Portrait

Love's Revenge

THE ORDER OF THE SICARI SERIES

Assassin's Honor #1

Assassin's Heart #2

Inferno's Kiss #3

About The Author

Monica Burns is a bestselling author of spicy historical and paranormal romance. She penned her first romance at the age of nine when she selected the pseudonym she uses today. Her historical book awards include the 2011 RT BookReviews Reviewers Choice Award and the 2012 Gayle Wilson Heart of Excellence Award for Pleasure Me.

She is also the recipient of the prestigious paranormal romance award, the 2011 PRISM Best of the Best award for Assassin's Heart. From the days when she hid her stories from her sisters to her first completed full-length manuscript, she always believed in her dream despite rejections and setbacks. A workaholic wife and mother, Monica is a survivor who believes every hero and heroine deserves a HEA (Happily Ever After), especially if she's writing the story.

Find all the ways you can connect with Monica

on the next page.

Connect With Monica

Follow For New Release Alerts

Bookbub

Monicaburns.net/BBpage

Amazon

Monicaburns.net/Amazon

Social Media

Facebook

Monicaburns.net/readergroup

Other Connections

Newsletter -Free Digital Book

Monicaburns.net/newsletter

Website

www.monicaburns.com

Email

monicaburns@monicaburns.com

9 781948 505130